Four Miles West of Burden's

Four Miles West of Burden's

DICK YOUNG

ISBN: 1544607822
ISBN 13: 9781544607825
Library of Congress Control Number: 2017903921
CreateSpace Independent Publishing Platform
North Charleston, South Carolina

For my grandchildren

Abigail Mary Young (Abi)
and
Alan Turner Young, Jr. (A.J.)

This story was written for you.

Acknowledgements

To my wife, Lynda, who was so patient with me while I was writing this book. You are, by far, my greatest source of strength and encouragement.

My warmest thanks to my brother, Phil; my sons, Richard, Jr. and Al; and my daughter-in-law, Mary Ann who spurred me along; Hugh Badger, Rev. Matt Matthews; Rev. Barrie Kirby; Paige Morse; Dean Richardson; and Gary Hipps.

My most special thanks to my late father and mother, Bill and Milo, who introduced me to the mountains and by their example, taught me to love them.

Contents

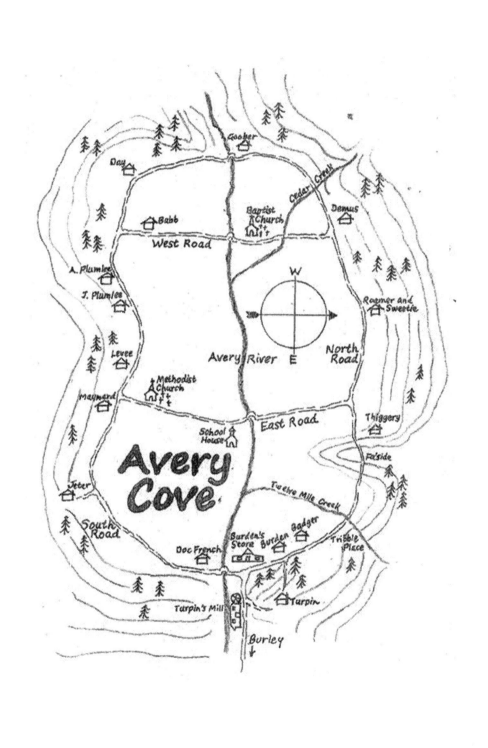

One

The first red hints of sunrise were appearing as Will Parker walked through the doors of Inverness Mill and stepped into the morning air. He stood for a few moments on the steps letting the cool freshness of October fill his lungs before he began his walk home—a walk of about a mile.

The streets of the mill village were mostly deserted. Fifteen minutes earlier, they had been busy with other night shift workers on their way home, and about ten minutes before that, they had been busy with the day shift workers going in. Now, the only movement other than his was that of the crews going to the sites of new mill houses under construction.

The carpenters, still groggy from a too-short night, were bundled against the morning chill. As some were unloading their tools, others were lighting fires from scraps of wood to warm their workplace.

The sun was climbing. The silhouettes of trees and buildings were taking on detail. He could see movement in the mill houses that were already occupied. Men, women, and children getting ready for another day were exposed to the outside through windows not yet fitted with curtains.

At the livery stable, a dark figure was bent over, cleaning the front stall as horses stood at the ready. Around back, behind the livery, the blacksmith was building the fire in which he would turn raw metal into horse shoes and tools.

The church and the school just beyond it were empty and silent, their fresh, new paint taking on a glow from the still-rising sun. In a year or so both would be filled to capacity, but for now, they could expect only a few to come, for the village was in its infancy.

The company store, the boarding house, and finally the homes of the mill management passed in review as he continued his journey.

Finally, he was on River Street and there was gravel beneath his feet. The mill village was past and he was nearing the outskirts of Charlotte, North Carolina, a town between the mountains and the coast, near the South Carolina border.

The newly cut dirt streets, the smell of freshly cut wood at the building sites, and the grassless, treeless land of new construction were behind him, and he was back in a more familiar place. There was something about the mill and the village that made him feel closed in—separated from all he had ever known. He wondered if he would ever get used to it.

———

Maybe it was the lift in spirit that he always got when he left the mill village, or maybe it was the smell of bacon cooking, but a rumble of hunger was sounding in Will's stomach. He cut diagonally across River Street at the intersection with Watt Street, and veered left and up the steps of Sarah's Cafe.

Sarah's was a small clapboard building standing alone near other small businesses. It was neat and painted white, and above the door was a sign that read, "Welcome All Ye Who Hunger."

Since eating at Sarah's was a regular morning ritual, he entered almost thoughtlessly. The air was thick with laughter and conversation weighted down with the smell of smoked bacon and warm bread.

"Mornin', everybody," Will called as he hung his coat and hat on the rack beside the door.

A cry of greeting rose in unison from the bachelor corps seated around the tables. "Mornin', Will."

Tommy Lee Jones stood, patted his stomach, and surrendered a soft burp as if to say, "We've had ours, boy, now you get yours."

Will walked to his regular place at the end of the counter and took his seat. Behind the counter was a large wood stove with a hood over the top. A table on the left of the stove held eggs, bacon, and patties of sausage on plates, loaves of freshly baked bread, and all the ingredients that would make a filling breakfast.

At the stove was a heavy, mature lady with her hair in a net. She stood with her left hand on her hip and her right hand wrapped around the handle of a spatula, flipping pancakes in a frying pan.

"Mornin', Sarah," he said to her back.

"Mornin', Precious," she returned. "Runnin' late again, I see."

"Yep, gettin' to be a habit, I guess. We still have looms that aren't running yet, and some of the weavers we have aren't worth the salt it would take to cure 'em."

"You're gonna' have the regular, I guess," Sarah said, still working her pancakes.

"Yep."

Prissy, the waitress, came to pour Will a cup of coffee, smiling her flirtatious smile. She was a girl of about 16, working to find a husband as much as a salary. Pretty she was, but as shallow as a puddle.

"Hey, Willie," she said in her soft, girlish voice.

"Prissy," Will said, "I've told you and told you not to call me Willie. It makes me feel like a shirt-tail school boy." Then he added with a grin, "But how are you anyway?"

Prissy blushed and turned to start clearing tables. It was obvious that she had a real crush on Will, and understandably so! He was the target of quite a few girls' affection—a young man of twenty-one, close to six feet in height, with sandy colored, neatly combed hair. He was thin yet muscular, but the thing that really made the girls' hearts flutter was the color of his eyes. They were the shade of blue that rivaled a robin's egg.

As Prissy walked away she glanced back at Will, and a careful observer would have noticed a little quiver in her breast as she took a breath.

Will stirred a spoonful of sugar into his coffee as he sat looking around. It was funny how he always seemed to see something new as he sat and waited at Sarah's. This morning, his eyes were drawn to a document hanging on the wall to the right of the counter. "Be It Known" it began. It was Sarah's high school diploma, dated June 1, 1862. *Let's see,* Will thought, *if she was seventeen when she finished high school, that would make her a little over fifty. Must have been the heat from the grill and the trials of being a widow that made her look more like sixty-five.*

"Dad-gum-it!" Sarah cried, rousting Will from his day dream. "I busted one of your yokes! I know how you hate that! You gonna divorce me?"

"Couldn't afford a lawyer," Will said, "and even if I could, good cooks are hard to come by."

Sarah turned, facing Will for the first time that day, and pointed her spatula in his direction. "You know what you need, young man? You need a wife … one that would straighten you out!"

Prissy stopped wiping the table in the far corner and turned slightly to hear what Will would have to say.

"No, Sarah," Will said, "I don't need a wife. What I need are some servants … one to cook and clean house, one to draw me a bath and scrub my back, one to hoe the garden and clean the horse stall, and oh yeah, one that would go to the mill and work my shift."

"That sounds about like a wife to me," Sarah said.

And with that, Prissy turned and continued wiping her table.

Will finished his eggs, bacon, grits, and fried bread and drank the last of his coffee. His stool groaned as he stood and pushed it back. He thought he heard the groan of his back too.

As he turned to leave, he placed two dimes on the counter—fifteen cents for the breakfast and five cents for Sarah.

"Have a good day, Sarah," Will said as he put on his coat and opened the door. "You and Prissy behave yourselves, now."

"Thanks, Precious," Sarah answered. "Get a good night's, uh ... day's sleep."

So, as he did every morning, Will closed the door of Sarah's Cafe, went down the steps, turned left, and continued his walk toward home.

It seemed that almost every day when Will left Sarah's, he left with a heavy heart. The brief, daily encounter that he had with Sarah, his bachelor brethren, and even Prissy—in whom he could muster no romantic interest— reminded him of the family life that he so enjoyed before the deaths of his parents and before his sister, Esther, moved to Wilmington. Today would have been like most every other day had it not been for an especially bright sun that was now fully above the horizon.

The dawn that began with a reddish glow had turned to an early day with a crystal-clear countenance. No sir, Mister, no "red skies in the morning, sailors take warning" today!

As his house came into view, Will's eyes searched for the only family he had left, his loyal friend, Dawg. Dawg had come to be with Will on his sixteenth birthday, a gift from his dad. He was bought as a coon dog, not because anyone in the family hunted coons, but because a neighbor had the pups for sale.

Dawg's mother, and supposedly his father, too, had a pedigree that could be traced back to the very beginning of the breed, but as Dawg grew from puppy to adult, it was plain to see that when the mother was in heat, there had been an outside visitor to the kennel! Dawg had grown to a size unknown in the coon dog world, and had as his foundation, feet as large as biscuits.

Despite Dawg's drawbacks, he was a good and faithful pal who had learned his lessons well. He waited at the end of the driveway, not putting so much as a toenail on the road. That was the way Will had trained him, and that was the way he carried out his training.

As Will got nearer, the excitement was almost too great for Dawg. He sat shaking his tail so hard that his backside raised dust from the dry dirt. He whimpered in anticipation and a little puddle of joy formed beneath him. Oh, the ecstasy of one's master coming home!

———————

The trees were clothed in their bright fall colors. The oaks, dressed in their brown remnants, were the only ones not celebrating the season. It was a glorious October day and would be warm and pleasant. Indian summer!

The walk home and the breakfast at Sarah's had put the time at 8:30 a.m., which on Will's schedule was early evening. There was only time for a few chores before bed.

He entered the house by the front door and went directly to the back porch where his grubby shoes and overalls were kept. A quick change put him on the back steps where Dawg was waiting.

First on the list were the buckets to be filled with coal to feed the pot-belly stove in the parlor. Dawg supervised the procedure. Filling the two buckets and carrying them to the porch would only take a few minutes, but that was enough time for Dawg to tire of his supervisory job and go to lie down beside his house.

Next on the list was his horse, Traveler. Traveler's home was a two-stall stable that stood about a hundred feet behind the house. In addition to the two stalls, the building had a tack room where Will also stored Traveler's oats, and above it all was a loft where the straw and hay were kept. The back of the stable opened to a fenced field of about two acres where the horse could meander and get in his daily romp.

Traveler was named for General Robert E. Lee's famous war horse, but Will was quick to point out to anyone who was interested that although Traveler was named for General Lee's horse, he had chosen to use the

American spelling with one 'l' instead of the British spelling with two 'l's' as Lee had done.

Aside from the spelling of his name, Traveler could have been Lee's horse reborn. He was iron gray with black tips and stood sixteen hands high. Will didn't know his weight but knew that he was more than half a ton. But more than anything, Traveler was a good friend, faithful and eager to please. A generous scoop of oats, some fresh hay and water, a quick cleaning of the stall including fresh straw, and Traveler was set for another day.

With his outside chores taken care of, Will turned his attention to the house.

With no one but himself living in the house, there wasn't a lot of daily work that had to be done. Hattie Jackson, who lived just off his route to work on Watt Street, did his laundry, and the only daily meal he had at home was a small one. Garden work would not come until spring, and even if it were the gardening season, the size of his plot didn't demand much time.

For a bachelor, Will wasn't messy. He had been raised by a mother who demanded that dirt and clutter not get out of hand, so fifteen minutes of sweeping, rug shaking, and dusting put everything in order.

Walking the mile from work and doing chores alone meant that there was a lot of time for thought. On most days, Will thought of his coworkers, the responsibilities of his management training, and all things related to his work.

He thought of his mother who had died when he was twelve, of his father who had been gone for two years, and of his sister, Esther. Oh, how he missed Esther! But today, the person heaviest on his mind was his employer and benefactor, Glenn Neil.

Two

The nineteenth century saw hundreds of thousands of immigrants land on the shores of America. On the west coast, there was an influx of workers from the Orient, coming to meet the demand for laborers on the railroads, in mines, and in the cities where the construction industry was booming. On the east coast, the "huddled masses" from the whole of Europe arrived to feed the industrial revolution with their talents, their inventiveness, and their sweat.

Coming in the midst of the throngs in 1845 was a 16-year-old Scotsman named Angus O'Neil. His was a common arrival, unnoticed and unheralded. He carried his possessions in two small bundles. Straight away, he changed his name to "Neil" as part of the ritual of Americanization.

Upon his arrival in New York City, Angus got a job in a dry-goods store owned by a man named McCray. There he met and fell in love with McCray's daughter, Jean, and after a whirlwind courtship, and with McCray's blessing, the two were married.

Angus was blissfully happy but longed for the mountains of the Scottish Highlands, and so with his small savings and Jean's dowry, they moved to Roanoke, Virginia, and opened their own dry-goods store. There he was reminded of the Grampian Mountains near his birthplace, Inverness.

The family grew as did the business, and before Angus was 21, he was the father of a son, Glenn, and the owner of two dry-goods stores.

Eventually, the family moved to Richmond, Virginia, to be more centrally located and opened a wholesale dry-goods business. Glenn remained an only child, and was his parents' pride.

When he was in his teens, Glenn went to work in his father's warehouse, quickly becoming an astute businessman. In 1870, the family business had expanded to cover a large region, and Glenn began traveling throughout the south selling his father's goods.

Glenn's business acumen soon led him to the booming textile industry. He invested in property and cotton mills, and eventually gave his full attention to the production of woven fabrics which his father's business sold to retailers.

In 1886, representing a large contingent of southern textile mills, the Neil family sold their dry goods business and formed Neil and Associates Textile Distributors, which devoted itself to investment in the fabric industry and the sale of textile goods. Glenn opened an office in Washington, D.C., where the business headquarters were to be.

Soon, that business was booming, and Glenn was not able to buy enough product to meet the demands of his father's clientele, causing him to make plans to do his own manufacturing.

All proceeded well until the financial crash and depression of 1893. The Neil family's progress was slowed but not stopped, and in 1895 Glenn began construction of a textile plant on land he had purchased in Charlotte.

Remembering his father's birthplace in Scotland, Glenn named the textile plant Inverness Mill. Since the plant was close to the cotton fields of the south, he abandoned the Scottish tradition of woolen fabrics and concentrated on the manufacture of cotton canvas and duck material in various weights. The growth and success of that mill led to the opening of several additional cotton mills in the southeast.

The Parker family came to know Glenn Neil in 1892, four years before the opening of Inverness Mill, when Mr. Neil came to visit Will's dad, Forrest, at his business in Charlotte. Forrest owned a small but productive brokerage dealing in items sold in general stores and hardware stores throughout the South. His business dealt in products such as household gadgets, pots and pans, cleaning supplies, and his showcase product, firearms.

It was the firearms that brought Mr. Neil to the front door of Parker Essential Products early one Monday morning. Forrest and his staff had just opened up, and Will was sweeping the receiving area when Mr. Neil came bounding in.

He looked around and inquired of no one in particular, "Is Mr. Forrest Parker here?"

Will nodded in the affirmative, walked a few steps toward the hallway, and called out, "Dad, there's a gentleman here to see you."

"Gentleman," Mr. Neil joked. "You noticed, eh?"

"Yes sir," Will said.

Glenn Neil was a large man—not as much in height as in girth, but not short either—about five-eleven and 260 pounds, Will guessed. He had a head of dark hair that made him look as though he were wearing a hat, even though he had a large, black Stetson in his hand. The most impressive thing about Mr. Neil, though, was his demeanor. He glowed with the light of confidence and success. Will had not seen many men like this!

Forrest entered the room from the hallway and walked to Mr. Neil with his right hand extended.

"Morning, sir … Forrest Parker. What can I do for you?"

"Mr. Parker," Neil said as he shook Forrest's hand, "You probably don't remember me, but I used to be in a business similar to yours. My name is Neil…Glenn Neil…and my family operated a wholesale dry-goods business up until recently. I think our paths crossed a few times."

"Goodness, yes!" Forrest exclaimed, "I talked to your daddy on several occasions. It sure left a vacuum when your business closed."

The two men talked about general stores and the mutual customers they had once had. They talked about the economy and the dark clouds of economic trouble on the horizon. They talked about Neil's father, Angus, and Forrest recounted a story he had once heard about how Angus fought off a gang of robbers with a peach tree sapling. The men had a good laugh, and then they got down to business.

Forrest directed Neil down the hall to his office and sat him in a leather chair in front of his desk. He then walked around the desk and sat in his creaky swivel chair.

"Glenn…I hope you don't mind me calling you by your first name… what brings you here?"

"Forrest…I hope you don't mind me calling *you* by *your* first name, but it does feel natural … I'm in town looking at some real estate, and while I'm here, I've come to beg a favor. I understand that you're the distributor for Colt and Winchester firearms. I wonder if you would do me the professional courtesy of selling me some guns at wholesale."

Forrest leaned back in his chair and stroked his chin with his right hand. A look of concern washed over his face.

"Glenn," he said, "I would love to sell you some guns, but I'm sure you know that as a distributor, I'm not supposed to sell weapons to anyone other than a licensed dealer. That's the agreement I have with both companies."

"I figured that was the case, Forrest, but there shouldn't be a problem. When we got out of the wholesale business, we didn't give up our license. Figured it might come in handy sometime. All you'd have to do is make me a dealer!"

A look of relief came over Forrest's face, and he rose from his chair to circle the desk with his hand extended. "You've got yourself a deal," he said. "Now what would you like to buy?"

"Well, sir … I want some nice rifles and revolvers to give to some of my customers, but I'll have to depend on your expertise as to what is the very best. I want top of the line, you know. I'm open for suggestions."

The look of concern came over Forrest's face again, and he sat on the edge of his desk. Then, as if he had had an epiphany, he rose and walked quickly to the door. "Will," he shouted, "come here a minute."

Turning back to face Neil, Forrest wagged his finger in the air and said, "You know, Glenn, if you want the particulars on firearms, you really need to talk to my son, Will … you know, the boy that was sweeping when you came in. I guarantee that he'll give you the very best advice, and when you've decided what you'd like to buy, I'll handle the paperwork."

Glenn Neil didn't know what to think. The boy that was sweeping when he came in was just a kid, he thought. Here he had come to Parker Essential Products to talk serious business, and he was being passed off to a boy janitor!

Neil looked at his watch and dropped it back in the pocket on his vest. *This is wasted time*, he thought. *Maybe I should just get up and leave.*

About that time Will came to the door with the broom still in his hand.

"You need me, Dad?" he asked.

"Will, Mr. Neil here is a *very* important new customer." Forrest's finger was wagging in the air again. "I want you to answer all his questions about Colt and Remington, and then take him out back and let him shoot as much as he wants to. And put down that broom! You look like a common chamber maid!"

Will's eyes brightened. Talking guns was just about his favorite thing to do, and he welcomed the opportunity to talk to a "*very* important new customer".

"Mr. Neil," Will said politely as he, like his dad, extended his hand, "my name is Will, and I would consider it an honor to show you some guns. Do you have anything in particular in mind?"

"Well, son, you know … I'm not a gun expert … but I've been told that the Winchester Model 1873 is a mighty fine rifle, and I've heard that the Colt 1873 Army Model revolver is the handgun to buy, so I think those are the models I want. I'm going to give them to some of my customers as gifts, you understand."

"Now you see, sir," Will said proudly, "you *do* know something about guns! Why, I have both of those pieces myself and they are *fine* weapons. I tell you what … you step out back through that door," Will pointed down the hall, "and I'll go get those two guns, and we will do some shootin'."

Will almost ran out of the room, his excitement evident.

Mr. Neil made his way out back where he found a shooting range. Bullseye targets and human silhouettes were set up at various distances, and behind them all was a tall, dirt berm to catch the bullets.

Almost instantly, Will appeared with two rifles and a handgun. He propped the rifles against the side of the building and proceeded to load the revolver.

"Mr. Neil," Will said as he loaded bullets into the gun's cylinder, "this is the Colt Model 1873 Peacemaker ... the gun that won the west. The Army version is a .45 caliber, but this one is the civilian version, a .44-40 caliber. I use it because the ammunition is a little easier to find. Now if you are going to give them as gifts, either would be okay. Each has its strong points."

Will had finished loading the Colt, and he quickly turned to face a silhouette target about 20 yards away. Instantly, he raised the gun with his right hand to the height of his waist and fired six shots as quickly as he could fan the hammer with his left hand.

The sound was deafening, and Neil recoiled in surprise. When he had sufficiently recovered, he could see that there were six neat holes in the chest of the target.

"Good lord, boy! Where did you learn to shoot like that?" was all that Neil could squeak out.

"Well, sir, I spend part of each summer with my grandparents up on a farm up near Galax, Virginia ... up in the mountains, and we do a lot of shooting and hunting and things like that. Course, it doesn't hurt to have a dad that sells guns and has a shooting range."

"Boy, you amaze me!" Neil blustered. "You know, I was born in Virginia! We seem to be finding some common ground here. By the way, I'll take six of those .44-40's."

Will beamed. "Now, Mr. Neil, I should tell you, those guns sell for ..."

"I don't care what they sell for ... make it eight. I want two for myself ... one for each hand. Now," he said, "how about those rifles?"

Will was almost breathless as he placed the revolver in his belt and hurried to pick up the rifles.

"Mr. Neil, this one," Will commented as he handed one of the rifles to Neil, "is your Winchester Model 1873, the largest selling rifle of all time … the one you said you wanted … and a good choice it is. It's loaded and ready to fire so why don't you take a shot at one of those targets."

Neil raised the rifle to his shoulder and fired a round at the target Will had used, hitting it in the arm.

"Smooth, isn't it?" Will said as he took the rifle back and handed Neil the other one. "Now, I want you to try the brand new Model 1892."

The difference in the two rifles was instantly apparent to Neil as he felt the lightness of the new model, and it had a look of refinement that was not seen in the other weapon. He raised it to his shoulder and fired a round that hit the target squarely between the eyes.

"Amazing!" Neil said. "Amazing! I'll take eight of those too."

Seated back inside in the leather chair, Neil looked across the desk at Forrest and said, "Forrest, this has been a good day! I came here looking for guns, which I got, and ended up with two new friends. I want to thank you for setting me up to buy those pieces, and I especially want to thank you for introducing me to that boy of yours. He's gonna do well, Forrest … yeah, that boy's gonna do *very* well.

"Now, to show my appreciation, I want to take you two out to dinner tonight. You name the place, and we'll make an evening of it."

"Okay, Glenn," Forrest said as he raised his finger in the air, "I'll name the place. My daughter, Esther, is fixing corned beef and cabbage for dinner. We'll go to my house!"

"Would you like another piece of apple pie, Mr. Neil?" Esther asked from across the table.

"My Dear, two pieces of pie is my limit. My wife is threatening to put me on a diet as it is ... and I can't imagine why!" Neil mused in mock wonder. "But I'll tell you what ... I'll have another cup of that coffee. You just can't get coffee like that in a hotel.

"You know, I'm on the road about three weeks out of every month, and I've always thought that I'd found the best of the hotels ... not the four-stars mind you, I don't need all that fancy service. What I look for is a clean room and good food. You can't do your best work if the food's not good. But the biggest shortfall of most restaurants is the coffee! And this is good coffee!"

It was late in the night before Glenn Neil and the Parker family parted company, and as Neil left, the house fairly rang with echoes of the laughter and frivolity that had marked the evening.

Yes, Neil had purchased his guns and had found three new friends, but Will was the big winner. He had gained a supporter who would help shape his life for years to come. Wouldn't Mama be proud!

Three

CHANCE OF A LIFETIME

July 1, 1894

Dear Glenn:

First of all, I want to tell you how I cherish the friendship you have brought to our family. Your first visit two years back, and the kind visits you have made to our home since, have added cheer and warmth to my life and to the lives of Will and Esther in a way I cannot describe.

In our first meeting, you asked a favor of me, albeit a small one, and I was pleased to oblige. Now, I am forced to ask a much larger favor of you.

My doctor has told me that my heart is failing. He has advised me that if I want to remain on this earth for more than a few months, I must sell my business and retire.

I would be most appreciative if you can help me find some-one willing to buy my company. I know that you still have ties to friends in the wholesale business, and perhaps you can think of just the right person to buy me out.

This could not have come at a worse time with the depression that is upon us. I can assure you however, that in spite of the awful business climate, Parker Essential Products is on reasonably good footing. We are fortunate to be the sole selling agent for several strong products that, as the name of the company implies, are essential to everyday life. I know that when this cloud of depression has lifted, P.E.P. will bounce back with ease.

Esther will soon finish her training and become a teacher. She would like to move to the coast to live and work.

Will seems to have interests that do not include P.E.P., and even if he were interested in staying with the company, he is not yet mature enough to manage a business of this size.

I know how busy you are, but if you could take a few moments to consider my plight and check with your long list of friends, I would be most grateful. to consider my plight and check with your long list of friends, I would be eternally thankful to you.

Your faithful servant, Forrest Parker

Western
Union

HA112 107DL= WASHINGTON DC 12   1150A
FORREST PARKER =
PARKER ESSENTIAL PRODUCTS CHARLOTTE   NC=

YOUR LETTER RECEIVED WILL ARRIVE TRAIN JULY 10 605PM
DO NOT WORRY ALL IS WELL=
GLENN

Will paced up and down the siding of the railroad station as he waited for the train that was now eight minutes late. Usually, he could set his watch by the sound of the whistle when the train reached Overbrook Crossing, but not today.

Finally the lonesome wail of the whistle arrived on the wind, and at last he saw the black smoke of the engine rising above the trees on the northern horizon. It was 6:15 p.m.

When the train had come to rest beside the platform, the conductor descended to place a step beneath the rear door of the lead Pullman.

First off was Glenn Neil, looking a little bedraggled. He was used to better service than this!

"Will, my boy," he said in greeting as he passed his valise from right hand to left, "I swear, every time I see you, you've grown an inch."

Will took the burden of the suitcase from Neil and greeted him.

"Mr. Neil, thank you for coming. Dad was sure relieved when he got your telegram. He's looking forward to seeing you. Did you make this trip just for him?"

"No, son," Neil said, "I made this trip for him, and Esther, and for you, and I must confess, a little bit for me too. We'll talk about that later. Right now, I need to find a toilet. I'm about to bust!"

Neil disappeared into the station to find the facilities, and Will circled the building to where the horse and buggy were waiting. Soon Neil emerged and the two were on their way.

The Parker home was across town in an upper-middle class neighborhood. The ride of about twenty-five minutes gave plenty of time for the two to catch up.

After some pleasantries about the weather, Neil turned to Will and said, "Son, let's see ... you're about 19 now."

"Yes, sir."

"Well, have you thought about what you're going to do with yourself? Are you planning to continue in the kind of work you grew up in ... you know, the wholesale business?"

Will thought about just how he was going to answer that question without sounding childish.

"All I know is I don't want to be shut up in an office all day long, chained to a desk, you know. If I could live out my dream, I guess I would go up to Virginia and farm like my grandparents did. They were two of the happiest people I've ever known ... just using the sun for their clock ... taking half-hour vacations on their porch ... and like that, you know.

"I guess Dad told you everything," Will said as he turned his eyes from the road toward Neil. "I mean, even if I did want to stay in his business, I wouldn't get to now."

"Well, son," Neil replied, "I've always followed my dreams, and sometimes they took me in directions that I didn't even know existed. And I've always been my own man, a lot like you, but it seems that every time I took a turn in the road, there was always someone there to give me directions ... sometimes directly, sometimes indirectly. I'm sure that someone will be happy to be there for you. I just know it!"

A look of calmness came over Will's face. He knew, sitting there by that big, impressive man, that even just the magic of Mr. Neil's presence would see him through the roughest part of his young life.

The horse picked up the pace on his own as the Parker home neared. He turned instinctively onto Will's street and trotted along until he reached the driveway. He made a left turn up the drive and around to the stable where he knew his oats would be waiting.

Neil climbed down from the buggy and grabbed his suitcase. "Will," he said, "I'll go on in and let your dad know we're here while you get the horse and buggy put up."

Forrest and Esther were waiting at the door. Esther was her usual shining self, and Forrest looked surprisingly good. Neil wondered if the situation was as desperate as Forrest had made it out to be, but when the men shook hands, he knew that Forrest wasn't well.

"Mr. Neil," Esther said as she turned toward the kitchen, "I'm just finishing up dinner. We'll eat as soon as Will gets in."

"Esther, whatever you're cooking smells like heaven must smell 'long about suppertime."

Neil headed up the stairs to the room that was always his when he came to visit. There was a comfort in this house that he had found in few places. He turned on the first landing to say, "I think I'll go freshen up a bit … you know, like the proper folks do."

When dinner was done, the two men retreated to Forrest's office with a cup of coffee. Forrest opened his desk and took out a bottle of brandy that he opened only on special occasions.

"Glenn," he said, "that quack that treats my heart won't let me drink this stuff, but I bet you'd like a glass."

Neil didn't answer, but he really didn't have to. The two men had become that close.

When Glenn had tasted the brandy, he turned to Forrest and said, "My friend, do you want to talk about it?"

"I find it very difficult, Glenn, but it must be done. I'm afraid I haven't been totally honest with you. I guess my letter made it sound like if I sold the company and retired, everything would be alright. Well, the truth of the matter is that things will progress whether I sell the business or not. It's imperative that I clear up my affairs as soon as possible. Do I have to say more?"

"No, we won't belabor the issue," Neil replied. "It's difficult for me, too. I just want you to know that you have absolutely nothing to worry about as far as Esther and Will are concerned. I love them both as if they were my own.

"Now, you said that Esther has plans to go to the coast to teach. She can call on me to help in any way, although I doubt that she will need to lean on anyone for much support. She is a remarkable young woman. Must take after her mother."

"That she does, Glenn."

"As for Will, Forrest, I'm sure you know that he is what drew me to this family." Neil swirled the brandy around in the snifter and tasted the elixir again. "With your permission, Forrest, I would like to offer Will a job."

Forrest sat forward in his chair. The words quickened his lagging pulse.

"As you know, I've been making a lot of trips to Charlotte over the last couple of years. You *ought* to know," he chuckled. "I've been eating your food every time I come. Well anyway, I have finally purchased the property I need to start building a cotton mill … a big one, latest technology. I want Will to be on the ground floor of the operation. I'll put him on a fast track to management. Now Forrest, you keep him with you as long as you need him. He'll be a big help to you."

"My head is spinning, Glenn," Forrest said as he sat back in his chair.

"I feel like the weight of the world has been lifted off me. Now if we can find a buyer for P.E.P., I'll finally be able to relax."

"Ah-ha!" Neil exclaimed as he moved to the edge of his seat. "I stopped in Richmond on the way down here and talked to Harold Jeffers. You remember Harold."

Neil was getting excited. "Your brokerage is just the thing Harold is looking for to enlarge his business. He's been thinking about expanding into the Carolinas, and you have some products tied up that he wants. Forrest, he wants to come see you. He'll buy your business in a snap. I guarantee it!"

Forrest slumped into his chair and buried his face in his hands. His body convulsed with sobs, and all he could manage to say was, "Thank you, Glenn … thank you."

———

Forrest William Parker, Sr. gave up his earthly life on August 27, 1894, with Will and Esther by his side. He had finalized the sale of his brokerage to Harold Jeffers just one week before, and he had spent his final days knowing that his house, the building where his business had been, and the proceeds from the sale of his business would give Esther and Will a strong financial foundation as they entered adulthood.

His funeral was held at St. Peter's Episcopal Church. Glenn Neil, as chief pall bearer, bore the right front corner of his casket.

———

"Will, it's time we had a talk," Glenn Neil announced as he bounded down the steps. "Hitch up the buggy and let's take a ride. There's something I want to show you. We'll talk on the way."

It had been three days since the funeral, and Will was close to depression. Esther was packing for her trip to Wilmington to begin her teaching career, and he didn't have a clue as to how he would spend the rest of his life. This trip of Mr. Neil's would be a welcome diversion, he thought.

Soon the horse and buggy were joined, and Neil bounded out the back door of the house.

"Will, do you know where North Avenue is?" he asked as he pulled himself up on the buggy seat.

"Of course," Will said.

"Well, get on North and turn onto Vandiver Street."

The fresh air and the company of Glenn Neil made Will feel new. For the first time since his father's death, he felt that life was worth living.

Neil sat on the buggy seat looking straight ahead. There was a look of deep concentration on his face that Will didn't want to disrupt, but his curiosity was getting the best of him.

"Mr. Neil," he finally said, "what did you want to talk about?"

Neil blinked, seemingly out of his daze. "Will, do you know anything about duck?"

"Roasted duck?"

"No, son, you don't eat it, it's a kind of cotton fabric … like canvas … real tough stuff. It's used to make tents and the like."

"That's what you wanted to talk about, Mr. Neil?"

Will turned the buggy on to North Avenue. Vandiver was just ahead.

"That's just part of it boy … the end result, you might say. I really wanted to talk about you. Your dad and I had a talk when I came in July, and I told him that I would be there to help you in any way I could. Will, I don't want to get in your way. You may have plans already made. You may want to go on up to Virginia and stake out a farm. If you do, God bless you!"

Will had turned onto Vandiver Street, which was lined with empty lots and vacant houses.

"Pull up right here," Neil said as he sat up straight to look around. "Will, I've bought all this property for several blocks around. In a few months we'll begin construction of a cotton mill to make that canvas cloth I was telling you about. This will be one of the first mills in the South to be totally electric … no water wheels, no gas lighting, no belts and pulleys to get caught up in. We'll run two shifts, as many hours as we need to get the job done. The mill must be completed and running by the end of '96. I've landed a big government contract for canvas of several weights to be used to make overalls for the Cavalry, wagon covers, tents, pontoons, awnings for barracks, and the list goes on. In addition to that I can sell all the light-weight canvas we can make in Europe for artists to slop paint on."

He turned to look directly at Will. "Son, I want to offer you a job … one that will train you to be a manager in this mill. I don't know where or how far it will take you; that's up to you. If you try it and don't like it, you can go on up to Virginia and live your dream. Does that sound fair?"

Will was astounded, and his answer was instant.

"Mr. Neil, *you've got yourself a deal*!"

"Have you ever been to Washington?"

"No, sir."

"Well, let's go home and pack a bag. I'll take you back with me to start learning the textile business. You can work for a while in the office to see the boring side of the business, and then we'll go around to some of the mills that I have an interest in and let you see how that fluffy white stuff that grows on stalks turns into cloth.

"And oh yes, while we're in Washington, I'll introduce you to President Cleveland."

Four

Jest Plain Goober

Will awoke to the sound of scratching at his back door, and for a moment he lay still beneath the covers, hoping it had been a dream. But there it was again, and this time he knew exactly what it was: it was Dawg wanting to be fed.

The clock by the bed said 4:55—five minutes before the alarm would have sounded anyway—dawn for a night-shift worker. He thought it ironic that he was getting up just as bankers and office workers were preparing to end their work day, but this was the schedule he had chosen. After all, night shift paid two cents more per hour!

He rolled out of bed and made his way to the back door, where he found Dawg waiting, thankful that his pleas had been heard, already licking his chops in anticipation of what was to come.

On his way home that morning Will had discovered that the butcher shop down the street from Sarah's had opened early, so he picked up a package of meat scraps and bones for Dawg's dining pleasure. With the addition of some scraps donated by Sarah, he had a supply of treats that would keep for several days in the icebox. Dawg was a well-fed animal.

With his pal fed, Will turned his attention to other matters. He coaxed some water from the pump by the sink, filling the kettle and Dawg's water bowl, and lit the kerosene kitchen stove.

While he was puttering around putting things in order, water came to a boil, and he prepared his regular "breakfast" of coffee and oatmeal, finished off with a grilled ham sandwich. Bachelor provisions. There was enough ham left to make a sandwich to take to work, and enough hot water left to wash and shave.

The trip to work tonight would be out of the ordinary. Traveler was going to the livery for a new set of shoes, meaning that Will would not have to walk to work. In two days, Traveler would be waiting re-shod in the livery corral when Will left work, and he would ride him home.

Mr. Neil's plans for the village had included a stable and corral to be built at the mill so that employees who didn't live in the village could ride to work, but so far, there were no signs of that happening. Will knew that it was more important to have housing built for the influx of new workers, and so he would be patient. He was quickly becoming a company man.

Mr. Neil had also promised Will a fast track to management, and he had promoted him to an assistant overseer position that most mill folks referred to as a "second hand." His job was to walk the floor of the weave room looking for problems, keep workers on their toes, and on occasion fill in for weavers who were absent. He was happy, and for the time being, thoughts of Virginia had been put in the dark recesses of his mind.

Mr. Neil had also fulfilled a promise he had made to Will's father that he would see to the needs of Will's sister too. Before seeing Esther off to Wilmington, he had agreed to buy the rambling house that would have been home to Will alone. "I'm going to need a place to stay when I'm in Charlotte," Neil had told them, "and besides, I've grown accustomed to the place."

In addition to buying the house, he had bought the building that had housed Parker Essential Products, telling them he needed it for ware-house space. With that done, Esther had the means to buy a nice home in Wilmington with a substantial nest-egg left over, and Will could buy the house and property in the country where he now lived and have his own substantial nest-egg.

"Now I can just step out my back door and shoot my guns," he had told Neil excitedly.

The trip to the livery was a real treat for Traveler. Will had been riding him only on Sunday, and that was in the fields nearby. His only trips into town were to church, and Will had not been attending every week.

One would have sworn that Traveler nodded to the few horses he passed, seeing them as friends and equals, but he gave the barking dogs a wide berth, lowering his head and sidestepping by them until he had left them behind.

With Traveler corralled at the livery, Will walked the final block or so to the Mill entrance, and as always, he was one of the first in.

The night time-keeper, Old Man Gunnelson, was seated behind his desk, feet propped up and eyes closed. Without looking up he said, "Evenin', Will. Heard you comin'. What is it they say about the early bird?"

Will greeted Gunnelson as he pulled his time card from the out rack and placed it on the desk. Gunnelson noted the time, initialed it, and put it in his basket.

"Hear you're gettin' a new man tonight, Will. He came in right 'fore you got here and headed off down to the super's office."

"Well, what did he look like?"

"Will, I swear, he's a *strange* one ... kinda hard to describe."

"Long as he can make canvas I don't care what he looks like," Will said, and he wished Gunnelson a nice evening and headed off down the hall.

As soon as Will entered the weave room, the day-shift overseer motioned for him to come to the far end of the room to see a problem with one of the machines. He walked by loom after loom, row after row, making his way through the cotton dust and the deafening clatter of the looms until he reached the overseer, who was standing over a broken shaft lying on the floor.

The overseer leaned over to Will's ear and shouted, "This one is off line until the fixers can make a new shaft."

Will nodded, made the "okay" sign with his hand, and took the repair slip from the overseer, then he turned and looked back toward the entrance just as the night supervisor entered the weave room with the new man in tow.

"I wish you'd look at what's comin'!" shouted the overseer.

There came the new man to the right of and a step behind the super, taking about a step and a half for every one the super took. He was not much more than five feet tall and couldn't have weighed more than 110 pounds. He walked with his toes pointed out, his chin held high, and his chest leading the way. His head was covered with a large, unruly shock of sand colored hair. He was as clean as a whistle and carried himself with confidence, but his trousers were a size too large and the sleeves of his flannel shirt were rolled up almost to his shoulders, exposing his long, red underwear.

The super guided the man up close to Will and shouted, "Will Parker, I want you to meet Makepeace Green. He'll be switching over to the night shift."

Will took the new man's hand and shouted, "Pleased to meet you, Mr. Green."

"How do, Mr. Parker. Likewise I'm shore," Green shouted back.

"Look, Mr. Green," Will said, "let's step into the spinning room where things are a little quieter, and we'll get acquainted."

"Much obliged, I'm shore."

Makepeace Green's voice was as strange as his appearance. It was a caricature of the voices Will had heard in the mountains of Virginia where his grandparents had lived—high and nasally—a sound that would cut right through you and yet an honest sound that recalled the memory of good, down-to-earth people.

With the weave room behind and the door closed, the noise level was a little more bearable. Will led Green to the overseer's area, which was not being used, and motioned for him to have a seat.

"Well, Mr. Green, we're glad to have you here tonight. In case you couldn't hear in the weave room, my name is Will Parker, but you can just call me Will."

"Mighty kind of ye, Mr. Parker."

"That's *Will*, Mr. Green. Is it alright if I call you Makepeace?"

"No sir, I'd druther ye didn't."

Will blushed. "Well then … Mr. Green it is!"

"Oh, no Sir, Mr. Will …Will … 'at ain't what I meant. Jest call me Goober. 'At's what ever'body back home calls me."

"*Goober?*"

"Yes sir, jest plain Goober."

"Well, okay … Goober. Tell me, how many looms have you been working?"

"I'm up t' 6. Course I only been weavin' fer a week."

Will was amazed! "You've only been weaving for a week and you're running 6 looms?"

"Yes, sir, I could do more, but they ain't enough hooked up yet. Soon as them new ones is up an' runnin' I kin do three times 'at many!"

Good lord, Will thought, *this ought to be interesting.*

———◆———

It had been a busy night in the weave room. Maybe it was the phase of the moon, maybe fate, but everything seemed to go wrong. Loom fixers weren't moving as quickly as some of the weavers thought they should, a sweeper accidentally jammed his broom handle into a loom, breaking some drop wires, and it seemed that machines were going down all over the room.

The only bright spot of the shift had been Goober Green. Will hadn't heard a peep out of him.

Late into the night during a period of relative calm, Will had parked himself near Goober where he could watch him undetected. Goober was a symphony of motion, darting here and there between his bank of looms, tying broken warp threads, pulling broken filling and repairing damage, replacing empty bobbins, and doffing rolls of finished canvas. He would pause when everything was running smoothly and watch his machines like a hawk, waiting to pounce on the next problem.

With production running smoothly for the time being, Will left the weave room and made his way to the supervisor's office. He knocked on the door and entered to find the super shuffling through some papers.

"Mr. Mooney," he said, "do you have a minute?"

Mooney motioned for Will to sit down. "Sure, Will, have a seat."

"Mr. Mooney, I wanted to ask you about the new man, Green."

"You got a problem with Green?"

"No, no," Will said, "Everything's fine. I just wanted to know how, with so many people looking for work, he got a job as a weaver. He just doesn't look like the type."

Mooney laughed. "Kinda like the frog that turned into a prince, isn't it? The only difference is, nobody kissed Green."

Will smiled and shifted in his seat.

Mooney continued, "The first-shift man said that Green came in looking for a job along with about a thousand other people, mostly women and children, and when they talked to him, he wouldn't shut up! Said he talked his way into a job as a sweeper and he did all right.

"Then one afternoon, it seems he was sweeping a row between a bank of looms and he found the weaver lying on the floor behind a stack of canvas passed out drunk! Well, Green looked around and there was thread goin' everywhere, and empty bobbins, and canvas rolls filled up needing to be doffed … so Green grabbed the weaver's reed hook and commenced to pullin' warp and replacing bobbins and getting things back on track. Seems he had been watching the weavers as he was sweeping. Even learned to tie a weaver's knot on his own.

"Then about that time the first-shift man came through the weave room and saw this sweeper up over a loom jerkin' out broken fill, and he screamed out, '*What do you think you're doin' there?*'

"So Green jumped down and ran over and got up in the first-shift man's ear and hollered back, 'I'm a-makin' canvas!'

"The first-shift man said he stood there for a minute watching Green work and about that time he saw the weaver's feet sticking out from behind the stack, so he went over and pulled the man out and fired him on the spot!

Went over and hired Green as a weaver … and like they say, the rest is history."

"Don't that beat all?" Will said, and he thanked Mooney and went back to work.

Near the end of the shift, he made his way over to Goober and shouted in his ear, "Goober, wait for me after you've signed out. I want to talk to you."

"Yes, sir, Mr. Par … I mean Will. I'll do 'er."

When Will had finished his paperwork and given his time card to Gunnelson, he stepped out the door and into another crisp October morning. Goober was seated on the steps waiting for him, his coat pulled up around his head. As Will approached he bounded to his feet.

"I ain't done nothin' wrong have I, Will?"

"Goodness no!" Will replied. "I just wanted to see if you would have some breakfast with me down at the cafe."

Goober looked down and kicked the dirt. "I'm mighty obliged Will, but I'm paid up down at th' boardin' house an' I 'spect I better eat there."

Will motioned in the direction of the street. "Come on Goober, I'm buying you breakfast as a welcome to the night shift. It's not every day that I meet a ball of fire like you! And besides, I like to get to know my weavers."

"Well, sir, in 'at case I'll shore be proud t' join ye!"

———————

Will held the door as Goober entered Sarah's Cafe. Goober removed his hat and clutched it in both hands as he looked around. It seemed to Will that the experience of going to a cafe must be a new one for Goober because his air of confidence had vanished. Right now, he seemed more like a child than the little rooster that had strutted into the weave room.

Will and Goober worked their way through the bachelor corps to a table near the counter, and the two were seated. The bachelor corps was taking the sight in.

Sarah turned from her stove and flashed a look of surprise. "Mornin' Precious," she said. "You're sittin' at a table this mornin'?"

"That's right, Sarah," Will replied, "and I brought you a new customer. Sarah, meet Makepeace Green."

The bachelor corps suppressed giggles and snickers as Makepeace leaned over and whispered to Will.

"'At's Goober … jest plain Goober."

"Sarah, make that *Goober* Green," Will said, and he looked around to see Tommy Lee Jones with his head on the table laughing.

As the introductions were being made, a new waitress appeared from the back room and came around to pour Will and Goober a cup of coffee. She was dressed in a uniform like Prissy wore, but she was closer to Sarah's age—a tall slender woman with a stern countenance. When she had poured the coffee, she disappeared into the back room again.

"Sarah," Will said, "you have a new waitress! Where's Prissy?"

"Prissy's in Raleigh with her mother, tending to her grandmother. The poor woman had a stroke. Looks like she'll be gone awhile. The new girl is Pearl. You gonna have the regular?"

"Yep, two eggs over easy with all the trimmings."

"How about you, Mr. … Goober?"

"I'll have 'em eggs myself with some trimmin's, an' make shore mine is chicken eggs!"

"*Chicken* eggs, Mr. … Goober?" Sarah asked as she turned to face him.

"Yes'm, I was jest makin' shore. Lots'a folks back whur I come frum eats guinea eggs an' turkey eggs an' th' lack, but they too rich fer me. An' if 'em trimmins don't include grits, I'd like a bowl o' them … an' a slice o' onion."

"Comin' right up," Sarah said, and she turned and tapped the edge of her spatula on the frying pan.

Will sat up and wagged his finger in the air—a mannerism he had inherited from his father—and inquired of Goober, "You keep saying 'back where I come from.' Just exactly where is that?"

"Hit's a little place back up west o' Burley called Avery Cove … purdy little place. Most folks don't know 'bout it. My house is at th' far end o' th' cove, 'bout four mile west o' Burden's General Store. If ye wuz at my place an' went up through th' woods t' th' top of th' mountain, you'd be in Tennessee."

"Good farm land?" Will asked.

"They's a river … right there, hit's called th' Avery River…an' it cuts right through th' middle o' th' valley … goes right by my house … an' 'at bottom land stays moist all summer long without gettin' soggy. And th' people there grows th' *finest* crops and th' *finest* livestock you ever saw."

Will was drawing a picture of Avery Cove in his mind, and he wondered why anyone would leave a place like that to come to work in a mill.

"People leaves thar 'cause hit's so dad-gum *fur* frum ever'thing," Goober blurted out as if he had read Will's thoughts. "And they ain't enough women thar to choose a *good 'un* frum!" Goober's face was red.

Sarah turned slowly and looked at Goober over her glasses, and by this time, the bachelor corps was through eating and had turned their chairs toward the pair, trying to figure out what was going on.

Will moved closer to Goober and lowered his voice so the audience couldn't hear. "Calm down, Goober," he said. I hope I didn't say something that upset you."

"Ain't nothin' you said, Will. I rec'on I jest git a little homesick ever' now an' then. I'll git over it." He was getting back to a more normal color.

"Here you are, boys!" Pearl had appeared out of nowhere and was placing their plates in front of them. "I'll be back to top off your coffee."

———◆———

The corps had finished eating and left. With no other customers in the cafe, Sarah came over and sat with Will and Goober while they finished their meal.

"Miz Sarah," Goober said, " 'at was th' most finest breakfast I have eat since I lef' th' cove. Much more finer than th' boardin' house. Them chicken eggs wuz good an' runny … jest th' way I like 'em."

Sarah was curious. "Who cooked for you back in the cove?"

"My mama did till she passed, an' then I et a lot o' m' Aint Sweetie's cookin'. Her an' Uncle Roamer lived a couple o' farms down fum me. They gettin' up in years so I swapped 'em work fer cookin'… even stayed with 'em fer a while. I plowed Uncle Roamer's garden an' cut their farwood, an' Aint Sweetie cooked a meal fer me most days an' give me a lot o' canned goods an' cured meat an' th' lack."

Will shifted in his seat and put his elbows on the table. "Who's looking out for Sweetie and Roamer while you're here?"

"People in th' cove looks out fer one another. They's a lot o' folk 'at'll barter fer whut Uncle Roamer makes."

Sarah perked up. "What does Roamer make?" she asked.

Goober thought carefully before he answered. "Oh, jus' stuff folks wants," he said.

Will had shifted positions again and was rubbing his eyes and yawning.

"Goober, this is nice, but I've got to get home and get some sleep. It's not long until we've got to be at work again."

"Yes sir, I'm tarred too," Goober said, and he got up and headed over to where his coat was hanging.

Will settled up with Sarah, and he and Goober headed out the door, but Goober quickly turned and started back inside.

"Will, I plum forgot t' tell th' ladies g'bye."

When Goober came back out the door his confident nature had returned, and he stuck out his hand to Will.

"Will, I want t' thank ye fer th' fine meal an' I 'specially want t' thank ye fer bein' nice to me. Most city folk looks right over m' head, but you look me right in th' eye! I got t' say though, fer a city feller ye ain't very careful."

"Really? How's that, Goober."

"Ye lef' 'is here dime a-layin' on th' table!"

Five

A Trip to Town

October 21, 1896

My Dearest Brother,

I felt that I must write to let you know that all is well here in Wilmington. My children (I like to call them that) are settling into their studies and it will be a good school year.

Please forgive me for waiting so long to write. I assure you that it has been only because my work load is so great. This year's class is large and the students have to learn on several levels. I get very discouraged at times. Right now, I am kept going by the fact that I will be with you at Christmas. How lonesome I am for your Company, and how I long to see home.

Now, I must grade papers. Please write often. My contact with you is vital. A longer letter will follow.

Please give Mr. Neil my love.

Your loving sister,

Esther

It had been awhile since Will had heard from Esther, such a long time in fact that he had been worried about her well-being. Homesick! But at least she was well.

He folded the letter carefully and continued his walk from the post office to the mill. The postal diversion had put him dangerously close to being late, and so he quickened his step, dodging puddles from the afternoon rain. As he neared the mill he was met by a line of workers coming in his direction.

"*Will! … Will!*" came a shout from the middle of the crowd. It was Goober.

"Goober … where's everybody going?" Will asked.

"Lightnin' struck th' 'lectricity, Will. They've closed th' mill. Said it ain't gonna be back runnin' till Monday."

Will had an instant feeling of well-being. He needed a day or two off.

"Let's see," he thought out loud, "with this being Friday, I have … 72 hours of free time."

In his exuberance he feigned a punch at Goober. "How 'bout it?" he said. "Come on out to my place and spend the weekend, and we'll see the town."

"Hot dang, Will, I'm fer that!"

They stopped at the boarding house for Goober to pick up a change of clothes, and they were off.

Darkness was upon them—too late today for much of anything but talk. Will was full of questions about Avery Cove, Goober himself, and Aunt Sweetie and Uncle Roamer, but he didn't want to seem nosy. He decided he would spring his questions a little at a time.

Goober had some questions of his own. As the two walked along, he asked Will about his family, how old he was—Goober didn't mind being nosy—and how he came to work at the mill.

It was easy to talk to Goober. Will told him about his family and how he had come to know Mr. Neil, and he told him about Esther's letter and how he couldn't understand why she would want to live so far away from the place she had always called home.

Then he told Goober about meeting President Grover Cleveland and shaking his hand.

"Why, I'd never warsch m' hand never ag'in!" Goober said.

Will did ask Goober how old he was and was surprised when he said he was 22, for in some ways Goober seemed to be much older. But then, as he pondered it, he seemed to be more like a boy of about 15.

They passed the livery stable, the church, the school, and the company store. All were dark and deserted. All that showed signs of life on the village were the boarding house and the mill houses that were occupied. There were no street lights, but the moon was rising and its light was all they needed.

The two were comfortable with each other, probably because each was comfortable with himself, and the comfort they shared was becoming that of friendship. Their talk and their laughter were flowing freely.

"Well, there's my house," Will finally announced. "And here comes my dog. He's not used to seeing me come home this time of day."

"Will, he looks lack a coon dog, but if he's a coon dog, he's the biggest un I ever saw. Looks like he's got some horse in 'im er somethin'."

Will bent down to scratch Dawg behind his ears, and Dawg showed his pleasure by squirming and making his puddle in the dust.

"What's 'is name," asked Goober.

"Dawg."

"Come on!" Goober said. "What's 'is name?"

Will laughed a hearty belly laugh. "His name is *Dawg*. D-A-W-G."

"I hope to my never!" said Goober.

While Will gave the dog some attention, Goober stood by the driveway and surveyed the house and property by the light of the moon and stars. He had seen lots of nice houses since he came to Charlotte, but this was the first one he could connect to someone he knew. While Will's house was modest by some standards, Goober saw it as a castle—much finer than most of the houses in Avery Cove, with the exception of Preacher Burden's house. The only finer structures in Avery Cove, he thought, were the barns on some of the larger farms. Most of the farmers there put a lot of importance on the size and quality of their barns.

"Will, whur's th' outhouse?" Goober asked?

"It's around back to the left of the stable," was the reply. "When you get through there, come on in the back door."

The two men talked through the night until shortly before dawn. When weariness finally took control, Will directed Goober to the room he had fixed up for Esther. The boarding house was very adequate, but this room was the finest that Goober had ever stayed in. It was clean and neat and had store-bought furniture even finer than Preacher Burden had in his home.

"You can spend the night here," Will said. "This afternoon we'll pick up where we left off. Sleep well."

On a cool fall evening a couple of years before, after a day in the fields, and after a warm bath, a good supper, and a sip of Uncle Roamer's elderberry wine, Goober had experienced a night of sleep as good as the one he had that night at Will house, but that was the "onlyest" one he could remember. Maybe it was the break from the clatter of the looms, or the casual talk with someone his own age, or a combination of things that converged like the planets do when magical things happen, but this had been a special day for Goober, and other special days were on the horizon.

———

G oober awoke to the sound of ham frying on the stove along with the smell of biscuits and some sort of beans.

"Now 'at's th' way a feller ort t' be woke up ever' day," he said to himself. "Hit's much more better than havin' a rooster squawkin' at ye."

Will had been up long enough to have a night-shift breakfast ready and on the table. He called out for Goober, and Goober came a-runnin'. Will had never seen such a diminutive person eat so much food. He wondered how he held it all.

With the meal devoured and the dishes washed, Will thought some entertainment was in order.

"Say, Goober," Will asked with his finger in the air, "do you like to shoot?"

Goober turned toward Will at the sink. "Shoot *whut?*"

"Targets ... cans, bottles, and such."

"Why, sure," Goober replied, "but first I gotta go t' th' outhouse."

"Well, while you're at the outhouse I'll get my .44 and I'll meet you out back."

When Goober exited the outhouse, hiking up his trousers as he walked, Will had just finished loading his pistol. As Goober approached, he raised it to eye level, pulled back the hammer, centered a tin can about 25 feet away, and fired.

"Man, 'at thing's *loud!*" Goober said. "Let me have a turn."

Will handed Goober the weapon without saying a word. He wanted to see if the little rooster knew anything about guns.

Goober looked it over, pulled the hammer back, and took aim at a can. When the gun went off, it flew out of his hand and landed on the ground behind him as he dropped to his knees and covered his head with his arms.

"*Man!*" he said. "'*at thing kicks lack a mule!*"

The gun was okay. Will examined it carefully and helped Goober to his feet.

"T' tell ye th' truth, Will," he said, "I'm more used t' a shotgun er a rifle."

"Good!" Will replied. "I've been watching a flock of turkeys about two fields over, so I'll go get you a shotgun and me a rifle, and we'll go see if we can shoot a big tom for Sunday dinner."

All was not well. Goober looked down and kicked the dirt as Will had seen him do before when there was a problem, but this time Will sensed that it was more serious than before.

"Will ..." Goober started out, "they's somethin' I been meanin' t' tell ye ...'bout th' real reason I lef' home."

"*O Lord,*" Will thought. He feared that Goober was in trouble with the law—that he was about to lose a new friend and a good worker. It had to be bad. Goober was trembling, and his eyes were clouding up. He directed Goober to the back steps, and they sat down.

"I'll start out at th' beginnin'," Goober said. "When I wuz jest a youngun, long 'bout six yars old, an' hit wuz th' first cold snap o' th' winter, my pa got me up one mornin' an' said, 'Git up, Goober, we gonna kill us a hog 'is mornin', an' I'm-a gonna let you shoot 'im!'

"Wal, 'at sounded real good t' me 'til we got out t' th' pig-pen whur Pa had been fattenin' 'at pig. …Wal, he got over in th' pen an' boarded him up in a corner … an' got a rope around' 'is leg and commenced t' draggin' 'im over t' whur I wuz … an' Pa had already give me th' gun … an' 'at pig wuz a-squealin' lack a youngun a-cryin' fer 'is mama, Will."

Goober wiped his eyes and pulled his knees tight to his chest with his arms, and then he continued.

"An' Will, 'at ol' pig looked up at me with 'em ol' beedy eyes …" Goober paused, and Will waited patiently. "… 'cause he knowed whut I wuz 'bout t' do. He knowed whut wuz happenin', Will … An' he was a-beggin.

"So I throwed down 'at gun an' I run fast as I could back behind th' barn an' I hid. … But I could hear 'at ol' pig a-squealin' … 'til finely, I heared th' crack o' th' gun … an' th' squealin' stopped."

Will was so moved by the story that he couldn't speak. Goober went on.

"Ye' know, Will, if ye gonna live on a farm, an' if ye 'spect t' eat an' feed a fam'ly, ye have t' kill a hog er a chicken most ever' day … an' ye need t' hunt turkeys and deer an' sech t' put meat on th' table. …Well, I can't do 'at, Will. … Now as long as somebody else is doin' th' killin' an' th' dressin' out, I'll eat it like th' next man, but I jes can't kill a animal. Ever' body in Avery Cove knowed how I felt about it, an' I wuz jest a clown to 'em … jest a clown … so I up an' lef'."

Goober looked Will in the eye, and Will had a sense of understanding that went beyond reason. There would be no more talk about hunting. He was angered that anyone would think of his friend as a clown.

Will sat for a moment and then put a hand on Goober's knee and pushed himself up.

"What say, Goober," he said. "Let's go to town."

Goober jumped to his feet and wiped his nose on his sleeve. "Hot dang, Will!" he said, "I'm fer that!"

C harlotte was a small, lazy town—a southern jewel surrounded by farms and forest—a place for farmers to come buy essentials, sell their goods, or see a doctor. Compared to New York, Washington, or even Richmond, it was just a wide spot in the road, but to Goober Green, it was Paris or London. There were buildings several stories high beside paved streets. There were restaurants and bars ... and there was a theater!

On the marquee of the theater a show was advertised. "Zim Blakey's All-Star Review," it read, and across the front of the theater were pictures of entertainers—musicians, an animal act, an actor in black face, a juggler, and the one that really caught Goober's eye, a seductive woman holding feathers over her body!

"I'm fer that, Will!" Goober hollered. "Can we see 'is show?"

"I guess we can," said Will, "but the tickets are 25 cents. Do you have any money?"

"I shore do!" said Goober, pushing his chest out with pride. "I got a dollar and 36 cent! I'll buy *you* a ticket!"

"I'm fer that," hollered Will, and he mockingly stuck out his own chest. "But it's over an hour till the show starts. Let's get something to eat."

———————

A ny new experience with Goober was an adventure. Will had come to find out that aside from two or three trips to Burley, and an occasional trip to Valle Crucis to sell herbs and chestnuts, this trip to Charlotte was Goober's first journey out of Avery Cove. The trip down the mountain and across new territory alone on uncharted roads must have been daunting.

Goober had studied the state of North Carolina in school and had seen pictures of places like Charlotte in books, but he had never seen a fine restaurant, a large church, a theater, or so many other things that the average person took for granted.

Will considered Goober's naiveté as he was choosing a place to eat. It must not be too expensive he thought, and it must not be overwhelmingly fancy, so with Goober's approval, he decided on a steak house—Buffalo Bill's—about a block from the theatre.

They were seated at a table in the rear near the kitchen. As the waiter pulled out Goober's chair, Goober said, "Lookie, Will, they got a bed sheet on th' table … an' ever'body gets a hanker-chief!"

The waiter thought that was a great joke, and Will didn't let on that Goober was serious.

Will ordered a New York strip steak, medium, with a baked potato, and a glass of wine.

Goober chose the large T-bone steak, well done, with a "tater", and since they didn't have elderberry wine, he had the same kind that Will got.

As Goober was gnawing the last bit of steak from the bone, he looked up at Will.

"Ye know whut, Will?" he said. "'at wuz th' most finest meal I ever had th' pleasure o' eatin'… an' hit shoulda been at sixty-five cent! With th' fifty cent fer our tickets, 'at'll leave me … 'et's see…twenty-one cent!"

Will left the tip since he didn't have the heart to bring up tipping at that moment. There would be time for refinement later.

As he had promised, Goober shelled out 50 cents for two tickets to the vaudeville show. He proudly gave Will his ticket, and they entered the theatre. Goober was incensed that the usher tore his ticket in half. "I wuz gonna press 'at in a book," he told Will.

After Will explained to the usher that this was Goober's first theater experience, the usher gave him an un-torn ticket along with a couple of tickets from other shows.

There were empty seats all over the theater, but Goober headed for front row center as Will tagged along.

Soon, the house lights dimmed, and the piano started playing the theme music. The emcee bounced out on stage to the applause of the audience and announced the first act, The Bailey Brothers, a song-and-dance team. Goober moved to the edge of his seat and was riveted to the stage. The Baileys did a rousing medley of popular songs ending with "Camp Town Races." To Goober's delight, the brothers ran a mock horse race around the stage as they sang, and when they hit the last soaring note, Goober sprang to his feet, stood on his seat, and shouted, *"Do 'er ag'in…. Do 'er ag'in!"* while the audience applauded.

The next act was a singer in black-face who played banjo and sang a sad song about his mammy. About midway through the second verse, Goober broke down into convulsive sobs that echoed through the hall, causing the audience to direct their attention to him rather than the singer.

Will turned to see the usher coming quickly toward the front to take care of the commotion, but he was able to breathe a sigh of relief when the usher, realizing that Goober was more entertaining than the singer, turned and went back to the lobby.

Goober's reactions to the jugglers, the animal act, and the female opera singer were equally demonstrative. Since Will doubted that there was anyone in the audience that would have known him, he allowed Goober to express himself, unbridled by decorum.

Finally the moment that Goober had been waiting for came. From stage right, the pianist began a slow, pulsating rhythm of seduction designed to magnify the animal instincts in any red-blooded man. On and on the rhythm pounded, gaining tempo and volume, and building to a frenzy that Goober could hardly bear.

His attention was glued to the pianist, who was bent over the keys, working his fingers in dancing motions, drawing out the last scintilla of passion that the upright box contained. So glued to the pianist was Goober that he didn't see the dancer entering from stage left with her feathers strategically positioned.

When she reached the center of the stage directly in front of Goober, his head snapped around, bringing her into full view, and he jumped up on his seat once again.

"Lookie, Will! Lookie!" he hollered.

The crowd roared, and the dancer, thinking the adulation was for her, went into her most excessive routine.

At the end of the performance, as Goober was nearing exhaustion, the dancer came to the edge of the stage, reached out with one of her minor feathers and tickled Goober on the nose. As she did, she failed to notice that she had come too close to one of the gas lights on the front edge of the stage, and as she dipped toward Goober, one of her feathers caught fire and the whole of her cover exploded in flame.

Fully exposed, she ran off the stage, and the audience joined Goober in what must have been the loudest show of appreciation the theatre had ever seen.

As Will and Goober left the theatre, the usher called Goober over and asked if he would be interested in joining the troop as a plant to stir up the audience. Goober thought about it for a few seconds and finally told him that he thought he would "keep on a-weavin' canvas" since he didn't think his heart could stand it.

The streets were mostly deserted when Will and Goober started home. Soon they were on the edge of the city. The street lights disappeared and once more the moon was their only guide. They agreed that there was a chill in the air that had not been felt that year. Winter was on the way.

"Ye know, Will," Goober said, "'at wuz th' most finest day I have ever had!"

"Glad you enjoyed it, Goober."

"Only problem is, I can't do much o' that. 'At boardin' house is takin' ever' thin' I make. Course, I git two meals an' a lunch in a poke to take t' work, an' hit's clean an' warm, but hit don't leave much fer other things. I wuz a-wantin' t' send a little back t' Uncle Roamer and Aunt Sweetie, but I ain't been able to yet."

"Things will get a little better when you get some more looms, you know."

"Yeah, an' I am happy here. Ye know, Will, when you uz a-talkin' 'bout ye sister an' ye said how she wuz home sick an' all?"

"Yeah."

"An' ye said ye couldn't understand why she'd want t' live so far away fum home?"

"Yeah."

"Wal, 'at made me feel a little teary-eyed myself … 'cause I'm s' far fum home. But a'ter today, I don't think I'll ever go back …'cept maybe t' see Uncle Roamer and Aint Sweetie. I think I found m' place in life, Will."

"That's great, Goob."

Goober's head snapped around, and he looked up at Will.

"Will, th' only other person 'at ever called me 'Goob' wuz m' uncle."

"I'm sorry, Goober, I won't do it again."

"Oh no, Will, 'at's awright. Hit makes me feel at home."

They were content for some time to hear only the sound of their feet on the gravel and the occasional barking dog.

Finally, Will raised his finger to the air.

"Say, Goob," he said, "if you wouldn't mind doing a little housework and cooking, and if you could help me with a garden in the spring … look, Goob, why don't you get your stuff and move in with me?"

Goober paused for a moment, and his face went blank as he checked with his ears to make sure he had heard Will correctly. Then he broke the serenity of the night air as he screamed, *Hot dang, Will, I'm fer that!*

Six

Goober Moves In

After their night on the town, Will and Goober turned in early. As Will was fluffing his pillow, the grandfather clock played its melody and chimed one o'clock. As he pulled up the covers, he heard Goober snoring softly in the next room.

While lying in bed winding down from the excitement of the day, Will wondered if his offer for Goober to move in had been a mistake. Only time would tell, but he had learned that his decisions made on instinct were usually correct.

Goober was a decent person in need of encouragement, honest in word and deed, and fun to be around. He hadn't laughed so much since the death of his father. And hadn't he heard that laughter was good for the brain, or heart, or some important part of the body?

His mind recycled everything that Goober had said about Avery Cove, and the picture he was drawing in his brain became brighter and more elaborate. The size of the community grew as did the scope of the fields and the height of the mountains that surrounded it all. And as he soared over the valley on the back of a huge bird, surveying the layout of the farms and houses, he fell asleep.

In sleep he continued his tour. He traveled up a mountain lane through an arch of overhanging trees—riding smoothly in a gilded landau coach.

The driver was dressed in morning coat and top hat, and he commanded a matched pair of black horses, each with a plume of feathers on his head.

Then suddenly, the archway of trees opened and before him lay the valley. The road continued through the center of the dale, straight and smooth, and beside it was the river, sparkling and rippling over rounded stones.

Beside the road and across the river lay fields of wheat and corn, and lush pastures nourishing horses and cattle.

On the wind there was the fragrance of flowers and new mown hay, and the song of a thousand birds.

It was Heaven on Earth, Paradise, and the garden of Eden, all rolled into one.

But all at once, the song of the birds was drowned out by the roar of an unfamiliar beast echoing between the mountain walls. It thundered and reverberated through the valley like nothing he had ever heard, pounding inside his head like a hammer, louder and more frightening with every cry.

And then he woke, and the sound continued. It was Goober snoring next door. The clock by the bed said 8:00, which for him was the middle of the night.

"*Goober!*" he shouted, and as if by magic the roar of the beast was silenced.

It dawned on Will that even though his schedule had shifted, he had gotten a normal night's sleep. It also dawned on him that it was Sunday and he had time to get his chores done, get dressed, and go to church. It had been so long since he had been that he hoped Father Millwood would remember him.

Will didn't spare the noise as he moved through the house. After all, Goober had gotten a full night's sleep too, but each time he passed Goober's room he heard the sound of the beast.

With Dawg and Traveler cared for, an egg sandwich eaten, and shaving and washing done, he put on his best Sunday suit and his blue bow-tie. A look in the mirror confirmed that all was well.

Traveler, seeing that Will was dressed and headed his way, pranced in the corral in anticipation. He liked to go to the places Will went when he was wearing his suit and tie, and he would walk with pride beneath his spruced-up owner.

Traveler was still as Will placed the blanket and saddle on his back and tightened the cinch. Finally, he pulled himself up on Traveler's back, and they were off.

———

W ill found a spot on the south side of the church that was warmed by the sun and sheltered from the wind, and there he tied Traveler, who welcomed the company of the other horses. Perhaps they too would worship the Creator as they waited.

The service had started, and the congregation was singing the hymn of praise:

Come, let us join our cheerful songs
With angels round the throne;
Ten thousand thousand are their tongues,
But all their joys are one.

As he walked toward the entrance he joined in the singing:

"Worthy the Lamb that died," they cry,
To be exalted thus!"
"Worthy the Lamb," our lips reply,
For He was slain for us."

He entered, made the sign of the cross, and found a seat near the rear on the left side, and the singing continued:

Jesus is worthy to receive
Honor and power divine;
And blessings, more than we can give,
Be Lord, forever thine.

Let all creation join in one
To bless the sacred name
Of Him who sits upon the throne,
And to adore the Lamb.

"In the name of the Father, and of the Son, and of the Holy Spirit," Fr. Millwood began as he called for God's blessing on those gathered, and his prayer reached into Will's heart to touch the hardness that had formed in his long absence.

Then the Scriptures were read—one reading from the prophet, *Isaiah*, one from *Psalms*, one from *First Corinthians*, and finally one from *The Gospel of John*.

As hard as he tried, Will could not concentrate on the Scripture readings, dwelling instead on the myriad thoughts that were racing through his mind. He was in the right place, but his mind was many miles away.

The pastor's sermon too was a blur with only a few words reaching his consciousness.

Then as the congregation recited the *Nicene Creed*, his mind clicked onto the purpose of his being there.

When the intercessory prayers were offered, he thought of those he knew who were in need, those who were sick, the bereaved—including himself—and in all the other categories of need or thankfulness, he offered a prayer.

In confession, in receiving the Holy Eucharist, and in all other parts of the liturgy, he was a full partner in giving, acceptance, and worship.

By the time the service had concluded, he had remembered that the act of worship takes practice if one is to do it well. He promised himself that he would be faithful to the task.

As he left he was greeted at the door by Fr. Millwood.

"Will! I feared that you had forgotten us. How wonderful it is to see you."

Fr. Millwood had remembered him after all!

"Thank you, Father," he replied, "I was afraid that you wouldn't remember me."

"Don't be ridiculous!" said the kindly priest. "How is Esther? Does she like Wilmington? There are so many things I would like to know."

The exiting crowd was backing up behind Will, and he wanted to push on, but Fr. Millwood continued pumping his hand.

"Congratulations, by the way. The superintendent at your work told me this morning about your promotion. I knew that good things were in store for you." And with that, the kindly gentleman released his hand, patted him on the back, and greeted the next congregant.

It wasn't until he walked around the corner of the church that it hit him. Why would the super mention a promotion that had happened months before?

Will and Traveler were nearing home when Will saw Goober coming from the direction of the mill shouldering the burden of his possessions.

"You didn't waste any time," Will hollered.

"Figgered I best get m' movin' done 'fore ye changed yer mind." Whur ye been? Ye look like a high-dollar preacher!"

Goober stopped, put down his load, and took a seat on his duffle bag.

"I don't s'pose 'at horse of yourn could help me tote this stuff, could he?" Goober asked.

"I s'pose he would if you'd ax proper," Will answered.

With Traveler carrying Goober's load, the two men walked the remainder of the way to the house.

"I started to get you up this morning and take you to church," Will said, "but I had mercy on you and let you sleep."

"I'll go another time, Will, but 'is mornin' I wuz sleepin' th' sleep o' th' dead! I don't know when I have ever slep' more better! Whut kind o' church do ye go to anyhow?"

"It's Episcopal," Will answered.

"I don't know nothin' 'bout them, Will. They don't take up th' serpent, do they?"

"Take what?"

"You know, handle snakes! I can't stan' snakes!"

"No, Goob, they haven't taken up snakes in years ... not since Saint Patrick came to Boston and drove all the snakes away. While he was there, you know, he dumped a shipload of tea in the harbor!"

"I hope to my never!" said Goober.

"By th' way, Miz Grant down at th' boardin' house sent me off with a bunch o' food ... 'nuff fer us both. I don't know if she wuz proud to get rid of me, er felt sorry fer me. She jest said I had it comin' since I wuz paid up fer th' week."

Goober put most of his things in Esther's room and stored the few remaining things in the barn. Then he returned to the house where Will was setting the table.

Mrs. Grant had sent food indeed! Fried chicken, sweet potatoes, pickled green beans, biscuits, and a jar of blackberry jam—and the jam was nectar for the gods—enough for a week of deserts.

As Will was finishing his third biscuit, this one with jam, he decided to run his dream past Goober.

"Goob," he said, "I had a dream last night about Avery Cove," and he told Goober all about the valley he had imagined—the landau, coachman and horses, the road and river, the layout of the homes and fields—all of it.

"Naaaw, Will," he said, "hit ain't lack 'at a'tall! I mean, hit's awful purdy an' all, but th' road don't run by th' river, 'cept at th' very first, an' they ain't no houses on th' river, 'cept mine, an' they ain't no fancy horse wagons, an' they shore ain't no horses w' feathers on their head! Tell ye whut ... I'll take ye' up 'ere and show ye th' place since ye so all-farred hot t' see it."

Will thought for a moment as he picked up biscuit crumbs with the tip of his finger. "Goob, tell me about your house."

"Wal, hit's ' bout the size o' this 'un ... hit's a frame house. My daddy wuz a carpenter. He built houses an' barns an' sech all over th' valley ... put a lot extry in 'is own. They's th' same number of rooms as this 'un has 'cept I got a spring house next to th' kitchen."

"A spring house?"

"Yep. They's a spring up above th' house … water as cold as winter … an' Daddy run a pipe fum hit to th' house. An' th' spring house has these cement troughs fer th' water t' run through, an' ye put yer food an' milk an' sech in thar t' keep it fum spoilin'. Good as yer icebox, an' ye ain't got t' buy ice. A pipe goes t' th' kitchen sink too. Ain't a lot o' city houses got runnin' water!"

Will sat and thought about that. The mountain people are pretty ingenious.

"How much land do you have, Goob?"

"160 acres—'bout 40 in fields, 20 in pasture, an' th' rest in a strip 'at runs right up th' mountain. They's a bald at th' top fer summer grazin' an' 'bout half way up, they's a stand o' chestnut trees that'll feed twenty hogs with 'nuff chestnuts left over t' pay th' taxes.

"Got a barn with six stalls, a smoke house, a crib, a chicken house, a pig sty, an' a house garden with a fence 'round it … oh yeah, an' a two-seat outhouse!"

"And you up and walked away from it!"

"Hit wuz jest about perfec' but I'd trade it fer this place 'fore ye spit could hit th' ground!"

"*Why*, Goober?

"Cause they ain't no *theaters* in Avery Cove! An' they ain't no *women* t' speak of." Goober paused to find just the right words. "An' ye know th' other reason!"

———

Monday evening came too soon. Will and Goober fixed a sandwich and lit out for work a few minutes early so that Will could drop off his laundry at Hattie Jackson's house. Goober wasn't ready to go the professional laundry route yet, so he had done his own "warshin" on Sunday afternoon.

Will noted, at least in his own mind that one advantage to having Goober stay with him was that he had someone to talk to on his way to and from work.

He had decided that he would continue to find out more about Goober a little at a time, and he had his question of the day prepared.

"Say, Goob," he said as they walked along, "how did you get your nickname … you know, 'Goober.' "

"Wal," Goober replied, "when I wuz 'bout four y'ar old, Mama was shellin' peanuts an' I got a-holt o' one an' et it, an' hit got stuck in m' goozel. I wuz chokin' t' beat all, an' Mama jerked me up an' went t' poundin' on m' back an' hit wouldn't shift, so Daddy put me on th' horse and run me down to Doc French.

"Wal, Doc French couldn't shift 'er neither, so 'e took me in th' back an' cut 'is hole in m' neck." Goober pulled his shirt back and showed Will a scar below his Adam's apple. "An' he reached down m' goozel with 'is pair o' pinchers 'bout two foot long an' pulled 'at peanut out!

"An' Daddy said he come out proud as a peacock holdin' 'at peanut in them pinchers an' showed it to 'im an' said, 'Little Papa an' goober doin' fine!'

"Wal, fum then on, I wuz knowed as Goober. Course, I liked 'at better'n Makepeace anyhow."

This was getting good, so Will went ahead and asked, "Well, where did the name 'Makepeace' come from?

"Wal, when I wuz borned, my mama didn't know whut t' call me, an' Doc French wuz a-reading' 'is book called *'Vanity Fair'* by William Makepeace Thackeray … I heared Mama tell it a hun'erd times … an' Doc said, 'Why don't ye call 'im William Makepeace? An' Mama said, 'at's too many names fer such a little feller! Makepeace'll do!' So 'ats whut Doc wrote down."

"I had to ask!" Will said.

"Mistah Will, you has got to buy yo'sef some new draws! Them you got is full o' holes! An' while you at it, buy yo se'f some new unda shirts an' socks. Dem is holy too!"

Hattie Jackson was going through Will's laundry, giving him an assessment of its state.

"I feels like I ain't washin' nothin' *but* holes when I does yo laundry. You evah thought about getting' yo'sef a wife t' tell you dem things?"

"Don't need a wife, Mrs. Jackson. I have you to tell me them things."

Hattie threw her head back and laughed till she shook.

The banter with Hattie was fun, but it was putting Will and Goober dangerously close to being late, and being late would not be a good thing for a second hand and an up-and-coming weaver.

They bounded up the steps in the midst of a crowd of night shift workers, pulled their time cards and placed them on Mr. Gunnelson's desk.

Will was half way through the door to the hallway when Gunnelson called him back.

"Will, Mr. Mooney wants to see you, and Mr. Neil is in there with him. Better get on the ball."

A message that the night supervisor and the owner wanted to see you was enough to get anyone on the ball! Will ran down the hall and turned left into the office wing and made his way to the super's office where he knocked and entered.

"Morning, Will," Mooney said.

Mr. Neil was seated in a chair to the side of Mooney's desk. He smiled and threw up his hand but didn't speak.

"Good morning, Mr. Mooney," Will replied. "Good morning, Mr. Neil. This is a pleasant surprise … I hope."

Neil smiled again and nodded and folded his arms across his broad middle.

"Will," Mooney said, "we can't help but notice that your work is exemplary. Can't thank you enough!"

Will felt his shoulders relax, and from the corner of his eye he saw Neil nod the affirmative.

The super went on: "Mr. Neil is building a new plant in Concord and your overseer is going to be transferring to that mill as a supervisor. That leaves us with an opening that we would like you to fill."

"You want *me* to be the night shift overseer?"

"Not exactly," the super said, "the day shift overseer wants to go to the night shift ... can't imagine why ... and since he has seniority, we'll let him do that, and we'll give you the day job ... that is, if you want it."

"Mr. Mooney, are you sure I'm ready for this?" Will asked.

For the first time, Glenn Neil spoke. "Will," he said, "a person never is ready for a promotion. Part of the job itself is learning how to do it. We expect that you'll make some mistakes just like you did when you took the job you have now, and we'll work through that. I don't know of anyone in this mill that is more qualified to be an overseer than you, and Mooney here agrees. What do you say?"

"Well ... of course I'll take it, but I don't even know all that an overseer does. The only time I see one is when he comes through to straighten out a mess."

"One of the first things you're going to have to do is train a weaver to take Ellie Ludwig's place," Mooney said. "She came in this morning and gave her notice. I don't know how many looms she runs, but it it's more than anybody we have."

Will raised his finger in the air and said, "I think I know just the person!"

Mooney got up from his desk and walked around where Will was standing.

"Will," he said, "go ahead and work your job tonight, take tomorrow off, and be here bright and early Wednesday morning. We'll start showing you the ropes."

Then Neil spoke up. "Son, since I'm here, I'll be going around tonight meeting workers ... you know, shake hands and lift morale, that sort of thing. I want you to go around with me to make the introductions in the weave room. I'll be down shortly."

Will walked out the door with his head spinning. And then it hit him like lightning—that's what Fr. Millwood was talking about!

Seven

GOOBER MESSES UP

Will walked calmly out of Mooney's office, looked back to make sure no one was looking, and broke into a run down the office complex hallway. When he got to the main hallway he skidded, turned left, and ran toward the weave room.

It was a good thing that no one was behind the weave room door when he bolted through, still in a dead run.

He shouted at the top of his lungs and waved his arms in the air, trying to get the attention of the workers who were oblivious to his racket because of the thunder of the looms. Those who did see him alerted the others, and soon everyone was headed toward him.

When everyone was together, Will called them in close so they could hear. "Listen up," he said, "Mr. Glenn Neil, the owner of this mill, is going to be coming through soon to see us work and have a few words for each of us. Stay busy, and look smart! He is a good man, and he will be nice to you, but I wanted to let you know he was coming so you could be on your toes. Any questions?"

Goober raised his hand. "Will, what are ye s'posed t' say t' th' man?"

"Just be nice, look busy, and smile. Everything will be all right."

Goober nodded and made the okay sign, and everybody went back to work.

In about a half hour Neil came to the weave room door and motioned for Will to come out in the hallway.

"Son, I don't see how you stand the noise in there. It gives me a headache! How about bringing your people out here one at a time, and I'll just say hello and say a few words and let 'em get back to work. Okay?"

Will gave the okay sign and went back out in the weave room. In a minute he returned with one of the weavers and held the door for her to enter the hallway.

"Mr. Neil," he said when the door had closed and the noise was at a more acceptable level, "this is Mrs. Taylor. She has been with us since the mill opened ... came over with her husband from Sandhurst."

Neil reached out and took the lady's hand. "Mrs. Taylor, I am so happy to meet you, and I want to tell you how much I appreciate your fine work."

"Oh ... thank you so much, Mr. Neil. I've worked in mills for twenty-one years, and this is the first time I've met an owner. This means a lot to me."

"Why, Mrs. Taylor, the pleasure is mine, I assure you. I just wanted to thank you for being a part of our family here at Inverness. I hope things continue to go well for you."

Will took Mrs. Taylor's arm and gently guided her toward the weave room. She backed away totally in awe of the big man.

In a few minutes Will was back with a loom fixer, Ernie Gaines, and Neil said the same kind things to him. Gaines went back to work with renewed vigor, anxious to please the kind owner.

Several more workers came—weavers, a slash tender, a doffer, a sweeper, a beam warper, a creeler and a drawing-in girl—and finally Goober. Will was saving the best for last.

Goober came through the door in his customary fashion, chest out and confident.

"Mr. Neil," Will said, "I want you to meet Makepeace Green, one of our hardest working weavers."

"'At's Goober, Mr. Neil ... jest plain Goober."

"Well, Mr. Green, I am very happy to meet you!"

"Likewise, I'm shore."

Neil bent his knees a little in an effort to better look Goober in the eye.

"I just wanted to thank you for your hard work and tell you how happy I am to have you as a member of our family here at Inverness."

"Likewise, I'm shore," Goober replied.

"You enjoy the weaving craft, Mr. Green?"

"You can jest call me Goober, Mr. Neil, and yes sir, I am most wonderf'ly happy a-weavin' canvas fer ye."

"Got any aspirations for any other job here?"

"Whut does 'at mean, Mr. Neil?"

"Well, Goober, would you like to move up in the company someday?"

"'Course I would! I'd lack t' have yer job, Mr. Neil."

"Uh-oh," thought Will. "This is getting off on the wrong track!"

Neil drew back and looked surprised. "That's good, Goober, but why would you want my job?"

Goober pointed to Neil's rotund middle and said, "Wal, hit don't look t' me lack you're missin' any meals. Matter o' fact, I'd say ye ain't missed none!"

A blank look came over Neil's face, and he couldn't speak. Will could see his neck turning red, so he grabbed Goober by the arm and said, "Okay Goober, you can go back to work now," as he led Goober toward the door.

"Much obliged, Mr. Neil," Goober sang out. "Hit wuz a pleasure a-talkin' to ye."

"How'd I do?" Goober asked Will as they went through the door.

"I'll talk to you later!" Will shot back.

Will stood for a moment reflecting on what had transpired, and when he went back out into the hallway, Neil was gone. He was filled with anger, embarrassment, and a combination of other emotions that he had not had to contend with before. "What am I getting myself into?" he thought. "This must be the kind of thing an overseer has to deal with daily. I don't know if I can handle it."

Just then, Neil came back down the hall looking resolute. Before he got to Will he sounded out. "Will, go get Green and bring him up to Mooney's office. Tell him to bring his stuff with him."

Will and Goober stood at the door to Mooney's office, each dreading to enter. Will had already given Goober the lecture of his life, and now they were about to enter the lion's den.

Goober was back to the state of being a little boy, his cocky attitude gone and forgotten. He was carrying his coat and hat and his lunch box.

"I still don't know whut I done wrong, Will," he said softly.

"Goober, if I haven't been able to explain it to you by now, I'm afraid you never will know. Let's go on in and hear what Mr. Neil has to say."

Will knocked and they entered. Mooney was seated at his desk doodling with pen on paper, and Mr. Neil was standing at the window looking out at the darkness. Mooney looked up as they approached his desk.

"Green, did you make an insulting remark to Mr. Neil?" he asked.

"Oh, no sir, Mr. Mooney!"

"Are you telling me that you didn't say that he didn't look like he was missing any meals?"

"Oh, 'at's whut I said, Mr. Mooney ... but 'at ain't no insult."

Will leaned over and whispered to Goober, "Speak up, Goober, so that Mr. Neil can hear you."

Goober walked over and stood behind Neil, who was still looking out the window.

"Mr. Neil," he said softly, "I shore am sorry that whut I said wuz a insult to ye. I didn't mean fer it t' be. ...Ye see, Mr. Neil, up whur I come frum, they's a awful lot o' people 'at goes hungry sometimes. Winters is hard, an' a lots o' times people's food runs out an' they're too proud t' axt fer help.

"Up in some o' them hollers they's people 'at's got a yard full o' youn-guns 'at's bowlegged frum th' rickets an' sech."

Goober was bent around trying to look Neil in the eye, and he was rolling his hat into a knot.

"Up thar, Mr. Neil, if ye tell a man he looks well fed, 'at's one o' th' most highest compliments a man kin give 'im.

"Mr. Neil, the most hardest thang fer me since I come down here is tryin' t' find th' right words t' say. Up whur I come frum, ever'body under-stan's one another. Down here, I can't make m'self understood."

Goober unrolled his hat and straightened it out, and then he turned slightly toward the door.

"Thank ye fer lettin' me work 'ere, Mr. Neil ... I'll get m' stuff an' go on now."

Neil turned quickly and circled around in front of Goober.

"Wait a minute, Green ... Makepeace ... Goober," he said. "I feel like a fool. ... I thought I knew a lot about human nature, but right now I feel like a ... injudicious dolt!"

"If ye say so, Mr. Neil ... whatever 'at means."

Will was exhausted. He felt like he had been on a storm-tossed ship. He was certainly thankful that he had tomorrow to rest, especially since it looked like he would be having a lot of tense days from then on.

Mr. Mooney spoke up. "Well, I think we've all learned a lot from this. I'm sure Mr. Neil will agree that we all jumped to a lot of conclusions. Green, you can go on back to work. I'm sorry we kept you away from your looms for so long. ... And Will, stay back and let's talk about that thing we were talking about earlier."

Goober gathered up his things, made a sort of half- bow of submission, and humbly backed out of the room.

When he was gone, Mooney spoke up. "Sorry about that, Will. I can see why Mr. Neil was upset ... I would have been too ... but I'm glad it worked out to everybody's satisfaction.

"Now, you said you had someone you want to train for that first shift weaver's job. Of course you'll have to talk to the first shift supervisor about this, but since it was brought up, you want to say who you have up your sleeve?"

"Yes, sir," Will said, "but before I do, there's something else I think we should discuss."

Neil came around in front of Mooney's desk, pulling a chair for Will and one for himself. He sat down and wiped his brow with his handkerchief.

Will chose to stand, leaning on his chair back.

"Mr. Mooney, Mr. Neil, I think you should know that Goober is living at my house. When he came over to my shift I sort of took him under my wing and tried to help him.

"He was struggling to make ends meet, and I gave him a meal and talked to him and found out that he really is a nice person, even though he's hard to understand at times.

"Everything was okay till now. With me accepting this new job, I'm put between a rock and a hard place, so to speak. I still want to help him, and I don't want to have to kick him out of my house, but I know it isn't normal for management to be socially involved with the hourly workers."

"That is awkward, Will," said Mooney. "I don't know ... What do you say, Mr. Neil?"

Neil shifted in his chair. "Right now I'd say that you've got more brains than I do, Will. If you have enough judgment to raise the issue, you have enough judgment to not let things get out of hand. Go ahead and befriend the fellow!

"By the way, Will, Green's dialect sounds familiar. Where is he from, anyway?"

"He's from a settlement in the mountains called Avery Cove. I understand that it's very remote ...somewhere just west of Burley."

"Well I'll be!" said Neil. "It's a small world!"

Neither Will nor Mooney knew what that meant, and neither asked.

"Well, that settles that!" Mooney said. "Now, about that weaver ..."

"Mr. Mooney, that man that just left here is the best weaver I have. The only thing that keeps him from being the most productive weaver in the mill is the fact that we don't have enough looms for him on night shift. I think we should move him over to first and give him Ellie Ludwig's looms!" As soon as the words were out of his mouth, he held his breath.

"Well, as long as Mr. Neil approves it, and since Green works for me now, I'd say done and done!" said Mooney. "I'll leave word for everybody about what's going on, and Green can take tomorrow off and start the day shift with you Wednesday."

"Stamped and approved!" said Neil. "And I'm glad that's over with!"

The rest of the night was a blur. Will experienced one of those times when a person runs on blind instinct, so deep in thought that he doesn't hear, feel, see, or in any other way sense the elements of his surroundings.

This night so far had given him the high of a promotion, the low of the realization that he might not be up to the task, the high of seeing Glenn Neil inspire his workers, and finally the low of seeing Goober crash and burn. At least Goober's crash was not fatal. At least he would survive.

Now Will was back to a neutral point. He would get through the night and take his day off to reset his clock and rest his mind.

Near the end of the shift he realized that he hadn't heard anything out of Goober. He walked to the far side of the weave room and found Goober seated on a roll of newly doffed canvas with his elbows on his knees, his chin in his hands, and his gaze firmly fixed on one of his looms.

Will sat down beside him on the roll and nudged him with his shoulder. "Are you hungry?" he asked.

"I ain't much o' nothin' rat now, Will."

"I want to tell you … that was a right powerful speech you gave in Mooney's' office."

"Hit was m' speech 'at got me in trouble in th' first place, Will. Thought I wuz doin' th' man a compliment, an' it turned out I wuz speakin' a for'n language."

"Well, Goob, it's not anything a few chicken eggs won't make right. When the whistle blows, let's go over to Sarah's and eat. I've got a few things to go over with you … good things, this time!"

"I'm fer that," Goober answered half-heartedly.

Goober was still in his little-boy state as he and Will walked toward Sarah's. They hurried along against a chilling wind that was the coldest of the year so far. It was hard to talk and half run, so Will saved his announcements for the warmth of Sarah's.

"*Mornin', Will, mornin', Goober*" rang out in chorus as they entered the café. All the regulars were there.

Will was glad to see an empty table in the far corner, and he pointed Goober in that direction.

"Will!" Sarah hollered. "Are you mad at me or somethin'? Why aren't you sitting at the counter?"

"Got high-level business to discuss with Goober, Sarah," he hollered back.

Goober reached in his pocket and looked at his change. "Will," he said, "you might have t' lend me a nickel. I'm runnin' a little short till payday … 'less ye want me t' jest git one egg."

"Well, Goober, that brings up an interesting subject. How many looms would you have to run to make enough money to not worry about pocket change, and then have enough left over at the end of the week to send some to Roamer and Sweetie?"

"Prob'ly 'bout 10 … but they ain't much chance o' 'at hap'nin' now … not after I opened m' big mouth t' Neil."

"I'll give you 10 looms, Goober' and even more as you gain experience."

"Thanks, Will, but you ain't got 10 looms t' give … an' no offense, but you ain't in no position t' be givin' out looms no how."

"I am now, Goob … got promoted to overseer tonight."

Goober slammed both hands down on the table and let out a "whoop" that caused all the bachelors to turn their heads and Sarah to drop her spatula.

"Only thing is," said Will, "you'll have to go back to first shift. Think you can handle that?"

"Rat now, I think I could handle a bobcat!" Goober answered.

About that time Sarah set the boy's plates in front of them and demanded to know "what all that hollerin' was about." Will told her, and against his wishes she made a general announcement about his promotion that was answered with cheers from the bachelor corps. Tommy Lee Jones ran over and got on his knees and bowed in mock praise to "the newly promoted one".

"He's jest jealous," Goober said.

The walk home was in sharp contrast to the walk from the mill to Sarah's. Will and Goober laughed and joked and discussed how they were going to spend their new-found money. They didn't even seem to notice the cold.

Finally, Will broke the playful mood.

"I have a feeling we better get plenty of rest," he said. "With you tending 10 looms and me taking on the pressure of a new job, we better get all the rest we can.

"'At's right," said Goober. "I hear 'at new overseer is a real whup cracker."

Eight

ESTHER'S CHRISTMAS VISIT

Western
Union

HC36   403DL= WILMINGTON NC 36 455P
WILL PARKER=
INVERNESS MILL CHARLOTTE NC =
DEAREST BROTHER WILL ARRIVE CHARLOTTE DEC 20 715 AM
ESTHER

The pall that had settled on Will in the last few weeks was lifted. Christmas was just around the corner. Esther would be with him for ten days, and during that period they would celebrate the season and all the joys that go with it.

Christmas this year would fall on Friday, giving him a total of three days in a row to visit with Esther and rest his mind and body.

On the days he had to work while Esther was there, she would joyfully cook, make his house a little more livable, visit with some of her friends, and finish her Christmas shopping.

And then, there was Goober.

This would be his first Christmas away from Roamer and Sweetie, the only remaining members of his family. It was hard to predict how he would react to the holiday, but Will was determined that he would make it a joyous season for everyone, Goober included.

Goober had put a crisp one-dollar bill in an envelope and mailed it to his aunt and uncle on the tenth of December along with a note that said, "Merry Chrismas from Goober".

If the roads were passable and there weren't any breakdowns in the postal system, it would be in the post office at Burden's Store in time. That would make a couple of old folks grin for sure!

True to his word, Goober had, in addition to the Christmas money, sent Uncle Roamer and Aunt Sweetie a total of $2.00. It was his goal to send back enough money each year to pay their taxes and give them enough left over to cover any medical costs they might have, and he took joy in being able to help them.

How he wished that either Roamer or Sweetie could write so that he could hear from them, but neither had the advantage of a formal education.

The week preceding the arrival of Esther's telegram had not been an easy one for Will. As an overseer, it had been his responsibility to terminate two employees, one a young farm girl who was chronically absent and the other a slash tender with a taste for whiskey. He was especially touched when the slash tender was met by his wife and children at the end of the shift, and he saw the man cry as he told his wife that he had lost his job. He knew when he took the overseer position that there would be times like that, but knowing had not made it easier.

As bad as things had been for Will, they were good for Goober. He was becoming a master weaver, and for the past two weeks when production was posted, Goober was on the very top of the list.

Even Mr. Massey, the plant superintendent who was known never to leave his office, had been seen peeking around a corner, watching Goober work. Massey had heard about Goober's magic, and the look of approval as he watched him was the talk of the weave room.

Goober would take it personally when a thread broke or a bobbin ran out. He attacked problems as one would attack an intruder or a bully picking on his little brother, but the magic of his work was that he anticipated problems. He seemed to be always standing over the very loom that was about to fail.

After Will had received Esther's telegram he walked out into the weave room and showed it to Goober. Although Goober was happy for Will, he raised the concern that he would be in the way.

"Let's talk about it after work," Will told him.

As they walked home, Will's mood was up and Goober's was down.

"Will," Goober said, "have ye thought about whur I'll stay when ye sister's here?"

"It's not going to be a problem," Will assured him. "Either you can come in and stay with me, or you can sleep on the sofa in the parlor. Esther is a very tolerant person, and I'm looking forward to her getting to know you. We'll have lots of fun."

"Tell ye whut, Will. I been eyin' a little corner in th' tack room. I think I'll make a pallet on th' floor an' spend m' nights out in th' barn. Ye know how I snore anyhow."

"Goob, you'll freeze to death out there!"

"If hit's good 'nuff fer th' horse, hit's good 'nuff fer me!" Goober shot back.

Will decided to let that matter rest, but he had another question ready for Goober.

"Say, Goob, what's Christmas like in Avery Cove?"

Goober tilted his head a little and got a faraway look in his eye.

"Ye might say hit's th' high point o' th' year, Will. Preacher Burden's store an' both churches an' all th' houses is decorated up with pine boughs an' popcorn on a strang an' stuff like 'at.

"An' Preacher Burden has oranges an' candy canes and little toys an' all at 'is store fer Santy to buy fer th' younguns. An' he has these tubs o' candied fruit an' nuts fer th' ladies t' make fruit cakes out of. Ever'body makes fruit cake at Christmas.

"An' they's always snow on th' ground fer Christmas. An' people goes aroun' visitin' with one another a-takin' pies an' cakes an' all.

"An' ever'body goes t' church on Christmas t' hear 'bout th' baby Jesus, an' they's singin' an' socializin' all day.

"An' here's th' part I lack best," Goober said. "On Christmas Eve night, ever'body goes outside an' starts a-shootin' their guns and a-whoopin' t' beat all!"

"What on earth for?" Will asked.

"Well, hit's t' get Santy's attention. ... Lets 'im know they's people down thar lookin' fer 'im t' come."

Goober paused and swallowed hard before he continued.

"Course, I shore do miss m' Mama and Daddy when Christmas comes."

Goober was getting teary-eyed, and though Will would not have admitted it, the part about missing Mama and Daddy brought tears to his eyes, too.

———

Friday, December the 18th. Two days until Esther would be there, and one week until Christmas.

Near the end of the shift, Will left the weave room to take his production numbers to the office. He walked down the main hallway and turned right into the office complex hallway and ran headlong into Mr. Neil's round belly.

"Will, my boy! I was on the way to find you," said Neil. "Didn't imagine I would run into you like this!"

"Sorry, Mr. Neil," Will said. "I was looking at the numbers for my weavers. Not bad, even if I do say so myself."

"I've been hearing about your weavers, son. They're getting the job done. Now, about why I was coming to see you ... when will Esther be home for Christmas? I do hope she's coming!"

"Yes, sir, she'll be here Sunday morning, bright and early. Can't wait!"

"That's wonderful news," Neil replied. "Now … I want you and Esther to come to my house Tuesday evening at 7:00 for a little Christmas gathering. Nothing fancy, but there'll be some food to eat and some good wine to drink and laughing and singing … and a good time will be had by all! Just some mill management and friends. And I don't think you'll have any trouble finding my place. You used to live there, you know!"

"I wouldn't miss it for the world, Mr. Neil, and I know Esther will be thrilled."

"Oh, and one other thing, son," Neil said, "be sure to bring Green with you. There's something about that boy I like, and I want to hear more about that place he's from … that Avery Cove."

O, no! Will thought. *What's going to happen this time?*

When he had caught his breath, Will asked, "You *are* talking about Goober?"

"One and the same," said Neil.

"We'll be there, Mr. Neil … with bells on."

Will didn't have a lot to say on the walk home. There was a lot going on inside his head.

Goober rambled on about his production numbers and how he was looking forward to meeting Esther, and he showed Will his new shoes at least twice. Will just grunted and kept rolling things over in his brain.

When the boys got to Watt Street they turned and headed to Hattie Jackson's house to pick up Will's laundry. The dim light of a lantern was showing through Hattie's front window when they knocked on the door.

Hattie answered the knock and immediately lit into Will.

"Mistah Will, I done tol' you that you got to buy yo'sef some new draws, and you ain't done it yet! All yo' underwears is fallin' apart, an' I ain't washin' nothin' but holes! Nothin' but holes, Mistah Will!"

Will took the neatly wrapped bundle and reached in his pocket.

"Mrs. Jackson," he replied, "I promise you that the next time I come I will have some nice new 'draws' for you to wash. And some socks and 'unda' shirts too. We just *can't* have you washin' holes!

"Now," he said, "here's a dime for the laundry … and here's a little Christmas present for you." And he pressed something into her hand.

Hattie opened her hand and took a breath that must have caused a vacuum all over Charlotte.

"Oh … Mistah … Will," was all she could utter, and her old dark body shook with emotion. She held a dime and a shiny silver dollar.

Will hugged her and gave her a kiss on the forehead, and he and Goober wished her a merry Christmas and left to continue their walk home.

———

Saturday, December 19th. The eve of Esther's arrival and six days before Christmas.

Will woke earlier than normal and quietly eased out of bed so as not to disturb Goober. He went in and filled the parlor stove with coal and put the coffee on in the kitchen.

Dawg was at the back door wanting to be fed, and when Will opened the door, he saw Goober in the yard lighting a fire under the wash kettle.

"Howdy, Will!" was Goober's greeting. "Gonna do m' warshin' an' warsh th' sheets on m' bed fer ye' sister. Then, I'm a-gonna move m' stuff on out t' th' tack room. Figgered I'd git a early start."

Will walked out to the fire and stood warming himself.

"I thought I'd go into town and finish my shopping and look around a little," he said. "Can you fend for yourself today?"

"I reckon I can," said Goober as he poked out his chest. "I might go down t' th' company store an' do a little shoppin' o' m' own."

With breakfast eaten and chores done, Will washed, shaved, and put on some of his better clothes, as was his custom when he went in to Charlotte.

Traveler did his customary dance when he saw Will coming with the saddle. He loved the trips into town where he could visit with other horses.

When Will and Traveler left, Goober was hanging the sheets on the line to dry.

———

The sun was setting as Goober approached Will's house carrying the fruits of his shopping trip to the company store. As he walked along he was overtaken by a horse-drawn surrey. The driver pulled up beside Goober and hollered out, "Hey stranger, want a ride?"

"*Will!*" Goober shouted, "*Is 'at you?*"

"Climb aboard," Will answered, "and I'll give you a ride home."

"Whur did ye git th' surrey?" Goober asked as he examined the rich leather upholstery.

"It's my Christmas present to me, but I think Traveler considers it a curse … he's not very fond of it. He's gonna have to get used to it though. Sitting up here sure beats sitting on a saddle."

While Goober was loading his packages and getting in his seat, Will explained.

"You know, Goob, I couldn't go to the train station and pick up Esther on horseback. And there are lots of times when you and I might have to go somewhere and not want to walk. Now, take Tuesday night for instance. It's going to push us to leave work, get home, get cleaned up, get Esther, and get to Mr. Neil's in time for the party."

"Whut?"

"Didn't I tell you? You and Esther and I are going to a Christmas party Tuesday night at Mr. Neil's house."

"You ain't tol' me 'bout no party! Will! I can't go t' no party at Mr. Neil's house! Why, I ain't got no nice clothes t' wear, and I wouldn't know whut t' say, ner *none* o' that!"

"Well, you're about like Traveler, Goob … you're just gonna have to get used to it. I'll talk you through it between now and then, and you'll be fine. Besides, Mr. Neil said to make sure you come because he likes you and he wants you to tell him about Avery Cove."

"Said 'e lacks me?"

"His exact words, Goob."

"I hope to my never," said Goober. "I'll prob'ly make a fool outta myself, but at least I'll be a-ridin' in style."

Traveler was relieved to get that surrey off his back. He didn't appreciate being hooked up to something that followed him so closely. He did concede, however, that it never did catch him, and since he trusted Will to do him no harm, he decided that he would go along with it in the future.

Will and Goober unloaded their packages, and when Traveler and the new surrey had been put in the barn, they went to the house. When they were inside, Will had lit a lamp and gotten a nice surprise. Standing in the parlor was a Christmas tree ready to be decorated when Esther was home.

"Mary Christmas, Will," Goober said.

———

Sunday, December 20th, 6:00 a.m. One hour before Esther's train would arrive, and five days before Christmas.

Will scurried through the house making sure that everything was as clean as a bachelor could make it. An inspection of Esther's room showed that everything was remarkably orderly. All of Goober's things had been moved to the barn, the sheets on the bed were clean and had the fragrance of sun and fresh air, and there wasn't a speck of dust.

Although Goober had his strange ways, Will had noted that he was clean in every way. He and his surroundings were always neat and tidy. Could it be he wondered, that Avery Cove is the same way—that Goober is the product of the environment in which he was reared? He promised himself that he would find out someday.

The parlor fire was burning warmly, Will and Goober had eaten their breakfast and cleaned the kitchen, the animals had been fed, and Will had put on his "goin'-to-town clothes" for the trip to the station. When he went outside he got another pleasant surprise. Goober had hitched Traveler to the surrey and was in the driver's seat, ready to take him to meet Esther.

"Yer coach is a-waitin', sir," the coachman said.

When Will and Goober were about a block from the station, they heard the train whistle at Pine Tree crossing. Two minutes early!

By the time they were on the platform, the train was pulling to a stop. In less than a minute, a porter stepped down with Esther's suitcase and hat box, and he took her hand as she descended.

She was lovely—lovelier than Will had remembered her. She was wearing her dark hair up, and it was crowned by a blue hat, tilted forward, with a long blue feather on the side. Her dress also was blue, and she carried a handbag covered in sequins.

When she spotted Will walking toward her, she ran to meet him. They embraced for a moment and then pulled back slightly to see each other's face. Esther's shined with tears.

It was time for introductions.

"Esther, I want you to meet my friend and housemate, Makepeace Green, known to most as Goober, and known only to Uncle Roamer and me as Goob.

"Goob, I want you to meet the most beautiful girl in the world and my favorite sister, Esther."

Goober jerked his hat from his head and started rolling it into a knot, while Esther blushed and laughed like one of her school-girl students.

Then Esther walked to Goober, who looked as though he was scared to death.

"I am delighted to meet you, Goober. Will has told me so much about you in his letters. He tells me you are a faithful friend, a strong worker, and a delightful conversationalist. I look forward to getting to know you."

"Uh … likewise, I'm shore … Miss Esther."

There are times in a fellow's life when he knows he's outclassed, like the time he sees the two boxers in the ring—tall, with muscles bulging, strength upon strength, power upon power—and he knows that he couldn't compete against either of them.

Or there's the time that he stands at the base of a tall mountain with vertical cliffs and an icy summit, and he knows he will never stand on the top.

This was one of those times for Goober. Miss Esther was the most beautiful girl he had ever seen—even more beautiful than the feather dancer at the theatre—but he knew he would admire her from afar. Aside from her beauty and sophistication, she was a good five inches taller than he. He would be lucky to know her only as a friend. Someday, he would meet his princess, but this was not the time.

"I'll git them grips fer ye, Miss Esther." The words flowed out rather naturally! Maybe he *would* know her as a friend!

The ride home was punctuated with talk and laughter. Will and Esther sat on the back seat of the surrey bundled against the cold, and Goober sat up front urging Traveler along, occasionally adding to the conversation. And each time he did, Will and Esther welcomed his involvement.

———

Tuesday, December 22nd. Three days before Christmas. Will noticed that Goober was restless as he tended his looms. For the first time ever at work, he seemed distracted. He thought he had better check on him.

"What's up, Goob?"

"Will, I don't think I'll go t' 'at shin-dig t'night. I won't fit in with 'at bunch o' big shots. I went through m' things 'is mornin' an' I ain't got nothin' decent t' wear."

"Tell you what, Goob, let's look again when we get home, and if we don't find something you're comfortable in, I'll make excuses for you and you can stay home. What do you say?"

Will patted Goober on the back and shook him a little.

"At sounds fair 'nuff, Will, but I'm a-tellin' ye, we ain't gonna find nothin'."

Since business had slacked off a little for Christmas, Mr. Neil had cut the shifts down from 12 hours to 10 for Christmas week, but was paying the employees for the full 12 hours. That was his way of giving a little extra to the workers and allowing them some extra time with their families.

And so when 5:00 rolled around, Will and Goober left for home. The anticipation of the party kept Will's feet moving swiftly, and Goober kept up.

When they reached the house, Will told Goober, "Goob, we have plenty of time. Let's go in and warm up before we look through your clothes."

"Suits me, Will," said Goober. "I'm 'bout t' freeze t' death. I got a hole in th' crotch o' m' pants."

Esther was dressed and radiant in her red gown. Goober talked to her while Will excused himself, and he soon determined that he could not be seen in the company of someone so lovely. He would definitely not be going to the party!

Shortly, Will reentered the room carrying a package wrapped in Christmas paper and tied with a ribbon.

"Goob," he said, "I want to give you your Christmas present early. When you open it, I think you'll understand why."

Goober wasn't expecting a present from Will, especially now, and he was taken back, to say the least. He accepted it, to Esther's delight, sat on the sofa, and pulled the ribbon. To his wonder and amazement, there, neatly folded, were a dark blue suit, white shirt, starched collar, and a red neck tie.

"Ooooh, Will," he moaned, "'at's beautiful. 'at's the first store-boughten suit o' clothes I ever had, an' hit's jest *beautiful*."

"Nice enough to wear to a party?" Will asked.

"Ooooh, Will, I hope to my never! Hit's so fine I fear t' put it on 'cause I might muss it up."

"If you 'muss it up,' I'll fix it!" said Esther. "Now go wash up and put it on and let's go to the party!"

Nine

The Christmas Party

Sunlight through snow clouds, muted and tinted blue, peaked in the window across from Goober's bed. It gently fell on the feather-filled comforter that lay atop a blanket and two quilts covering Goober's sleeping form.

Quietly he lay, dreaming of fruit cake, oranges, and wooden toys—visages of Christmas past. And warm he lay, securely held by the gentle weight of his covers, and by the love of the season.

"Goober!" The far-away sound of his father's voice gave him a feeling of security.

"Goober!" Nearer now his father must be, watching over him, guarding him as he slumbered.

"Goober ... git up and see whut Santy brung ye!"

His eyes snapped open to reveal morning—Christmas morning!

"Hit's out in th' barn, boy! Santy left ye a present out in th' barn!"

Feet move quickly when the promise of a Christmas gift from Santy moves them, and overalls and shoes fly on with the speed of Santy's sleigh.

The snow was not deep, but it was gathering, enough already to leave impressions as deep as the soles of his shoes. And the impressions of his shoes were far apart, for that is how it is when a six-year-old boy is running.

Goober swung open the door of the barn, and there in the light of Christmas morning stood his dream—a white, floppy-eared goat hooked to a two-wheeled cart, ready to take him on adventures to the ends of the earth—as far as to school even!

"Goob … Goob … how's it coming? Do you need any help with your tie?"

In an instant Goober was back in Charlotte, washed and dressing for Mr. Neil's party, his memory of a Christmas past back in the security of his brain.

Will and Esther were dressed and ready—the appointed hour was near —when Goober stepped from the kitchen, dressed in his finery. The shirt and suit fit to perfection. His sandy shock of hair was parted in the middle and combed back, revealing his forehead.

" Somebody's gonna haf t' he'p me w' m' tie," he said. And Esther hurried over to tie it in a fashionable bow.

"So help me," declared Will, "I wouldn't have recognized you! You'll be the best dressed person there … other than Esther, of course."

Traveler and the surrey stood at the ready, and the lap blankets lay on the seats as the trio boarded—Will and Esther in the rear, and Goober in the driver's seat.

"Will, I still feel like I'm-a-gonna mess up an' say somethin' stupid," Goober said as he took the reins. "I jest know I will!"

"Tell you what," Will said, "if you'll limit your conversation to 'yes, no, thank you, and please,' and only talk about things you know about, everything will be fine. And remember, Mr. Neil already knows you speak a foreign language, and he's going to be a whole lot more tolerant of you than he was before."

"Thanks a *lot*, Will!" Goober said.

As Traveler neared his former home, he picked up the pace.

"Give him his head," Will told Goober, "and see if he'll go to the barn." And he did!

In minutes, Will stood at the front door with Esther on his arm, and Goober hiding behind. He was back to his little-boy stage.

"Will and Esther … lovely Esther!" Mr. Neil said in greeting. "Merry Christmas to you … and you've brought a guest … that's wonderful!"

Neil gave Esther a hug, shook hands with Will in his regular, vigorous style, and then thrust his hand past them to take the hand of the stranger.

"Merry Christmas, sir, and welcome to my home."

"Howdy do, Mr. Neil, likewise I'm shore, an' you can jest call me Goober."

Neil drew back. "*Green! Green, is that you?* Green, you look *wonderful!* I would never have known you … I've only seen you in your … work clothes. Come in! Come in all!"

The house was alive with guests milling about, talking and laughing.

In the parlor, a lady in a green formal dress was playing a Christmas song on the piano, and in the dining room was a table laden with food and bottles of wine.

Goober was in a fantasy land of color and light. Green pine garland and red ribbon hung everywhere, and scores of candles, each giving off a gentle flicker, brightened the house. His eyes darted back and forth, experiencing a feast of decorating excellence.

Will proudly directed Esther around the room, introducing her to the management of the mill—Mr. Mooney and Mr. Spann, the shift supervisors and their wives; Mr. Massey, the plant superintendent and his wife; several overseers and their wives; and finally, Mrs. Neil.

Mrs. Neil was a lovely lady, most worthy of her successful husband, and a gracious hostess. Will had met her only once before but thought of her fondly. Will and all the management team from the mill were flattered that she had made the trip to share Christmas with them.

It was clear to Esther—she said later—that Mrs. Neil had been at the home for some time, decorating and furnishing it with a touch of refinement.

No man, especially a man as busy as Glenn Neil, could have brought together the colors, furnishings, and accessories as well as it had been done. Esther had always been fond of the way her mother had decorated the house, but she had to admit that Mrs. Neil had outdone herself. Will had told her about the Neils' Washington home and how fine it was, but it was hard to imagine a second home as beautifully decorated as this one.

While Will and Esther were taking care of their social obligations, Goober was busy filling a plate with food. Some of the delicacies were new to him, but he was anxious to try each one. He heaped his plate full, and a servant who was minding the wine filled a glass for him. He asked, but they didn't have elderberry.

With plate and glass in hand, he was looking around for a place to sit when he heard a "psssst" behind him.

He turned to find Mr. Neil at the door to an adjoining room, motioning for him to come.

"Green … Goober, let me see you for a minute," Mr. Neil said softly.

Neil held the door open, and Goober entered a study area with a desk, chairs, and shelves of books. The door closed.

"Goober," Mr. Neil said, "I know this is probably not the time, but I just have to talk to you."

"Did I do somethin' wrong, Mr. Neil?"

"O, no, Goober. I need to ask your advice about something. Sit here at my desk where you can put your food and wine down, and talk to me while you eat … please."

"Oh Lord, Mr. Neil. Whut on earth could I be a-tellin' *you*."

Neil pulled a chair up to the desk, sat down, and leaned forward toward Goober.

"Goober," he said, "my father was from Scotland … came to America when he was 16 years old and made a success of himself. He went in the dry goods business and eventually, I joined him in the business, and we became interested in turning good old southern cotton into cloth to sell in dry goods stores. All the while my father never forgot the Scottish tradition of finely woven woolen fabric … but he went to his grave having never woven a single strand of wool!

"Now, here I am a successful cotton mill owner and investor with Scottish blood coursing through my veins, and by golly, I'm going to take up the challenge and build me a woolen mill and raise the sheep to furnish the wool!"

Goober swallowed a bite of some unknown delicacy and said, "Wal, Mr. Neil, I don't know nothin' about weavin' wool, ner wool mills, ner sheeps, ner none o' that."

"I didn't expect that you would, Goober," Neil said. "What I want to ask you about is this place you're from … Avery Cove. I've been reading and hearing about that region, and from what I can tell, it's prime sheep country up there. Then too, I remembered what you said about people there who might be in need. I want to see if Avery Cove might be a location to consider buying up some land to raise sheep, and then build a small woolen mill … not a lot of employees … to weave some high quality, specialty woolen fabric."

Goober looked interested.

"Another thing, Goober. I am to the point where I want to cut back on my work. I want a spot in the mountains where Mrs. Neil and I can go to live out our days. The mill and the sheep would be a small enough thing that I could consider it a hobby and a large enough thing to keep me busy."

"I can't understand why anybody-ud want t' live in th' mountains …
Hit's s' far frum ever'thing," Goober said.

"Goober, do you know anything about Henry David Thoreau?"

Goober looked up from his food. "Whut did 'e throw?"

"Tho-reau, Goober. He was a writer who went to live in a wilderness place called Walden Pond. He said that he moved to the woods to live *deliberately*. That's what I want to do ..,. live *deliberately*. Maybe that's why you moved to Charlotte … you know, live in a place that would challenge you mentally."

"One o' my teachers said she thought I wuz mentally challenged."

A blank expression flashed over Neil's face followed by a stifled grin. "Suppose we get on with it," he said. "How many people live in your valley?"

"Wal … at one time they was 'bout 700 people lived up 'ere, but hit's down t' 'bout 250 now. They's a lot o' people leavin' like me, 'specially the young folk, cause they hear 'bout all th' stuff in th' city that they ain't got in th' cove."

"Is there land for sale there?"

"Wal, hit seems like ever' parcel that comes up fer sale, Preacher Burden buys it. Him and some others is gettin' into cattle purdy heavy."

"But do you think there would be enough land available for a few thousand sheep, and enough people in need of work to support a small mill?"

Goober pushed his plate to the side, took a sip of wine, and thought carefully.

"Mr. Neil," he said, "I hate t' tell ye this, but I don't think Avery Cove's yer place."

"Why not?"

"Wal, first off, they wuz this feller, Smithfield, raised some sheeps up 'ere sev'ral years ago. His wife an' daughters would fix up the wool and spin it up into yarn t' sell fer knittin' an' sech ... did purdy good, I understand. But th' folks up 'ere raisin' cattle didn't take too kindly towards him an' 'em sheeps, 'cause th' sheeps 'ud pull th' grass up by th' roots and kill it ... make the land warsh, whur as the cows 'ud clip it off with their teeth an' hit 'ud grow back."

Then Goober went on to tell Neil about the roads—how bad they get in the winter or after a heavy rain.

"An'," he said, "they ain't no 'lectricity up 'ere neither."

But his most stinging indictment concerned the number of potential workers. He pointed out that of the 250 people who lived there, many were "younguns" and "old folks," and that didn't leave a very large pool from which to draw workers.

"Any suggestions?" Neil asked.

"Wal, 'at feller Smithfield moved 'is sheeps up t' a place north o' Burley. They ain't no cattlemen up 'ere, an' pastures is plentiful, an' they's a lot more folks in Burley. Some of 'em might be lookin' fer a job!"

Neil sat back in his chair and rubbed his chin. He had a look of disappointment on his face.

"Green, once again I feel like a fool! I should have asked you about this in the first place. What do you say we go out and join the party?"

"Imagine that," Goober thought as he exited the office carrying his empty plate and wine glass. "Found somethin' I'm a expert on!" His chest led the way out of the room and his head was high.

When Will saw him come out with Neil, he went over to see what was going on.

"Goob, is everything all right? There's not a problem, is there?"

"Naw, Will! They ain't no problem. Mr. Neil jest had some business questions he wanted to axt me about. I got 'im straightened out!"

Just then, Mrs. Neil came over and introduced herself to Goober and told him how glad she was that he could come. "Mr. Green, my husband tells me that you're a master weaver and an expert on the mountains west of here."

" Wal ..."

"But I must apologize to you, Mr. Green. Here you were kind enough to come to our home, and Glenn has been keeping you from the party, trying to get business advice … I just know it."

"Aw, 'at's awright, Miz Neil, I wuz jest tellin' Will here that I got 'im straightened out. He can come t' me anytime 'e wants to an' I'll set 'im straight. An' you can call me Goober … jest plain Goober." And with that, Goober went back to the table for more food.

"Oh, Lord," said Will under his breath.

Will's fear that Goober would really embarrass himself never materialized. As a matter of fact, things went rather well, and if anyone there looked down on Goober, it didn't show.

Before the evening was over, he had danced with all the ladies, joked with all the men, and consumed most of the food and about a bottle and a half of wine.

When it came time to leave, he shook Mr. Neil's hand, kissed Mrs. Neil's, and told them both how much he enjoyed the "shin-dig," and to say that he was the hit of the party would be an understatement.

Thursday, December 24th, Christmas Eve.

The mill whistle blew at 3:00. It was just as well—with all the Christmas spirit, not much work was getting done. There would be no night shift, and to even things out, on the first day back from Christmas, the day shift would be off and the night shift would come in at the regular time.

Will had circulated through the various departments of the mill, wishing everyone a merry Christmas. He had gone to the office to turn in his paper work and had wished all the office workers the same. He gathered his things together and walked down the long hallway, wished the time keeper a happy holiday, and walked through the door.

Goober was waiting as usual, and the two started for home. At the road they got a nice surprise. Esther was waiting with the surrey to give them a ride. She had gone to the company store earlier to get the last of the grocery items she needed, and on a whim, she had stopped by the mill offices to see if the workers would be coming home early. She was told that they would be, and she waited.

"Esther," Will said as he climbed aboard, "stop by the store on the way out. There's something else I need to get."

Traveler moved willingly under Esther's light touch, and in minutes Will's shopping trip was completed and he was climbing back aboard the surrey with a package wrapped in brown paper and tied with string. This time he took the reins.

"I need to make a stop on the way home," he said, and he turned the surrey to go out into the village.

Soon he stopped in front of one of the mill houses and called for a boy playing in the yard to come over.

"Hey, Buddy," he called out, "give this to your Mama and Daddy and tell them a man said 'Merry Christmas.' " He handed the boy the bundle and drove away.

"Whut wuz 'at all about?" asked Goober.

"I guess you could say that was another Christmas present to me," said Will. "You remember that worker I had to fire ... the one with the family? That was their house. They'll have to move soon. The package was just some things to make Christmas a little better for them and a way to ease my mind a little. The farm girl had a stable family to go back to and she'll be all right, but all this family has is each other. God bless 'em."

Traveler's hooves clicked on the roadway as the trio moved along, each deep in thought about how much they had and how lucky they were to be together.

Life wasn't perfect for any of them. Esther wasn't happy living so far away from Will, Goober worried about Roamer and Sweetie and was still looking for the right woman, and Will, though happy and secure on the outside, successful in his work and a friend to everyone he knew, silently hungered for the simple life of the farm and the majesty of the mountains. Yet in this time and place, each in some way was blessed.

Suddenly Will had a thought. "We'll go to the Christmas Eve service at church!"

"That's a wonderful idea!" said Esther.

"Long as 'ey don't take up th' serpent!" added Goober.

It's easy to forget the true meaning of Christmas. After all, Santa Claus is an imposing figure! The parties, decorations, and secular trappings of the season cause one to forget the tiny Infant surrounded by shepherds, angels, and wise men in a stable setting. Forgotten too is the purpose of His coming; so it is that churches celebrate Christmas Eve with a service of remembrance to refocus the thoughts of believers on the Christ Child.

Will, Esther, and Goober arrived at the church at 6:50 p.m. and walked up the steps to be greeted by an usher with a joyful "Merry Christmas!"

They entered and found seats about halfway down, on the right side. Esther entered the pew followed by Will, and Goober entered last and proudly sat on the aisle, dressed in his new suit.

As he had been so many times since he came to Charlotte, Goober was amazed, but this was perhaps the most amazing place he had ever seen! His eyes darted around to take in a host of people dressed in their finest.

Above his head were mighty hewn beams spanning the sanctuary, supporting, it would seem, the very sky. Suspended from them were large chandeliers with electric lights illuminating the room.

Stained-glass windows depicting stories from the Bible stood at constant attention along the walls, and one, depicting the birth of Jesus, was circled with candles and greenery.

Before him was the alter decorated with greenery and a crèche, and behind the alter, the most impressive of the sights, what seemed to be a large pump organ surrounded by tubes of various sizes made of gold and silver metals and elongated, square wooden tubes of various lengths.

"Will," Goober whispered, "whut are 'em tubes up 'ere 'round 'at big ol' pump organ?"

"That's a pipe organ, Goob," Will whispered back. "The organ sounds come out of those pipes."

Goober then picked up the *Book of Common Prayer* and began leafing through it. His lack of understanding of the book was evident.

As he was placing the prayer book back in the rack, the organ sounded the thunderous first chord of *Joy to the World* and Goober dropped the book and jerked to the upright position where he remained with eyes glued to the organist. Oh! The magnificence of the sound that enveloped his body as the organist played a verse of the triumphant carol!

Then Goober rose with the rest of the congregation as they began singing:

Joy to the world, the Lord is come!
Let earth receive its King;
Let every heart prepare Him room
And heaven and nature sing.

Goober's attention was focused on the organist—his fingers flying over the keys, pulling stops, working the pedals—and did not see the crucifer leading the procession up the aisle until he was beside him. When he sensed his presence, Goober's head jerked around to see him and the rest of the religious procession coming at him.

The fixtures of worship—the cross, the Bible, the censer with its sweet smelling incense, the priest and lay clergy, and finally the choir, all in their robes and vestments, passed beside him, close enough to touch. And he was in awe!

For the entire service Goober watched Will and the others around him and did as they did. He stood, kneeled, sat, and bowed on cue. He received communion and didn't even ask if they had elderberry. The refinement of Makepeace Green had begun!

Traveler walked slowly home, minding the darkened streets. Will, Esther, and Goober sat silently for several blocks, letting the impact of the service work within them.

Finally, Goober spoke.

"Will, 'at church service an' all 'at's took place lately has done it fer me. I've made up m' mind ... I ain't goin' back t' Avery Cove 'cept maybe t' visit m' aint and uncle. Might even try t' git 'em t' move down here. Course, I reckon I'll haf t' go back sometime an' sell m' house an' land, then come back here an' try t' get a place like yourn."

"Kind of ironic, isn't it Goob? Here you want to take root in Charlotte, and I want to find a simpler time and place ... sort of like Avery Cove. Here you want a place like mine, and I want a place like yours. You want action, and I want peace and quiet. You want to work in a mill, and I want to farm. Life isn't fair, is it?"

Again there was silence, but Esther finally said it: "Why don't you just swap. Sometimes I wish I had someone I could just swap with."

Suddenly it was so quiet that Traveler's hooves against gravel sounded like gun shots.

Finally Will spoke. "What say, Goob ... do you want to swap?"

And Goober answered, "Hot dang, Will! I'm fer that! Let's do 'er!"

As Traveler pulled into the yard and circled toward the barn, Will jumped from the surrey and ran toward the house.

"You two wait here," he called back. "I'll be right out."

The excitement of the moment was great for everyone, but Goober and Esther must have both wondered if Will had gone over the edge. Where had he gone and why?

All at once Will burst through the back door with his Colt .44 in one hand and a shotgun in the other. He ran into the field beside the barn and emptied the pistol into the air. As soon as he had thrust it into his belt, he raised the shotgun and fired both barrels upward. All of his shots were accompanied by whoops and screams like none Esther and Goober had ever heard, and Esther was frozen in fear.

"*Will! Will!*" she cried. "*What are you doing?*"

"*Just lettin' Santy know we're here,*" he shouted. "*Just lettin' him know we're here.*"

Ten

THE BLIZZARD

January brought snow and bone-chilling cold to Charlotte. The old timers agreed that the January siege was the fiercest since the winter of 1874.

It started on the evening of Tuesday, January 12th as snow showers that fell intermittently until Will and Goober were in bed and asleep, but in the night it came in earnest.

Will woke about 4:00 a.m. to the sound of Dawg scratching on the back door. When he opened the door to investigate, Dawg rushed into the house and cowered in a corner of the parlor near the stove. He knew by the layer of white on Dawg's back that the first real snow of the year had arrived.

The commotion awakened Goober, who came to see what was going on. When he saw Dawg's white coat he commented under his breath, "Didn't think I'd have t' put up with 'at mess down 'ere."

"Goob" Will said, "I just peaked outside, and it's already several inches deep. We might as well get ready and leave for work early. The going could be slow today."

Although the snow was an inconvenience to Will and Goober and was sure to cause some hardship, it was still a welcome diversion from the one thing that had totally occupied their recent conversations.

In the days since Christmas neither Will nor Goober had cooled off in their determination to make a property swap, with Will moving to Avery Cove to farm, and Goober staying in Charlotte to work in the mill. They had spent countless hours going over the details of what each owned in the way of property, what kinds of furniture and equipment each would leave behind, who they would get to handle the legal transaction, and so forth.

Goober assured Will that when his parents died he had gone to the county seat on the advice of Preacher Burden and had the deed to the property transferred to his name and that he owned the property free and clear with all taxes paid in full.

Whereas Will had shown Goober the deed to his property and Goober had been able to inspect it, Will was at a distinct disadvantage in that he had to trust Goober's word that he owned any property at all. Beyond that, he also had to trust Goobers assessment of the scope and condition of the property and the furnishing and fixtures that went with it.

Because of the uncertainty of all that was involved, it was decided that they would have the Parker family attorney, Creighton Williams, devise a plan.

Mr. Williams suggested that since Goober could not leave his job to go with Will to inspect the property, Will should take a leave of absence and go inspect the property on his own.

He further suggested that Will take a notarized letter of explanation from Goober to Preacher Burden, who in addition to being the Methodist minister, storekeeper, and postmaster, was the local justice of the peace. Preacher Burden, in turn, would introduce Will to Roamer and Sweetie and request that they show Will the property and the deed they were holding for Goober.

If Will was satisfied with the trade, Mr. Williams would carry out the transaction in Charlotte and in Avery Cove through an attorney he knew in Burley.

There were still plenty of details to work out, not the least of which was Will's getting a leave of absence to make the trip, but for now, all efforts and energy would have to be directed toward dealing with the snow storm.

Much to Dawg's delight, Will charged up the parlor stove and got a fire roaring, and while Goober was making a trip to the outhouse, Will started cooking a breakfast of eggs, bacon, grits, fried bread, and coffee.

"Mus' be below zero out thar," Goober announced as he rushed back into the kitchen. "I like to-a stuck t' the seat. Didn't think I'd have t' put up with 'is mess down 'ere."

"Does it snow a lot in Avery Cove?"

"Up 'ere we'd call 'is a skifflin," Goober said. "I've saw times when ye couldn't even git t' th' barn t' feed th' animals fer three days. An' they was 'is one time hit wuz s' cold, we had a cow froze t' death standin' up. Daddy went out t' feed 'er, an' shoved 'er on th' butt to move 'er over, an' she fell over stiff as a board!"

Will turned from the stove with a look of utter disbelief on his face, but he didn't—or couldn't—say a word.

"Then, they wuz this other time when th' river froze over solid. Ye could drive a wagon an' team 'cross it an' not fall through. Then, they wuz the time …"

"*Goober!*" Will said, and he put his hands over his ears. "Are you trying to talk me out of moving to the cove?"

"Oooo, nooo, Will," Goober said, "I'm jest bein' fair an' honest. Thought ye ort t' know whut ye wuz gettin' into. They wuz this time when hit got so cold that Mama stuck t' the outhouse seat, an' Daddy had t' pry off th' boards an' bring th' whole shootin' match inside t' thaw."

"*Goober!*" Will was shouting this time. "*I don't want to hear about your mama freezing to the outhouse seat!*"

"Okay, Will. But ye shouldn't git s' touchy."

By the time the breakfast dishes were washed and Dawg had been fed, Goober had taken care of Traveler's needs. With the fire banked in the stove, Will and Goober put on their warmest clothes and left for the mill.

The snow was falling at a moderate rate, and by the time they reached the road, it looked like about five inches were on the ground.

"Unless it gets worse, we should be all right," Will said.

It's strange what snow does to sound. Everything became eerily silent. The birds, dogs, and other animals were hiding in the warmest places they could find, there were no horses and wagons clopping along the road, and the blanket of snow was absorbing everything else that dared make a peep.

By the time the boys reached the bridge at Silar Creek, the snow was falling harder and the wind had picked up. Conditions were almost to the white-out stage. The only bright spot was that the wind was to their backs.

Suddenly, a stark, white figure appeared, coming toward them from out of the wall of white. It turned out to be a night-shift worker on the way in to town.

"You men going to the mill?" he asked.

"If we don't freeze to death first," Will answered.

"Wasting your time," the white figure said. "Power's out. Mill's shut down."

Will and Goober stopped and searched each other's face to find looks of frustration behind their own white features.

"Whut we gonna do?" Goober asked. "I don't think I can make it back t' th' house."

"Let's see if Sarah's is open. At least we can warm up before we head back," said Will.

When they reached Sarah's, they almost passed it by. The landmarks that they had always unconsciously used to find it were obliterated by what was now a full blown blizzard. Only a dimly lit window signaled that it was there.

The steps leading to the cafe were laden with snow, and there were no tracks that would indicate that anyone had been using them. When they opened the door and stepped inside, they found Sarah, who was in a panic, and no one else.

"Am I glad to see you!" she said. "I sent Pearl to the company store over two hours ago to get some eggs, and she's not back yet. I was just about to close up and go looking for her."

"She's probably holed up at the store or in someone's house," Will said, "but if it will make you feel better, Goober and I will go out and make sure she's not lying in a snow bank."

"*Will*! Don't say things like that! And yes, I would be eternally grateful if y'all would look for her."

"Keep the coffee hot. If we survive, we shall return and drink the pot dry!" Will exclaimed melodramatically as he threw his coat around himself.

A smile came to Sarah's face as Will said to Goober, "Off with you then, Porthos! Off, you Musketeer! We shall slay the dragon storm and rescue the fair Pearl, then return to quaff all the coffee in the land!"

"I hope to my never!" said Goober. "Whur did ye come up with 'at mess?"

As the door was closing behind them, Will and Goober met Pearl coming up the steps, tired and covered with snow, but carrying three dozen eggs. Will took the eggs, and Goober helped her up the last step.

When they opened the door and came in, Will exclaimed, "We have slain the dragon storm and rescued the fair Pearl!"

"And all the coffee in the land is yours for the drinking!" Sarah cried as she greeted Pearl and helped her with her coat.

———————

The school house clock on the wall of Sarah's Café chimed 11:00 o'clock. Will and Goober had been there for four hours. For the first hour or so they had talked to Sarah and Pearl about the storm and storms past, and Pearl had recounted her adventure of going to get the eggs.

Goober retold the story about the cow freezing to death and started to tell about his mama and the outhouse, but Will stopped him there.

For the next couple of hours, Will and Goober napped with their heads on the table while Sarah and Pearl spent time in the back room, and for the last hour Will and Goober sat at the front window watching the snow fall. In all that time not one person ventured in.

Finally, Will got up and found a long wooden spoon under the counter and went outside to measure the accumulation. When he came back in he announced, "Looks like about 11 inches to me."

"How's th' sky look?" Goober asked.

"Black as a pirate's heart," was the reply.

"Do ye think we better try t' git home?"

"I think we better stay put as long as Sarah will have us," Will answered. "By the way, is your turning plow in good shape?"

"Ain't no time t' be thinkin' 'bout no turnin' plow!" said Goober.

"An' yes, hit's in dandy shape … handles an' all. Sittin' in th' barn with th' harrow, a cultivator, th' latest seed drill, an' sev'ral other very fine implements, thank ye very much!"

"Okay," said Will. "But ye shouldn't git s' touchy."

"Why'd ye bring 'at up anyway?" Goober asked.

"Goob, do you realize that farmers will be doing their spring plowing in about three months? And here I sit in Charlotte without a plow, or a team, or seed, or any soil to plow for that matter. If we're really gonna make this change, I need to get started. I need to be in Avery Cove in early spring to start breaking soil, or I won't have anything to eat, and my animals won't have anything to eat come next winter."

"Whut ye gonna do, Will?"

"As soon as we get home, I'm going to write Mr. Neil and tell him my plans, and then I'm going to see if the mill will give me a leave of absence … and if they don't … I'll give my notice and start getting my things together."

Goober got up and walked to the window. "Will, I'm startin' t' wonder if we'll ever make it home. Hit ain't slowed up a lick."

———◆———

The following morning found Will and Goober sleeping on the floor of Sarah's Cafe, with Sarah and Pearl sleeping in the back room. Sarah had rounded up all the towels, table cloths, flower sacks, and any other fabrics she could find to fashion make-shift beds.

The clock on the wall said 8:20 when Will rolled over and got up to look out the window. The snow had slowed to sputters and flurries, but the sky was still a dark shade of gray. When she heard someone stirring about, Sarah emerged from the back room looking disheveled.

"The building creaked and groaned all night long," she said. "I started to fear that it might collapse under the weight of the snow. Have you measured it yet?"

She reached under the counter and handed Will a yard stick. Will opened the back door, pushing snow aside, and made his way out to flat ground. He stuck the yard stick into the snow and placed his thumb at the 19-inch marking.

"Is this what you'd call a skifflin up in the cove?" he hollered to Goober.

"Didn't think I'd have t' put up with 'is mess down here," Goober hollered back.

"Hello! Are you open?" A voice was coming from the front door.

"Sheriff! Come in!" Sarah called back. "We're open for you anytime. Do you want something to eat? Thanks to Pearl, we have eggs."

"That would be nice, Sarah," he said. "And some coffee!"

Just then Will came in stomping snow off his feet. "Sheriff, what brings you out? Somebody rob a bank?"

"Hey, Will! You know bank robbers don't get out in this kind of weather. They're too smart. I'm headed into town, lookin' for stragglers."

"How on earth are you traveling, Sheriff?" Will asked.

"Two-horse sleigh," the sheriff answered. "The county bought one years ago for weather like this. I think it's only been used once before, but it does the trick. It's a little tricky to drive though."

"Would you consider giving Goober and me a ride on the way out?" Will asked.

"I'd consider it a pleasure," the sheriff said, grinning. "Especially since elections aren't far off!"

Breakfast never tasted better, and the coffee was never more warming. To top it off, Sarah fixed everybody some food to take and a bag of scraps for Dawg, and said that it was all on the house!

After everyone's hunger was satisfied, Sarah closed up and the sheriff walked her to her house two doors up. Then he loaded up Pearl, Will, and Goober and headed for Pearl's house.

Will had never ridden in a sleigh, and it was a completely new experience. The runners made a high-pitched sizzle on the snow while the horses' hooves were silent. The only sound other than the sizzle was the clatter of the harnesses and the breathing of the animals.

The sheriff kept the speed of the sleigh to a walk since he was not accustomed to driving one and since the horses had a good distance to go.

Soon, Pearl was safely home, and Will and Goober were getting off the sleigh at Will's house.

"Thanks, Sheriff!" Will called out. "We'll see you at the polls come election time."

———

January 14, 1897

Dear Mr. Neil

I am writing to let you know that I will be requesting a leave of absence from Inverness Mill so that I can look into the possibility of moving to Avery Cove, North Carolina.

If my request is granted, I will be leaving Charlotte in the early spring and be gone for two weeks. While in Avery Cove, I will inspect the property belonging to Goober Green, and if I find it satisfactory, I will exchange the property I have here in Charlotte for the property there. If I decide to stay, I will be submitting my resignation from Inverness Mill.

I am sure you remember that one time you told me how you followed your dream, and you encouraged me to follow mine. That is what I am doing, and I hope I can do it with your blessing.

No matter how this turns out, I want to thank you for all you have done for me. You offered me a chance to be a part of your textile business at a time when I did not know how I would make a living, much less how I would survive, and more than that, you gave me hope that I could be happy and successful in whatever I chose to do.

Thank you again for your kindness and help.

Respectfully yours,

Will Parker

With the burdensome letter written, Will could think of the things he and Goober could do to start recovering from the storm and protecting themselves from the bitter cold.

Traveler and Dawg were fed as soon as they got home, and Dawg was let out to do his business. He had a hard time going in the small space that Will had scraped off for him, so Will's first priority was to find his coal shovel and clear off a large area to act as Dawg's outhouse. He shoveled off an area about ten feet square just outside the back door, and Dawg showed his appreciation by christening it.

Then Will turned his attention to Traveler. After he had moved Traveler into the isle of the barn, he cleaned his stall and put in a fresh bed of straw. He supplemented the hay that Goober had given him with a generous serving of oats and the core of an apple he had eaten, and he drew a bucket of water from the well. Traveler showed his appreciation by nuzzling Will's chest and giving a soft "whinny."

While Will was tending to the animals, Goober had been busy clearing some of the snow off the roof with a rope and chain, cleaning the steps, and shoveling paths to the barn and outhouse.

The coal supply was a concern to Will since he was afraid the coal wagon would be stopped, or slowed to a crawl at best, so he and Goober sawed down a dead oak tree at the edge of the lot and split it into firewood.

A check on the food showed that they had a generous supply if they didn't mind doing without some of the store-bought items such as eggs.

"I'll tell you what, Goober," Will said, "I'll sure be glad to get to where I have a chicken house and don't have to buy eggs."

"They was 'is time in th' cove whur hit got s' cold that some o' Mama's chickens froze on th' roost and flopped over upside-down still hangin' on t' th' perch."

"*Goober!*"

"Man! Ye sure are touchy."

Throughout the day and into the night, flurries and sputters of snow fell, but there was no further accumulation.

When Will awoke at about 4:00 the next morning, he went to the front steps and looked up to see stars—millions of stars glittering in a clear sky.

A trip to the back porch confirmed the chill he felt. The thermometer read 10° Fahrenheit. Nothing would be moving today.

Eleven

DON AND MOLLY

The mill reopened the following Monday, much to the delight of Will and Goober. They had developed a bad case of cabin fever as their only trip out of the house was to the post office to mail Will's letter to Mr. Neil, with a stop at the store to get some essentials.

Mr. Massey had informed the supervisors and overseers that the plant would run seven days a week until production was caught up. That meant that if anyone wanted a day off, everyone had better put extra effort into their jobs.

The weather over the last few days had warmed to a point where the snow was melting and the roads were a mess.

Will and Goober decided to drive the surrey as far as the livery stable and leave Traveler there during their shift. Traveler would enjoy getting out and visiting other horses, and they would enjoy riding above the mud.

When Will went to mail Mr. Neil's letter, he had a letter from Esther telling him that she had gotten back to Wilmington, and thanking him for taking such good care of her during her Christmas break—although she had done most of the care-giving—and she thanked him especially for the cameo broach and the fur lined gloves he had given her.

She told him, too, how she hoped he would find happiness in Avery Cove and how she wished she could follow a new dream.

He was saddened thinking how she was so far away without family or even a close friend to share life with her, and he hoped in his heart that she would find a special someone with whom she could build a family.

Goober was back in his element. He was hovering over his looms like a mother hen hovering over her chicks. He would dash from one to the other checking, tweaking, repairing, and otherwise nurturing his machines, and the looms were paying him back! They were clacking, and thundering, and spitting out canvas at a blistering pace. Goober wasn't going to miss a day off if he could help it! No sir, mister!

When break time came, Will went down the hall to the office wing, looking for Mr. Spann. He, like Will, was on break, and Will asked for a minute of his time. As much as he hated to, he would have to talk to Spann about the leave of absence.

"Sure," Spann said. "We'll go back to my office and spread out our lunch on my desk."

They entered the office, and Mr. Spann went to his seat behind the desk. Will chose to stand.

"Mr. Spann, I've written Mr. Neil and told him that I would be requesting a leave of absence from my job to look into relocating to another area. I know I haven't been at the mill long enough to have any vacation time coming, so of course I'd be going without pay. If I decide to relocate, I'll be resigning, but if I decide not to stay there, I really would like to come back to work here. I figure it will take me two weeks to make the trip."

"That's a bold move," Spann said. "I guess you know how hard jobs are to come by right now … especially an overseer's job."

"Yes sir, I know."

Spann took a bite of his sandwich. "I don't want to hold you up, but I would really like to talk to Mr. Neil and Mr. Massey before I give you an answer."

"I understand, and I'll be glad to wait."

"When do you want to go?"

"Early spring."

"Then I'll get back to you as soon as possible. For now though, keep those weave room hands hustlin'. We need canvas."

"You've got it, Mr. Spann." Will breathed a sigh of relief.

One more load was lifted. One more step was taken. A few more and he would be in Avery Cove.

When the shift ended, Will and Goober slogged to the livery stable to pick up Traveler and the surrey. On the way back to Traveler's stall, a tall horse in a front stall caught Will's eye. In the stall next to it was another horse matching the first in color and size.

He opened a gate and walked inside to find one of the largest horses he had ever seen—taller than he at the withers by several inches. It was a gelding and had a dark, heavy coat and long feathery hair surrounding its hooves.

He then went to the other stall and found a mare that was equally impressive.

"Goober! Look at these creatures!" Will said.

"Them's the biggest horses I've ever saw, Will!"

The livery keeper heard them talking and came out of his living quarters to see what was going on.

"Whadaya think about *them* animals?" he asked.

"Biggest horses I've ever seen," Will said. "I've only heard about horses like this. What are they?"

"They're Clydesdales ... Scottish draft horses. The gelding's name is Don, he's four, and the mare is Molly, she's six."

"Are they for sale?"

"Yep! But you wouldn't have any use for 'em. These are farm animals. Why, they'd pull that surrey of yours apart. I'll probably have to go north or west to find someone to take 'em. They'd do real good in a cold climate."

Will took another look at the mare. "How did you get them?"

"Artis McGreevy is sellin' 'em. Too much for him to handle at his age. I hope I find a home for 'em soon. You've heard of eatin' like a horse? These eat like two ... each!"

"I'm afraid to ask," said Will, "but how much does he want?"

"Hundred and twenty-five each," said the livery man. "It's a package deal ... includes all the tack and rigging, and a good, heavy wagon if you buy both."

Will backed away shaking his head "no" and waving his hands back and forth in front of his face as if to say, "This is crazy. I can't afford these animals. I can't even afford to feed 'em." But the look in his eye was saying, "I'll be back. I can't live without 'em."

The livery man understood and said, "You come back and see 'em in the light. You can even hook 'em to a plow and see 'em pull, if you want to."

———◆———

Will spent a restless night, and the next morning during his lunch break, he ran up the street to see the horses again.

"You're back, I see," the livery man said. "Something told me you would be."

Will told the livery man that he was possibly moving to the mountains to farm and would need plow horses, and he would need strong animals to pull his possessions up the mountain. Telling him that was a mistake.

"Two-fifty for the whole deal?" Will asked.

"Yep, two-fifty."

"Isn't that a little steep?"

"Nope! I can take 'em up in the Shenandoah Valley and get three ... maybe three-twenty-five."

"That's a long trip."

"Not so far for fifty dollars extra!"

Will felt beaten. He was going to have to work on his trading skills if he wanted to be a farmer. "I'll be back tomorrow," he said.

"I'll be here. Don't know about the horses."

———◆———

That evening, Will and Goober walked to the livery stable and got the surrey and Traveler, making as little noise as possible. Will wasn't prepared to talk with the livery man any more that day about the Clydesdales. He did check to make sure they were still there, and they were.

Goober had been acting strangely since they left the mill. On the way out of town Will asked him what the problem was.

"Ain't no problem," Goober said. "Gonna court a girl nex' Sunday, 'at's all."

It was dark and Will couldn't see the expression on Goober's face, but he sensed a note of pride in his voice. "*What? You're going courtin'... with a girl?*"

"Yep, if th' mill ain't a-runnin'."

"Anybody I know?"

"Hit's a little girl in spinnin', purdy as a pitcher ... little farm girl, 'bout 16, I guess. She's 'bout as big as me. Got brown hair an' brown eyes. Talks funny though. Sounds a lot lack you an' yer sister."

"What are you going to do with her?"

"Gonna walk 'er t' church if we ain't a-workin'. She's a Babdist same as me, but ye know, I been thinkin' 'bout jinin' 'at church o' yourn."

"Tell you what, Goob. If the mill isn't running, you can take Traveler and the surrey. How about that?"

"Hot dang, Will, I'm fer that!"

Things were coming together for Goober too! He was starting to make a living wage, he loved Charlotte, he was learning city ways, and he had himself a girl!

As for Will, there were more hurdles to clear, but things were looking good. Very good.

———

Will and Goober left for work a few minutes early the next morning so they could go by Hattie Jackson's house and drop off some laundry. Goober had decided that it was time to have Hattie do his laundry too, especially since he might be having to work seven days a week for a while. And then too, there was this thing about having a girlfriend: he wanted to look especially nice.

The surrey pulled up in front of Hattie's house, and Hattie was sweeping the front porch. She looked up at the Surrey, wondering who this could be, and then her eyes brightened.

"Law, Mistah Will! I almos' didn't realize you in dat buggy!"

"You'll be glad to see me too," Will said. "Goober gave me a new pair of drawers, an undershirt, and a pair of socks for Christmas, and I went out and bought some more to go along with 'em. Everything's new! *And*, I brought you a new customer! You remember Goober, don't you?"

"Law, Mistah Will! I needs all th' laundry I can git! Thankee, thankee! An' thankee too fo dat silvah dolla'! It's gonna come in *mighty* handy!

"Now, Mistah Goobah, is yo underwears full-a holes? I don't like holes!"

"I think you gonna find mine in purdy good shape, Miz Jackson. An' I want mine done up lack ye do Will's. Don't put no starch in my shirts, same as his."

The banter with Hattie Jackson put them behind as usual, and they had to hurry to get to work under the gun.

Will ran past Goober, who had stopped at the timekeeper's desk, and he was scurrying down the hall when he heard a familiar voice call out from behind him.

"*Will*."

It was Glenn Neil!

"Will, get Goober Green and meet me in Spann's office!" he shouted.

"Hey, Mr. Neil!" Will shouted back. "We'll be there soon as possible."

O Lord! Will thought. *This could be bad ... it could be good ... and why did he want to see Goober? That could be bad ... or good. Was Neil smiling? Was he frowning?* He didn't know.

Will went into the weave room and got his paperwork started; then he caught Goober's eye and motioned for him to come.

"Goob, I don't know what it means," he shouted in his ear, "but Mr. Neil wants to see us in Spann's office."

Goober's countenance fell. "Did I do somethin' wrong?' he asked.

"Not that I know of," Will answered, "but I guess we better go see. We might both be in trouble."

It's a long walk to the front offices, but it goes really quickly—kind of like the walk to the gallows, Will supposed.

Will knocked on the door and they entered.

"Will and Goober!" Mr. Neil said. "Two of my favorite characters! Sit down, boys, and let's talk."

They sat down silently, afraid to say anything.

"Will, I'll start with you. I am very disappointed that you may leave us, and I mean that lovingly, son."

He walked to the window and looked out. Then he turned back to Will.

"I do remember telling you to follow your dream, and even though we may lose you … I'm glad you're doing it."

Will moved uneasily in his chair. Goober was sitting stiffly with his hands on his knees. His feet were bouncing up and down uncontrollably.

"About your leave," Neil continued, "I'll give you two weeks, but that's all we can afford. It's not fair to the people running the mill to have you out while production's behind. I hope you understand."

"Yes, sir, I do."

"I want you to either do this thing or get it out of your system, so I'm going to help you all I can. I'll say more about that in a minute.

"Now, Green, let's talk about you."

"O Lord," Goober muttered.

Neil sat on the edge of the desk looking down on Goober's small frame. Goober's feet bounced higher.

"Goober, after I talked to you, I went up to Burley to look at the lay of the land. I found that fellow, Smithfield and his sheep that you were telling me about, and do you know what he did?"

"No, sir."

"He called me a 'city slicker' and told me to get off his property. Said I was dressed up like a dandy and talked like a Yankee … he said a lot of other things I won't go into now. He even pointed a gun in my face … a Winchester 1873—I learned that from you, Will. I feared for my *life!*"

Goober's eyes were as big as saucers.

"So then," Neil continued, "I went around asking about buying property and got the same reception everywhere I went. Nobody would talk to me."

Goober broke in. "'At's cause ye ain't one o' them, Mr. Neil."

"*Exactly, Goober!*" Neil pointed his finger in the air. "That's where you come in! I need someone like you to go up to Burley and talk to those people—talk their language in a way they can understand—and help me buy some property. I tell you, I love that country up there but the people are strange!"

Neil got up and paced back and forth. Then he sat back down on the edge of the desk.

"I need about 3,000 acres, more or less, and I found an area that's ideal. There are about 15 landowners involved, according to the tax records, and if I … we … can get that land, I'll be set to raise sheep and build my mill and a summer home. Another thing I learned is that I don't want to live up there in the winter," he added.

Goober's feet had stopped bouncing, and his confidence seemed to be returning. "Why would them people sell t' you, Mr. Neil? Whur would they go?"

"That's the part that's good for them, Goober. Even though I'll own the land, I'll allow them to stay in their homes as long as they live, and I'll guarantee them jobs as long as they want to work. I think their lifestyles will improve dramatically. The only difference they'll experience is they'll be seeing sheep when they look out their windows, and they'll have to figure out how to spend their new-found money!"

"I hope to my never!" Goober said. "But just zactly whut am I s'posed t' do?"

Neil leaned in closer and spoke softly. "Goober, I want you to be my agent. I want you to go up there in the spring and stay as long as it takes to buy that property for me. I'll pay you what you're making here plus expenses. As soon as things are sewed up, I'll give you a bonus of $100 …"

Goober sat up straight and whistled.

"… and then, you can either come back to work here, or you can stay in Burley and work at the woolen mill. If you stay there, you can help get the locals organized and recruit workers until the mill is opened.

"*Now!*" Neil walked to the window and looked out again before he continued. "This is what I'm thinking: In the early spring, you can go with Will to Avery Cove, show him around, help speed his trip, and when things are settled there, you can go over to Burley, meet me, and we'll get started!

"The only thing that bothers me is the time element. It'll be a push for you to get up the mountain … those roads are bad up there, especially in the winter and spring … and get things settled in two weeks. Will, are you planning to take your things with you in case you stay?"

"Yes, sir," Will said. "I was going to buy a wagon and team and take some essentials, and then if I stay, I'll come back later and get the rest."

"Okay then, here's what we'll do. I'll arrange for the railroad to carry your team and wagon and you two, of course, up to Virginia and back down to Burley, and unload you there. The train trip will take two days. Then, you can get over to Avery Cove in another two or three days if things go well. That would save you a lot of time and keep you from having to go up that mountain road from Lenoir to Burley."

"Since Goober is going, I'll take my horse and surrey too, and my dog," Will said.

"No problem, we can load them up too," Neil answered. "So … what do you think?" and he held out his hands in a questioning manner.

Will and Goober turned to each other with looks of amazement on their faces.

"It's no wonder you've been so successful, Mr. Neil," Will said. "I would have never been able to come up with a plan like that, and I want to thank you once again for helping me out. Maybe someday I can return your kindness."

"I've got all I need, son. Just pass it on to someone else," Neil said.

"I thank ye too!" Goober crowed. "An' I'll take 'at job! I'll tawk 'em hillbillies in t' sellin'!"

The morning was a blur for Will. His mind was racing with plans for the trip, even though it was still about two months away.

When the lunch break came, he ran out of the mill, turned left and ran to the bank up the street. He made a withdrawal of $125 from his savings and requested that they give it to him in one $50 bill and the rest in ones. Then he went to a counter and wrapped the $50 bill around all the others and tied the bundle with a string.

Then he was off in a trot to the livery stable. The Clydesdales were in the corral next to the building, and there was a sign on the fence advertising them for sale. "I made it!" he said to himself.

The livery man was forking straw in the loft, and he climbed the ladder to talk to him. "Them horses still for sale?" he asked.

"Yep, they're in the corral."

"Let's talk," Will said, and as he spoke, he pulled his hand out of his pocket and the bundle of cash fell to the floor of the loft. He looked around as if he couldn't find it, and directly, the livery man found it and picked it up. He had a serious look on his face as he handed it back.

"Thanks!" Will said. "Tell you what I'm prepared to do. I'll buy the horses if McGreevy will pasture them till spring, and give them their oats and make sure they're taken care of. I want them strong and healthy when I come to get 'em."

Come on, Mister," the livery man said. "He wants to get 'em off his hands."

"I understand," said Will, and he turned and started down the ladder.

"Wait! Come back! Maybe we can work that out after all."

Will climbed back up the ladder. "Okay," he said, "I give you half now and the other half when I pick them up ... that is, if the horses are all right and the wagon and tackle are what you say they are. Otherwise, I'll want my money back."

"No way," said the livery man. "No deal! He won't mind if you inspect the wagon and gear, and I guarantee the horses will be okay, but you'll have to pay it all ... now."

"I'll get back to you," Will said, and he started down the ladder again.

"Where are you going?" asked the livery man.

"Going just this side of Concord to see a team of Shires. I think I'd just as soon have them as Clydesdales." He continued down the ladder. "I'll see you tonight when I pick up my horse and surrey."

"*Wait!*" The livery man said as he came down behind him. "You've got yourself a deal. McGreevy will probably kill me, but the horses are yours … on your terms."

———

That evening when Will and Goober stepped out into the darkness to walk to the livery stable, the air smelled a little sweeter, and even though the sun had set, the day was a little brighter.

For Will, the giant step had been taken; he had been granted his leave. Only the final step—the move—remained.

For Goober, the unexpected job opportunity was a vote of confidence that would cement him even more firmly to Charlotte.

At the livery stable, the "for sale" sign was gone and the Clydesdales were back in the stalls, but the livery man was nowhere to be found. Will called out for him, but he wouldn't come out.

"He's probably in his quarters, licking his wounds," he told Goober.

When they had joined Traveler to the surrey and were climbing aboard, the livery man stuck his head out of his door and hollered, "I'll be taking the team back to McGreevy tomorrow. Thanks for the deal. The truth be known, I'm glad I didn't have to go to the Shenandoah Valley."

"Thank you too," Will said. "I'll see you tomorrow, and we'll settle up for Traveler's room and board."

"You ain't gonna try to beat me down on the price, are you?"

Will didn't answer, he just laughed and nudged Traveler into the road. The sky was clear and the air was cold. Will gave Traveler his head so he could make his way through the frozen spots. He made his way slowly, still not totally used to the surrey, especially at night.

"Will, do ye think we'll be caught up come Sunday?" Goober asked.

"We're making headway," Will answered. "Are you going to be disappointed if you have to work all day?"

"I'll be sore disappointed, Will. Judy Ruth will be too, I'm assured."

"Judy Ruth! Is that her name?"

"Judy Ruth Roach!" Goober answered. "And she's purdy as a pitcher."

Traveler walked on, mindful of the icy patches. Will was deep in thought.

"Goober, I'm going to crack the whip tomorrow through Saturday. I guarantee that at least our department will be caught up by Sunday. I want us to have a day off, and I want Judy Ruth Roach to see that new suit of yours!"

Twelve

GOODBYE, CHARLOTTE

Winter left Charlotte with a sigh. The January storm that closed the mill brought the only heavy snow of the season, and February could only add some spits and flurries to the wintry mix.

March was, as the old saying goes, coming in like a lamb. The old saying also held that when it came in like a lamb, it went out like a lion. Will certainly hoped that it wouldn't since the end of March would be so close to his mountain journey.

When they weren't making canvas, Will and Goober had spent most of their time preparing for the move. Plans had to be made for closing Will's house for an unknown period of time. There were plans to be made about putting crops in the ground once they got to Goober's place, but most of all, Will had to decide what he would take with him.

In late January Will had gone to McGreevy's farm and inspected the wagon that he would be getting as part of the horse deal. The wagon was in good shape but smaller than Will had thought it would be, and he was convinced by seeing it that he should leave many of his treasures in Charlotte to be retrieved later. That was for the best anyway, he thought, since anything hauled up the mountain would have to be hauled back down if things didn't work out. He merely altered his plans to include a trip back to Charlotte in the fall after the crops were in to retrieve items like some favorite furniture and the clock that had been passed down through the family for several generations.

On his trip to McGreevy's farm, he found an old man and his wife who were grateful to him for giving their horses a good home. They were pleased that he was concerned that the horses got ample food, and they had shown their appreciation by feeding, watering, and sheltering the animals to perfection. In turn, Will was pleased that the extra time the McGreevys were having with the horses was giving them the opportunity to say goodbye to the faithful beasts.

Goober's romance with Judy Ruth had been flourishing. He had worn out the road between Will's house and hers anytime there was a church service to attend, and he was working on her father, trying to get him to allow Judy Ruth to go into town to the restaurant where he and Will had eaten.

So far the old man was convinced that church, the dinner table, and the parlor were the only proper places for a young lady to court, but Judy Ruth's mother, who happened to like Goober, was working on her husband, too, by quoting the Scripture, "Train up a child in the way he should go, and when he is old, he will not depart from it." She added to that, "You've brought her up right, and she's not going to run off to town and do something foolish." Quoting the old man Scripture was a powerful tool, and there were signs he was bending.

Goober was tight lipped about what he and Judy Ruth talked about, but Will wondered if there was talk of marriage since Goober was beginning to voice regret that he would be away from her so long on his trip to Avery Cove and Burley.

To forestall any thinking along those lines, Will had told Goober, "Goob, don't you let Judy Ruth stop you from going to Burley! This could mean a lot to you and her both in the future. Just remember how good Mr. Neil has been to me. He'll be that good to you, too!"

Goober's reply was "Hit ain't that simple, Will. She's a-tuggin' at m' heart somethin' fierce!"

It was now March first, and Glenn Neil was nowhere to be found. He had not been back to Charlotte since the mid-January meeting where he laid out his plans for Will and Goober to make the trip by rail to Burley. Will was understandably concerned that he had either forgotten about the deal or had changed his mind about sponsoring it.

The time had come, Will thought, to find out where he stood. He chose to go to his supervisor, Mr. Spann.

Having chased Spann down in the carding room, Will motioned him to a quiet corner and asked, "Mr. Spann, I'm getting concerned about Mr. Neil. Have you heard anything from him lately?"

"He hasn't contacted you?" Spann asked. "Massey told me that he would be here this week. This is the first week of March, isn't it?"

"You don't know exactly when?"

"Will, you probably know Neil better than I do. He'll blow in one of these days, get the job done, and blow back out like a whirlwind."

For the time being, Will would have to be satisfied with the fact that Neil hadn't let him down before. He would remember that Neil was a very busy man.

On the walk home that evening, Will told Goober that he had thought of something that hadn't been taken care of.

"Goob," he said, "I need to get out to McGreevy's and get the horses and wagon, and get the blacksmith to check 'em out … better get Traveler and the surrey checked out, too."

"How d'ye think 'em horses is gonna like ridin' on a train?" Goober asked.

"You sure it's the horses you're concerned about and not yourself?" Will wanted to know.

"I got to affirm, Will, I ain't never rode a train b'fore. 'Em things make a lotta noise. Do they ride rough?"

"The passenger cars ride like a boat on water, but I don't know about a cattle car. I guess that's where we'll be riding. I want to be with Dawg and the horses in case they get spooked."

"O Lord!" Goober said.

The following morning Will and Goober took Traveler and the surrey in and left them at the blacksmith's shop for a checkup. During lunch break Will checked on them and found that Traveler's shoes were all right, and that the smithy had greased the wagon wheels and tightened some nuts and bolts.

"If you do come back, have the blacksmith up there check 'em out again before you leave, but what I done will get ya there, no problem," the smithy said.

Just as Spann had predicted, Glenn Neil came blowing in the next day. He went out in the weave room himself to get Will, but only after he had gone to the carding room to get some cotton to stuff in his ears.

"Will, my boy!" he shouted as he approached. "Are you packed and ready to go? You are still going, aren't you?"

"Hey, Mr. Neil!" Will shouted back. "Am I glad to see you! I'm not packed yet, but I'm working on it."

"Well, let's go out in the hall, and I'll tell you what the plans are."

Will's pulse quickened. It was actually going to happen!

Neil put his arm around Will's shoulder and walked him through the door into the hallway.

"Boy," he said when the noise level was more manageable, "I don't see how you can deal with that racket! It's a wonder to me why everybody in that room isn't making plans to farm!"

They walked a little further down the hall before Neil spoke again.

"Son, do you know how hard it is to lease a livestock car ... I mean, a *single* livestock car?"

"No, sir, I can't say that I do."

"Well, let me tell you, it's *hard!* I thought that with as much material as I shipped in and out of here by rail, I could snap my fingers and find a livestock car sitting on the siding downtown. *No, sir,* it took an act of Congress to get one sent in here and another act of Congress to get a flat car hooked up to it.

"Now, the livestock car and the flat car are sitting on a siding downtown waiting for you to load up. The only problem is time. You and Green will

113

have to have your horses and wagons on them and be ready to leave by about this time day after tomorrow. The livestock car has to be in Chicago in ten days."

Will looked toward the front door and sighed deeply. The reality of the move was hitting him.

"Look at me, Will," Neil said. "Is that going to be a problem?"

Will turned to face him. "No, sir," he answered. "We can do it, but we'll have to leave work now to get it done."

"I'll cover for you with Spann," Neil said. "Will … I sure hope you're doing the right thing. Now go get Green."

Will's legs were like jelly. It hadn't crossed his mind that when the time finally came it would be like this. As he walked toward Goober, he thought about how he was leaving the only home town he had ever known —leaving the graves of his mother and father, his high school, friends, and a good job, and he was frightened.

When Will delivered Goober to Mr. Neil, there were some equally stirring words for him.

"Green," Neil said, "I'm putting a lot of responsibility on you. Helping me convince those stump-jumpers in Burley to sell their property is a small task compared to the other thing I want you to do. I want you to deliver Will here to Avery Cove in a timely manner, show him around, and get him happily settled. If you fail me there, I'll nail your skin to the front door of the mill. Any questions?"

Goober cowered underneath Neil's lofty presence, looking like a flea that had been shaken off a large dog. All he could utter was a weak "No, sir."

Then Neil's softer side returned. "Now boys," he said, "you had better get packin'. Go on and leave, and I'll tell Spann what's going on. On my way out of town I'll tell the railroad people that you'll be at the station at 10:00 a.m. the day after tomorrow. Check in with them and they'll tell you what to do."

"Green!" he said, and Goobers head snapped up. "Meet me at the Burley Lodge on March the 19th … that's two weeks from when you leave here. I'll get a horse for you, and we'll get started."

With those things said, Neil encircled the boys' shoulders with his big arms and said, "I guess that's about it, fellows. May God watch over you and give you a safe journey. Will, don't forget to write, and oh yes, one more thing ... on your way out, go to the loading dock and get enough heavy canvas to cover your wagon. You've both done a good job making it ... you might as well use some of it."

Neil then turned and walked toward the offices without looking back. The boys stood and watched him lumber away.

"O Lord, Will," Goober said, still shaking from the comment about his skin being nailed to the mill's door, "kin I go tell somebody goodbye?"

"I think you should," Will replied.

———————

Instead of going home, Will and Goober started their walk toward the McGreevy farm. They ate their lunches on the way and said little, both reticent in light of the moment.

McGreevy had been expecting them and had the wagon at the ready with all the horses' gear laid out in the back.

As expected, the horses were fat and healthy, well groomed, and grazing in the pasture. McGreevy whistled, and they immediately turned and walked to him. In quick order, they were hooked to the wagon and ready to go.

As a parting gesture, McGreevy threw three bags of oats in the wagon. Then he patted the mare on the neck and went in the house to join Mrs. McGreevy at the window. The boys were off.

Will hadn't driven a farm wagon and a team since his days on his grandfather's farm. It was so much noisier than his surrey—the ride was rougher—and the horses—these horses—were so powerful! They walked as if they were pulling nothing even as they ascended the grade coming up McGreevy's drive into the road. Will urged them on with the reins, and the horses picked up speed to a fast walk, glancing at each other as if trying to judge the exact rhythm of the other's gait.

As they moved along, he thought of his grandfather sitting beside him, teaching him how to hold the reins, laughing and exhorting him to let the horses work. "Don't pull s' hard, boy," he had said. "Give 'em some slack and let 'em work!" And he thought of other lessons he had learned on the seat of the wagon. "Yer corn should be knee high by the fourth of July!" he had said.

The memories were still coming as they pulled up at the blacksmith's shop, but when the wagon came to a halt and the noise subsided, the memories were replaced by the distant thunder of the mill. "Would it ever go away?" Will wondered.

While the wagon and the horses were being checked, Will settled up with the livery man. He and Goober walked up to Sarah's Cafe to say goodbye. Nothing would do but that Sarah pack some food for them, and then she gave them tearful hugs and sent them on their way.

Back at the blacksmith's shop, they found the smithy re-nailing a shoe on Don's left rear hoof. The wheels on the wagon had been recently greased, so all was ready to go.

"We've got two more things we need to do on the way home," Will told Goober. "We need to pick up that canvas, and we need to say goodbye to Hattie Jackson," and he turned right out of the smithy's yard and started for the mill.

"Will, do ye think I could go back an' see Judy Ruth one las' time?" Goober asked.

"I thought you already told her goodbye."

"I did, but they's somethin' else I gotta tell 'er."

"I think you had better write her a letter," Will said. "It's getting late. What did she do when you told her goodbye this morning?"

"She cried real big and kissed me on the jaw right in front o' the whole spinnin' room. Embarrassed me s' bad I couldn't say nothin'."

Will turned the horses to the left onto the driveway that led to the loading dock. Then he returned to the conversation.

"Goob, I think that for greatest effect, you should wait and write Judy Ruth a letter and say what you have to say. You know . . . if you go back, she might kiss you on the jaw again and make a big scene and get people talking about her."

Goober didn't like Will's advise, but he took it and kept his eyes forward as they pulled out of the mill drive with the full roll of duck that Mr. Neil had marked for them.

Hattie Jackson was broken hearted that Will and Goober were leaving, but they promised they would be back to see her.

"I won't be gone real long, Miz Jackson," Goober said, "an' I promise t' bring ye a lot o' laundry when I get back ... real dirty too."

Back on the wagon, Will asked Goober, "Goob, do you have a wash pot and clothes line up at the Cove?"

"Shore do," Goober said. "Down by th' river whur ye kin wrench out ye stuff in crystal clear water."

"O Lord," Will said.

———

The day of departure came quickly and dawned with skies of gray. Will woke as usual to scratching at the back door, and this time Dawg was seeking shelter as much as food. In the west storms cast sheets of orange and yellow lightning across the sky followed by low rumbles of thunder.

The wagon had been packed the night before with clothing suitable for all seasons, food, a few pieces of light furniture, family pictures, feed for the horses, blankets, two lanterns and kerosene, toiletry items, the prized clock that Will decided at the last minute to take, Will's firearms with ammunition, a few pots and pans, and some of the farming implements that Goober said he either didn't have or were in poor repair.

Goober had packed all of his clothes, including his Christmas suit and a few things he had accumulated, and put them in the surrey.

All that remained to be loaded were Dawg, a barrel of water, and Goober and Will's warm bodies. The canvas had been cut to cover the bed of the wagon and the surrey with several layers to save from having to pack the roll, and one piece had been cut to provide shelter on the nights they were to camp along the road.

"Goober!" Will shouted after he had let Dawg in. "Get up and get dressed. We're going to the mountains!"

"I hope to my never!" Goober muttered as his feet hit the floor.

The boys busied themselves getting breakfast cooked and cleaned up and the house put in order. "I don't want any food left out to rot," Will said.

Finally, Will looked around and decided that everything was in order, but then he saw the coffee pot sitting on the stove and realized that it and the coffee hadn't been packed. That raised new worry that something else might have been left out.

Goober reassured him by saying, "Hit ain't lack ye gonna die fer somethin' ye left! You'll be back in th' fall anyways."

On his way to the wagon with the coffee and pot, Will noticed that the sky was still dark and the thunder was closer. Hopefully, that wasn't a portent of things to come.

The horses were standing at the corral fence, probably wanting to be fed, but he decided to wait until they were on the train to feed them, thinking that some oats and hay might give them a bit of security.

Back in the house, he called for Goober. "Hey Goob, it's early but let's get going before the rain starts."

"Be right with ye, Will. I gotta go to the outhouse."

While Goober took care of his morning ritual, Will started getting the horses hooked to the wagon. In a few minutes, Goober came out of the outhouse carrying the last piece of equipment to be loaded—a very important piece of equipment—the remainder of the Sears Roebuck catalog. "Glad you remembered that," Will said.

When the Clydesdales were harnessed to the wagon and Traveler was hooked to the Surry, Will closed up the barn and went back to the house to check on it one last time. Doors and windows were locked, all fires were out, and everything was eerily still.

He looked around and spoke out loud, "Goodbye, house. You've given me warmth and comfort. You've sat up with me through sleepless nights like the good friend you are. I'll be back to see you soon, but before I return, Goober will be back to take care of you. I know you'll care for him too." And so then, he left and locked the door behind him.

Leaving Charlotte to follow his dream was supposed to be a happy time for Will, but it was turning out to be anything but that. On top of the sadness he felt leaving home, the foreboding sky wasn't giving him any comfort. It looked like the bottom might fall out at any moment.

Adding to his sadness was the pressure to make a success of the exchange. Even though there was the loop hole that would let him back out of the deal once he had seen Goober's farm, he was trying to convince himself that the move would be permanent. He had to make it work, and not just for himself, but for Goober as well. The security of the mill could never outweigh the happiness he had experienced on his grandfather's farm.

The sky seemed to be boiling and thickening. He looked back at Goober in the surrey and pointed upward, but Goober just looked up and shrugged his shoulders. Goober's surrey had a top, scant protection for a blowing rain, but still, the only covering Will had was the new Farmer Brown straw hat he had bought for the occasion. It would shield him from the sun, but there was no guarantee that it wouldn't fall apart if it got wet.

When the rain finally started, Will reached back and got the piece of canvas he had cut for a camp shelter. He wrapped it around himself and was protected from the cold shower. Goober was not as fortunate. The flat top on the surrey was meant to shed sun more than rain, and he was getting soaked. The only one totally protected was Dawg, who was snug under the wagon's canvas cover.

By the time they had pulled up to the depot, the rain had subsided. The sky overhead was still dark, but a glint of sun shone through the clouds on the western horizon.

Will climbed down and went into the station. In a few minutes he came out with an employee who pointed to a spot a few hundred feet down the track.

"He wants us to go to a siding down the track where the flat car and the livestock car are parked," Will called back to Goober.

They circled the wagons around the depot and down a path that led to a siding beside their cars. The siding had a long dirt ramp covered with gravel that led to a heavy wooden platform. There was a wooden bridge secured between the platform and the flat car, and another bridge that led into the cattle car. A caboose was attached to the flat car.

A worker directed Will's wagon up the ramp and had him stop short of the flat car. Then he had Will set the brake and unhook the horses. He and Will led the horses into the livestock car and into stalls with moveable partitions.

"Them's some fine animals," the railroad man said.

The worker then asked Will to get out of the way while he and his helper loaded the wagon. It was clear that the railroad men had done this job before. They hooked a rope to the front axle of the wagon, and as the helper turned the tongue to guide it, the other man winched the wagon onto the flat car. The brake was set, the wagon tied down, and everything was secure.

The process was repeated for the surrey and Traveler, and everything was ready to go.

"Now," the railroad man said, "get everything you want to have with you and put it in the livestock car. Once the train gets going you won't be able to get to your wagons until the first stop. The engine will be here in …" he looked at his watch, "one hour and five minutes."

The workers removed the bridges between the ramp and the cars, and they were gone.

Goober and Will watched the railroad men walk down the dirt ramp and up the road toward another job. It was strange how when the men were out of sight, they felt so alone. With a town surrounding them, with a busy depot only a few hundred feet away, and with houses and businesses in sight, they were a world away from civilization—alone and deserted—two orphan boys out on their own.

Goober snapped Will out of his trance. "What do ye think we ort t' bring in th' horse car with us, Will," he asked.

"Uh … yes, Goober," he answered. "Let's start by getting a bag of oats and some hay for the horses."

They uncovered the wagon and found Dawg sleeping in comfort among the horses' provisions. Will rousted him up and took him to be tied in the horses' car while Goober brought a bag of oats and went back for a bale of hay. They brought their blankets, water, the piece of shelter canvas, and their jackets and put them on the fresh straw that the railroad had provided.

Will went back to the wagons, checked their moorings and retied the canvas coverings. "So far, so good," he said out loud.

When the horses had been fed and watered, Will and Goober sat on the straw pallet to wait for the engine to come.

"O Lord," Will said. "I just remembered that I didn't leave a forwarding address at the post office!"

"Preacher Burden kin take care o' that," Goober said.

"That Preacher Burden can take care of just about anything, can't he?"

"Might near," Goober affirmed.

"Goob, you mentioned his daughter one time. Could she be courted?"

"Preacher Burden ain't let nobody near 'er yet. Some say he's a-waitin' fer a preacher boy t' come ridin' through and he'll marry 'er off t' him. Others say she's th' world's only Methodist nun. I wouldn't git m' hopes up 'bout her, if I wuz you."

Silence prevailed for about a minute before Goober said, "Now ye got me thinkin' 'bout Judy Ruth. I wonder whut she's doin' 'bout now."

"She's probably fightin' one of those spinning machines and thinkin' about you, Goob."

"O Lord," Goober said.

Will lay back on his straw bed and pulled his Farmer Brown hat down over his eyes. "Goob, let's get some rest," he said. "We might not sleep much for the next two days."

"O Lord," Goober said again.

———

A soft but steady rain had drummed on the metal roof of the cattle car and sung the boys to sleep. Peacefully they rested, as did Dawg and the horses, until a locomotive sounded its whistle, signaling that it was about to back onto their siding.

They raised up and looked through the openings in the end of the car and saw the engine pushing several cars their way. Closer and closer they came until they felt the mighty jolt of the cars joining.

The horses reared and whinnied, reacting to the unfamiliar feel of their foundation moving. Dawg whined and cowered, and Goober said, "Lord, Will! 'at wuz a mighty blow!"

For a minute, the train was still as the switchman checked the connection, and then, the cars started moving. "We're on our way," Will said.

Goober moved to the rear of the car and looked through the openings to see a man pull himself up onto the caboose. The train was jerking and making moaning sounds as slack was taken up between cars. Hissing sounds were coming from the brakes, and the locomotive was puffing and churning to get the mass moving. Will rushed to calm the horses in their stalls while Goober and Dawg comforted each other.

Soon the train moved onto the main track and began to pick up speed. Charlotte was parading before their eyes as the movement smoothed out, and the clanging and banging became a steady hum.

"*We're on our way, Goob ... we're actually on our way,*" Will sang out, and he looked up through the openings in the car to see the sun pouring through the clouds.

Thirteen

Riding the Rails

There is a tavern in the town, in the town
And there my dear love sits her down, sits her down
And drinks her wine 'mid laughter free
And never, never thinks of me.

A song Will sang with his chums in high school came pouring out as the train set a rhythm on the track. It started out slowly—a flat spot on a wheel just below him clicking with each rotation, click, click, click, click—building slowly and steadily, musically chiming a pitch as well as the beat.

He sang louder as the clicking grew faster, his spirit leaping out of the doldrums that had pinned him down earlier in the day.

Fare thee well, for I must leave thee,
Do not let the parting grieve thee,
And remember that the best of friends
must part, part, part.

Adieu, adieu, kind friends adieu, friends adieu,
I can no longer stay with you, stay with you.

I'll hang my harp on a weeping willow tree,
And may the world go well with thee.

He reached a tormented high note on the last word of the song as the train sounded its whistle at Overbrook crossing. It was a fitting postlude to his life time in Charlotte, he thought.

"And now," he said out loud, "I must find a suitable song to sing as I enter Avery Cove!"

"I hope to my never!" Goober muttered under his breath. "If ye go in t' Avery Cove a-caterwaulin' lack 'at, they'll tar an' feather ye!"

Goober and Dawg were beginning to calm down, having decided that the train wasn't going to wreck and scatter their brains across the countryside.

"'Is ain't s' bad," Goober said. There was a pause while he double-checked with himself to make sure that statement was indeed true, and then he asked, " Wha'che got t' eat, Will? My breakfas' has wore off."

There are times in life when one's world comes crashing down. It may be a time when certain stars and planets align to bring catastrophe, it may be when a plague or a natural disaster such as a flood suddenly descends, or it could be when one realizes that the food was left in the wagon—in plain view, but totally out of reach. This was one of those times.

"Goob, you didn't bring the food over to this car?"

"*Me!*" Goober stated incredulously. "*I thought you wuz in charge o' th' food!*"

There was a long pause as Will looked around, seemingly at nothing in particular. "Well," he said, "we've got water … and we've got oats."

At least the rain had stopped, but as the train left the town and gained speed in the country, the wind, pouring through the openings in the sides of the livestock car, was dropping the temperature.

"I don't guess ye brought a lantern t' warm by either, did ye?" Goober asked.

"No."

"Well ain 'is a fine howdy do! No food, no heat, an' no tellin' how long till we git t' whur we goin'. Do ye know when th' train's gonna stop?"

"No."

"*Will!* We could be goin' to Californy fer all *you* know!"

Fair thee well, for I must leave thee,
Do not let the parting grieve thee,
And remember that the best of friend
must part, part, part.

"*Will!* 'is ain't goin' right! Stop yowlin' an' let's tawk 'is thing through. Do ye even know whur 'is train's headed?"

Will was disoriented. Maybe it was the motion of the train, or the shock of leaving home, but most likely it was just the realization that he had loaded himself onto a train not even knowing its destination. He knew it was headed north when he really needed to go west, but he knew too that traveling by rail meant sometimes taking strange routes since train tracks didn't connect every city and hamlet.

"Goober," he said calmly as he struggled to regain his composure, "I've put my trust in Mr. Neil many times before, and he hasn't let me down yet. Has he ever let you down?"

"Not in my 'membrance."

"Well, he planned the trip—made all the arrangements—so we're just gonna sit back and go where this train takes us. If it's 'Californy' then so be it. We'll pick grapes and oranges and live in the sun. How does that sound?"

"'At don't sound ha'f bad, Will."

"Now about the food … this engine is going to have to stop for water if nothing else. When it does, I'll jump off and go get us something to eat. I'll get us a lantern too. Till then, let's wrap up in this wonderful canvas that you made and try to get warm."

"Hot dang, Will," Goober said as he grinned. "You come up with a answer fer ever'thing, don't ye?"

"We try, Goober. We try."

The train rumbled on, around curves and down long straight-aways, through the North Carolina Piedmont. As the sun peeked through the clouds, Will could tell by its orientation that the train was indeed headed north. He could peek through the slats of the car to see farms, forests, and small villages file by, but no signs of a town or city.

"How long we been travelin', Will?" Goober asked.

"I'd say about an hour and a half, Goob. We should have to stop for water soon."

"I'm gonna have to find me a outhouse or a clump o' bushes when we do!"

Before long, the whistle of the train sounded a series of blasts signaling a stop was ahead. It began to slow as signs of a town came in view through the cracks. Goober and Will took opposite sides of the car and began to announce the sights.

"There's a road w' lots o' houses," Goober announced.

"Same over here," said Will, "and a church and cemetery ... a big one ... looks like we might be coming to a town."

Finally, there were more houses, some large buildings that looked like some sort of industrial setting, and more roads and crossings. The whistle of the engine had gone into overtime announcing the train's arrival.

There was a jolt as the cars moved to a side track. They slowed further and finally came to a stop.

Goober slid the door open and looked out over a grove of trees surrounded by portions of a small town.

"'Is looks lack a good spot," he said, sounding pleased, and he hopped down and scampered into the trees.

Will hopped down, walked back, and was pulling himself up on the flat car when he heard a shout from behind him.

"*You there!*" the voice barked. "*What are you doin' on my train?*"

Will stopped and looked around to see a man approaching him at a brisk pace. He had a pistol strapped to his side and was holding a billy club in his hand.

Will was stunned! He was being taken for a hobo.

"Mister," he said, "this may be your train, I'm not disputing that, but these two cars here are mine … bought and paid for. These two wagons are mine, and the horses and dog in that car are mine, and I'm going back to *my* wagon to get some food, and if you hit me with that stick you'll be in a heap of trouble."

Will was shaking with fear. By this time, Goober was through with his business in the trees and was peeking out from behind a bush watching the action.

The detective wasn't used to being talked to like that by a hobo and he relaxed his club hand. "Why are you ridin' in a cattle car," he asked.

"I'm there to keep my animals calm."

"What kind of animals?" the detective asked.

"A large coon dog, a Saddlebred, and two Clydesdales."

The detective looked in the car and seemed satisfied. "What's in the wagons?"

Will rattled off a list of the contents down to the number of canvas covers over each wagon; then he and the detective pulled themselves up, and the detective looked under the coverings and again seemed satisfied.

"Can't be too careful," the detective said. "Lots of hobos ridin' the rails these days."

Will motioned for Goober to come out. "That's my friend, Goober," he said as Goober approached. "Soon as I use the bushes myself, we'll be getting back in the livestock car."

"Have a good trip then," the detective said, "and if you get questioned by another detective just say 'empty bucket'."

"Empty bucket?"

"Yeah, that's a sort of code that'll get you through. We use those for employees and folks like you and change 'em every now and then. You shouldn't have any more trouble."

"Thanks," Will said, and he hopped down and ran off toward the trees.

"By the way, where are we?" he hollered back.

"Statesville, North Carolina," was the answer.

Just as he was finishing up, Will heard a blast of the whistle and looked toward the train to see Goober pulling himself onto the livestock car with it moving. He ran as fast as he could and caught the train as it was picking up speed. The gravel was rolling under Will's feet, and he was beginning to think he wouldn't make it. Then, Goober lay down on his belly, stuck his hands out the door, and caught Will, helping him swing up through the opening.

Will lay on the scattered straw, breathing heavily and thanking God and Goober that he was in the car.

"I don't want to go through that again," he said. "You heard what the man said about 'empty bucket,' didn't you?"

"Yep, I heared it, an' I tell ye whut else I'm a-hearin'. Hit's my stomach growlin'. Ye didn't git th' food, did ye?"

———◆———

It seemed like the song, "There Is a Tavern in the Town", had been coursing through his brain for days, and Will was beginning to wonder if he would ever get rid of it. Hunger and cold were also taking their toll on his psyche as well as Goober's, and even though it was still daylight, it seemed like sleep would be their only escape.

Sleep came easy with the constant drone of the train wheels singing to them as they nestled in the straw, covered with the canvas. They slept so soundly in fact that they didn't even realize the train had stopped for water until they felt the jolt of it restarting. Another stop without food, and night was approaching.

"Goober, do you realize what just happened?"

"I do, an' my stomach ain't pleased a bit!" Goober replied irritably. "Whur do ye think we are?"

Will got up and looked through the slats. "We're out in the country, probably just a water station. I expect we'll be in Virginia soon."

When Will had settled back down in the straw, Goober said, "I shore would lack t' have some o' Aint Sweetie's biscuits."

"What else does Aunt Sweetie cook?" Will asked.

"'At woman could make a meal outta sawdust," Goober said. "Next t' my momma, she's the most finest cook I ever saw. Why, she kin cook up a rabbit an' hit tastes jest lack 'em steaks we et in Charlotte. In the fall, she puts up all kinds o' vege-tables an' fruits an' things like 'at, enough t' feed a army. An' she raises chickens an' pigs, an' her an' Uncle Roamer fixes 'em up an' she cooks 'em an' there ain't no finer. Will, she makes food as good as Uncle Roamer makes ..."

"Uncle Roamer makes what?" Will asked.

There was a long pause while Goober collected his thoughts.

"Will, let's not tawk about food no more," he finally said. "Hit's jest makin' me more hungrier. Let's tawk about Judy Ruth. I wonder what she's up to long 'bout now."

Will looked thoughtful in an exaggerated way.

"She'll be getting off work pretty soon, I guess. She'll probably go home and purdy up for some boy to come a-courtin."

Goober jumped to his feet and faced Will. "You take 'at back, Will Parker," he snarled. "Don't never say nothin' like 'at agin!"

Will was shocked. "Goober," he said. "I'm truly sorry. Of course I know that Judy Ruth is true to you!" And to try to shift Goober's mood he added, "She's probably going home to write you a letter. Does she know where to send a letter to you?"

Goober sat back down on the straw. "I told 'er t' send me a letter t' Avery Cove an' then t' send 'em t' gen'ral delivery at Burley."

"You're a lucky man, Makepeace Goober Green," Will said. "A lucky man! Got ya a good job, a house ... just don't know which one yet ... and a girl waiting for you in Charlotte. I'm beginning to wonder if I'll ever find the right girl for me. To hear you tell it, the pickin's are pretty slim in Avery Cove. Sounds like I might as well be moving to a monastery."

"I don't know whut a monusturry is," Goober said, "but they are a few girls in the cove an' ye never know when another un's gonna move in."

"That makes me feel a whole lot better," Will said sarcastically.

Soon, twilight crept into the livestock car. The sky, still overcast with the remains of the morning's storm clouds, offered no light. Will got up to check on Dawg and the horses one last time before total darkness came. He watered them and gave the horses a small portion of oats, as much to comfort them as to ease their hunger. Dawg gave no indication that he was hungry, probably off his feed because of all the commotion.

The train lumbered on in total darkness, its speed reduced with the coming of the night. As it came to bends in the road and the light on the front of the engine shown to the right or the left, Will could make out the shapes of trees and bushes, and occasionally he could see in the distance faint light from a house.

Finally, the light from houses became more plentiful, and the train began to slow. "Goob, I think we're coming into a town," he said.

Sure enough, the lights of a fair sized town began to appear with more and more regularity. The train passed a depot, continued on to a side track on the left, and finally stopped.

Will slid the door open and jumped down. Then he reached up, cradled Dawg in his arms, and set him down on the gravel.

"Get off, Goober," he said. "I don't know where we are, but whatever I'm standing on ain't moving!"

Dawg wandered off into the high grass beside the track pulling his rope tight, and Will tied him off to a bush.

He was looking around, stretching, when saw a man with a lantern coming toward him. "*Empty bucket,*" Will cried out.

"Back at ye," the lantern man said. "Are ye travelin' with some wagons and animals?"

"Sure am," Will said.

"Is yo name Parker or Green?" the lantern man asked.

"I'm Parker, Will Parker, and this is Goober Green, but how on earth did you know?"

"Got a wire from a man named Neil. Said to look out for ye. Wanted t' make sure we got ye on th' right track goin' outta here. You'll be sittin' on this sidin' most of th' night an' then we'll make up a train goin' back the other direction. You'll go outta town on th' track ye came in on, then fork off and head out toward the mountains ... Burley. That's right, ain't it?"

"Boy, is it ever!" Will said. "Boy, is it ever! Is there a place around here to get something to eat?"

"Yeah, they got sandwiches an' stuff up at th' depot. Not bad fer depot food, I guess."

"Thanks, Mister," Will said. "Thanks a lot."

Will lifted Dawg back up into the car and told him to stay. Then he turned and started toward the depot.

"Come on, Goober," he said. "Let's eat!"

———

"Goober, do you remember that meal we had at Buffalo Bill's in Charlotte?"

"Guess I'll 'member 'at meal th' rest o' m' life."

"Juicy steak, potato cooked to perfection, fine wine, all the trimmings?"

"I'll always 'member 'at meal, Will."

"This one was better, wasn't it Goober?"

"Yep ... ham and cheese samwich, luke-warm coffee, dried-out cake ... best meal I ever had."

Will and Goober were walking back to the livestock car after their meal at the depot. It hadn't been gourmet fare, but it had filled a mighty empty spot. Will had even asked for some scraps for Dawg and was given a piece of butcher paper full of scrapings.

"Whut time do ye figger it is," Goober asked.

"I figure about 10:00 o'clock."

"'At's past my bed time," Goober said.

"You've been sleeping all day long."

"Sleepin' wears ye out, Will ... plain an' simple."

The gravel crunched underneath their feet as they walked along the siding. The lights that had been so plentiful were going out, one by one.

"Goob, I'll tell you what we're going to do before we sleep. We're going to get a lantern and some food to go with us the rest of the way. I'm not going to go through that hunger mess again."

131

"I'm fer that, Will."

"*Empty bucket!*" Will shouted as he saw someone with a lantern walking up the track.

"You the men in that cattle car?" the man asked.

"That's us," Will answered.

"You guys important heads of state or somethin'?" he asked.

"Just two ol' country boys," Will answered. "Why do you ask?"

"'Cause we been told that if we get you on the wrong track, our hides will be nailed to the door of the depot," the man said.

Goober bent over and slapped his legs just above his knees. "I know whur 'at come frum!" he chimed out.

The man continued walking toward them. He wasn't as amused as Goober was.

"The engine will be here in about two hours to pull you off this siding," he said. "You'll be on the way to Burley by 1:00 a.m."

"Thanks for the information, and have a good night," Will said.

When they reached the livestock car, Will opened the paper wrapper and laid out Dawg's meal. Dawg ambled over, sniffed it, and gulped it down in two bites.

Then Will felt his way along the sides of the cars and crawled up on the flat car. He made his way along the side of the wagon until he felt the back wheel. Beside the wheel, right where he had put it, was the lantern. With the lantern giving an abundance of light, Goober hopped up, and they dug down to a package of food—precious food.

Back in the livestock car, they settled down with the warmth of the lantern between them to wait for the next leg—the final leg—of their rail adventure. Only now, with light and warmth for comfort, and with hunger satisfied, did they sense the movement around them.

From the north came the sound of a train approaching the town, while in the train yard, the bell on an engine rang, reminding the boys that the railroad was a working organism, even at night.

People came and went in lighted coaches—going north, going south. Freight cars carrying unknown commodities rumbled by in darkness, destinations unknown.

"Whur ye think 'at train's a-goin?" Goober asked.

"I think that train is bound for Charlotte," Will replied, "with new machinery for the mill ... maybe some of those new looms we've heard about. Or maybe it's carrying the food that Sarah will be serving in the cafe in a couple of days. Maybe iron for the blacksmith's shop."

"Sometimes ye shore do think strange thoughts," Goober said.

———

The lantern was off and the talk had slowed to random comments when they heard the rumble of an approaching engine. Will got up and looked through the slats of the car to see a worker walking down the track with a light ahead of a freight car.

As it neared, the worker waved his light, and the engine slowed before hooking to the caboose. In short order, the caboose was unhooked from the flat car and livestock car, and it disappeared into the night.

Soon, the train reappeared and hooked to the flat car, reversed direction, and Will and Goober began moving once again.

Twice more the trained stopped, backed on to a siding, and picked up cars to build a train about 10 units long.

"I'm 'bout t' git sick goin' back and forth lack 'is," Goober said.

As the train passed the switchman for the last time, Will leaned out of the door and shouted, "What town is this anyway?"

The flagman shouted back, and as he did, the whistle on the engine sounded a warning blast. All they heard was "Virginia."

"How 'bout that," Will said to Goober. "When we get to Burley, we'll have gone several hundred miles and not even know where we've been."

The engine eased slowly out of the train yard pulling harder than before. It seemed to know and care that people living along the tracks were sleeping. Its bell was silent; the sound of its whistle was short and muted.

Will lit the lantern and checked on the horses. They were secure but restless.

"I know these animals will be glad to get out of this rolling barn," he told Goober. "To tell you the truth, I'll be glad myself."

"What we got t' eat?" Goober wanted to know.

"Biscuits and jelly."

"How 'bout some meat an' taters an' beans?" Goober asked.

"Biscuits and jelly."

"How come we don't have no meat an' taters an' beans?"

"We have potatoes and beans in the wagon, but I didn't bring any meat. I didn't have any and didn't have time to buy any. You'll have to get by on biscuits and jelly until we have a way to cook the beans and 'taters'."

"I hope t' my never," Goober complained. "I figger I'll starve t' death 'fore we git t' Aint Sweetie's."

The train took a sharp-right hand turn as it was leaving town, and from what Will could tell, they were on a different track than the one they had come in on.

"Will, how fast do ye think 'is train goes?" Goober asked.

"I'd say 40 or 50 miles an hour."

Goober shifted up on his elbow. "'At's hard t' even think on, ain't it? Goin' 50 miles in one hour! A feller could almos' get sommers 'fore he lef'."

The train rumbled on, picking up speed.

"They wuz some boys in the cove that would race horses … they bred 'em jest t' run. People said they could go over 40 mile a hour … an' here, 'is big ol' train can go faster 'an 'at."

"Why Goob, there are trains out west where the tracks are straight and flat that go 100 miles an hour."

"You'd lie too, wouldn't ye?"

"No, Goob, that's the truth, so help me."

The train moved on, cutting the darkness, putting miles behind them.

"All I kin think 'bout is a train full o' cows an' pigs goin' to th' butcher," Goober said. "I shore would like t' have a chunk o' meat t' gnaw on."

Finally, sleep took control as Will and Goober gave in to the hum of the wheels. They weren't even aware when the train stopped for water or when it dipped and swayed as it crossed the long trestle over the Green River.

They slept as the train moved through farm land that was just now yielding to the plows of spring and forests that were awaking to the warmth that comes when winter ends.

They slept as they passed cattle and horses in the fields waiting patiently for dawn and farm houses where children were dreaming of adventures of their own.

Under the cloak of darkness they moved into the foothills of the Blue Ridge where the train began negotiating curves and rises, working a little harder now to keep a steady momentum.

At about the crack of dawn, the changes in the movement of the car became greater than even a heavy sleep could ignore. The centrifugal force of a sharp curve shifted Will from his back to his side, even threatening to roll him across the floor. The horses braced themselves and complained about the annoyance with deep grunts.

Alarmed by the unfamiliar movement, Will crawled to the right-hand side of the car and looked out between the slats. The sun was up enough for him to see a high-cut bank rising out of sight only a few feet from the track. He moved to the left-hand side of the car and saw a deep precipice falling away, it seemed, into the very bowels of the earth. They were on the side of a mountain where a roadbed had been cut away.

"*Wake up, Goober!*" he shouted. "*We're in the mountains!*"

If the scenery were not enough to illustrate his point, the chilled freshness of the air was.

"'At's whut I figgered," Goober said. "Hit's cold!"

Will pressed his face to the slats on the left-hand side of the car as the train continued to bend to the right until all at once, there was nothing beneath them. He rushed to the right-hand side, and there, too, was a void beneath the train. They were on a trestle crossing a deep gorge filled with the dark outline of trees, their tops at least 75 feet below.

He fell on the floor of the car, disoriented and frightened by the abyss that had so quickly appeared.

"Whut's wrong with you?" Goober inquired.

"Look for yourself."

Goober rolled over and looked out across the chasm. "Lord, Will," he said, "we're a-flyin'!"

As quickly as it appeared, the gorge was gone and they were on a flat mountain top. On their left was the rising sun highlighting fields and farms —the plain of the Piedmont. On their right were the mountains rising one behind the other—green into dark green, blue into purple.

Will slid the door on the right side open about two feet and sat in the opening feasting on the view. He was joined by Goober who, even though he was a mountain boy, was also moved by the sight.

Presently, the train sounded its whistle and slowed for a stop ahead. A house and water tower came into view with the tower keeper waiting by the tank. They slowed to a crawl and finally stopped with the engine under the spout.

The engineer and fireman hopped down with their oil cans and began servicing the moving parts while the engine took on its supply of water. Will, Goober, and Dawg got down, too, and took advantage of some nearby bushes.

"How far to Burley?" Will shouted to the engineer.

"Two hours … about 60 miles." He walked toward them. "Look," he said, "I ain't supposed to do this, but if you boys want to, move on back to the caboose and ride. We've got some mountains to climb and it'll get colder. You'll have a better view too."

"I'm fer that!" Goober said.

The caboose was a box car that had been converted to a traveling apartment for the conductor and off-duty crew. The box had been shortened to make a porch on both ends, and a box with windows had been added on the top to serve as an observation deck.

The engineer escorted Will, Goober, and Dawg up the steps, onto the porch, and finally through the door on the end into a comfortable room that was fitted with a sofa, some upholstered chairs, a table with kitchen chairs, and a pot-bellied stove. In one corner there was an ice box, and in another a tall cabinet with full length doors. There was a ladder in the center of the room that led to the observation deck where one could sit on benches around the perimeter, legs hanging down, and see the sights.

At the far end of the room there was a short hallway leading to the other porch, and on either side of the hall were doors that opened to small bunk rooms.

One of the bunk room doors opened, and a little old gentleman stepped out rubbing his eyes.

"Boys," the engineer said, "this is Jessie, the conductor. Jessie, I want you to meet some guests of the railroad, Mr. Green and Mr. Parker. Take good care of 'em." And with that, he gave Jessie a wink and departed.

"That dog don't bite, does he?" Jessie asked.

"No, sir, he's as gentle as a lamb," Will replied.

"Well, make y'selves to home then. Ya want somethin t' eat?"

"'At shore would be good," Goober answered.

"Too bad," said Jessie. "I ain't got a thing. Guess we'll get somethin' in Burley."

Jessie scratched, slowly turned, dawdled back through the bunk room door, and closed it behind himself. As if that were a signal to the engineer, the train jerked and started its roll toward Burley.

Goober plopped down in an overstuffed chair. "Ye know whut we done, don't ye Will … ag'in?"

Will didn't answer. He let the growl of his stomach answer for him. He merely climbed the ladder and sat himself on one of the seats where he could take in the full panorama that changed with every curve in the track.

From the ridges, he could see the farms below with barns and houses and livestock the size of ants. He saw a farmer in the field plowing a yoke of oxen, changing the color of the land from tan to almost black as he broke the soil. He was reminded that he would be plowing his own field as soon as he was settled in Avery Cove, and he could almost smell the fragrance of newly plowed dirt.

When Goober was through pouting about his empty stomach, he climbed the ladder and settled across from Will. For several minutes he sat, silently taking in the view, marveling as much at the miracle of the train as the scenery.

"Well, Goob, what do you think of rail travel?" Will asked.

"I tell ye what, Will, 'is here's th' way t' go. I think sometime I'll git on a train an' take me a trip all th' way t' Californy. Might even git me one o' them sleepin' compartments."

"That would make a good honeymoon for you and Judy Ruth, wouldn't it, Goob?"

Goober slapped his leg. "Aw, Will, I wish you hadn't a-said that," he moaned. "I'm a-missin' 'er somethin' fierce. Whut do ye think she's doin' right along now?" And then he caught himself. "Now that I think on it, I'd jest as soon ye didn't tell me!"

Fourteen

Burley

Dear Judy Ruth

    This is Goober writing to you. Me and Will are on the train riding and we are near to Burley. I will tell you of the trip when I git back to work at the mill but it has been a adventure for shure. It is good for Will to have me to keep things going smooth for it has got out of hand at least too times at least. I will writ to you agin when we git too Avery Cove and let you know when we git their. I did not git the chanch to say to you I love you befor I left to go but I thing you know it any how so I will say good by for now and I will think about you for all the time I am awake and not sleping.

Love Goober Green

The conductor had told them to make themselves "to home" and so Goober had rummaged around and found paper, pen, and an envelope and had penned a heart-felt letter to Judy Ruth.

"Will," he hollered up the ladder, "come down 'ere an' read 'is letter an' tell me if hit's too mushy."

"This I've got to see," Will said under his breath as he scampered down the ladder and sat down at the table.

"Tell me whut ye think," Goober said as he handed Will his manuscript.

Will put on his serious face and read the letter silently. He knew that he dared not give any indication that he thought it was light or humorous, so he scanned it diligently, nodding his approval as he went.

"This is an excellent letter, Goober!" he said, and he shook it in the air toward his friend. "I wouldn't change a thing, and no, it isn't too mushy!"

"I figgered you'd lack it," Goober said, poking his chest out. "Soon as we git t' Burley, I'm gonna take it t' th' post office."

Will scampered back up the ladder and was getting seated when the train sounded its whistle. He looked to the right to see a team of horses with a wagon waiting at a crossing, the driver sitting motionless as the train passed.

A farm house came into view on the right and another on the left. A hazy smoke in the distance signaled some sort of settlement approaching.

"Will," Goober said up the ladder, "have ye noticed th' frost on the winders? Hit muss be gittin' cold outside."

Will hadn't noticed the frost, but he had been keeping an eye on the dark gray skies that were blocking the sun. "I figured it would be cold," he hollered down to Goober, "but I don't like the look of those clouds. They have that steely look that snow clouds have."

A hacking cough came from the hallway, and Jessie emerged from his bunk room, scratching and yawning. "Accordin' to my watch we ought to be comin' into Burley long about now," he announced as he took his coat and hat from the hook on the wall and started pulling them on. "Time to git to work."

The town of Burley came into sight from almost nowhere. The train rounded a long sweeping curve to the right, and there it was, sitting slightly below the grade of the tracks. The hazy smoke that signaled its presence from a distance hung heavy, pushed down by the cover of clouds.

The tops of the mountains must be there, Will thought, but they were hidden by the low-flying curtain of gray. Still he could tell that they were in a valley, surrounded on three sides by hills and on the western side by mountains of unknown height.

As the train came into the station, the town was hidden by the depot and the buildings surrounding it. The train stopped briefly to unload the mail and then continued down the track to a staging area with a turn-around loop. They paused and were then pushed onto a side track where they finally came to rest at a ramped siding surrounded by livestock pens and chutes.

Jessie walked up beside the caboose from the rear and announced, "This is where ya get off, boys."

As Will and Goober stepped onto the front porch of the caboose, they were hit with a blast of freezing air accentuated by the altitude. It was cold for sure, but there was a freshness in the air along with a light fragrance of wood smoke.

"Goober, smell that air!" Will said. "The smell of oak and hickory burning sure beats the stench of coal smoke."

"Ye got a point thar, Will."

A crew of four was waiting for them when they climbed down. "These yo' wagons an' all?" the boss man asked.

"Yeah, and the horses in the livestock car."

"Well, if y'all will jest step over here outta th' way, we'll have 'em off in a jiffy. Be best a man does this work!" and he grinned at the others.

The men put down a bridge and proceeded to muscle the wagons off the flat car, lining them up to be pulled off the siding by the horses.

"You've done this before," Will said.

"Once 'r twice."

Then they opened the door to the livestock car.

"Lord-o-mighty!" The boss man said. "Them's the biggest horses I ever saw ... Tell ya what ... I think you better handle 'em ... I don't want one o' them buggers steppin' on me!"

"Jest step outta th' way, boys, an' let us handle 'is," Goober said as he stepped forward with his chest poked out. "'Em horses is mean as a snake an' I wouldn't want you boys t' git hurt none." He brushed his hands together and strode into the car with Will following.

"Guess I showed 'em yahoos a thing 'r two," he said quietly to Will.

With the railroad men looking on, Will and Goober hitched Don and Molly to the wagon and Traveler to the surrey. They retrieved all their belongings from the car; then Will climbed up on the wagon and swung the horses around into one of the holding pens with Goober following in the surrey.

"Nice doin' business w' ye boys," Goober hollered as they exited the siding.

The horses seemed to be very relieved to be out of their rolling barn and on firm ground, and they showed it by dancing as they pulled. When they were well clear of the siding, the boys pulled up and got down to talk.

"Goob, do you know the way out of here?"

"Long as I keep m' eye on 'at mountain yonder, I kin git us outta town an' on th' road," he answered. "But first things first. I gotta find me a out-house and th' post office."

———

There wasn't an outhouse nearby but there was a clump of trees, and the post office happened to be across the road from the depot. With those two things taken care of, and with Goober in the lead, they headed out of town toward Goober's landmark.

"Will," Goober shouted back, "there's th' Burley Lodge whur I'm s'posed t' meet Mr. Neil."

They continued on past a general store, the court house, the jail, a Baptist Church, and several businesses. There was a doctor's office, a livery stable with blacksmith shop out back, and a row of neat houses.

Just past the edge of town, Goober stopped and motioned for Will to come along side. "Will, 'ese horses is wore out frum riddin'. I figger we best find a spot and set up fer th' night … give 'em a chanch t' rest. 'Sides, I'm powerful hungry. Let's cook up some o' them beans and taters."

"Good idea, Goob."

"An' Will, they's one more thing I ort t' mention. 'Is road don't git a lot-a travel and they's been robbers 'long here in th' past. If I wuz you, I'd have 'at pistol o' yorn handy jest in case."

"Robbers! That's all we need!"

Will reached back in the wagon behind the seat and pulled out a bundle wrapped up in an old flower sack. It was holding his Colt revolver neatly secured in its holster with belt.

"I feel like an old-west cowboy," he said as he strapped it around his waist.

They proceeded on with Will on the lookout for bad guys. He sat upright, bundled against the cold, eying rocks and trees as if he were trying to see through them.

About a mile outside of town they came to a flat, grassy area on the left side of the road. It was circled by a grove of hickory trees, and a small branch trickled along the near side, disappearing down a ditch that had been cut to channel it away.

"'Is looks lack a good place," Goober hollered back to Will. "'Et's set up down near 'em trees."

They circled their wagons to the back side of the clearing and pulled up. Their first order of business was to stretch a hitch line in the shelter of the trees and tie off the horses that were then fed and watered. While Goober was gathering wood and building a fire, Will unloaded the cooking utensils and food.

It was good to be on solid ground even if the ground was cold. There was a nurturing feel to the spot with the trees surrounding them, and the fire, though not large yet, was giving warmth to the soul as well as the body —until Will sensed that he and Goober were not alone.

In the undergrowth, back in the trees away from the horses, Will saw from the corner of his eye a wisp of movement. And then, there was the unmistakable rustle of dry leaves from that very spot. Dawg, who was sitting beside the right front wheel of the wagon perked his ears and emitted a soft growl. "Down and stay," Will said softly to him.

He dared not alert Goober, who was bent over the fire, for fear that he might jump up and fall into the flames. There was the possibility, too, that it may have been his imagination, which, he admitted to himself, had been heightened by Goober's warning about robbers.

And so, he eased up and walked slowly around behind the wagon, giving himself some degree of cover and getting Goober out of the direct line of fire should there be any.

There he waited while Goober fanned the flames, enjoying the warmth that was beginning to come. There was the noise again, and the slight movement, coming closer to the edge of the thicket.

His hand moved slowly to his holster and closed around the handle of the revolver, and the instant that Goober stood and took a step away from the fire, he drew the gun and cocked it in one swift motion—and fired!

BLAM. The sound was like that of an artillery piece—felt as much as heard—shattering the stillness of the place with finality!

"*Goodgodamighty!*" Goober screamed as he grabbed his hat and attempted to pull it down over his ears. He charged toward the center of the clearing and ran in a circle, whimpering with fear. Will stood and solemnly looked toward his target, ignoring Goober for the time being.

He held his gun at the ready, hammer cocked, muzzle still smoking from the first shot, and eased around the wagon. His eyes were glued to the underbrush.

Goober was standing in the clearing, speechless, trembling, and watching as Will advanced. Dawg had run behind the wagon wheel where he cowered in distress. Will eased toward the spot slightly crouching, but as he neared the place, his body relaxed, he stood erect and re-holstered his weapon.

Finally, he stood over the victim of his shot, reached down, and picked up the plump, gray rabbit, its head cleanly severed from its body. And then, he got a bonus that he wasn't expecting. Behind the rabbit was a second one, killed by the single bullet that had claimed the first. Two for the price of one!

Goober had at last regained his voice. "*Will! You idiot!*" He hollered. "*Whut has got into you? Why did you far 'at shot right in my ear lack 'at?*"

Will walked out into the clearing toward him, holding his prizes. "You said you wanted some meat, didn't you? Well, here it is. We're having rabbit stew for supper!"

———

Twilight was falling, and the rabbit stew was simmering over the fire. A canvas shelter had been erected at the edge of the clearing, Dawg, who had enjoyed about half of one of the rabbits, was asleep in his bed in the wagon, and the fire was burning brightly when Goober saw the first flake of snow.

"I shore do hope 'at wuz a speck o' ash frum th' far," he said. And then, he saw another and another. "Will, do you see what I'm a-seein'?" he asked.

"Yeah … I'm afraid I do."

"It's 'at little hard snow too," Goober said. "Usually, when hit starts lack 'at, hit lays firm on th' ground."

"What do you think we should do?"

"They ain't a whole heck-of-a-lot we can do, Will. Hit may peter out. Sometimes hit sputters an' spits lack 'at up here in th' spring. Other times, hit'll come up a blizzard lack 'at time th' cow froze…. Seems lack 'at wuz in th' spring."

It did "sputter and spit" for a few minutes, and then it started coming in earnest—hard little pellets of snow that stung when they hit bare flesh and sizzled when they hit the fire. Within minutes, darkness had fallen, and by the light of the fire they could see little patches of white gathering on bare earth.

For the first time since he had left Charlotte, Will longed for home, and for the first time since he had left the cove, Goober wished he was back in the shelter of the house his father had built. Now, home was a piece of canvas stretched across a rope; their kitchen, a pot on the camp fire; their bed, the hard, cold ground.

But in the light of the fire, with snow falling, each of them tried to think his own positive thoughts—thoughts of the future and of the final destination.

Goober, as he gathered more firewood by the light of a lantern, thought of Judy Ruth—of her laugh and the fragrance of store-bought soap that surrounded her. He imagined their wedding in the big Episcopal church with the organ playing and the wedding party dressed in their finest. He saw in his mind their children playing in the yard of the Charlotte house, well fed and happy in their security. And on the wings of hope his spirits rose to a level of content.

And Will, as he stirred the stew, revisited his dream of Avery Cove. Once more he entered the valley, not in a Landau coach this time, but in his wagon pulled by Don and Molly, traveling along the road beside the river, drinking in the smells, sights, and sounds of Paradise. He saw the house at the far end of the cove, four miles from Burden's store, shining in its perfection and waiting to enfold him in warmth and security, and he, too, was lifted on the wings of hope.

"*Supper's ready!*" Will hollered. Goober turned from the underbrush and hurried to the fire with an arm load of wood that he dropped on the pile.

"Will, I don't know when I have smelt nothin' more better 'an 'at stew," Goober said as he squatted by the fire.

Will spooned out generous servings on the plates as he alternately glanced up at the snow coming down. "Let's get under the canvas to eat," he said.

The canvas shelter was oriented with it's opening toward the fire, and there they sat, silently enjoying their stew consisting of beans, potatoes, onions, salt, mountain branch water, and rabbit. There was an abundance, and Goober's second helping still left enough for another generous meal.

When supper was finished and the dishes and leftovers were put away, they turned their attention to preparing for the night. "We best git t' sleep," Goober said. "Hit may be a struggle gittin' up th' mountain tomorrow … 'at is, if we kin move a-tall."

Sleep came easy in the canvas shelter. Will had coaxed Dawg to join them and share his warmth, and with the flap down on the end of the shelter, the atmosphere was surprisingly cozy. The only sound was the pepper of the hard snow pellets on the canvas, and it, like rain on a tin roof, sang a gentle lullaby.

———

Will woke before dawn to silence. He lay still for a moment, wondering if the snow had stopped or if it had turned to the soft, silent kind, and though he dreaded to look, he rolled out from under his covers and peeked outside. It looked as if the snow had stopped completely, but there were about four inches on the ground.

He pulled on his boots and eased out of the tent to find the fire still smoldering from the previous night. The wood they had put under the wagon before going to bed was dry, and he was soon able to get the fire roaring again. By then, the sun was up enough to start getting some coffee brewing and a breakfast of leftover rabbit stew warming.

With his own nourishment warming, he turned his attention to the horses that had fared well through the night in the shelter of the trees. As he was feeding them, they all raised their heads, directing their attention toward the road and a sound they had heard.

Out of the shadow of the trees and around the bend came a wagon pulled by a yoke of oxen. It lumbered slowly up the road and came to a stop at the clearing. In the dim light of dawn, Will could make out the form of a single person on the wagon seat, bundled up against the cold. The wagon was carrying a large wooden crate, and from the way the oxen had been pulling, Will guessed that it was a heavy load. "Good morning," the driver shouted out.

Will threw up his hand in greeting. He couldn't imagine that this lone individual on a burdened wagon would be a robber. "Good morning to you, sir. Would you like some coffee?"

The driver set his brake and climbed down from the wagon, and as he did, he answered Will's greeting. "You are a welcome sight, sir," he said, "and

I'd be delighted to share your coffee. I can tell by your voice that you're a friendly sort."

As he walked toward the fire, the snow crunched under his cautious steps, and Will could tell by his gate that he was not as nimble as he possibly once was. When he had finally crossed the clearing, he extended his gloved hand. "Thank you for your generous offer, sir," he said. "My name is Burden ... Eli Burden. Most folks call me 'Preacher'."

"*What?*" Will looked at the man in amazement. "You're Preacher Burden ... from Avery Cove ... the Preacher Burden I've heard so much about? *Goober, get up and see who's out here!*"

"Did you say 'Goober'?" the preacher asked. "Goober Green?" and his amazement equaled Will's. The scene would not have been richer if two neighbors had met unexpectedly on the other side of the earth.

Goober clamored out of the canvas shelter, hopping on his left foot as he pulled on his right boot. "I hope to my never!" he said. "Preacher Burden, is 'at really you? Whut are ye doin' out 'ere in th' middle o' nowhur?"

"I could ask you the same thing, Goober." He ambled over and gave Goober a warm hug. "I thought we had lost you, son," he said, holding him at arm's length and looking into his eyes, "and I sure have missed you."

Will quickly caught the essence of the good man, knowing instantly why Goober had always seemed so fond of him. There was an air of kindness that enveloped him—a tone in his voice that gave a feeling of comfort. While Goober and Preacher Burden caught up on what had been going on in each of their lives, Will went about the business of getting breakfast ready and breaking camp.

"So, Goober," the preacher asked, "where have you been and what have you been doing?"

"Wal, Preacher, ye see 'at canvas over yonder? I made 'at canvas, an' 'at coverin' th' wagons an' all. I got me a job in a mill a-weavin', an' rat now, I'm on a spacial mission fer the owner o' th' mill, Mr. Glenn Neil. In a couple o' weeks, I'll be a-goin' 'round buyin' up land t' build a mill in Burley."

"Goober! I'm astounded! One of our Avery Cove boys has gone off and done well in the world! I am so proud of you, son, and I know Roamer and Sweetie are proud of you, too."

"Got me a girl, too!" Goober said, poking out his chest. "Purdy as a pitcher! Her name's Judy Ruth Roach! An' people in Charlotte respects me … hit ain't lack it is in Avery Cove."

"Breakfast is ready." Will said. "Preacher, there's plenty, and we'd be honored if you'd join us."

"I'm the one who's honored," the preacher said, "and would you mind if I said a little blessing before we eat?"

Will assured the good man that a blessing was in order, and the preacher prayed. He thanked God for safe travel and a good night's sleep, he thanked God for Goober and the one traveling with him, he prayed a blessing on the remainder of the trip back to the cove, and finally, he prayed a special blessing on the food—that it would give them strength for the trials that were ahead.

As Jesus blessed and multiplied the five loaves and two small fishes, the leftover meal of potatoes, beans, onions, salt, branch water, and rabbit was multiplied to a quantity sufficient to satisfy the three men, and as they stood around the camp fire and ate, they talked.

"You know, young man," the preacher said to Will, "in all the confusion, I didn't get your name."

"I'm sorry. My name is Will Parker."

"Well, Mr. Parker, what brings you to these parts?"

Will explained to Preacher Burden that he and Goober were looking into the possibility of exchanging properties, and that more than likely, he would be moving to Avery Cove. He told him about working on his grandparents' farm and his love for the soil and how he had always dreamed about having his own place in the mountains.

Preacher Burden stopped eating for a moment and looked thoughtful. "Well, we would certainly be proud to have a young man of your obvious refinement living in the cove," the preacher said. "How old are you, son?"

"I'm 21 years old," Will replied.

"Well now," the preacher said, looking thoughtful again, "are you by chance a Methodist?"

"No, sir, I'm Episcopalian."

"Really! Well, we don't have an Episcopal Church in the cove, but you know, the Methodists are about the same thing. They sprang out of the Episcopal Church back in England."

"Yes, sir."

"Tell me, Mr. Parker, are you married?"

"No, sir, never married."

"Good Lord," Goober said under his breath. "Preacher's tryin' t' hook 'is daughter a husband."

Before the conversation could progress further, Will suggested that they should break camp and start the journey up the road, especially in light of the weather. It was agreed that it was to their advantage to stay together both to help each other along and to guard against robbers, and in a matter of about 15 minutes, they were ready to leave. It was decided that the oxen would lead the other two wagons since they would have difficulty keeping up with the horses' pace.

The preacher made his way through the snow and climbed up on his wagon and waited for Will and Goober to get to the road.

"Don't mean to pry," Will said as he pulled in behind the preacher's wagon, "but I've been wondering what you have in that big crate you're hauling."

Preacher Burden looked ahead in thought, and then he climbed down and walked back toward Will and Goober, stopping to rest his foot on Will's wagon wheel. "Boys," he said thoughtfully, "this was supposed to be a surprise, but word will get out anyway … so I might as well go ahead and tell you. That crate contains a water-powered electric generator. We're going to have electricity in Avery Cove!"

"I hope to my never!" Goober declared.

"I've gone in with Caldwell Turpin, and we're going to install this thing at his mill and supply ourselves and our businesses with power, and if anyone else wants to buy power for themselves, we'll string the wires and sell it to 'em. Hope to be up and runnin' in about two months."

"I hope to my never!" Goober declared again. "Kin you imagine Uncle Roamer an' Aunt Sweetie havin' 'lectric lights?"

"And that's not all," Preacher Burden said. "Did you notice those long skinny poles that are being set along the road coming out of Burley?"

"I did notice them," Will said, "but I didn't think much of it."

"Well, those are for a telegraph line going all the way to Avery Cove. In six weeks, we'll be hooked up to the whole country. And wait till you hear this ... someday, we'll have a telephone!"

"Lord have mercy!" Goober said as he slapped his leg. "In Avery Cove? Kin you imagine Aint Sweetie a-talkin' on a tele-phone?"

Preacher Burden put both feet down in the snow and raised his hands upward as if he were preaching from the pulpit. "Boys," he said, "we are about to enter the twentieth century. Our country is coming together after a long and terrible struggle. This is both the information age and the industrial age, and we will not be left behind!" Then he showed his excitement by extending his left hand outward and striking at it with his right fist—pounding the metaphorical Bible of progress! *Avery Cove will not ... be ... left ... behind."*

Goober jumped up from his seat on the surrey and threw his own arms toward heaven. "*Hallelujah! Praise the Lord!*" he shouted.

———

As they traveled upward, the sun peeked from behind the clouds and cast shadows of still-bare trees across the road. It wasn't long before rivulets of melted snow began running to the ruts, combining to make tiny streams that trickled into the ditches.

The mountain air, which was pristine from the start, was as clear as crystal now that the wood smoke of Burley was far behind. The land fairly sparkled as water droplets formed on the icy snow crystals and shimmered before they fell to the earth. It was the magic time of mountain spring that Will had never experienced, having spent only summers with his grandparents.

The road snaked through the mountains, curling around one hill and then another—rising all the while. Puffing and straining under the weight of the pull, the oxen emitted huge clouds of steam but kept a steady pace, and the horses with their lighter load had no trouble keeping up.

At the top of a ridge near midday, Preacher Burden stopped his team and stood on the footboard of his wagon, surveying the view. "Mr. Parker," he hollered over his shoulder, "come here and let me show you something."

Will, ever anxious to learn about the hills, jumped down and slogged to the preacher's wagon.

The preacher pointed to a spot in the distance and looked down to make sure Will was looking in the right direction. "You see that little notch yonder between those two high hills?"

"Yes, sir."

"Well, my boy, that is Avery Pass ... the entrance to the cove. You can't see it from here but there's a river running down through that notch with a road running beside it. We'll go down this mountain and back up the other side and through that pass, and we'll be home." And when he said "home," he said it is a reverent sort of way that made Will even more anxious to see it.

"I've got to tell you, son," the preacher said, looking down at him, "the road gets rough from here, but it's worth the trouble. ... Now, before we start down, let's have a bite to eat."

He reached back in his wagon and from beneath a canvas cover he pulled out two gallon-size tins. He called for Will and Goober to join him on the seat, where he opened the tins and shared homemade hardtack from one and venison jerky from the other. "This'll test ya teeth!" he said. "I keep these provisions for folks I find along the road...unfortunates, you know... and you boys look unfortunate enough to me!" He and Will laughed at the joke, but Goober didn't get it.

"Do you think we'll make it all the way in tonight?" Will asked.

"No ... it's usually a one-day trip ... but with the roads the way they are, and with this heavy load, I guess we better stop in the valley and rest for the night. We'll get up early and go on in the morning."

Will was disappointed, but he was tired too. He had waited months to enter the cove, and he told himself that one more day wouldn't matter.

The trip down the mountain was not as easy as the trip up since they were now on the western-facing slope and the snow was deeper. Preacher Burden fought with his wagon to keep it on the road, and at times when he had the brake fully applied, the wagon would slide down long stretches, held back solely by the brute force of the oxen and the grace of God.

The horses didn't fare much better. Their loads were lighter, but their strength could not match that of the oxen. Twice, Goober stopped and went forward to calm Traveler, who had never seen anything like the sheer cliffs that fell away just inches from the road's edge. Molly and Don fared better, having been fitted with blinders to block their side vision, but still, their instincts told them to proceed with caution, and their steps were halting at times.

Finally, they reached the bottom of the mountain, and the most perilous part of the journey was behind. When Preacher Burden's team was on level land, he pulled up and went back to talk to Will and Goober. "Goober, you know that meadow just ahead by the river?"

"Shore do, Preacher."

"Don't you think that would be a good place to spend the night?"

"I think 'at would be a very excellent place."

About a half mile ahead they came to a meadow on the right bordered by a grove of trees. Ahead and flowing toward them from the west was the Avery River. As it reached the valley, it turned to their left, where it joined another river flowing down the mountain behind them to blend and move southward.

The sun and the warmer air of the valley had melted the snow so that only traces remained. On the eastern edge of the meadow was a well-used campsite situated on a raised, snow-free spot, and it was there that they set up camp.

Since the spot was surrounded by natural boundaries, Will and Preacher Burden decided they would set the animals loose to graze for the remainder of the daylight hours, a decision accepted joyfully by all of the beasts, especially the horses.

With the horses romping in the pasture, Goober resumed his role as the gatherer of firewood, the preacher began constructing a shelter, and Will, with rifle in hand, walked into the grove of trees. In the space of about ten minutes, three shots rang out and Will emerged holding three squirrels by their tails. "*Supper!*" he hollered, holding them up for the others to see.

It was plain to see that the preacher, like Glenn Neil before him, had singled Will out as a special person. Here was a young man of 21, tall, strong, and handsome, in good health, and with obvious refinement. Although worldly possessions were not of prime importance to the good preacher, he had noted that Will was well heeled for a man of his age, and able, it would seem, to live comfortably. He wasn't a Methodist, but he did profess to be an Episcopalian —"about the same thing"— and wasn't ashamed of it, and that *was* a matter of importance to the preacher.

As Will worked around the campsite, Preacher Burden watched his every move. He observed him as he tidied the space around himself, as he cooked the meal, as he cared for his animals, as he communicated with Goober, and communed with God's earth—and he was impressed. "If this young man moves to our cove," he thought to himself, "we will be truly blessed."

When the meal was finished and darkness had fallen, the three men sat around the fire watching the moon and stars parade across the sky and listening to the rush of the river in the distance. They told stories, shared experiences, and learned a little more about each other, and a stranger happening upon the group would have probably thought, "Now this is a happy bunch ... a friendly sounding lot."

Finally, Preacher Burden pronounced the benediction: "Boys," he said, "this old man had better get to bed. Tomorrow we have a mountain road to climb. And Will ... tomorrow, you'll be home!"

Fifteen

As the first signs of dawn came to the valley, the gentle sound of the river was joined by another.

Coo-OOH, Ooo-Ooo-Ooo…Coo-OOH, Ooo-Ooo-Ooo. The distant call of a mourning dove drifted out on the morning air, causing Will's head to turn slightly on his pillow.

Coo-OOH, Ooo-Ooo-Ooo. There it was again.

In his half-awake stupor, Will imagined that the dove that had nested near his bedroom window in Charlotte had followed him to this faraway place. It had to be his dove, he thought. The sound was unmistakable.

And then, from the opposite direction came the sound of another dove, sounding exactly like the first … Coo-OOH, Ooo-Ooo-Ooo.

With the curtain of sleep lifting, Will realized that the doves he was hearing were not ones that had somehow followed him from home. He turned to lie on his back, and he rubbed his eyes.

How is it, he wondered, that these birds who had lived here their entire lives sound exactly like their cousins who live hundreds of miles away? And since birds speak instinctively, why don't people? Why do those reared in Avery Cove speak in such an odd way, he wondered—or was it he who

155

spoke oddly? He decided that he wouldn't waste his time on that riddle that day. There were other things to do that were far more pressing!

As he lay there collecting his thoughts, the sounds of the river and the birds were joined by still another sound. Preacher Burden was reciting his morning prayers. Will was a little embarrassed to be overhearing a message intended for God alone, but he couldn't help but hear snippets of the good man's supplication.

"... and for safe travel, the warmth of this shelter ... through the night ... strength for the beasts-of-burden and for ourselves ... food for mind and body ... we thank Thee ... especially Goober and Will ... and that ... join us to live in Avery ... in Jesus' name we pray ... *Amen.*

"*Willllll! Goooober! Wake up, boys! It's time to get crackin'!*" The tender, almost silent prayer had turned to a roar. "*I just realized that today is Saturday and I haven't finished my sermon!*"

Will rolled out from under his covers and sat up with his arms stretched over his head. Goober on the other hand sprang to his feet and immediately pulled on his boots.

"Tell you what," Preacher Burden said, "I'll go round up the animals. Will, how about starting a fire and gettin' us some breakfast together. The leftovers from last night's supper would be good. And Goober, why don't you start breaking camp and loading the wagons. If we get hoppin', we can be at the store by noon or a little after."

The preacher adjusted his pants and started scurrying about like a man half his age. "I'll tell you boys," he said, "I'm looking forward to Naomi's cooking." He turned slightly in Will's direction and clarified his statement. "Naomi is my wife, Will. Course Rachel...that's my daughter...cooks some things better than Naomi does!"

"O Lord!" Goober muttered. "Will's a goner fer sure!"

Oblivious to Goober's comment, Will pulled on his boots and stepped out into the morning. He was greeted by a warm, southerly wind that had already blown away the low-hanging mist of the night. As he had slept, the last traces of snow had melted from the valley floor and the damp earth had been dried by the southerly breeze.

The shelter of the valley and the song of the river had given him a wonderful night's sleep, and he was feeling a calm relief about finally seeing Avery Cove. But beneath his calmness was a sense of anxiety. Had his imagination been playing tricks on him? Was Avery Cove just another place? At least the wait to find out was down to hours—not days or weeks.

Soon, the shelter and bedding had been loaded on the wagon. Goober and the preacher had rounded up the oxen and horses. A fire was roaring and steam was rising from the cook-pot. By the time the stew was re-warmed, the entire valley was bathed in its aroma.

"I tell you what, Will," Preacher said, "you've just *got* to give Rachel your recipe for squirrel stew. I'd say give it to Naomi, but she's kinda like me … gettin' old and set in her ways. Now Rachel, she's cooperative and eager to please. She'd take this stew of yours and add some of her secret herbs and such and have it ready to be served to the crown heads of Europe 'fore they could tuck their napkins under their chins!"

"I wish you'd listen t' him spoutin' 'at mess," Goober muttered.

———

The road leaving the camp rose as it came to the junction of the two rivers. When the wagons reached the apex of the rise, Will looked to his left and saw the swirling convergence of the near-equal flows butting heads. The spot was marked with worn boulders that appeared to have washed from the east and the west—probably in great floods that surged from the hills eons ago. He was thankful that they didn't have to ford these waters that looked so cold and inhospitable.

Past the convergence, the road turned downward and slightly to the left to come to the edge of the Avery River. At that point, it turned slightly upward and began its climb through the pass.

"It's all up hill from here on, Will!" Preacher Burden shouted back.

The sun was up but still behind the mountain to their backs. Will figured that it must be about 7:00 o'clock.

The road was narrow but relatively smooth. Deep ruts had been worn into the path from years of wagon travel, but the ruts were clear of large stones. It was customary for travelers to stop and remove large rocks that had washed into the traces, and stones too small to remove were eventually pounded into gravel by burdened wheels.

In about a mile, as the road began to tilt to a steeper grade, a bank began to rise on the right, and the trees growing on its top began to form a canopy over the way. Some of the trees were already sprouting their new greenery, drawing a roof over the procession.

Because of the tunneling effect, Will began having a flashback of his dream of being on the Landau coach, gliding beneath the canopy that opened into the cove. Once more he rode behind the elegant, black horses, until he was jolted into reality by a large rock under the wheel of his wagon.

Slowly but steadily the three wagons proceeded until the preacher halted the party at one of the few flat spots on the road. He got down from his wagon and looked at the sky. "Must be about 10:00 o'clock," he said. "We're a little over half way there. Let's rest the animals for a bit and stretch our legs; then we'll slog on in."

Will was getting a sense of what these mountains were really like. His grandparents' mountains were in an area that was more open, with terrain that undulated gently from hill to hill. These mountains were steep and desolate. They were remote and secluded. It's no wonder, he thought, that Goober has such a strange way of speaking!

Now that the sound of the wagons had been quieted, the sounds of the forest could be heard. It seemed that hundreds of birds were singing a hundred different songs. The bright colors of numerous species shone in the trees and on the forest floor. In every direction he could see the movement of squirrels racing through the branches, celebrating the arrival of spring—the time for courtship.

"Hit's rat purdy up here, ain't it, Will?" Goober observed. "I'd plumb forgot how purdy it can be up 'ere in th' sprang o' th' year."

"You got that right, Goob," Will answered. "I've never seen so many birds."

"They's a lot, awright, but they'll be a lot more when the weather warms," Goober said.

While Goober and Will were talking, the preacher had filled two buckets with water and given the animals a drink. Dawg had hopped down from his wagon bed, done his business, and gotten himself a drink from the river. When he had hopped back on the wagon, the Preacher had taken his action as a signal to continue on up the mountain. He climbed aboard his wagon seat, thrust his right hand toward the sky, and shouted loudly enough to silence the birds, "*Onward and upward, boys! Onward and upward!*" Then using his whip to both urge on the oxen and direct an imaginary choir, he broke into song:

Onward! Upward! Christian Soldiers
Turn not back nor sheath thy sword.
Let its blade be sharp for conquest
In the battle for the Lord.
From the great white throne eternal,
God Himself is looking down.
It is He Who now commands thee.
Take the cross and win the crown.
It is He who now commands thee.
Take the cross and win the crown.

—————

When the sun was high in the sky, Will began to hear the sound of rushing water over the rumble of the wagon wheels. The preacher, as if he had sensed Will's curiosity, stopped the procession and climbed down from his wagon.

The road had now risen to about a hundred feet above the river gorge and had once again flattened to a gentle slope.

"Will," Preacher said as he walked back toward the others, "we're coming up on Coon Tree Shoals. That racket you hear is the river going over the falls. Caldwell Turpin's mill is just ahead, and I think what I'll do is leave the wagon and generator there. If you have room, I'll load my mail sacks and the few provisions I have into your wagon and ride on in to the store with you."

"How much further to the store?" Will asked.

"Only 'bout a mile."

Will felt his stomach muscles tighten. He was almost to the mythical place.

While Will and the Preacher were talking, Goober had gotten down to inspect the surrey. "Will," he said, "we got a problem. We got a tar 'bout t' come off the lef' rear wheel. I reckon we can tie it on with some rope an' I'll go on straight t' Karl Badger's shop an' leave 'er t' be fixed. I'll walk back t' th' store and we kin ride on up t'gether."

With the iron tire lashed to the wheel rim, the procession moved forward once more.

In less than a minute, a building—the first building since Burley—came into view. It was a large, two-story structure sitting on the left between the road and the river. As they came closer, Will could see the movement of a big water wheel on the back side of the building. The wheel turned slowly and steadily, going nowhere, but transferring its energy to the machinery inside that ground corn and wheat into food. On the side of the mill facing the road was a sign that read:

TURPIN'S MILL and LUMBER WORKS

There was a long, flat-roofed shed on the up-river side of the building that housed the machinery to cut logs into lumber. It ran—as Will would later see—on shared energy from the water wheel. It sat silent for the time being, as most people preferred not to have lumber cut in the spring when the sap was rising in the trees. Between the shed and the river, the long wooden trough that supplied the wheel's water ran up the river and out of sight.

The odd parade came to a stop in front of the mill, and Preacher immediately began calling to the miller.

"*Caldwell! Caldwell!*" he shouted. "*I'm back! Come see the power works!*"

Right away, Caldwell Turpin scampered through the mill door, wiping his hands on his denim apron, and went straight to the wagon to admire the large wooden crate. He was a slender man of average height with a full head of graying hair cut short on the sides. He had a large nose that reminded Will immediately of a Greek ruler he had seen pictured in a book.

"Law, Preacher," he exclaimed, "'at thing looks heavy! Do ye think we can muscle it down onto th' mount?"

Will heard the same twang in Turpin's voice that he heard in Goober's.

"Caldwell, if a few men could move that water wheel into place, we can sure as fire find a way to shift the generator," the preacher replied. "Now, I want you to move your attention back to that surrey and look at who's come back to see us."

Turpin looked back and focused his eyes on the figure sitting on the surrey's seat. "Law, Goober! I heared ye had gone to th' big city to seek ye fortune! Did ye bring some back t' share w' ye old friends?"

"I've done real good, Mr. Turpin," Goober answered as he stuck out his chest. "Got me a job in th' mill a-weavin! Got me a girl too ... purdy as a ..."

"And I want you to meet a new-comer to our cove," the preacher interrupted. "Caldwell Turpin, meet Will Parker."

The oxen had been unhooked from their wagon and attached by ropes through their nose rings to the rear of Will's wagon. As soon as the preacher was settled on the seat beside Will, the Clydesdales took their turn leading, and the procession moved forward again.

From the mill, the grade of the road rose above the river again and moved to the right to avoid a large bolder. Steep banks rose on both sides of the road leading up to even higher hills. They were in a narrow canyon on a narrow road with the river rushing on the left below them.

Before Will realized what was happening, the banks on either side receded, and the road reached the crest of the rise. There before him was the valley, held on all sides by mountains. He stopped the wagon and viewed the scene before him.

"Pretty, isn't it?" Preacher Burden asked.

"It's beautiful," Will answered, "but it's …"

"It's what?"

"It's … it's just not what I expected, I guess. I had pictured black earth and lots of green. … I'm seeing fields of brown and gray … and the hills … they're only spotted in green."

"Will, my boy," the preacher reasoned in a calm, gentle voice, "it's only March … and early March at that! In a week or two, you'll see fields turn as black as soot as farmers begin turning the soil. And the pastures will turn as green as green can be. And those hills," he motioned all around with both arms, "those hills will be a dozen shades of green with patches of sourwood blossoms and chestnuts in flower, and the rebirth of the land will *amaze* you!"

Will looked at the valley again in the light of its potential, and this time, he saw Eden.

———

From the crest of the hill, the road entered the cove and continued for about a quarter mile to where it forked into the road that circled the rim of the valley. In the fork of the road sat Burden's General Store, and to the right of the store was the Burdens' home.

Just beyond Burden's on the road to the right—North Road, as the locals called it—was the home and shop of the blacksmith, Karl Badger.

About a hundred feet out South Road, a wooden bridge crossed the river and continued past a house on the right where Doc French lived and practiced the art of healing both humans and animals.

This small group of buildings, Will was to learn, was the center of town —the hub of commerce in Avery Cove. All other business dealings were carried out at the mill or on various farms throughout the valley by farmers who plied their specialty trades, bartering or selling their goods and services.

As the two wagons approached the store, two men seated on the south end of the porch soaking up the sun rose to greet the procession.

The first man, tall, thin, and straight, was dressed in a black suit and a white shirt with no collar.

"That tall, skinny man is Doc French," the preacher said.

The other man was shorter and heavier, but advanced in years like Doc French. He wore faded overalls and a heavy canvas coat.

"And the other man is Jasper Jeter," the preacher explained. "Lives about a half mile up the south road. He's a farmer like most folks and runs a tannery on the side."

At the fork, Will continued into the parking lot of the store, and Goober turned right toward the blacksmith shop. Will couldn't hear the conversation between Doc and Jasper, but he could see their animation, looking and pointing at him, his Clydesdales, and at Goober.

"Howdy, fellers," the preacher hollered as the wagon came to a halt.

"Howdy, Preacher," Doc hollered back. "Where on earth did you get those horses?"

"Whut I want t' know," Jasper chimed in, "is, wuz 'at Goober Green drivin' 'at surrey? I heared he wuz gone fer good."

Preacher climbed down from his seat and stretched his back from side to side. "Goober's home to take care of some business, and I want you boys to go easy on him. He's living in Charlotte, and I understand he's doin' well. As for these horses here, they belong to this young man. I want you to meet Will Parker, who might be moving here, and I want you to be especially nice to him. Ain't every day we get a cultured person move to the cove! Mostly all we have here is scallywags and miscreants like you two!

"Now, since you boys don't have anything better to do, help me get my supplies and mail sacks into the store. ... *Naomi! Rachel!*" he hollered as he opened the door.

Will walked up the steps and shook hands with Doc and Jasper, exchanging grins over the preacher's mock tirade, and then he entered the store.

In the center of the room sat a large pot-belly stove shedding its heat on three men sitting around it in straight-backed chairs. They stared intently, maintaining their blank expressions. They were old and worn—wrinkled it would seem, by years in the fields. Will nodded, but they didn't return his greeting.

The room was ringed with glass counters displaying what seemed at first glance to be anything the heart could desire.

Behind the first counter on the left was a bank of pigeon holes, some of which contained envelopes and small parcels. Above the cubicles was a sign that read:

UNITED STATES POST OFFICE

Continuing down the left wall and across the back were shelves lined with food staples such as sugar, coffee, salt, and canned items. Along the right hand wall were shelves and racks holding tools, mops, brooms, buckets, and all sorts of farm and home supplies. Crowding the center of the room were barrels of salt pork and fish, crackers, and pickles, as well as tables displaying clothing and fabrics. Everything was neat and organized.

As Will was looking around, Preacher Burden hurried in the back door. "Naomi and Rachel are in the seed house moving some sacks of feed," he announced." They'll be in shortly. I guess you met these boys?"

Before Will could answer, Preacher walked over and put his arm around his shoulder and said, "Now, son, if there's anything you need, I've got it. If you don't see it here, it's out back in one of the storage houses. Your credit's good here, and we can settle up when you get situated."

"That's kind of you," Will answered. "I see several things I want, and I'll be back the first of the week after I see what's needed at the house."

He turned to point out some items he wanted, and there stood Rachel.

———

Goober was standing on the side of the road in front of Karl Badger's house when Will started up the road from Burden's.

"Why didn't you walk down to the store?" Will asked as he stopped to let Goober climb aboard.

"Didn't want t' listen t' all 'at mess 'bout me comin' back."

"Does it affect you that much?"

"'At's why I lef', ye know."

"What about the surrey?"

"Hit'll be ready first o' nex' week."

Will handed the reins over to Goober and reached around to pat Dawg, who was lying on the canvas cover.

"Here, Goob," he said. "Give me the guided tour ... and don't leave out anything."

"I'll do 'er," Goober said as he took the reins. "By th' way, did ye meet Rachel?"

Will gazed out across Badger's pasture. "Yeah, I met her," he said unemotionally.

"Ye don't seem so all-fard happy 'bout it."

"I don't think we hit it off too well, Goob. I don't know what I was expecting, but I did expect her to speak. Her daddy introduced us, and she just stood there with a vacant look on her face ... didn't even smile."

"'At's Rachel! She ain't got a lot t' say t' nobody. Whut did ye think otherwise?"

Will thought for a few seconds before answering. "Hard to say, Goob! All I could see was a tall skinny girl with a vacant look on her face. I don't think she likes me ... I don't think I like her too much either. ... You say she's the only single girl in Avery Cove worth looking at?"

"'At's about it 'less somebody moved in whilst I wuz gone."

Will thought about the girls he had known in recent years. On the one hand, there were those like Prissy, the waitress who wouldn't leave him alone, and on the other hand, there was Rachel, who wouldn't even smile at him. Surely, he thought, there must be a girl somewhere between those two extremes.

The wagon rolled slowly up the road with Will taking in the sights. On his left were pastures fenced in barbed wire, some holding cattle and horses grazing on winter grasses. The land between the road and the river that wasn't fenced lay waiting for the farmers' plows. Some still showed the remains of the previous year's corn stalks.

On the right, the mountain rose gently, with room enough for gardens, livestock pens, and an occasional house on the edge of the woods. Behind the houses, the forest towered with hardwoods showing the first green of spring. At the tree line, the mountain moved suddenly upward toward the rim of the bowl.

Goober took seriously his role as tour guide, giving Will the names of creeks, homeowners, and points of interest. "'At chimbley rat yonder is th' only thing lef' o' th' Tribble house," he said at one point. "Hit burned some time back along w' the Tribbleses. Preacher Burden bought th' land t' raise cattle on."

Soon the road rose over a finger of land that jutted out from the mountain. From the crown of the rise Will looked out over the valley.

"'Is here is jest about th' best view they is o' th' valley," Goober said.

And the view was magnificent. The entire valley was laid out before him in a patchwork of field and pasture bordered by the forest and the mountains. Down the center of the valley snaked the Avery River, glistening in the mid-afternoon sun.

Goober pointed out two roads, East Road and West Road, crossing the valley and the river, creating shortcuts from one side of the valley to the other. On West Road, the one furthest away, the steeple of the Baptist church pointed heavenward. On East Road, the Methodist church with its large cemetery gave witness to its strength and longevity. Across from the Methodist church stood the valley's school house.

"'At's whur I got m' learnin'," Goober said proudly! "Finished all eight grades! An' Will," Goober said, "if ye look up yonder whur th' river comes down out o' th' mountains, 'At's my house up in th' trees, next t' th' river."

Will couldn't see any details, but at least he could see that Goober had a house of some kind.

"'At house t' the lef' o' mine is whur th' Days live, an' th' one this side o' mine belongs t' a half-breed Indian named Nicodemus Whitedeer. ... Ever'body calls him 'Demus'. He's sort of a hermit, an' he ain't too sociable, but if ye leave him be, he'll leave you be!"

Goober picked up the reins and started to urge the horses forward, and then he stopped. He tied the reins to the brake handle, placed his hands on his knees, and stared ahead. "Will," he said, "they's somethin' I need to talk to ye about."

Will had one of those sinking feelings in his stomach that he got when Goober wanted to talk seriously about something. "What's wrong Goob?" he asked.

"Wal … I want ye t' know first off that I love m' Uncle Roamer 'bout like I loved m' daddy. I purely do! But ye know how most ever'body in th' cove has a spacial trade t' make tax money an' spendin' money an' sech?"

"Yes, I know that."

"An' ye know how I tol' ye 'bout how Uncle Roamer makes stuff that people wants?"

"Yes."

"Wal … Uncle Roamer makes his money by makin' moonshine whiskey, Will. … Oh, he does some other things too that's legal, like makin' chawin' terbackie. … He's got people that comes up from Burley t' git his terbackie. An' his whiskey is famous over three states … 'cept people don't know whur hit comes frum!"

"Has he ever gotten caught?"

"*Uncle Roamer? Caught?*" Goober was amused. "His still is so well hid, a hound couldn't find 'im! Th' folks in the cove pertects him too."

"I guess I shouldn't be surprised," Will said.

"But they is one problem, Will." Goober was back to his serious side. "We'll be at Uncle Roamer's purdy soon, an' 'fore we leave there, he'll be a-wantin' ye t' sample some o' his whiskey. He does 'at t' ever'body 'at comes aroun' that he knows ain't th' law."

"It's alright, Goober, I'll taste his whiskey."

"'At ain't all, Will." Goober was very serious now. "He'll be a-wantin' ye t' sample a bunch o' differ'nt batches. He'll want ye t' sample his wine too! 'At's th' way he is. He'll have ye snockered 'fore ye kin turn aroun'!"

Will laughed and gave Goober a gentle shove. "Don't worry Goob," he said knowingly, "I can handle your Uncle Roamer."

Sixteen

Roamer and Sweetie

"Will ... I wuz jest sittin' here thinkin' 'bout you an' Rachel," Goober said soberly as the wagon rolled along. "Maybe ... jest maybe ... ye ort t' call on 'er an' take 'er a sack o' candy er somethin' t' show yer good faith. ... Seems I remember she favors horehoun' candy."

"I thought you didn't approve of Rachel, Goob."

"Wal, I got t' figgerin', ye need a woman t' look after ye ... an' since she's th' onliest one aroun' ..."

"I appreciate it, Goob," Will said, "but let's let it rest for now. I promised Preacher Burden I'd come to church tomorrow, and I'll see if she's any more friendly there. ... Maybe some candy wouldn't be a bad idea though. ... It might fatten her up a little."

The road wound further around the edge of the valley, with Will taking in the sights. He noticed that although the houses were modest, they were neat and well kept. The fields and pastures, even those that lay fallow, were clear and healthy looking.

But as he traveled further into the valley, the things that impressed him more than all the others were the barns. In Charlotte, and even where his grandparents had lived, barns were utility structures built solely for function.

Here, they were works of art! They were oversized and unique—painted and decorated—statements of pride and dignity.

He looked at each of the buildings and imagined the motion and sound of the community coming together to raise the massive timber frames. As he pictured the completion of each structure, he could smell the food the ladies had laid out on tables for the workers.

As the wagon rattled up the road, Will noticed that Goober's legs were bouncing up and down on the foot board. He had come to know when Goober was worked up over something, and this was one of those times.

"Goob," he said, "is everything okay? You seem nervous."

"I'm jest a little excited, I guess. 'at house up yonder … 'at's Uncle Roamer and Aint Sweetie's house. I'm kinda anxious 'bout seein' 'em."

Roamer and Sweetie Robinson's house sat in the edge of the forest, a couple of hundred feet from the road. It was an unpainted frame structure sitting on stone pillars with a wide porch across the front and down the right side.

In a clearing to the left of the house were several outbuildings including a stable, a chicken house, a smoke house, and a corn crib. Behind the house and to its right were several other structures.

As they approached the house, a figure kneeling before a flower garden in the yard stood up to see who was coming. As the old gentleman rose to his feet, Will got his first glimpse of Uncle Roamer.

Roamer was an elf of a man, about the height of Goober, but broad around the middle. His bare head was bald on top and was fringed with a rim of snow-white hair. He stood, staring at the wagon headed toward him, until Goober threw up his hand.

When he recognized his nephew, Roamer threw down his small spade, turned, and ran toward the house. He paused after every three or four steps to look back, making sure that Goober was still there. The boys could hear him hollering as he went but couldn't make out what he was saying.

Before he could reach the porch steps, a little old lady came out the front door wiping her hands on her apron. When she saw the source of

Roamer's excitement, she stopped and covered her face below her eyes with her hands.

The reunion of Goober, Roamer, and Sweetie was one of the most touching things Will had ever seen. Tears flowed freely as they embraced. Roamer and Sweetie held Goober tightly as if they feared he would vanish as suddenly as he had appeared.

"Goober, I knowed ye'd come back ag'in … I jest knowed it," Roamer said, staring at him through tears of joy.

"Boy," said Sweetie, "ye mus' be starved! Have ye had ary a thing t' eat whilst ye been gone?"

"Ain't et nary a thing since I lef' Avery Cove, Aint Sweetie," Goober answered, "an' I could eat a whole pan o' yer cat-head biscuits."

Sweetie turned and shuffled into the house, wiping her tears on her apron, and as she walked away, Roamer pulled Goober close to him and whispered, "Who is 'at feller ye brung with ye? He ain't snoopin' 'round, is he?"

———◆———

"I tell ye, Goober," Aunt Sweetie said as she mixed biscuits on her dough board, "when I seen ye a-comin' up th' road, I got th' all-overs. You wuz purdy as a pair o' red shoes a-sittin on 'at wagon."

The celebration had moved inside and was centered on the kitchen where Sweetie was cooking a feast for her nephew. "Ye once't wuz lost, but now yer *found*," she told Goober again and again as she labored over the wood stove.

After Goober had explained that Will was the one who had taken him in and "sirfistercated" him, Roamer and Sweetie accepted him as one of the family. They had hated to lose Goober, but they were thankful for his new-found happiness and for the one who had befriended him. They even reluctantly accepted the possibility that Goober and Will might exchange properties.

Will's grandmother was a wonderful country cook and he was no stranger to food prepared in the old-time way. He was reminded of his grandmother as the aromas of home cooking filled the house. When they finally sat down to eat and after Roamer delivered an impassioned prayer of thanks for the blessing of having his "boy" home, Will ate the best meal he had eaten in years.

"Mrs. Robinson," he said when he was finished and was pushing back from the table, "that was a delicious meal. If you weren't a married woman, I'd be trying to court you!"

Sweetie giggled and flashed a toothless grin. "An' if hit wa'n't fer 'at ol' man a-sittin thar, I'd court ye back!"

"'Fore we git too lovey here," Roamer said as he stood and reached in his pocket for his chewing tobacco, "I'd like t' axt ye a question thar, Will. Do ye have any pastimes that ye perticalarly enjoy?"

"You mean what I do for fun?"

"Yep! Like th' feller said, ever'body looks at 'is spar time through 'is own knot hole."

"Well, I guess it would be hunting. I'm gonna do a lot of hunting if I move here."

"Do say!" Roamer said as he put a cut of tobacco in his mouth. "Wal, if ye go huntin'… an' ye could bring me an' Sweetie back … one o' 'em wild pigs 'at lives up above Goober's house?" He paused to spit a stream of tobacco juice in the wood stove. "I'd be a-owin' ye."

"You want a pig, do you?"

"'At's right … a little un … a young an' tender un."

Will got up from the table and walked around the room thinking. "Goob," he said, scratching his head, "can you show me where those pigs are? Maybe we could go up in a day or two and get a couple … one for us, and one for the Robinsons."

"Course I can," Goober declared. "They'll be a-rootin' aroun' 'em ol' chestnut trees. They'll prob'ly be a bunch of 'em too! Ever'body knows them is my pigs an' they wouldn't shoot one 'less they axt me first."

Roamer flashed a toothless grin that matched Sweetie's. Here at winter's end, with the pork he had cured in the fall almost gone, he could use some fresh ham and side meat. A small pig would last a couple of weeks in his ice cave.

With that settled Roamer shuffled over to where Will was standing and looked up at him with his big eyes. In a low voice, he asked, "Ain't ye gonna axt me 'bout my pastime?"

"O Lord!" Goober said to himself.

Will looked down at Roamer and lowered his own voice. "Sure," he said, "I've been wondering about that."

Roamer grinned and walked to the center of his front room and kicked away a rug. There, where the rug had been, was a trap door that he lifted to expose a hole with a ladder descending into darkness.

"Come on, boy," he said as he stepped down onto the ladder. "I'll show ye m' doin's."

Will followed Roamer into a cellar, with Goober, muttering under his breath, close behind. Soon a lantern was lit and the dim room came into focus.

It was nearly as large as the Robinson's front room and kitchen combined, with walls of well-fitted stone work. The dirt floor was dry and cleanly swept. Along one of the walls were shelves lined with jars of preserved vegetables, fruits, and juices—enough, it would seem, to last for years. Along another wall were wooden bins containing apples, pears, and both Irish and sweet potatoes.

But Roamer's pride—his pastime, his "doin's" as it was—was displayed on shelves lining two entire walls. There were pint jars and quart jars filled with liquid ranging in color from clear to dark amber. There were jugs and wooden casks containing goodness-only-knows what, and there were several shelves of wine bottles—filled, corked, and lying on their sides.

"Wal, sir," Roamer said, motioning with reverence, "'ere she is…some o' th' finest fixin's t' ever pass over a man's gums!"

He shuffled over to a wall of shelves and looked up and down. "What say we have us a little nip!"

Goober buried his face in his hands and muttered to himself.

Roamer then selected a quart jar of clear liquid and announced, "Now this-un here is some o' m' latest. Hit'll show ye how new fixin's goes down."

He screwed off the lid and handed the jar to Will. As Will smelled and then sipped the liquid, Roamer looked up at him with his head tilted back. His lips formed a small, round opening, and his tongue darted around the inside of his mouth as if it were searching for a way to escape the darkness.

"How'd 'at go down?" he queried.

When Will grimaced, Roamer returned to the shelf and looked again. "Let's try 'is-un here," he said. "Hit's a mite more meller."

Will found this amber liquid to be a little milder, but remembering Goober's warning, resisted the temptation to take more than a sip. When Roamer saw Will's nod of approval, he returned to the shelf and selected a jar of an even darker colored liquid.

"This 'un here set up in a barrel fer six yars 'fore I bottled it," he said. "Hit wuz made in 1887! Have a nip o' hit."

Sure enough, this whiskey was mild and smooth—and it went down with amazing ease! He took another sip.

Roamer returned to the shelves several more times, selecting various bottles of liquid, and with each he gave a history of its vintage, the number of years it was aged, and the type of grain that was used—all from memory. Each of the samples was like his child. Some were babies, some were older and more mature, but like any father, he loved them all equally. More than that, Will loved them too.

It wasn't clear when Will passed out. Goober thought that he was out on his feet a good five minutes before he hit the floor, but at some time during the evening, he succumbed—as Goober had predicted—to Roamer's "doin's".

———

Will awoke the next day in bed, covered with a layer of blankets and quilts. He had no idea where he was or how he had gotten there. Light filled the room and bored into his eyes like sharp sticks, making his head pound.

Goober stood above him, looking down on his sorry frame. "Thought ye said ye could handle Uncle Roamer," he said mockingly.

"Where am I?"

"Yer at my house."

"How did I get here?"

"Ye don't 'member? Me and Uncle Roamer pulled ye up out'a th' cellar with a block 'n tackle—'at's th' way he gen'rally gits people out. Then we loaded ye on th' wagon an' brung ye here."

"I feel like I'm gonna be sick."

"They's a slop jar under th' bed."

Goober retreated to the kitchen and started cooking some food that his aunt had sent along, and before long Will was at the kitchen door asking for coffee.

"I've got to get myself together and get to church," he said, remembering his promise to Preacher Burden.

"You kin fergit about goin' t' preachin' today. Hit wuz over long ago. Hit's might near th' middle o' th' afternoon."

Will sat down at the table where Goober had placed a cup of hot coffee. "I guess I'm in trouble with the preacher then," he said.

"'At kind o' trouble we'll git over," Goober said, turning away from the stove. "We got trouble of a differ'nt kind."

"Like what?"

"I went out early 'is mornin' lookin' 'round, an' we got some stuff missin'. My turnin' plow's gone, they's some boards missin' off the side o' th' barn, an' worst of all, th' split-rail fence I had 'round my garden is gone. Ever' single rail. Hit took me an' my daddy weeks t' split them rails."

"Who would do a thing like that?"

"Ain't but one feller I kin settle on," Goober said, "an' 'at's Demus Whitedeer. Soon as dark comes, I think we better go over an' snoop aroun' 'is place ... see whut we kin find. Got another mist'ry, too."

"What?"

"You ever heared 'bout rocks fallin' frum th' sky?"

"What on earth ..."

"I wuz out lookin' 'round th' place, an' a rock 'bout th' size of a peach pit hit me right twixt th' shoulder blades an' fell down on th' ground. Skeert th' livin' daylights outta me! Hurt, too! I looked aroun' an' nobody wuz there! It had t' be one o' them shootin' stars!"

"Goob, a shooting star would have gone straight through you. You think Whitedeer could have done that, too?"

"I don't know, but ye best strap on 'at six-shooter o' yourn till we find out."

———

Two cups of coffee and some of Sweetie's leftovers began to clear Will's head, and when he went outside to take care of Dawg's needs, his head was cleared further by the fresh mountain air. Only then was he able to come back inside and begin assessing Goober's property.

True to Goober's description, the house was very much like his house in Charlotte, and it was surprisingly well built. There were two bedrooms, a parlor, a dining room, and the large kitchen downstairs.

To the side of the kitchen was the indoor spring house that Goober had described. The masonry troughs were dry since Goober had not restarted the water flow, but they were clean and ready to chill food and milk. Sure enough, there were a sink and spigot in the kitchen, but they too were dry for now.

In the back bedroom, a ladder led up to loft area that could be used as another bedroom or for storage.

Outside, things were equally impressive. The house was painted white, and the shake roof was neat and solid. There was a porch on the front of the house with masonry steps and handrails leading up to it.

The porch was high enough to stand under, and beneath it, in the rock wall that held up the front of the house, was a door leading to a root cellar.

All the outbuildings Goober had listed were there and in relatively good condition.

Then his eyes were directed to the crowning glory of the entire property, which was across the road in the edge of the field. There, standing tall and erect, was a magnificent barn covered with red iron-oxide paint. It looked to be more barn than he would ever need, but if things went well, it would be there waiting to be filled with hay, straw, and animals. But as Goober had told him, there was an area of about ten feet by twenty feet on the front of the barn that had been stripped of its outer skin.

As Will was gazing out over the field and pasture, Goober walked down from the house. "Whut do ye think?" he asked.

"Goober," he said without taking his eyes off the fields, "I feel guilty. This place is more than I ever expected ... much more than my place in Charlotte. Are you sure you still want to trade? Are you sure you want to give this up?"

"Will," he answered, "ye heared th' way Caldwell Turpin took off on me...an' he ain't near as bad as th' others. ... In Charlotte, even th' mill owner gives me some respect! Up 'ere I ain't nothin', but down thar I'm somethin'. So yes sir, I still want t' trade if you've a mind to."

Goober stuck out his hand, and Will took it to seal the deal. The papers would be filled out and registered at a later date. Preacher Burden would notarize the transaction, and the court houses in Burley and Charlotte would record the fact that an exchange of property had taken place. All of the wherefores and whereases would be handled by the attorney to make it official with the courts, but Goober and Will had shaken hands, and it was official with them—and then, they had embraced.

As soon the sun set and the moon appeared in the eastern sky, Will and Goober left the house and started back down North Road toward Demus Whitedeer's property.

When they were a few hundred feet down the road, Will raised a question that had been bothering him. "Goober," he said, "who is this Whitedeer fellow, and where did he come from?"

"Wal," Goober said, "I'm shore ye studied in ye hist'ry 'bout how th' soldiers come back in th' 30's an' rounded up all th' Cherokees an' took 'em out west."

"Yep ... the trail of tears."

"Ye know, they wuz a few of 'em 'at run off an' hid in th' mountains whur th' soldiers couldn't find 'em."

"I remember."

"Wal, 'bout 1836 'is sixteen-yar-old boy named Joseph Whitedeer run off an' hid in a ol' broke-down gold mine up north o' my place in th' hills ... up above whur Demus lives now."

"There was a gold mine here?"

"They was several of 'em! Why, ever' now an' then, somebody'll still find a nugget in th' river! But anyhow, Joseph Whitedeer hid in 'at cave an' mite near starved t' death till he wuz found by Seth Leggery that used t' own th' property.

"Wal, sir," Goober continued, "Seth Leggery took th' youngun in an' put 'im t' work long side 'is slaves, 'cept he treated th' boy more lack a son."

"People up here had slaves?"

"Seth Leggery did! An' when Joseph Whitedeer wuz 'bout 26, he married one of, 'em, an' soon, they had a boy ... Nicodemus."

"So ... Demus is half Indian and half Negro?"

"'At's right, an' when Seth Leggery died, he left th' whole shootin' match t' Demus ... jest lack he wuz his own gran'son."

"How come he's such a loner?"

"Most folks don't lack 'im 'cause o' 'is mama an' daddy."

Goobers voice trailed off to almost whisper, and he lightened up on his steps. "'At house up yonder whur ye see th' lights ...'at's 'is house."

The Whitedeer house was about halfway between Goober's and Uncle Roamer's, and like most other houses Will had seen in the cove, it sat back from the road at the edge of the trees. Unlike others though, Demus had allowed new tree growth to surround his house and partially hide it.

Will and Goober used the trees to their advantage as they worked their way up close enough to the house to be able to see Demus inside. By the light of a lantern, they could see Demus pacing back and forth, drinking from a cup. He was a large man—thick and muscular. His skin was dark and his black, curly hair fell to his shoulders.

"Let's look around the yard," Will whispered.

They eased back from the house and made their way through the trees to a cleared area near the road where Demus had started preparing a garden. Sure enough, between the clearing and Demus's house were several large stacks of split rails.

Goober hurried over and closely examined a number of them, feeling along the edges, and looking at them closely by the light of the moon.

"These is *my* rails!" he declared.

"How do you know they're yours?"

"Come 'ere an' look," Goober said as he crouched over the rails again. "Ye see here along th' bark side whur th' limbs was cut off with a ax?"

"Yeah. So what?"

"Wal, Look at th' angle o' th' cut. See how hit comes in frum 'is direction? Them limbs was cut off by a lef'-handed man. I'm lef'-handed, an' so was my daddy! Demus is right handed!"

"How do you know that?"

"Didn't ye see 'im drinkin' out'a 'at cup? He helt it in 'is right hand!"

Will stood up and looked down at Goober. "Goob," he said, "how did you come up with that? Instead of bein' a weaver, you should-a been a police detective. Let's go on home and get some sleep. We'll come back and see Mr. Whitedeer in the morning."

"O Lord," Goober said.

———

Morning brought more of the warm winds that had melted the snow and dried the earth. Spring had arrived.

It seemed that as each dawn came, green was literally drawn from the trees. Buds were bursting on branch tips in profusion, hiding the brown of the limbs and trunks.

Will rolled out of bed at dawn, dressed, and went outside to continue his tour of what was now his property. He examined each of the outbuildings carefully and made mental notes of repairs each would need.

The smoke house was the one in greatest need of repair since it had not been used since Goober's father died. It would need new chinking around the firebox stonework, a new door, and new roofing tin.

The chicken house was in need of a thorough cleaning and would have to be whitewashed inside to kill an infestation of mites.

The corn crib had some rotted logs around the bottom where the rain splashed up.

But the first thing that he would do was get water running back to the house again.

As he was completing his inspection of the outhouse, Goober came out the back door and hurried that way. It was time for his morning outhouse ritual.

"Mornin'," he intoned as he scurried inside, latching the door behind himself.

"Mornin' yourself," Will said after Goober was inside. "You ready to go see our neighbor?"

"I been thinkin' 'bout that very thing, Will. Don't ye think hit would be best t' let Preacher Burden handle it? I mean, him bein' Justice o' th' Peace an' all?"

"No," Will answered. "He'd probably tell us to try to handle it ourselves before involving him. I intend to pay a nice, civilized visit and tell the man what we want. If he gives us a hard time, then we'll see what Preacher Burden has to say. If you don't want to go, I'll handle it by myself."

"No, I'll go," Goober said. "I ain't skeert of 'im."

———

Will decided that Goober was dragging his feet. He had been puttering around the house finding one thing after another to do, putting off the inevitable. No one in the valley had ever stood up to Demus Whitedeer, and Goober was having a hard time convincing himself that he should be the first, even if Will was with him.

While he was waiting, Will picked up a Bible that was lying on the mantle and opened it to the front where he found the name of the name of the original owner—Marta Green, Goober's mother.

On the liner page, Marta had chronicled the history of many of the family's members.

It turned out that Goober's father, Laddie, and his Uncle Roamer were half brothers. From the names and dates of birth that were listed, it appeared that Goober's grandmother bore children from two separate marriages. Roamer was the son of her first husband, Claude Robinson, and Goober's father, Laddie was the child of Adolphus Green, her second husband.

He found another interesting fact. A history was given of a Russian prince who came to America in exile and settled in western North Carolina. In 1820, the wife of his son gave birth to Anastasia Larisa Petrov. Beside Anastasia's name in parenthesis was the name "Sweetie"! Aunt Sweetie, it would seem, had descended from royalty!

"I guess I'm ready t' go," Goober announced as he entered the parlor. "I brung ye yer pistol. I reckon ye best take it with ye."

"I'll take it if it'll make you happy," Will said, "but I don't plan to shoot somebody over some fence rails."

As they headed out the door, Will strapped the .44 around his waist and covered it with his coat.

"You figgerin' t' walk to 'is house?" Goober Asked.

"No," Will replied, "Let's ride Don and Molly over there. I think we might look a little more serious if we ride up on some big horses."

As they were about to cross the road to go to the pasture, a stone flew by Will's head, nicking his ear. It whistled on across the road, and hit a fence post on the other side.

He grimaced in pain and wheeled around just in time to see a young boy disappear into the woods between his house and the river. Overcome with pain and anger, he ran through the yard and into the woods where the boy had disappeared.

The sounds of the boy crashing through underbrush and dry leaves told Will exactly where to go, and he was gaining on the boy when they reached the river.

Without hesitation, the youngster hopped across boulders in the river, running almost as fast as he had on dry ground, and before Will could decide which course he should take, the boy had vanished into the woods on the other side.

Will met Goober in the woods as he was returning.

"Did ye catch 'im, Will?" Goober asked.

"No, he got away, but I think we can safely say that it wasn't Whitedeer that was chunkin' the rocks. It was a young boy."

"Hit was Matthew Day's boy, Sonny," Goober said. "He's growed since I've saw 'im, but 'at was him! 'At little feller has got a *mean* streak!"

Will stopped to catch his breath, and he looked back in the direction of the river. "Well," he concluded, "I guess that after we talk to Demus Whitedeer, we better go talk to the boy's daddy."

When Will walked into the pasture and whistled for Don and Molly, his mind flashed back to Artis McGreevy, the man who had raised and trained the two giant horses. "What a gentle and patient man he must be," he mumbled to himself. He knew the McGreevys must miss the animals, and he added them to his mental list of those to whom he would write.

The two horses, remembering their training, responded to Will's call and trotted to him instantly. They stood motionless as he placed a bridle on each of their heads, and they walked with him to stand beside the fence where he and Goober could climb up and mount them.

As the two rode off down the north road, new vistas greeted Will. This was the first time he had seen this section of road in the light of day. He took in every sight and flooded Goober with questions about points that interested him. One of his questions, however, didn't concern their surroundings. "Did you say the boy's name is Sonny ... Sonny Day?"

"'At's right."

Will shook his head. "With a name like that, no wonder he has a mean streak."

Beyond the mist that hung over Cedar Creek, Demus's farm came into view. In the garden patch between his house and the road, Demus was walking behind his mule, plowing the soil for his spring garden. At the edge of the garden nearest the boys, he turned his mule and positioned his plow to cut another row.

"*Will*," Goober howled, "*'at's my plow he's a-usin'!*"

Will stopped his horse in the road and looked intently. "What makes you think that's your plow, Goob?" he asked.

"Ye see how the lef' handle is a lighter color than th' right un is? I made 'at handle an' fixed it on th' plow right 'fore I come t' Charlotte. When ye git up close to it, you'll see hit's made outta ash, and the right un is made outta hickory. 'At's how I know!"

Before Demus started down the next row, he turned in the direction of the boys, wiped his forehead on his sleeve, and looked, wondering who it was coming his way. He stood where he was, holding the plow handles as the boys brought their horses up to within a few feet of him and stopped.

"Mr. Whitedeer," Will said, "my name is Will Parker. You know Goober here," and he nodded in Goober's direction.

"What do you want?" Demus said in a dark voice. He had a look of fear in his eyes.

"Well, the first thing we want is that plow there that you borrowed from Goober. As soon as you're finished with it, Goober needs to plow his garden."

"Why do you think it's your plow? I'd thank you to leave."

"Will, 'et's go," Goober whispered.

Will sat up straight up on the back of the horse and looked in the direction of the rails. "And we want those rails over there ... and the boards off the barn. I'll expect you to have them put back where they belong in three days."

"Those rails are mine, and I have no boards. Now, I said for you to leave!"

Goober tightened the reins on his horse and whispered again, "Please, Will, 'et's go!"

"Then I'll have Preacher Burden handle it," Will said.

Demus dropped the handles of the plow to the ground and started walking toward Will. "And what if he believes me instead of you?" he said as he hastened his pace. "Then what?"

Before Demus could take another step, Will had the pistol out from beneath his jacket and pointed between Demus's eyes. "Then I guess the real owner will have to blow your brains out and take 'em back himself!"

For several seconds, Will and Demus froze with their eyes locked on each other. The only sound that could be heard was their heavy breathing.

Goober was frantic. He finally made a little whimpering sound as he pulled his horse around and started for the road. "*Will, I'm a-telling ye! 'Et's go!*" he yelled.

Will pulled hard on his reins, backing his horse away. With his eyes still locked on Demus, he slowly lowered the gun. Finally, when he had backed off a safe distance, he turned his mount and trotted off to catch Goober on the road.

"Will, I hope t' my *never*! 'at wuz about the most *dumbest* thing I've *ever* saw you do!" Goober screeched. His voice was high and strained. "Tellin' him you'll blow 'is brains out. I'm here t' tell ye … he'll be *layin'* fer ye!"

"I said no such thing," Will said calmly, "and he won't be layin' for *me*. What I said was, 'The *real owner* will blow your brains out,' and as far as he knows, *you're* still the real owner. He'll be layin' for *you* … so you can just relax!"

Seventeen

THE HUNT

When Will and Goober got back to Cedar Creek, the mist had lifted. Will hoped that this was a good omen. Goodness knows he needed one.

Since his outburst over the set-to with Demus, Goober had been silent, but he was still seething. He could see no humor in Will involving him with his comment about "the real owner."

Will knew that what Goober needed was something to take his mind off the confrontation. He knew, too, that this was not the time for them to see Matthew Day, so he said, "Say, Goob, I don't think I'm up to seeing Sonny's dad today. The boy probably won't bother us again anyway because I put a real scare in him. Why don't we go find those wild pigs instead?"

Goober remained silent, but the furrows in his brow relaxed. He was thinking. Finally, he broke his silence. "'At's the first smart thing ye've come up with t'day! I wa'n't lookin' forwards t' seein' Matthew Day anyhow … 'specially a'ter all 'at mess w' Demus!" He thought for a little longer. "Tell ye whut," he said, "I'll take ye up thar, but you'll have t' shoot um and dress 'em! Is 'at fair 'nough?"

"'At's fair 'nough!" Will replied, and then he thought to himself, "I've got to be more careful. I'm beginning to talk like Goober."

He wondered as they plodded along how he would adjust to this strange environment. He wondered if he would lose the language of his parents as he grew comfortable with the place.

And what of his sister? Would she know him if she saw him years from now? If in the future they were to meet on some faraway street, would she see him as just an unfortunate mountain man, forlorn and out of place? A change like that was something he would have to guard against.

Further up the road, as his new property came into view, Will's thoughts turned to his surroundings.

By approaching the barn from this angle, he could see the masterful workmanship of Goober's father. In the high eves there were patterns of delicate design that served no purpose other than to beautify.

He marveled at the scale and balance of the building, and he reasoned that with the right training and education, Laddie Green could have built high-rise buildings and grand cathedrals.

With all that he saw, he decided that the risk of adopting a backwoods dialect was outweighed by the beauty of his newfound home.

By that time, Goober had calmed down and was thinking about Will's hunting proposal. "I think we ort t' leave Don here an' jest walk up," Goober said. "We kin take Molly along t' carry th' pigs back, but hit's purdy overgrowed up 'ere … too growed over fer horse ridin'."

Back at the house, Will went inside to exchange his revolver for a rifle and a handful of ammunition. Since Goober had told him that a pig hunt was no place for an untrained dog, he brought Dawg inside where he would not be tempted to follow them.

While Will was in the house, Goober turned Don out to pasture and found a coil of rope that would be used to tie the pigs to Molly's back.

When they met at the road, Goober told Will what was ahead. "Whut we'll do," he said, "is t' foller th' river up t' whur th' trail ends. We'll prob'ly have t' leave Molly thar an' walk on up t' th' chestnut grove.

"Now Will," he continued, "wild pigs is mean. Some of 'em boars has tusks long as ye foot, an' they kin rip a man t' pieces. Keep ye gun handy, 'cause sometimes they'll charge ye. Whut we're a'ter is the little shoats, an' they should be a bunch of 'em."

"Don't you want a gun?" Will asked.

"No, one gun's a-plenty. I'll scamper up a tree if need be."

Then Goober put on his reflective look. "I 'member when I wuz a boy, Uncle Roamer got treed by a bunch o' pigs deep up in th' woods whur he wuz a-workin', an' they wouldn't let 'im down!"

"What did he do?" Will asked.

"He fin'ly farred three shots frum 'is pistol …'at's th' distress signal up 'ere … an' a couple o' hunters come t' he'p 'im. One o' th' fellers shot th' biggest boar an' 'e weighed over six hundr'd pounds … that wuz th' boar, not th' feller."

"Why didn't Roamer just shoot the pigs himself?"

"'At little ol' pistol Uncle Roamer totes wouldn't hardly kill a squirrel, much less a pig."

At the river, they turned onto a trail that branched off to the west along the river's bank. The slope of the trail was gentle but steady as it climbed beside the river into the thickening forest.

Birch trees, still bare from winter, stood on the left between the trail and the river, holding the bank in place. To the right of the trails were silver maples. They too were leafless, but they held in abundance the odd seeds that would drift down in whirls later in the spring.

Beyond the maples were oaks and poplars intermingled with dozens of under story species filling the voids where giant trees had fallen.

All at once a flash of color that seemed out of place caught Will's eye. It was on the right, almost hidden by the undergrowth. And it was red—barn red.

"Goob, look up in the clearing beyond that patch of laurel," Will said. "Is that what I think it is?"

"I hope to my never!" Goober answered. "'At looks like th' boards off th' barn. Somebody has built a shack out o' 'em missin' barn boards!"

Quickly, Goober found a trail leading to the shack, and he pushed his way through the undergrowth with Will close behind.

Sure enough, what they found was a lean-to fashioned from the boards taken from the barn. Inside was a floor of freshly cut pine boughs, and lying by the opening was a slingshot and a pile of stones about the size of peach pits.

"Looks like we owe our friend Demus an apology," Will said. "He may have taken the plough and the rails, but not the barn boards ... and it looks like we still owe Sonny Day's father a visit."

"Firs' things firs'," Goober replied. "'Et's go git them pigs, then we'll worry 'bout Sonny Day."

Not far up the trail, the sound of falling water came within earshot. At that point, the terrain jutted upwards and the river fell over a series of waterfalls. The trail turned right, away from the river, but after a steep, crooked climb, it rejoined the river beyond the falls.

A few hundred feet from there, the trail ended at some large boulders.

"Rat here is whur we'll haf t' leave Molly an' walk on up," Goober said. "Th' chestnuts is up at th' top o' th' ridge."

It wasn't long before their progress was blocked by a deep, dry gully coming from high on the right and running to the river. It was strewn with boulders and thick underbrush tangled with leaves, dead limbs, and fallen trees that had washed down from the hill above.

When they stopped to search for a way across, they were startled by what seemed to be a large animal coming up the gully through the thick growth and debris.

"Git down," Goober whispered, and they both instantly crouched on the side of the crevasse.

For a moment, the movement stopped, and the only sound they could hear was the wind and an occasional bird call. But then it started again. The steps were slow and heavy, breaking limbs and crushing the dry leaves. It would take a few steps toward them and stop for several seconds as if it were listening for them too.

"'At sounds like a pig," Goober whispered. "Could be a mama pig with 'er younguns. Sometimes 'ey nest in gullies."

They waited for at least a minute to see if the animal would show itself, but all was quiet. The movement had stopped.

Finally, Will rose slightly from his crouched position and looked up and down the ditch. When he was satisfied that he could see nothing, he lowered back to the crouched position and whispered to Goober, "I'm going to go down into the gully and see if I can flush 'em out. Keep down in case I have to shoot."

"Be careful," Goober whispered back.

Will crept down the side of the gully toward the river, where he found a spot with a ledge about six feet from the top. He motioned, and Goober joined him.

He held out his rifle toward Goober and whispered, "Hold my rifle while I climb down to that ledge, and then pass it down to me."

"Be careful," Goober whispered again.

With his hands free, Will lay down on his stomach, put his legs over the side, and dropped to the ledge below. He was now about three feet from the bottom.

When he turned and looked up to receive his rifle, a terrible sound erupted below him. As he wheeled around, a huge black body burst through the underbrush and charged at him, roaring in a fit of rage!

"*Bar, Will! Hit's a bar!*" Goober screamed in terror!

Before Will could react, the bear knocked him off the ledge to the bottom of the gully and smothered him with its body. Instinctively, Will covered his head and neck with his arms, defending his face and neck from the attack.

The air was filled with chaos! Will was screaming in pain and horror. The bear was roaring with rage, tearing at Will's arms and hands with claws and teeth, and shaking his body from side to side. Goober was helplessly running about, screaming in fear.

"*Shoot, Goober! Shoot!*" Will screamed. "*Get him off of me!*" But Goober couldn't shoot for fear of hitting Will.

And then, for one glorious moment, all rational thinking flew from Goober's mind. All the fear he had ever known was gone, replaced with the anger that had welled up inside him since he was a child. His feelings of inadequacy vanished as the fear of losing his friend took control.

With no other option, Goober crouched at the edge of the gully and dove head first onto the back of the bear. Before the animal could react, he locked his arms around its neck and squeezed with all his might.

Now the bear was on the defensive. Sensing mortal danger and feeling pain itself, it abandoned Will and turned its attention to saving its own life. It thrashed around, crashing against rocks and debris, trying to shake the thing that was depriving it of breath. It rolled and tumbled with Goober desperately hanging on, his arms around the bear's neck and his legs now latched around its body.

The bear could do nothing to free itself from this parasite that smelled like man. It could do nothing to restore its breath. And so, after several agonizing minutes it lay still, covered by Goober's sobbing body.

Goober continued to squeeze the bear's neck until he knew it was dead, and when he finally did let go, he continued to lie on the animal's back, exhausted and crying.

At last, he remembered Will. Fearing what he would find, he reluctantly raised his head and looked around.

Will was about twenty feet away, raised up on an elbow, covered with blood. The only sound he could make was a gurgling "whoosh" coming from a hole that was torn in his neck. When he saw that Goober was all right, he lay his head down and lost consciousness.

All the emotions known to man rushed through Goober's mind. His heart pounded, fueled by a rush of adrenaline.

Forgetting the bear, he crawled to Will's side and hovered over him on his knees, pleading, "Don't die, Will. Please don't die. I'll git he'p, Will. Please don't die."

It was only then that Goober felt the searing pain that burned in his right hand. He looked to find that it was distorted and twisted between his little finger and his wrist. The pain was excruciating.

A glance back at Will though made him forget his pain long enough to begin looking for a way out of the gully. Knowing that he would not be able to climb out with an injured hand, he ran down the gully, dodging rocks and bushes, until he was almost to the river. There, the gully was shallow enough for him to pull himself out with his left hand alone.

Once he was out of the chasm, he ran back to the spot where the rifle was lying. Somehow, he managed to fire it into the air, chamber another round, fire it, chamber a round, and fire it for the third time.

After a brief rest, he began the laborious walk toward the trail head where Molly was waiting. As he walked, his mind flashed back to better times. He recalled the Christmas Eve service he attended at Will's church. He remembered the comfort and happiness he felt there, and the joy he felt as he, Will, and Esther rode home in the surrey, laughing and singing carols.

He thought of Preacher Burden and how he had been kind to him when others weren't. How he wished he could call on the good preacher to pray for his friend at that very moment.

Molly was waiting when he reached the river. He needed to ride her, but he knew he wouldn't be able to mount her with his injured hand.

Just as he started to lead her away, a voice called out. "*Goober! Goober Green! Did you far them shots?*"

He turned and saw Ansel Falwell standing on the opposite bank of the river with an ax in his hand. "*Mr. Falwell,*" he called back as he began crying again, "*please … I need he'p!*"

Doc French's house served as the community's hospital. His back bedroom was the surgery and patient quarters combined, and his parlor was his office and waiting room.

A small gathering waited in the parlor while Doc tended to Will's injuries. While they waited, the preacher's wife, Naomi treated Goober's hand with cloths soaked in cold water to prevent swelling. Doc had already given him a dose of laudanum for pain.

"I wuz a-cuttin' wood when I heared three shots, an' went t' runnin' in 'at direction," Ansel Falwell related to Preacher Burden. "When we got t' th' boy, I figgered he wuz dead till I seen 'im twitch. So we got 'im up on 'at big ol' horse an' brung 'im here as quick as we could."

"What about the bear?" Preacher Burden asked.

"Oh, 'at bar wuz dead ... dead as a rock! I reckon 'em shots I heared wuz Goober a-shootin' 'im."

"I didn't shoot 'im ... I choked 'im," Goober said quietly.

The preacher and Ansel exchanged silent looks.

Ansel raised up, resting his elbows on his knees, and he looked over at Goober. "I know they wuz a lot goin' on up 'ere," he said. "You prob'ly don't 'member most of it, but a man jest don't choke a bar t' death ... he jest *don't*!"

"'At's whut happened," Goober replied as he looked straight ahead.

"Look," Preacher Burton said as he stood, "why don't we just let this thing rest for now. There'll be plenty of time later to sort it out. I've got to say though that just *killin'* that bear was a brave act."

The preacher walked over and stood above Ansel and looked down at him. "Ansel," he said, "I've known Goober his entire life and I've always known him to be honest. I've never known him to flat-out lie. So if he says he strangled a bear, I guess I'll have to believe him 'til it's proved otherwise. Now, I'll say it again, let's just let it rest for now."

Ansel jumped to his feet and set his hat on his head. "Well, I'll tell ye whut I'm a-gonna do," he said. "I'm a-gonna git Jasper Jeter, an' we'll jest go up 'ere an' skin 'at bar an' *see* whut kilt it!"

As Ansel left, slamming the front door, Goober looked at the preacher and nodded. "Thank ye, Preacher," he said.

Finally, Doc French came from the back room. He pulled the swivel chair around from his desk and sat down in front of Goober and the Burdens.

"I've gotten the boy patched up," he said. "The good news is that the injuries themselves aren't life-threatening. He has bites and claw wounds on his arms and chest along with that bad one on his throat. I've cleaned them and stitched them all except for the one on through his windpipe. It'll have to stay open until the risk of infection has passed because if it swells, he wouldn't be able to breathe. For the time being, he'll have to breathe through the wound. As soon as he's out of danger, I'll sew it up too.

"Now, he's lost a lot of blood and he'll be weak for a while because of that, but the biggest threat to his life now is infection. About the dirtiest thing in nature are a bear's claws. If you think about it," he said, "they tear into carrion with their claws, they scratch their urine into the ground with 'em, and they never get cleaned or trimmed. I'll take a bite wound over a claw wound any day."

"He'll need nursing care, won't he?" Naomi asked.

"He'll need lots of it."

"Then I'll stay with him as long as need be," Naomi replied as she stood and went into the back room.

"Now," Doc said as he rolled his chair over to Goober, "let's take a look at you."

He took Goober's right hand and gently examined it, turning it one way and then the other. "You know, there are a lot of small, delicate bones in the hand," he said as he took Goober's left hand to demonstrate. "You've broken this bone right here on your other hand. I'll set it and put a splint on it, and it'll heal up fine. How did you break it anyway?" he asked as he looked into Goober's eyes.

"When I grabbed th' bar 'round 'is neck," he replied, "I grabbed my right han' with my left-un an' jest pulled as hard as I could. I reckon I jest pulled too hard."

Doc stood and helped Goober to his feet. "A man can have extraordinary strength when he's facing adversity," he said, and he led Goober toward the surgery.

———

The morning found Naomi standing over Will's bed, with Doc asleep in a chair in the corner.

Will was still sleeping soundly under the influence of a strong dose of morphine. His breathing was slow and labored, entering and exiting through the hole in his throat.

Naomi held her hand to Will's brow and turned to wake the doctor. "Doc," she called out, "he has a fever!"

Doc rose to his feet and hurried to the bedside. He looked at Will and felt his head for himself. Then he gave Naomi her instructions.

"Naomi, start putting cold compresses on his head and chest. Be sure to change the water often enough to keep it cold. I'll go over to the store and get Rachel to help you, and while I'm there, I'll pick up some things we'll need."

Doc left by the front door, putting on his coat as he went. He walked quickly across the bridge, down the road, and up the steps of the store which was already open for business.

When he walked in, he was met by Ansel Falwell, Jasper Jeter, and two other men who were standing around the stove talking. Their talking ceased when Doc entered.

"Preacher!" Doc called out.

The preacher immediately came from the back room with a broom in his hand. Doc pulled him to a back corner and spoke to him in a whisper. "Preacher, I need a package of bleached cotton, about two yards of white linen, and I want at least a pint of Roamer Robinson's whiskey."

"But Doc," the preacher said, "I don't think I have …"

Doc looked at the preacher sternly. "Don't tell me you don't have the whiskey. I know where you hide it! Now I need it for the boy!"

The preacher turned and headed out the back door, and Doc went to sit by the stove and wait.

"Uh, Doc," Ansel said after he the doctor was seated, "how's th' boy a-doin'?"

"He's developed a fever, Ansel. I've sent the preacher for some supplies."

"Whur's Goober?" Ansel asked.

"I set his hand and got him a ride up to his uncle's house. They'll take care of him."

"Well, Doc," Ansel said sheepishly, "hit's like 'is. Me an' Jasper here went up an' skint that bar. Hit wuz a female … not real big, 'bout two-hunderd-fi'ty pounds."

"That's still more than twice Goober's size," Doc said.

"Wal, anyhow," Ansel continued, "we found a dead cub in the under-growth … looked t' have been dead two 'r three days. I figger th' mama bear wuz jest a-guardin' her youngun."

"Makes sense," Doc said.

"But here's th' kicker," Ansel said. "Shore 'nough, 'at bar wa'n't shot a-tall … hit's neck wuz crushed jest like Goober said. I swar, Doc," he said excitedly, "'at boy *choked* 'at bar t' *death*!"

"An' I'm a-gonna tan th' hide fer 'im!" Jasper proudly added.

Doc leaned back in his chair and clasped his hands behind his head. He thought for a moment and finally said, "Fellows, I think we've all learned an important lesson from this. We've learned trust, respect, and love for one's fellow man. We've learned another thing too … and it's a scientific fact! A man can have extraordinary strength when he's facing adversity."

Eighteen

A New Hero

Goober's first night after the bear attack was a sleepless one. Too many things were going on inside his head.

Having known more than one person who died from infection, he was deeply concerned about Will's survival. He just couldn't get Doc's comments about claw wounds out of his mind.

He worried too that if Will survived, he might be handicapped in some way. He could imagine Doc having to remove an arm that became infected. "How kin a man plow an' make hay w' jest one arm?" he thought.

Then he thought of his own injury. The pain had been really bad, and although the laudanum he had been given brought some relief, it also caused hallucinations. Worry, pain, and hallucinations make for a sleepless night!

To try to put his mind at ease he decided to think of the most pleasant thing he could imagine—Judy Ruth Roach. He thought of her at work in the mill and how she always looked pleasant and happy as she worked. He smelled the air and recalled the fragrance of her hair. He imagined her at home—their home—cooking, cleaning, and caring for their children.

Then, through the magic of a laudanum-induced hallucination, he saw her float out the door of their home and across the yard to greet him as he returned from his job as mill supervisor.

When Uncle Roamer's clock chimed at 3:00 a.m., Goober gave up on the night and got out of bed. By a dim lantern's light, he found a tablet and pencil and sat down to write.

Dear Judy Ruth

This is Goober writting to you. I am thinking of you tonite for I am not abel to sleep for you see me and Will was attackted by a bear in the woods. Will is hurt real bad and mite even die. I have a broke hand but I am manely fretting over Will. I am spending my time thinking about you to eze my pain witch is in my hand but mostly in my hart because I am hear and you are their. Things was going reel good untill the bear attackted us but thar is good news. Me and Will is going to swap houses so I will have a house and land in Charlott reel soon that is if Will dont die witch I did not think of til now. When its morning I will go to the store and male this letter and look for a letter from you. Like I told you befor writting on the train I love you and I wont to git a letter from you soon.
Love Goober Green

Roamer had gone to Goober's house the evening before and put Molly out to pasture. While he was there, he retrieved Dawg and brought him back to stay with him while Will was on the mend.

He fixed a bed for Dawg in his woodshed and tied him up by the opening with a piece of rope. With a belly full of leftover cornbread, Dawg had settled down happily for the night.

When Goober finished his letter, he dressed and went outside to check on Dawg. His rope was there by the opening and his bed was in the woodshed, but he was gone.

A wave of panic washed through Goober's mind! Here was Will injured, unconscious, and clinging tenuously to life, and his dog was on the loose in an unfamiliar place. "What else can go wrong?" he thought.

He circled the house, calling and searching. He walked to the road and gazed in both directions, but there was no sound except the far away howl of a wolf baying at the moon.

A second wave of panic washed over him as he began to see flurries of movement. Ghostly apparitions appeared, floating up from openings in the earth then darting from tree to tree and bush to bush.

He turned and ran toward the house, followed by the drug-induced demons. They roared and morphed into bears with needle-sharp claws. They became wolves that snarled through bared teeth. He tried to scream, but no sound would leave his throat.

Goober was met at the front door by Roamer and Sweetie, who had heard his distress and come to see what all the commotion was about. As he ran in, Roamer seized him and held him closely until he was able to speak. "*Uncle Roamer,*" he cried, "*th' whole valley is full o' bars an' wuffs! They come an' got Dawg ... an' now they a-comin' fer me! Hide me, Uncle Roamer! Hide me away!*"

"Settle down, Goober! Jest settle," Roamer said as he held Goober tightly. "They ain't no bears ner wuffs neither a-comin' fer ye! Hit's all in ye head, boy ... all in ye head. Somethin' has got ye addled, an' I fear hit's 'at potion Doc give ye."

"I'll go an' see 'bout that dog o' Will's," Sweetie said as she turned and shuffled out of the room. "'At orter he'p ease 'is mind."

Roamer guided Goober into his bedroom and sat with him on the bed. He held him and rocked back and forth with him as he spoke soothingly. "'At's awright now, boy," he cooed. "Ol' Uncle Roamer ain't gonna let no bars ner wuffs git ye. Hit'll be awright. Hit'll be peep o' day soon."

"At ol' coon dog's gone fer certain," Sweetie announced as she shuffled back into the house. "Must-a gone off lookin' fer a coon er a possum."

"He most likely took off fer Goober's a-lookin' fer Will," Roamer answered, "but he'll prob'ly be back fer s'more cornbread soon as th' sun's up."

Soon, the smell of coffee and ham filled the house as Sweetie labored over her stove. She knew that what Goober needed to chase the demons from his head was a good "fry-up".

Sure enough, some eggs, ham, red-eye gravy, grits, a slice of onion, and a couple of cat-head biscuits cleared the last of the laudanum from Goober's head. The demons were gone, but the pain was back.

"I got to go see Doc an' git me some medicine," he told Roamer and Sweetie. "Shorely he kin gi' me somethin' 'at won't fill m' head w' bars an' woofs an' sech."

"Ye don't need none o' his medicine," Roamer said, and he got up and walked to the kitchen cabinet. He reached up on the top shelf and retrieved a quart mason jar of dark amber liquid. "'Is here'll set ye free," Roamer concluded.

Goober dropped off to sleep a few minutes before 6:00 a.m. and slept free of pain and demons until almost 3:00 a.m. the following morning. When he woke, he got a lantern and went immediately to the outhouse. Then, he went to the wood shed and found that Dawg was still gone.

When they heard him clatter back in, Roamer and Sweetie got up to see how he was.

"Soon as light comes, I'm a-goin' t' Doc's an' check on Will," Goober told his aunt and uncle. "If I go early, I won't be as likely t' see any o' 'em ol' boys 'at hangs aroun' th' store. I shore don't want t' hear no more o' Ansel Falwell's mess."

"I'll go w' ye," Roamer said, "case ye need me ... which I hope ye don't."

"After that, I'm a-gonna see if I kin find Dawg," Goober continued. "I'd hate t' haf t' tell Will his dog has run off. Then, I'm a-gonna check on th' house an' git th' water t' runnin'."

Sweetie raised up from wiping the kitchen table and waved her dish rag in Goober's direction. "Ye best go easy," she warned, "'r *you'll* be laid up at Doc's too."

———

Roamer's mule-drawn wagon rumbled slowly down his drive and turned left onto the road just as first light was appearing. Roamer controlled the reins, gently urging the mule onward. Goober sat beside him, bundled up against the chill of dawn. His right hand was wrapped in an extra layer of warmth and buttoned up inside his coat.

As they rode along, Goober shared his experiences in Charlotte with Will, telling Roamer again how kind Will had been to him. He cried when he recalled the night they walked back from their evening at the theatre and Will invited him to move to his house. "Ain't another man on earth would-a did that," he said.

He told Roamer about Christmas in Charlotte and the suit that Will had bought him. "I'm a-gonna dress up in 'at suit fer you an' Aunt Sweetie t' see," he promised.

Roamer nodded his approval.

He recounted his experience at Mr. Neil's party and how Neil had asked his advice about the sheep. "Hit was all 'cause Will had took me in," he declared.

"Don't need no sheeps up here," Roamer affirmed.

As they approached East Road, Goober's banter ceased. He looked to his right down the road as they passed and recalled the legend of Daniel Boone

Stories had it that Daniel Boone was introduced to what would later become Avery Cove by a friend with whom he served in the Revolutionary War. After the war—as the story goes—the two men, along with some friendly Indians, came to the cove to hunt. They established a camp on the river and built the foundation for their living quarters from rocks they gathered there.

Down East Road by the river there were the remnants of the very spot where Daniel Boone had camped. It was a favorite gathering place for the boys when Goober was in school, and they would run down the road to play there at recess time.

Ever since the valley was settled, Daniel Boone had been the hero of the local boys. As the boys grew up and had boys of their own, the story was passed along and the legend remained.

When Goober finished his eight years of school, he left the stories and the camp site to the boys who would follow him, but unbeknownst to him, things were about to change. Avery Cove was going to have a new hero.

All was quiet at Doc French's house. Goober stood on the front porch, hesitated, and then knocked gently at the door. There was no answer, so he knocked again.

When the door finally opened, he was greeted by Rachel Burden. "Oh … hello, Goober … hello, Mr. Robinson," she said. "I … wasn't expecting anyone this early. Please … please come in."

Goober removed his hat and twisted it into a knot as he walked into the parlor with Roamer following. The only light to show the way was the one coming through the door to the back bedroom where Will was.

Goober looked around at the parlor, which seemed so different in the soft light. "I was jest a-wonderin', Rachel," Goober said haltingly, "how is Will a-doin'… I mean, is 'e …"

"He's just the same," Rachel said. "He slept through the night, but he has a high fever. Doctor French, Mother, and I have been with him, keeping him cooled with cold compresses … and praying … lots of praying."

Roamer tip toed to the door where Will was sleeping and peeked in while Rachel opened the curtains on the front windows. She turned and for the first time that Goober could remember, she looked directly at him. "How is your hand, Goober?" she asked.

"Hit's been a-hurtin' like crazy, but hit'll be awright, I guess. … I was hopin' t' see Doc."

"He's sleeping right now," she said, "but maybe I can help you. Are you hurting anywhere else?"

Goober twisted his upper body around as if to ease his pain. "Well, I'm sorter stove-up in m' back and shoulders frum all 'at thrashin' about," he answered. "I figgered Doc could gi' me some pills er liniment er somethin' 'at wouldn't snurl me up lack 'at ol' lordymun did."

Rachel took on a look of femininity that Goober had never seen in her. She fairly glowed as she tried to think of a way to help him. "Doctor French has some ointment that might help, Goober. Would you like me to rub some on your back and shoulders?"

Roamer's head jerked around at the sound of that, and he eased back toward the parlor and sat down in an overstuffed chair.

By this time, Goober's hat was twisted into an almost impossible knot, and his ears were as red as fire. "If hit's all th' same to ye ... Rachel ... I'm kinder worried 'bout Will," he sputtered. "Kin I jest look in on 'im fer now?"

"Sure, Goober, whatever you want," she said.

Goober followed Rachel into the dimly lit room where Will lay sleeping. He was greeted by Rachel's mother, who was wringing water out of a piece of white linen. "Come in, Mr. Green," she said softly. "Will needs to wake up. It would be good for you to be here when he does."

Goober circled around the bed, watching Will as he lay motionless. The covers were pulled up to his upper chest. He had a pillow beneath his shoulders, and his head lay flat on the bed exposing the opening in his throat. His arms and hands were heavily bandaged with only the tips of his fingers visible.

"Doctor French wants Will to wake and sit up for a spell so that he won't develop pneumonia," Naomi said. "Why don't you talk to him and see if he'll respond? I'm sure he'll come around for the man who saved his life."

It wasn't until that instant that Goober considered the fact that he had indeed saved Will's life. He had thought about having killed a bear, and having saved himself from being seriously hurt, but he really wasn't prepared to assume the mantle of life-saver.

He decided that he would have to ponder in private how he would handle all of this, but right now, there were more important things to think about.

"Will," he said softly, his voice trembling, "'is here's Goober a-talkin' to ye. Kin ye hear me, Will?" He paused and listened to the whooshing sound coming from Will's throat.

"Kin ye hear me, Will?" he said again, this time a little more firmly. "Ye need t' wake up now an' git t' stirrin'. We got a lot o' stuff we need t' do, Will. ... Ye know, we got t' git some seed in th' groun', an' they's animals 'at need tendin' to. ... Ye ain't gonna lit ye ol' buddy down, now are ye?"

Will's eyelids fluttered and his fingers moved. Naomi came and stood by Goober, and she put her arm around his shoulder.

"Open 'em eyes, Will," Goober said, even more forcefully this time. "We got far wood t' cut, an' pigs t' hunt an' sech … got t' git some boards back on th' barn."

Will's breathing came quicker and stronger, and he opened his eyes and blinked. Finally, his gaze settled on Goober and his lips moved.

When he found that he couldn't speak he became agitated. Goober could see fear in his eyes.

"Rachel, go get the doctor," Naomi said. Rachel hurried out of the room.

"'At's awright now, Will," Goober said. "'At ol' bar made a hole in ye goozel an' ye can't tawk rat now… so I'll do ye tawkin' fer ye. Is 'at awright?"

Will's stare remained on Goober's face, and his head nodded slightly to the affirmative.

Doc French entered the room wiping sleep from his eyes. He moved to Will's side and bent over the bed, examining his face and throat. "Decided to wake up, eh?" he said. He held his hand on Will's head and examined the wound in his throat. "You're looking a whole lot better. … Been gettin' some excellent nursing care, I hope you know. … Soon as we get that fever down, we're gonna have a barn dance," he quipped.

A week smile crossed Will's face, and his eyes darted around the room before closing in sleep again.

"Goober, let's go out and sit in the parlor," Doc said. "I want to talk about Will, and see about you, too."

After they seated themselves near Roamer, Goober began the conversation. "Is Will gonna be awright, Doc?" he asked.

Doc crossed his legs and breathed out a deep breath. "Waking up just now was a good first step," he said. "He's young … strong … and he seems motivated. I think his chances for a full recovery are very good. Now," he continued, "let's talk about you. How's the hand?"

"Hit still hurts, but I can stan' at better'n 'at lordymun ye' gi' me. 'At stuff gi' me th' heeby-jeebees somethin' *awful!* I wuz a-seein' bars, an' spooks, an' woofs t' beat all!"

Doc got up and went to his cabinet and got out a box. "I have some powder from Germany called aspirin that Felix Noren, a doctor in Burley, sent me," and he measured some into an envelope. "It's made from willow bark. Take a quarter teaspoon every four hours and see if that works. I guarantee it won't cause hallucinations."

"'At's good," said Goober.

"I noticed you're a little bruised up too," Doc said. "It'll also help with any muscle pain you might have."

Doc gave Goober the envelope and sat down beside him again. "Now," he said, "I want to talk to you about something else."

"Have I did somethin' wrong?" Goober asked.

Doc laughed. "Not at all … quite the opposite. Let me ask you, have you seen anyone other than Naomi, Rachel, and me since all this happened?"

Goober looked perplexed. "No, sir. I've mos'ly slep'."

"Well, Goober," he said as he leaned forward, "I've got news for you. Word has traveled like wild fire all over the valley about what you did. No one … *no* one has ever heard of a man killing a bear with his bare hands. People are comparing you to Davey Crockett and Daniel Boone Why," he said excitedly, "Ansel Falwell is even comparing you to King David in the Bible!"

Goober's eyes were as large as dinner plates. "Lord he'p! I hope to my never!" he said. "I didn't mean t' git nothin' lack 'at started. All I wuz doin' wuz tryin' t' he'p Will!"

Doc sat back in his chair and clasped his hands behind his head. "I know," he said chuckling. "That's what makes it so special."

Goober stood and untwisted his hat. His face was pale and had the look of disbelief. "Doc," he said, "kin ye do somethin' fer me?"

"Sure, Goober. Anything for you."

Goober reached in his coat pocket and pulled out his letter to Judy Ruth along with two pennies. "Could ye mail 'is letter fer me when ye go t' th' store?" he asked as he handed the letter and coins to Doc. "An' could ye see if they's a letter fer me?"

The doctor flashed a warm and compassionate smile. "Sure, Goober. Anything for you."

G oober had been a special lad growing up. He was much smaller than the other boys his age, and he was quiet and shy. Usually, he was shunned by his peers.

After news got out about him not wanting to kill animals, things got worse. He was teased and taunted by the other children and even some adults. Those who didn't openly taunt him ignored him as if they were afraid his peculiarities would rub off on them.

To compensate for his shortcomings, he adopted the mannerism of walking about with his chest poked out. Not understanding that he was being singled even more for that quirk, it soon became a habit.

The love of his parents and of his aunt and uncle brought protection. They would shelter him from unfriendly adults and children as much as possible, and though it wasn't their intention, he withdrew even further.

His day of redemption came when he left Avery Cove and made a fresh start. Free of his past, he pulled himself up and started a new life, but now, attention was coming to him again. He would shun it, for he feared notoriety of any kind from the people who had once harassed him!

Knowing the lifelong problem, and at Goober's insistence, Roamer turned to the right as they left Doc's yard and started up South Road. "I ain't ready t' go by th' store yet," Goober had told him.

They rumbled along without a soul in sight just as Goober had planned, until they reached Perry Maynard's farm. Perry was in the yard feeding his chickens when he heard the wagon coming up the road. He stopped and stared at the figures sitting on the wagon seat until he recognized Goober.

Perry set his feed bucket on the ground and took off in a trot toward the road. "*Goober! Goober!*" he hollered. "*I want t' tawk to ye, Goober!*"

Roamer pulled back on the reins and brought the wagon to a halt as Perry approached.

"Goober! I want t' tawk to ye," Perry said breathlessly. "I heared what ye done ... killin' 'at bar an' all." He paused for a moment to catch his breath. "Why don't you an' Roamer come up t' th' house, an' th' wife'll fix up some coffee ... warm ye up, don't ye know."

"I'm rat grateful, Mr. Maynard," Goober replied, "but ye see, we best git on along 'is time. We got chores t' do an' all. Maybe next time we're by …"

"Well, let me jest axt ye this," Perry said. "Whut's hit lack fer a man t' kill a wild bar with jest 'is bar hands? I wuz jest a-wonderin'."

Goober looked out across Perry's field before he answered. "I ain't settled on 'at yet, Mr. Maynard," he replied. "Don't know if I ever will neither."

Goober nudged his Uncle Roamer, and the old man released the wagon brake and clicked the mule onward.

Perry trotted alongside the wagon for several feet, waving as he ran. "Now Goober, you come on back any time ye kin. I want ye t' tell me 'bout that bar."

The sun was up above the mountain now, following Goober and his uncle up the road. They passed houses on the left and barns on the right, bumping along South Road. To Goober's relief, no other farmers were in their yards or fields.

Eventually they came to East Road. Instead of continuing up the loop to Goober's house, they answered the call of their stomachs and took the short cut out East Road toward Roamer's house. They knew a late breakfast would be waiting.

As they approached the school, the laughter of the boys and girls could be heard on the playground. To Goober's dismay, one of the children saw him seated on the wagon and sent up an alarm. "*Look*," the boy hollered, "*hit's Goober Green, th' bar killer!*"

The laughter ceased, and all heads turned in Goober's direction. Like a flock of birds, they broke and moved as one body toward the road, calling his name and pleading for attention.

"Lord have mercy, Uncle Roamer," he called out, "please don't stop! I ain't ready fer all 'is mess."

Roamer clicked his tongue and snapped the reins on the mule's rump. The mule responded by picking up the pace to a fast walk.

Instantly, the children surrounded the wagon, calling out Goober's name and asking a hundred different questions at once as they ran along.

Goober raised his good hand, waved, and gave a faint smile, but he had no word of greeting for them. His indifference only added to his mystique!

The children would have probably followed along for miles had it not been for the ringing of the school bell. They answered the call to learning, and Goober was free once more.

———

Roamer's wagon pulled out of his yard and turned right toward Goober's house. With their stomachs satisfied by another of Sweetie's fry-ups, they were ready to tackle the job of finding Dawg.

"Ye've been awful quiet," Roamer said when they had straightened out on the road. "Are ye cogitatin' on somethin'?"

"Tell ye th' truth, Uncle Roamer, I ain't lookin' forward t' goin' by Demus Whitedeer's house. Las' time I seen 'im, Will had a gun pointed in 'is face."

"Well, ye can rest easy," Roamer said. "I got m' pop gun in m' boot, an' if 'e messes with us, I'll clean 'is plow!"

"Well 'at makes me feel jest a whole lot more better!" Goober shot back.

As they neared Demus's farm, they could see no sign of activity. The plowing had been finished, the barn door was closed, and there was no sign of Demus.

With that worry behind him for now, Goober picked up on his banter. He told Roamer more about Judy Ruth and how he planned to ask her to marry him. "Wouldn't 'at be a hoot up th' holler," Roamer said.

Roamer had things to discuss too. He told Goober that it was almost time to get his "terbackie" plants out of the house and into the cold frames. About three weeks there and they'd be ready to go to the field, he reasoned. "My chawin' terbackie is makin' almos' as much money as m' other," he told Goober. He told Goober too—with some concern—that he might have to quit making spirits and turn to tobacco farming full time. "I'm a-gettin' too old t' tote corn an' empty jars up th' mountain an' tote full jars back down," he said.

"Why, you'd put th' revenuers outta business," Goober declared.

As they neared Goober's farm, the conversation returned to the confrontation at Demus Whitedeer's farm. "I'm worried 'bout whut Demus might do in the middle o' th' night," Goober said. "You know how crazy he is, Uncle Roamer. He's jest as likely as not t' sneak up on ye while ye sleepin' an' cut ye throat frum ear ..."

Goober paused and stood up on the footboard of the wagon. "I hope to my never!" he declared.

"Whut?" Roamer wanted to know.

Goober pointed toward his garden plot. "My rails is back," he exclaimed.

Sure enough, the fence around his garden was standing exactly where it had been before, and there was another surprise. The garden had been plowed, and the plow was sitting beside the gate.

Roamer stopped the wagon and looked around. Not a soul was in sight —not a sign of life around except for Dawg who was sitting by the road in front of the house.

When they got closer, Dawg's tail went to work, stirring up the dust. His master may have been gone, but he hadn't forgotten his manners. He wasn't about to leave the yard.

Nineteen

CALL ME "MAKEPEACE"

Goober awoke early Thursday morning with a burning pain in his hand. It was the kind of throbbing agony he experienced when his hand was first broken. He got out of bed, and as he was pulling on his pants, Roamer's clock chimed 4:00 o'clock.

"Is 'at you, a-stirrin', Goober?" Sweetie called from her bed.

Goober struggled to button his trousers. "Hit's me," Goober replied.

"Are ye awright?"

"My hand's a-hurtin' real bad, Aunt Sweetie, I'm goin' in t' see Doc."

He slipped his feet into his shoes and eased out the back door toward the outhouse. When he returned, Sweetie was shuffling around the kitchen, getting some breakfast together. "Ye got any more o' them powders th' doc give ye," she asked.

"Them powders is gone," Goober said. "I need somethin' stronger 'n 'at anyhow."

"Got jest th' number," Roamer declared as he entered the kitchen dressed in his night shirt. He walked to the kitchen cabinet, reached up on the top shelf, and brought down his quart jar of dark amber liquid. "I'll put a mite o' this in ye coffee," he said. "Hit'll fix ye up!"

Roamer's "mite" was about half a cup. The half cup of coffee Sweetie added was enough to warm it and make it go down smoothly.

Little by little, the pain was reduced to a dull ache.

When breakfast had been eaten and the morning chores had been done, Goober and Roamer hitched up the wagon and pulled themselves aboard for the trip to Doc's.

"'Is headin' out 'fore daylight's gettin' t' be a burden," Roamer said as he clicked the mule into motion. "Course I'm full willin' t' do whatever's needed t' he'p ye out ... you bein' my nephew ... an' th' new Dan'l Boone an' all."

"Now you ain't gonna start up with 'at mess are ye, Uncle Roamer?" Goober asked impatiently.

Roamer spat a stream of tobacco juice into the darkness and wiped his mouth on his sleeve. "Wal, I reckon ye ort t' know," he answered, "'at's all 'ey tawked about at prayer meetin' las' night. Preacher Babb couldn't hardly git a word in edgewise."

"I hope to my *never*," Goober exclaimed, and he gave Roamer a hard stare. "You didn't egg 'em on, did ye, Uncle Roamer?"

"Naw, I didn't egg 'em on. I tol' 'em you didn't want no big t' do over killin' 'at bar ... an' I tol' 'em ye shore wouldn't want 'em changin' th' name o' th' valley t' Green Cove. ... 'At's *right*, ain't it?"

Goober grabbed the reins from Roamer and pulled the mule to a stop. He stood up on the foot board, and his small frame hovered over Roamer.

"Are you a-tellin' me that some fool wants t' call 'is place 'Green Cove'?"

"They's a bunch o' folks wants t' call it that," Roamer replied, and he sent another stream of tobacco juice into the shadows.

"Wal, jest wait 'til ye hear whut I tell 'em 'bout *that*," Goober snarled as he flopped down on the wagon seat.

Roamer jerked the reins back out of Goober's hand and took his turn standing on the foot board. This time it was he towering over his nephew who was sitting with his knees pulled up against his chest.

"*Now you look 'ere, boy*," Roamer said—his voice booming into the darkness. "*Ye growed up w' people a-makin' fun of ye! Ye went off an' made good, an' when ye come back, they was some folks noticed ye come back a man an' ye turned ye back on 'em! Then, ye done whut nobody's never done b'fore—chokin' 'at bar t' death—an' ye won't even let em pat ye on th' back fer it!*"

The mule pawed the ground impatiently, not knowing at whom the tirade was directed. Roamer was in an uncharacteristic rage as he released his frustrations.

"*If yore s' fixed on turnin' folks agin' ye, I think ye ort t' jest pack up and git out o' here...git out! Go on back whur folks don't know ye.*" Roamer paused to catch his breath before he delivered his most stinging remark. "*I'm ashamed of ye, boy!*"

In the distance, a dog took up where Roamer had left off, piercing the silence with angry barking.

Roamer clicked, and the wagon lurched and rolled away.

D oc French came to answer the knock on his door with a bounce in his step. "Goober, Roamer, I'm glad you're here," he said as he motioned them in. "You're gonna love what I have to tell you!"

Doc motioned for his guests to be seated as he pulled up the chair from his desk. When all were seated, he gave the glad news: "Will's fever broke during the night. I think I can safely say that he'll be all right!"

"Glory be an' hallelujah!" Roamer exclaimed.

Goober sat up in his chair and craned his neck toward the back room. "Kin 'e tawk yet?" he asked.

"No, he still has the hole in his throat," Doc said, "but if the fever stays down until tomorrow, I'll close that up and he'll be able to speak … softly at first … but he'll soon be back to normal.

"In the meantime," Doc continued, "I've given him a slate and some chalk. He's been writing like crazy … wanting to know what happened, and asking about you, Goober."

As Doc was finishing his statement, a loud banging sound came from the back room.

"Our patient is calling," Doc said as he rose and pushed his chair back. "Come on back, and we'll see what he wants."

Goober entered the room to find Will propped up in bed looking alert and relieved. Naomi Burden was drying his face after having helped him shave.

Goober made his way to the foot of the bed where he stood, twisting his hat into the customary knot. "Howdy, Will," he said.

Will grabbed his slate and began writing furiously. When he turned it around for Goober to see, it read, "Howdy yourself, Goob. How's your hand?"

"Oh, hit's fine, Will, jest fine. Ever'thing's *real* fine now. Got a lot t' tell ye. 'Em fence rails is back 'round th' garden, an' th' plow's back. Guess ye was right 'bout takin' Demus on an' all ... I shore have missed ye, Will ... Worried 'bout ye, too."

Will cleaned the slate with his bandaged arm and began writing again, and as he wrote, a serious look came over his face. When he turned the slate around, it said, "Thank you, Goob. They say you saved my life."

"Oh, Will," Goober blurted out, "hit watten nothin'. You would-a did the same fer me," and he brushed a tear from his face with his sleeve.

Roamer, who had been standing in the door, moved over and put his arm around Goober's shoulder. "We real proud o' Goober here," he said. "Th' whole valley's proud of 'im."

As Goober stood before his friend, his expression took on a look of softness—a look that some would have called acceptance. Gone, at least for now, was the air of defiance that had enveloped him for years—an aspect that had intensified since the bear attack.

He flashed back to his mother's pleas for him to try to fit in. "Hit's like ye standin' on th' outside, lookin' in on ever'body," she had told him. "Sometimes, hit's like you're part of another world, and we're all strangers to ye," she had said. "Won't ye come on in an' be with them that love's ye?" she had pleaded.

Despite his brief look into reality and the feeling of relief in seeing Will on the mend, Goober had to turn back to his original intent for coming. The effect of Roamer's whiskey was wearing off and the intense pain was back.

"I'm gonna go out here an' tawk t' Doc fer a minute," he told Will. "When I finish up, I'll come back an' jaw w' ye s'more."

Doc followed Goober to the parlor and they sat down. "Is something wrong?" Doc asked.

Goober held his bandaged hand out to Doc. "'Is hand's 'bout t' kill me, Doc!" he said. "I want ye t' look at it an' see if somethin's the matter."

Doc took Goober's hand and carefully unwound the binding that held the splint in place. When the splint was off, it was plain to see that something was indeed wrong. Goober's hand was badly swollen, and there was an indentation in the area of the break.

"Can you move your fingers?" Doc asked.

"No."

"Can you move your wrist?" Doc asked as he gently tried to rotate it himself.

"I can't move it neither," Goober said, "an' I wish you'd jest leave it be."

Doc placed the hand back in Goober's lap and leaned back in his chair. "Goober, your hand looks bad … the kind of bad that I can't help. You're going to have to go to Burley and see a surgeon who'll probably have to operate on it and reset it from the inside."

"Oh Lord," Goober said, "what'll happen if I don't?"

Doc leaned forward and looked deeply into Goober's eyes. "It'll heal up and stop hurting in time," he said, "but you'll never regain the use of it. I don't think you have any choice but to go."

Goober stood and walked over to his uncle. "Whut d' ye think I ort t' do, Uncle Roamer?" he asked.

Roamer was calm in his reply. "I think ye better go home an' git ye stuff t'gether, an' git t' Burley as quick as ye can."

Goober turned back toward Doc to plead his case. "Doc," he said, his voice shaking, "I got t' meet Mr. Neil in Burley next Wednesday. My job hangs on it … an' I got t' take care o' Will, Doc. … Mr. Neil said he'd *kill* me if anything happens t' Will. … An' I gotta git crops in th' ground fer Will an' Uncle Roamer …"

"It's all right," Doc interrupted, "We'll take care of Will! I know Roamer and Sweetie will be glad to take him in 'til he heals up enough to be on his own."

Roamer shook his head vigorously. "'At's right, Goob," he said. "You ain't got t' worry 'bout Will. Me an' Sweetie'll treat 'im lack fam'ly."

"And as for the crops," Doc said, "there is a group of men in the Baptist church that does plowing for those that can't. I'll talk to Preacher Babb about that."

Then Doc walked over to his desk and found a pen and paper. "Now, while you're getting things ready to go," he said, "I'll write a letter to Dr. Noren about your condition, and I'll write another letter for Mr. Neil explaining the situation. When you get to Burley, leave Mr. Neil's letter at the place where you were supposed to meet him. I'll tell him where you'll be, and I guarantee everything will be all right by him."

Doc sat down at the desk and started making some notes. Without looking up, he asked, "Any questions?"

"Can I tawk t' Will ag'in?"

"Sure, but don't stay long," Doc replied, still writing. "He needs his rest."

Goober walked back to Will's room and circled around by the bed. "Will," he said, and he cleared his throat. "Doc says I need t' go t' Burley an' git a operation on m' hand. He says I need t' go now."

Will gave Goober a concerned look.

"Doc says him an' Uncle Roamer'll take real good care o' ye and not t' worry," Goober continued. "He says Preacher Babb'll take care o' plantin' the crops, and Uncle Roamer says ye can stay w' him an' Aunt Sweetie till ye git able t' stay on ye own … that is, if ye still want t' live here."

Will wiped his slate clean and started writing.

"I want to <u>stay</u>," he wrote. "Get the papers Preacher Burden is supposed to handle and we'll sign them <u>now</u>."

He cleaned the slate again and continued writing.

"You know where my money is. Get enough to pay Doc for me <u>and</u> <u>you</u>."

He wiped the slate again and continued.

"Get enough for the Doctor in Burley. Doc will tell you how much, and enough for the surrey repair."

He wiped the slate again as Goober watched.

"The surrey and Traveler are now <u>yours</u>, Goob. To keep. I know you'll take good care of Traveler."

"Will!" Goober said. "Why are ye a-doin' all 'is?"

"This is just a start," Will wrote. "I'll never be able to fully repay you."

Goober laid his head on Will's chest and sobbed deeply. As he cried, the sun peeped in through the bedroom window, illuminating Naomi's face. She rose from her chair in the corner and quickly left the room, wiping tears from her eyes.

———◆———

G lenn Neil sat in the office of Superintendent Massey discussing Mill business with the senior staff of Inverness Mill.

"By the way," Mr. Spann asked Neil, "have you heard anything from Parker and Green?"

"No, I don't really expect to hear anything until I see Goober in Burley next Wednesday."

"Do you have any idea if Parker will be back?" Massey asked.

"I sort of doubt it," Neil said. He absentmindedly tapped his pen on Massey's desk as he thought. "I can imagine those two out plowing the fields right now," he said. "Either that or chasing around behind some of those mountain gals. Oh well," he sighed, "I'll know for sure Wednesday, and I'll wire from Burley."

———◆———

"W al, how much do I owe ye fer fixin' th' surrey an' boardin' th' horse?" Goober asked as he stood across from Karl Badger's forge.

"Owe me!" Karl declared. "Why, Goober, ye don't owe me a cent! Not one red cent!"

"Why not?" Goober asked. "Didn't ye fix th' wheel ... an' didn't ye feed th' horse?"

"Course I did!" Karl declared. "But ye still don't owe me nothin."

"I don't understan'," Goober said a little impatiently. "When did ye start workin' fer nothin'?"

"'Is is how I got it figgered," Karl replied as his hammer fell on a horse shoe. "I fix wagons, an' you kill bars!" He stopped his hammering and looked Goober in the eye. "Now if you hadn't a-kilt 'at bar, he might-a come down th' valley an' kilt one o' my calves ... might even a-kilt *me*! So I figger we even ...'cept I might still owe ye a shoein' er somethin'."

Karl stuck the horse shoe in the fire and propped against his anvil while it re-heated. "Any more dumb questions?" he asked.

———

Preacher Burden stood in the river chasm behind Caldwell Turpin's mill, straddling a masonry sluice. Water rushed down the channel, splashing up on his legs.

"Ease 'er down, Caldwell," he shouted, "and if you drop it on me, I'll come back to haunt you."

He looked up as the power generator slowly descended, held only by a thick, manila rope.

"Any time today, Caldwell," he cried. "I'm freezing to death down here. How did I get stuck down here in the water anyway?" he demanded.

"'At's as fast as I can lower it without droppin' it, Preacher," Caldwell shouted down. "You jest be ready t' turn it and sit it on th' supports! Ye hear?"

Power was coming to Avery Cove. When the turbine generator was in place, the man would come up from Burley to hook it up and begin running the wires that would bring light to the valley.

Preacher Burden had already planned a ceremony to be held at the store with everyone in Avery Cove in attendance. He would stand on the porch of the store with his hand lifted to a string that would switch on the first glimmer of electric lighting that some of the folks had ever seen. At the moment he pulled the string, he would quote from the first chapter of the Bible. "*Let ... there ... be ... light!*" he would declare ... and everyone would be in awe!

———

Tommy Lee Jones looked in both directions as he crept out of the carding room into the spinning room.

Judy Ruth Roach was perched on a step ladder, removing bobbins from the top-most rack of a spinning machine as Tommy Lee tiptoed up behind her.

When he was sure that no one was looking, Tommy Lee reached up and grabbed Judy Ruth by her waist, pulling her down into his arms.

Judy Ruth gave out a little squeal and giggled with delight. "You stop that, Tommy Lee," she said. "You're gonna get me in trouble."

"Ain't nobody lookin'," Tommy Lee replied. "I didn't do nothin but grab you a little, anyway. I just come over to ask if you wrote that letter to Goober Green yet."

Judy Ruth looked down and the smile left her face. "I don't know what to tell him," she said.

"Just tell him you can't be his girl no more."

"It'll purely break his heart," she replied.

Tommy Lee threw his arms in the air and grinned his big grin. "Aw, he'll get over it real quick," he said.

———

Will woke from a short nap to find a man standing at the foot of his bed. He was slightly startled by the stranger with the big smile, and he began to feel around for something to bang on.

"Mornin', young feller," the man said. "I'm Brother Billy Babb ... th' preacher up at th' Baptist church ... th' one where yer friend Goober's a member." He lay his hat on the foot of the bed and circled around by Will's side. "I just came by to see you," he said, "to make sure you know that we're a-prayin' for you."

Will nodded and pushed himself up slightly on his elbows. A blank expression came over his face.

"And how 'bout Brother *Goober*," the preacher raved, "killin' a bear with his bare hands! I ain't never heard of such a thing! Have you?"

Brother Babb stood above Will with his teeth shining through his wide smile. Will pulled himself a little further up on his elbows and shook his head from side to side.

With the pleasantries taken care of, Brother Babb shut off his smile and got down to business. "Now," he declared, "Brother Doc tells me that you're gonna need some plowin' done!"

Will nodded to the affirmative and continued his blank look.

"Well I'm here t' help," the preacher announced. "We've got a group o' men in our church that calls themselves 'The Plowsharers'." Brother Billy bent over Will and lowered his voice. "That's a mighty catchy name, ain't it?" and he came to the upright position and gave Will a wink.

Will nodded to the affirmative again, and the blank look intensified.

"Those boys have got six fields and six gardens t' plow next week," he continued, "but they can bust yours and Roamer's out 'fore you can turn over in bed!" The smile was back. "And if you'll buy the seed, they'll put them in the ground, too."

By that time Preacher Babb was fairly bursting with pride! Will felt an instant since of relief, and he settled back on his pillow and put on a smile of his own.

"Tell you somethin' else too," the preacher continued. "We got a bunch of younguns in the church called 'Brother Billy Babb's Baptist Bible Buddies'!" He leaned over Will and lowered his voice again. "Bet ya can't say that three times real quick!" Then he winked and straightened back up.

The blank look came back to Will's face, and as the room got silent, the whooshing sound from his throat could be heard.

"Guess not, huh?" the preacher uttered. "Well anyway, those little clod kickers'll go through yer field and pick up rocks and sticks and so forth, and tote water for the Plowsharers ... just another part of th' service, don't you know!"

Just then, Preacher Burden came bounding into the room, and a look of relief came over Will's face. "*Preacher Babb!*" Preacher Burden called out. "I've been wonderin' when you'd get by t' see this boy."

"Well, here I am, Brother Eli," the Baptist preacher answered. "I was just tellin' Brother Will here that we're gonna take care o' his plowin' and plantin' ... put his mind at ease, don't you know."

"Long as you're not here t' sheep-steal," Preacher Burden said. "You know, we've already claimed him for our flock!"

Preacher Babb took on a mock look of surprise. "Brother Eli," he exclaimed, "you know us Baptist don't sheep-steal! Why, the way our church women cook, folks just smell our Sunday dinner on the grounds, and come a-runnin'! Ever'body knows we got the best cooks in Avery Cove ... 'cept of course fer your lovely wife and that sweet daughter."

Then Preacher Babb got a faraway look in his eye and added, "That Rachel makes the best peach cobbler I ever put in my mouth."

"*You got that right,*" Preacher Burden sang out, and both preachers broke out in laughter.

———

Goober and Roamer had gone directly to Goober's house and gotten the money, the papers for the land transaction, and Goober's clothes and personal effects. While they were there, they had checked around and found that everything was in order. Finally, they had fed the horses and closed up the barn.

As they had pulled away, Goober looked back at the farm and bid it farewell. He figured it would be a long time before he would see it again.

He knew in his heart that leaving was the right thing to do. He had a job, respect, and a house in Charlotte, but more than that, he had a girl waiting. The future was bright!

Now they were back at Roamer's house, and he realized that the day was half spent. There wasn't enough time left for him to make Burley that day.

"I 'spect ye better jest make ye self t' home an' light out early in th' mornin'," Roamer told him, "'specially with 'at busted hand. Hit's gonna be hard 'nough a-drivin' 'at rig o' yourn in th' daylight, much less at night!"

Goober parked the surrey in the shed and made a place for Traveler in the stable. He fed the horse and curried him down, talking to him all the while.

Then just before Goober left him to go inside, Traveler turned and gave him a knowing look. It was as if he had figured out that Goober was his new master—and he approved.

Goober entered the house and sat down at the kitchen table. Armed with his tablet and pencil, he began composing a letter to Judy Ruth.

Dear Judy Ruth
    This is Goober writing to you. Doc French has tol me

There was a knock on the door—a very small knock. At first Goober thought it was the wind, or a mouse, or some other small creature, but then he heard it again. He pushed his chair back and made his way through the parlor. When he opened the door, he came face to face with Rachel Burden.

The shock of seeing her was almost too much for Goober. For a moment he stood motionless and speechless, shocked that she would come to see him. Even more shocking was the fact that her father would let her come to the home of a moonshiner.

"Hello, Goober," she finally said. "Can I come in?"

"Wal ... shore," he blurted out. "You kin come in."

Rachel entered the parlor, looking around as she came, and as she brushed by, Goober detected the fragrance of store-bought soap. He motioned toward the sofa, and Rachel sad down.

"Doctor French wanted me to make sure you were all right," she said. "He was concerned that he hadn't given you the full instructions for the morphine he gave you."

"He jest said t' take a pill ever' four hours if I need it," Goober said.

"I know," Rachel replied, "but he wanted to make sure you knew that you shouldn't have anything with … alcohol in it while you were taking it."

"You mean like Uncle Roamer's tonic?"

"Exactly," she said.

"Wal, I jest want ye t' know I don't tetch 'at stuff 'less I need it fer medicine," Goober declared. "'At's th' only reason Uncle Roamer makes it anyhow, ye know."

Rachel nodded gently. "I understand, Goober," she replied. "My daddy gave me some mixed with honey for croup when I was just a little girl."

"Your daddy gave you whiskey … I mean tonic?"

"Do you need anything else?" Rachel asked.

"No," Goober said thoughtfully, "but it's mighty nice of ye t' come … I mean, me bein' a Babdist an' all."

"When are you leaving?" Rachel asked.

"First light."

"Are you ever coming back?"

Goober stood and walked to the front window. He didn't like what he was feeling. It frightened him.

"I'm sorta puzzled 'bout that rat now," Goober said. "Ye see, I got a girl in Charlotte. Her name's Judy Ruth Roach … an' I reccon I'll be gettin' married. … Whut I mean is, I ain't really axt 'er yet, but I reccon I will."

Goober turned back and Rachel was looking up at him with sparkling eyes—eyes that sparkled with tears, not joy.

"I'm glad that you're okay, Goober … and happy," Rachel said, "and I'm sorry it took me until now to get to know you."

She stood and walked to the door, and as she brushed by, Goober once more breathed in her fragrance.

The morphine brought sleep and dreams, but no nightmares. The dreams were of Christmas and toys, blueberry cobbler, Daniel Boone's campsite, and his father—pleasant memories that had been filed in the back of his mind.

And in his dreams he flew, not as Will had flown on the back of a bird, but as a bird himself.

He would race along close to the earth, traveling at breathtaking speed. Then he would turn and climb upward toward the clouds, passing hawks and killdeer, swooping and rolling far above the ground.

It was while he was cavorting with a hawk that Sweetie bent over his bed and softly said, "Goober Honey, hit's time t' wake up."

He teetered on the edge of reality as he slowly became aware of his surroundings.

"Goober," she said again, "hit pains me t' wake ye, but ye got t' git up an' start fer Burley. I got ye some eggs an' grits cooked up."

He awoke enough then to smell a mixture of bacon, coffee, and wood smoke from Sweetie's kitchen stove—smells that had greeted his mornings in the valley his entire life.

It was a bittersweet time. It was bitter because of its finality—the last of Sweetie's meals for what could be a long time. It was bitter because of the uncertainty of what lay ahead with the doctor in Burley. But it was sweet in that leaving was a first step back to Charlotte.

"Said I watten gonna bawl," Roamer declared when it was finally time for Goober to leave, "but I jest can't hep it." Tears ran down his face and spotted the front of his clean overalls.

Sweetie was the stoic one. She held Goober at arm's length where she could focus on him, and she brushed a strand of horse hair from his collar.

"You write us a letter, now, boy," she said. "We'll git Preacher Babb or Preacher Burden to read it fer us. Ain't even no need t' put no money in it!"

And so, he was off.

———◆———

By the time Goober passed Karl Badger's house, the sun was shining behind the mountain. Its indirect glow highlighted Karl's silhouette as he headed for his shop.

Preacher Burden was also on the move. As Goober neared his house, the preacher was leaving his yard, walking toward the store.

"You came along at just the right time," he hollered as Goober pulled up beside him. "Understand you need some papers signed."

Goober nodded, and the preacher pulled himself up on the surrey. The surrey leaned heavily toward the preacher's side and relaxed in the tilted position.

"Preacher, have I got any mail at th' store?" Goober asked.

"No," the preacher replied. "But I'll tell you what, if you get any, I'll make sure it's sent to you in Burley."

Goober was concerned about not getting any mail from Judy Ruth, but he was thankful that Preacher Burden would look after his interests. "I shore am thankful to ye, Preacher," he said.

"I've asked Doc and Caldwell Turpin to witness the land transaction," the preacher told Goober. "Hope you don't mind."

Goober shrugged.

"Head on over to Doc's," the preacher added. "Caldwell's gonna meet us there."

Goober would have rather not had Caldwell Turpin involved, but he was willing to proceed without protest. Anything that would speed the process along and get him on the way to Burley would have to do.

Caldwell and Doc were waiting in Doc's parlor when the preacher and Goober arrived. Through the front window they could be seen seated facing each other, engaged in conversation. The preacher opened the door without knocking and entered with Goober following.

"Wal, here's th' bar-slayer now!" Caldwell chimed.

"Mornin', Mr. Turpin," Goober replied softly.

"Well, let's get down to business," Preacher Burden said as he took charge. "I assume Will's awake and alert."

"He's awake and chompin' at the bits," Doc said. "Let's go on back."

Will was propped up on the bed, freshly bathed and shaved. He had a look of uneasiness on his face, but when he saw Goober, it was replaced with a smile.

"How ye been keepin', Will," Goober asked.

Will scribbled on his slate and turned it toward the group. "Great! How is your hand?"

"Hit's gettin' better an' better," Goober replied. "Doc gimmie some medicine 'at's real good, an' he tells me 'at doctor in Burley'll fix me up quick as a bunny."

"Give me the papers!" The preacher said as he stepped forward. His voice sounded anxious. "Goober's got t' git on th' road."

He looked over the transfers of title and the accompanying requests for deeds. When he was through, he shuffled through them again.

"Now," he said to Will, "I want you to sign here and here," and he pointed to two blanks on separate pages.

When Will had signed, he moved to Goober. "Goober, you sign here and here." He watched intently as Goober signed where his name had been printed.

"Now, Doc, you sign here as a witness, and Caldwell, you sign on this line."

Doc signed and the papers were passed to Caldwell, who wrote his name in the assigned place.

"Wal look here!" Caldwell declared as he looked over the papers. "Hit says 'Makepeace Green' here. I thought your name wuz Goober, *boy*."

Silence filled the room as Doc, Will, and Preacher Burden held their breath. They all knew the gravity of Goober's state and sensed that he could explode just as he did when he jumped on the back of the bear.

Will especially felt for his friend and wished he could get out of bed and throttle Caldwell with his bare hands, bringing some degree of relief to Goober.

All eyes turned in Goober's direction as he lifted his head and slightly extended his chest. He took a slow, deep breath.

"Mr. Turpin," he said calmly, "my name *is* Makepeace Green an' fum now on, 'at's whut I want ye t' call me. Matter o' fact," he said, "'at's whut I want ever'body t' call me. Ye can joke 'bout me killin' bars an' th' lack, but I don't want ye jokin' 'bout m' name cause 'at's 'bout th' only thing I got lef' that my mama give me."

"Uh … okay … Makepeace," Caldwell said, "if 'at's whut ye want."

A loud whooshing sound came from Will's throat as he tried to shout. He clinched his fists and pumped them in the air in celebration of Goober's statement. He then raised his slate and wrote feverishly. When he turned it for his friend to see, it read, "Can I call you Make?"

Makepeace's grin reminded Will of the one that "Goober" had flashed when he invited him to live in his house in Charlotte. And it reminded him, too, of the one he wore as he recounted their night on the town.

Then for the first time since he arrived at Doc's, Will swung his feet over the side of the bed and stood. He walked to Makepeace and hugged him goodbye.

Makepeace Green stood on the porch of Doc's house and breathed in the crisp, mountain air. He felt that he had walked out into a new world—one where all was right, and calmness and reason prevailed.

The anger and resentment were gone—replaced with quiet acceptance.

There was a peace in his heart for Roamer and Sweetie. With Will and Preacher Babb to look out for them, they would be okay.

He was satisfied that his friend would heal. Will had demonstrated his recovery by standing and walking, and his hug had shown that strength was returning to his body.

As for himself, he had been reassured by Doc that his hand would mend. Doc had told him that his surgery would be easy and his recovery swift. Now he could continue with his life.

As he stood on the porch, he noticed, for the first time that spring, the song of the birds. They were singing their anthems of morning as if their hearts could fairly burst with joy. From every direction the music came—building in a jubilant chorus—and as he listened, a mockingbird sang, "Make-peace, Make-peace, Make-peace."

Twenty

Makepeace Has Surgery

"Can you breathe all right?" Doc asked as Will drifted back into consciousness.

Will nodded his head yes.

"Can you say anything?"

Will shook his head no.

"How do you know if you haven't tried?" Doc asked.

Will gave Doc an unpleasant look. He was waking up after having a mild dose of chloroform so that Doc could sew up the hole in his throat, and he was too groggy to perform tricks.

As the fog lifted and he began to sense his circumstances, Will realized that for the first time in days, he was breathing through his nose and mouth. It's funny, he thought, how we take things like that for granted. Breathing through a hole in one's throat may get the job done, but there's just something about breathing through one's nose that is so much more satisfying!

"Doc," he said softly without thinking.

Doc turned from the table where he was cleaning his instruments and gave Will a smile. "That's more like it," he said. "Got a question?"

"When can I go home?"

"Couple of days, if you keep improving."

226

A couple of days sounded like a lot to Will. He wanted to walk in the fresh air. He wanted to reach down and feel the dirt and pet his dog. By George, he wanted to plow!

Doc lifted the last of his instruments from the tray of disinfectant and wrapped it with the others in clean linen. He turned as he dried his hands and looked down at his handiwork on Will's throat. "I should have been a tailor," he said. "I sew a pretty mean stitch."

When his hands were dry he rolled down his sleeves and buttoned them at his wrists. "Tailors don't have to get up in the middle of the night and deliver babies either," he concluded.

"Speaking of babies," he said, "I've got to go up and see Sue Levee … she's expecting any day. I asked the preacher to have Rachel come over and sit with you while I'm gone. Maybe you can use that new-found voice of yours, and the two of you can get to know each other."

"She doesn't seem like much of a conversationalist," Will murmured.

"Aw, she's just shy," Doc said, "and with you being a stranger and all, she probably just can't find much to say. By the way, you want to use the chamber pot before she comes?"

"Not a bad idea," Will muttered.

Will woke from a light sleep as Doc's front door closed with a thud. "Go on in, Rachel," he heard Doc say. "He's been asleep but he'll probably wake up a little from time to time."

"Does he get medicine or water or anything while you're gone?" Rachel asked.

"One of those little white pills by the bed in about two hours if I'm not back," Doc answered, "and all the water he wants."

Before she entered Will's room, Rachel peeked around the corner to make sure he was prepared for visitors. Will was lying in bed, propped up on pillows with his eyes focused on the door.

"Good morning, Will," she said. "Can I come in?"

"Sure," Will replied weakly.

Rachel was startled. "Oh! You can talk," she declared, and she entered the room and nervously began to open the window curtains.

Will was in a quandary for something to say. It was, after all, an awkward situation—a single man alone with a single woman—she, being shy—he, lying in bed.

"Looks like a pretty day," he finally murmured.

"It is ... it is."

With sunlight now streaming into the room, Will worked up the courage to start a dialog. "Look," he said softly, "I want to thank you for all you've done ... for all your whole family has done."

"It was mostly Doctor French and Mother," she replied. "I stayed home and cooked for Daddy while you were unconscious. I really wasn't around much."

There was a long pause while both Will and Rachel tried to think of some way to extend the conversation. Finally, Rachel spoke. "I've known Goober all my life," she said, "but when all this happened, I discovered that I had never really known him."

There was another awkward pause as both parties tried to find words to say. Finally Will said, "He wants to be called Makepeace now."

"What?"

"Makepeace. He wants to be called Makepeace ... his real name, you know."

"I'd forgotten that," Rachel replied. "Makepeace!"

Things came a little easier then. They had found a subject they could discuss freely.

Will told Rachel how Makepeace had come to Charlotte and, against all odds, landed a job, became a master weaver, and began working his way into city culture. He told her about their adventures and how they had become the best of friends.

When he realized that his vocalizations were down to a whisper, he turned the talking over to her.

"Who is Judy Ruth Roach?" she asked out of the blue.

"He told you about her?"

"Yes, sort of."

"She's a flighty little girl in Charlotte that he's fallen over," Will whispered. "Hope she doesn't let him down."

"You seem to think she will."

"Just a feeling that keeps eating at me," Will muttered, and he drifted off to sleep again.

———

Dr. Felix Noren was a German immigrant, who, at twelve years of age came to America with his parents. He eventually graduated from the University of Michigan Medical School and, after two years of private practice, returned to the medical school for further study in surgery.

He was a talented physician and surgeon who could have found a position at most any hospital in any major city, but he came to Burley to be in mountains like those he left behind in Germany. He, like thousands of other immigrants, chose his settling point by the strength of his memory—the memory of home.

In spite of his remote location, Dr. Noren attracted patients from all over western North Carolina and eastern Tennessee. Makepeace, like all his other patients, was lucky to have him there.

Makepeace arrived in Burley on Friday afternoon after his long, hard trip across the mountains. He had found it necessary to stop several times during the trip to rest and wash his face in cold water. When he rolled into Burley, he was exhausted.

His first stop was the Burley Lodge, where he left Doc's letter to Glenn Neil. Then, he went to the livery stable, where Traveler found a clean, warm stall and he parked the surrey under a shed. The livery keeper directed him to Dr. Noren's house, and with a few possessions tossed over his shoulder, he finally stood at Dr. Noren's front door at the stroke of six o'clock.

After a knock and a short wait, Makepeace was greeted at the door by Dr. Noren's wife, a gentle lady who reminded him of Naomi Burden. She cheerfully seated him in the front room, and after having heard his reason for coming, she disappeared into the rear of the house.

Moments later, Dr. Noren appeared and walked directly to Makepeace with his hand extended. "Velcome to my home and clinic," he said with a slight German accent. "I am Doctor Noren. How can I help?"

Makepeace introduced himself to the doctor and gave him Doc French's letter. Noren sat down at a desk, switched on an electric lamp, and began reading it.

"Ah! Dr. French," he said as he read. "A goot man!"

As the message of the letter unfolded, the doctor reacted with amazement. "My *gootness!*" or "I haf *nefer!*" he would say with eye brows raised.

Finally, the doctor's arms went limp with feigned exhaustion and a page of the letter fell to the floor. He then turned and shook the other pages toward Makepeace and said loudly, "It says heere that you keeled a bear by schtrangulation! Ver you a gladiator in a past life? Are you Davie Crockett cum back to us?"

Makepeace was amused by the good-natured physician. Moreover, he found comfort in the fact that he wasn't offended by the doctor's teasing. As a matter of fact he was finding acceptance in recognition. He relaxed and laughed along with the doctor.

"I'm jest a mountain boy 'at did what he had t' do," he said.

"I haf *nefer!*" the doctor replied.

Doctor Noren showed Makepeace to a room that was more like a bedroom than a hospital room. Then he escorted him to the family table where he ate a dinner prepared by the doctor's wife.

In the course of the conversation he found out that he would be one of three patients in the clinic that evening. The other two had recently had surgery and were taking their meals in their rooms.

The doctor told him that he would be examined early the next morning, and if surgery was needed, it would be performed that day. He also learned that the meal he was eating would be his last until after his hand was repaired.

After Makepeace had retired to his room, a nurse came and did some preliminary tests. She told him what to expect from his surgery and assured him that he was in good hands. When she was finished, the nurse bid Makepeace goodnight and left him alone with his thoughts.

O n Sunday, Will had recovered to the point where he could be left alone while Doc attended services at the Baptist church. The silence of the empty house and the absence of traffic on the road were a welcome relief to him. He had missed his privacy and longed to be at home on his own.

When the noon hour had passed, he worked his way out of bed, wrapped himself in a blanket, and walked to the front porch. He was as in need of nourishment as fresh air, and he sat on one of Doc's rockers to look for the return of passers-by, which would indicate the end of church followed by Sunday dinner.

At about half past one, he saw a buggy followed by a wagon coming down South Road. As they neared, he made out the buggy driver to be Doc, followed by Roamer and Sweetie in the wagon.

When the caravan arrived, Doc proceeded around the house to shelter his buggy and put his horse out to pasture. Roamer and Sweetie pulled up in the yard and busied themselves removing a basket from the bed of the wagon.

When everyone was gathered on the porch of the house, Doc announced, "Will, I have some good news for you. You're going home with Roamer and Sweetie today!"

"That *is* good news," Will said, and he turned to the couple and thanked them for their generous hospitality.

"Ain't nothin'," Roamer allowed, "you bein' a friend o' Goober's an' all."

"An' I got a surprise fer ye," Sweetie said. "I brung ye a plate o' food frum th' church dinner. Whatever ye like'll be there, fer there's 'bout six kinds o' meat, an' 'bout eight vege-tables, an' three kinds o' pie."

There's something about the combination of hunger, mountain air, and home-cooked food that turns a normal man into a glutton. The plate of food —actually three plates of food—mostly disappeared in short order. Will saved the pickled pig's foot till last and used a too-full stomach as an excuse for passing it up. Roamer, not one to waste food, ate the pig's foot himself.

After Doc had examined Will and changed the dressings on his arms and throat, the trio prepared to leave.

Back on the porch, Doc put his arm around Will's shoulder and pulled him back. "Will," he said, "I want to thank you for settling yours and Goober's...I mean Makepeace's bill. I don't see a lot of cash money, and it sure comes in handy."

"Least I could do," Will replied. "I'm convinced you saved my life."

"Well," Doc concluded as he gave Will's shoulder a little shake, "unless you need me before then, I'll see you at the meeting Thursday evening."

Will had started down the steps, but he stopped and turned abruptly. "Meeting?" he said. "What meeting?"

Doc looked puzzled. "Preacher Burden didn't tell you?"

"Tell me what?"

"Why, you've been appointed to the Avery Cove Council! The members are unanimous in your appointment."

"I can't be on a council," Will said. "I just got here. I don't know any-thing about the valley."

"You'll learn about Avery Cove real quick at the council meeting!" Doc declared, and he turned, went in the house, and closed the door.

———

Makepeace woke from surgery with pain in his hand and nausea from the ether he had been given. "Vell, how do you feel?" the doctor asked him.

"I'm sick ... an' I hurt."

"Dat is to be exchepected," the doctor said.

"My head's goin' round an' round in circles."

"Dat is to be exchepected, too."

Blessed sleep was the only relief for the nausea and pain, but the sleep was intermittent. Relief from the nausea came late in the day, and the nurse was able to give Makepeace a dose of morphine. With that, sleep lasted through the night.

Early the next morning, Dr. Noren came bounding into the room. He stopped and spread his arms wide into the air. "Vell, how do you feel?" he asked.

"I'm glad ye come," Makepeace said. "What is 'is thing on m' hand? Hit weighs a ton!"

"That," Noren answered, "is the latest thing ... a plaschter cast. It vas developed by the Dutch Army. It vill hold your hand together vhile it heals!" The doctor smiled and punctuated his comment by swinging his arms upward again.

"Well then," Makepeace continued, "kin ye tell me whut ye done t' m' hand? It shore does hurt."

"Of course," Noren said. "Dat little metacarpal bone on the side of your hand vas shattered. I assembled the parts and bound them up vit a golden vire. Your hand vill be as goot as new! *As goot as new!*" he exclaimed and he swung his arms in the air once more.

"Now," the doctor said as his excitement abated, "you vill eat breakfast?"

"T' be honest w' ye, I am a mite hongry," Makepeace said. "Hit's been more'n a day since I last et."

"Vonderful!" Dr. Noren exclaimed. "And vhat vould you like to eat?"

"Couple o' eggs with all the trimmin's, I guess."

The good doctor turned to leave the room, and Makepeace added, "'At's chicken eggs ..."

The doctor stopped abruptly and turned to get that statement clarified, and Makepeace added, "... an' a slice o' onion."

Will spent all day Monday writing letters. He wrote his sister Esther and let her know what was going on. He told her that in spite of the bad thing that had happened he had no regrets about moving there. "It's like I went to heaven without dying," he told her.

Next he wrote to Mr. Neil and told him that he would be staying in Avery Cove. He thanked him again for all he had done and invited him to come and see the valley as soon as he retired to Burley.

He wrote a note to Sarah at the cafe and asked her to tell everyone hello. He asked about Prissy's aunt and if Prissy had come back to work, and he asked about Pearl and the bachelor corp.

Then he wrote to Hattie Jackson. He didn't know if Hattie could read or if she ever checked to see if she had mail, but he wanted to let her know that he missed her.

The writing wasn't strenuous exercise, but it left him exhausted both mentally and physically. He therefore pledged that he would keep increasing his physical and mental output until he was back to normal.

On Tuesday afternoon, he persuaded Roamer to take him to check on his house and the horses. Roamer's mule had a slow and steady pace that allowed him to take in more of the valley sights.

Roamer was more of a historian than Makepeace had been. He told Will about the early settlers, and he knew the chain of ownership of every farm. He pointed out obscure trails that led off into the hills and painted a mental picture for Will of each one's destination.

As they passed Demus Whitedeer's farm, Roamer spun a tail about Seth Leggery and his slaves. He pointed out a trail that led to the old gold mine where Demus' father, Joseph, had hidden as a runaway boy of sixteen.

"Best ye don't go 'round 'at ol' mine at night," Roamer said. "Hit's haint-ed by 'em ol' slaves! Why, they wuz a bunch o' ol' boy's went coon huntin' up 'at trail one night . . ." He paused to send a stream of tobacco juice off the side of the road." . . . an' they run up on 'em spirits, an' they come down off 'at mountain lack 'ey wuz shot out'n a gun! Why, hit wuz s' bad, a couple o' 'em ol' boys coon dogs died o' fright … jest thought ye ort t' know."

Will gave Roamer a look, but he didn't comment on that revelation.

As they approached Will's farm, Roamer raised up on his seat and said, "Well, lookie yonder. The Plowsharers is a-bustin' yer field."

True to Preacher Babb's word, two teams of mules were pulling turning plows across the field.

The rich, black earth was boiling up over the iron blades, and a group of children were following along, picking up stones and loading them onto a pony sled.

Roamer pulled his wagon down to the edge of the field, and he and Will sat and watched the annual ritual unfold. Back and forth the plowmen went, painting the field the color of soot. Closer they came until they ended the job by stopping next to Roamer's wagon.

"Howdy!" one of the plowmen shouted. "I'm Artis Plumlee an' 'is here is m' brother James Plumlee, an' you mus' be th' feller 'at was eat up by 'at bar."

"Sorry to say I am," Will replied. "I'm Will Parker, but mostly I'm thankful ... thankful for what you're doing."

"Hit's our callin', Brother Parker," James replied. "But say ... we was jest admirin' 'em horses in th' pasture."

James turned and motioned toward the Clydesdales grazing in the distance. "'Em's some o' th' biggest an' finest horses we've ever saw!"

"Thanks," Will replied, "and I was just thinking ... if you care to do me one more favor, you could hitch up those horses and plow 'em a little. They need some work."

James and Artis exchanged glances before Artis said, "Why, hit'd be a pleasure t' walk back o' 'em animals, 'at is if ye ain't jest a-jokin'." Then Artis paused to rub his chin and think. "Hit'd speed things up, too," he concluded.

"Tell you what," Will said. "Use 'em till your spring planting is done, and share 'em with anybody else that needs 'em. That would do us all a favor."

James and Artis looked at each other again. "Ye got y'self a deal 'ere, Brother Parker," Artis chimed. "Ye got y'self a *deal*!"

Tuesday afternoon found Makepeace sitting on Dr. Noren's front porch wrapped in a robe, soaking up the sun.

His hand was healing, and the pain was down to a dull ache. Dr. Noren was treating that with his new aspirin powder, but Makepeace was convinced that the sun shining on him through the thin, mountain air was better medicine still.

The sun was beginning to drop behind the western ridge, and he was about ready to go inside and smell supper cooking when his eyes were drawn to Main Street about a hundred feet away.

There, coming from the train station headed toward the Hotel, was Glenn Neil, lugging his suitcase.

A cold chill ran up Makepeace's spine as he saw the big man, and he was reminded that he was to meet him the next day. What would Neil say if the doctor wouldn't release him to begin his work? Would Neil fire him on the spot, or grind him into the earth? After all, this man's time was valuable, and he wasn't accustomed to waiting.

He sank back into his rocker and propped his feet on the porch railing, contemplating his fate. The essence of life had been sucked out of his body.

He had come so far and endured so much to be cut loose in Burley without a job.

Just as he was getting up to retreat to his room, he glanced down the street and saw Neil headed in his direction. He was walking swiftly and had a determined look on his face. Makepeace stood, and Neil spotted him.

Neil's pace quickened, and before Makepeace could react, the big man was on the porch.

A look of concern was on his face, and he was breathing heavily as he stood above Makepeace. "My boy," he said, "you *are* hurt." He looked down at Makepeace's cast and took on the aspect of a father looking down at his son.

He removed Doc French's letter from his pocket and held it out between them. "Is what I'm reading here true?" he asked.

"I ain't read it," Makepeace replied.

Neil opened the letter and began to scan it, "Will Parker…while on a hunting trip was attacked by a bear…seriously mauled…Mr. Green threw himself on the bear's back and fought with it, eventually killing it with his bare hands. … Green went for aid, though injured himself … fired distress shots … with the assistance of a woodsman, carried Mr. Parker five miles to get medical attention."

Neil paused and looked down at Makepeace, who was shivering in the chilling air. "I'm sorry," Neil said. "Let's go inside where you'll be warmer."

Makepeace turned and walked into the parlor with the big man following. They sat down, and Neil continued reading the highlights of the letter.

"It says here, 'Had it not been for Mr. Green, Will Parker would not have survived the vicious attack. No one in Avery Cove has ever seen such an act of bravery and strength'."

Neil lowered the letter and looked in Makepeace's eyes. His countenance softened, and there was a hint of perspiration on his brow. "Is this true, son?" he asked.

"I can't answer on th' part 'bout bein' brave an' all," Makepeace said.

"I jest done whut I … had t' do an' didn't stop an' think 'bout bein' strong an' all. Th' rest o' whut 'e said … is true enough I reckon. I 'member whut ye said 'bout takin' care o' Will an' all, an' I done m' best."

A door opened, and Dr. Noren entered the room. He held his arms out and announced, "Ve haf a visitor!"

"Dr. Noren, 'is here is Mr. Neil that I tol' ye 'bout," Makepeace said.

Neil jumped to his feet and offered his hand to the doctor. "Dr. Noren, it's a pleasure to meet you. Now, I want to know how this man is doing!"

"He is doing vell, and he shoot be as goot as new in a few veeks."

Neil shook his finger in the air and blustered, "You give him anything he needs! Expense is no object! I need him, but I want him healed."

"I underschtand," the doctor replied. "Our greatest fear is infection, but if he is vell on Thursday, he may go vith you."

"*Excellent!*" Neil thundered. "*Excellent!*"

By Thursday afternoon Will was much stronger, due in most part to Sweetie's home cooking. Now his greatest fear was getting fat with all the food intake and no exercise.

He had mixed feelings about the council meeting being held that evening. He felt that he had no business there, being so new to the community, but he knew that by going, he could gain insight into the workings of the valley.

Roamer too was mindful of the importance of Will's attendance, and he volunteered to give Will a ride.

Since the meetings were open to the public, Roamer's plan was to sit in the back of the room and then give Will a ride home. "I'll jest sit back 'ere an' try t' keep m' yap shet," he explained to Will. "'At way, I won't shame m' nephew."

The custom had always been that the preachers of the valley's two churches would act as moderators of the council on alternate years. The valley residents had not yet fully grasped the concept of separation of church and state.

Since it was Preacher Babb's year, the meetings were being held at the Baptist church.

Will and Roamer rolled into the church yard as the sun was setting behind the mountain. There were about six wagons and a few saddle horses there already.

The building was an average sized country church, painted white. Beside it were the graves of many of the valley's departed. Each of the sites was marked with a neat, simple gravestone.

The interior of the church was also painted white. There were hand-hewn benches lined up in two rows with an isle down the center. Along the walls between the windows, oil lamps burned, radiating a soft light.

All heads turned, and those who were seated stood as Will and Roamer entered the sanctuary.

"There's our newest member now," Preacher Babb announced, and several men led by Preacher Burden walked over to greet him.

As the crowd milled about laughing and back-slapping, Preacher Babb pounded the pulpit with a gavel and called the meeting to order. Then in accordance with another custom, he called on the other preacher to lead in prayer.

Silence prevailed as Preacher Burden poured out the feelings of his heart. He thanked, blessed, and pleaded his case, and before he finished his powerful supplication, the meeting had taken on the feel of a church revival.

Then before the "amen" was fully out of Preacher Burden's mouth, the gavel fell again, and the meeting was in session.

"Any old business?" Preacher Babb asked.

"Caldwell Turpin!" someone declared.

The crowd laughed and knee-slapped while Caldwell folded his arms and looked disgruntled. Will decided that must be an ongoing joke.

Preacher Babb pounded his gavel to silence the crowd. "*Cut out the foolishness*," he demanded. "Any new business?"

Preacher Burden's hand shot up and he raised about half-way up. "I've got a point of new business," he said. "Want to make a motion that we give a generous welcome to our new member, Will Parker."

"Second!" Doc French declared.

"All in favor?" Preacher Babb shouted. "And it's unanimous! Put in the records that Brother Will is welcomed with open arms! Any other new business?"

Paul Thiggery jumped to his feet. "Preacher, I declare I ain't in favor o' that 'lectricity comin t' th' valley! I think hit ort t' be stopped *rat now!*"

"Look," Caldwell Turpin said as he jumped up, "ain't nobody a-forcin' you t' hook up. If you don't want 'lectricity, *burn oil!*"

"I'm a-thinkin' 'bout 'at stuff gettin' loose an' burnin' th' whole valley down!" Thiggery barked.

"Ain't no danger in 'at a-happenin'," Caldwell shot back. "Jest axt Will here. He come frum a city whur ever'body had it! Ain't that so, Will?"

"*Chair recognizes Brother Will Parker*," Preacher Babb shouted, and he pointed his gavel at Will's face.

Will rose slowly and looked around. Every eye was looking back. "Well!" he said rather softly. "First, let me thank you for your welcome. Didn't expect that. And let me tell you how much I love your home. Everybody has been wonderful to me ... and I thank you.

"Now about electricity: the best part of it coming here is that you can take it or leave it. If you take it, I think you'll like it because it solves a lot of problems."

Will looked around at the crowd before he continued. "If you don't want it right now, then you can be happy doing what you've always done."

All eyes remained on Will as he stopped to clear his throat before continuing again. "In thinking back, I can't recall any fires being started in Charlotte by electricity. There may have been one. I do recall several fires started by oil lamps though.

"So I think you'll find that it's safe," he said. "I know that when the lines get up my way, I'll hook up."

The crowd remained silent as Will was seated.

"You got anything else to say, Brother Paul?" Preacher Babb asked.

" I guess 'at answers my question," Paul said sheepishly.

"*Next!*" The preacher shouted.

"I want t' know whut Will has t' say 'bout th' roads!" someone said.

Will looked around, and all eyes were on him again. He stood and cleared his throat. "Well, I'm afraid they're pretty bad. Of course, you'd expect them to be here at the end of winter. I know of a man who considered opening a small manufacturing business here in the valley, but the condition of the roads was a sticking point. It seems to me that if everyone worked together for a day or two, we could get them smoothed out. If everyone wanted a business here, we could talk about something more permanent later."

A murmur moved through the crowd. No one had ever even considered having a manufacturing business in the valley.

"*Next Saturday, dawn till dusk!*" Preacher Babb shouted. "Them that lives on South Road works on it. Them that lives on North Road works on it. Baptists do West Road, Methodists do East Road. *All in favor?*"

"*Aye!*" The council shouted.

"*Opposed?*"

The crowd was silent.

The meeting continued in the same manner with members raising questions, Will coming up with a solution, and everyone agreeing.

When the gavel fell for the last time and the meeting was ended, Will thanked each member for letting him be a part. He then cornered Preacher Babb and apologized for talking so much. "I'm sorry," he said. "I felt like I was talking the entire time, but folks kept asking questions."

"That's all right, Brother Will," the preacher said. "They were sorta feelin' you out, I guess. You know, they really like you."

"They don't even know me," Will protested.

"Yes, they do," the preacher declared, "and I'll tell you how. When you loaned th' Plumlee brothers those horses of yours, you put your trust in 'em. Those are the finest horses the Plumlees had ever seen, and you gave 'em your permission to just walk off with 'em. Then, when you told 'em to share those animals with anybody else that needed 'em, you put your trust in th' whole valley.

"*Strangers!*" the preacher said emphatically, and his teeth glistened through his big smile. "You put your trust in strangers, and that kind o' thing goes a long way up here. These folks know that a man that'll trust a stranger is gen'rally trustworthy himself, so when the Plumlee boys spread the word 'bout what you did, ever'body figgered you were a good man. Simple as that!"

Twenty-One

A Refined Gentleman

Despite objections from Roamer and Sweetie, Will decided on Friday morning that he was going home. "It's time to start getting my house in order," he told them.

Roamer couldn't believe that Will would try to make it alone in his weakened state, and he resisted. "Ye ain't even got no horses t' pull ye wagon," he argued.

Sweetie added, "Ye ain't got no food put up neither!"

Will ran his fingers through his hair and thought. "Roamer," he said, "if you'll just take me to Burden's store, I'll stock up on essentials, and I can hunt and fish until my garden starts coming in. I thank you for all you've done, but if you were in my position, wouldn't you want to be in your own house?"

Roamer finally gave in to Will's argument. He figured that he could find some excuse to check on him regularly until he was back to full strength. He remembered too his own youth and how he had been so anxious to get out on his own. "Wal, git ye stuff t'gether," he said, "an' I'll take ye."

Sweetie turned away and smoothed the front of her apron with her hands. She had already lost Goober, and now she was going to lose another surrogate child. "I'll git ye some jars o' food t' tide ye over," she said as she walked out on the back porch to retrieve a wooden box.

Will busied himself getting his things together. He didn't have much at Roamer's house, but what he did have was spread out between his room, the pile of dirty clothes on the porch, and the clothes in Sweetie's room waiting to be ironed.

When everything had been collected, he cleaned and straightened his room and made the bed.

Finally, when he was ready to leave, Sweetie held him at arm's length as she had held Goober, and gave him his instructions. "Now you eat good and git lots o' rest," she said. "Ye best come t' see me if ye git short o' food. An' keep ye clothes warshed an' arned so ye kin impress th' gals. An' be careful with them ol' guns o' yourn an' don't shoot y'self ..."

"Sweetie, let 'im be," Roamer whined. "He ain't no youngun! He's a growed man!"

"Well, I appreciate you looking out for me, Aunt Sweetie," Will said, "and I'll be around a lot. I promised Makepeace...Goober...that I'd help you out like he always did."

"An' we'll be here, if'n ye need us," she answered.

Roamer's wagon rolled down the drive and onto the road just as the sun peeped over the mountain. Its brightness promised a warm day— the kind of warmth that would push leaves out of the buds on the trees and sprouts of spring wheat out of the soil. It too, Will hoped, was the kind of warmth that brought healing to the body.

When Roamer had the wagon pointed down the road and firmly in the ruts, he declared, "'Fore we go t' th' store, I'm a-gonna take ye by Doc's an' see whut he has t' say 'bout ye lightin' off on ye own."

Will looked ahead pensively and remained silent. He knew it would be best to let Roamer have his way since he didn't feel like walking. Maybe, he thought, Doc had been young once himself and would understand.

On the way Will got another history lesson as Roamer recounted the story of the first settlers to the valley. He told about battles with Indians and starvation through harsh winters. He took great joy in telling how families survived the first winter on corn meal, squirrel, mother's milk, and whiskey.

He told how the settlers cleared the bottom land and drained swamps to make the rich fields and pastures that survived to that day. He recounted in great detail how they built houses of logs and lived off the land by hunting and gathering.

When they neared the old Tribble place, he told about how he went to the porch late one night to get a drink of water and saw in the distance the glow of the Tribble house burning. He said that he ran down the road and arrived at the fire to find that the only remaining life was an old hound circling the burning house, crying in vain for his master. The effect of the tragedy was reflected still in Roamer's eyes.

"Twelve Mile Crick," he announced as the wagon rolled through a stream of water, but he had no clue as to why it was called that. It was just another mystery of the valley.

The history lesson ended as the wagon passed Burden's store. The men who were gathered on the porch hailed the pair as they passed but settled back down when Roamer hollered that they would be back shortly.

To Will's relief, Doc was not at home. A note on the door said that he had gone to Sue Levee's house and that he didn't know when he would be back. "Doc'll sometimes be gone fer days when they's a baby a-comin'," Roamer offered.

Back at the store the morning gathering of men had dissipated. Inside only Preacher Burden and Perry Maynard were in attendance, and they were busy poring through an implement catalog.

When Perry saw Will come in, he snapped to attention. "Will thar," he exclaimed. "Got t' plow 'em horses o' yourn yestiddy. 'Em's th' mightiest beasts I ever worked. Pulled a gang plow like hit wa'n't nothin'."

"I'm looking forward to workin' 'em myself," Will replied.

"Well, son," Preacher Burden said as he closed the catalog, "you're lookin' better. What can I do for you this fine day?"

"Need a few things to stock the pantry," Will said.

He clicked off a list of items including coffee, flour, corn meal, salt, black pepper, baking soda, and sugar. Then he selected a bar of lye soap, a tub of lard, some honey, and a jar of James Plumlee's black strap molasses.

"A dollar and seventy cents," the preacher announced as he finished totaling the purchase. "I declare," he said. "I'm amazed every day how things are goin' up. Used to be, that much would have been 'bout a dollar and a quarter. I'll put it on your bill!"

When Will got home he realized that he might have made a mistake by striking out so soon. He retreated to the bedroom for a nap, and when he woke, Roamer was gone.

The day that started on a warm note was changing. In the west above the mountain, clouds were gathering, obstructing the late-day sun.

Will made a trip to the outhouse and found that a cold, biting wind was bearing down on the valley. On it rode the smell of winter weather.

In his more cognitive state, he realized that not only was it supper time, but that he had missed lunch. *Not good to miss a meal while trying to heal,* he told himself.

Back inside he sorted through the things he had bought at the store, assigning them to their niches on the kitchen shelves. He then began to investigate the contents of Sweetie's wooden box. It was a wealth of country food.

On the very top was a cluster of brown eggs wrapped in a scrap of woolen material and a half loaf of bread wrapped in butcher paper. Beneath that was a portion of side meat, and deeper down were jars of preserved vegetables. Hidden in a corner was a jar of amber liquid that Will decided must have been something Roamer contributed. All in all it was a treasure- trove of nourishment.

Soon a fire was burning in the kitchen stove, two eggs had been selected, and a portion of side meat had been cut. Nothing to do now but wait for the stove to heat and get a bucket of water.

As he was walking to the sink to get his bucket, he heard a knock on the door—a slow but deliberate knock. Thump … thump … thump. "Why would Roamer be knocking?" he immediately asked himself. "He should just walk on in."

The fading sunlight that was filtering through the kitchen window was shielded from the front room, and as Will walked through he had to be careful not to trip on some still unfamiliar object. The door handle itself was hidden from light, and he groped for it in the half darkness.

When he finally found it and swung the door open to let Roamer in, he was confronted not by Roamer, but by the unmistakable, shadowy bulk of Demus Whitedeer.

He instantly froze, not knowing what to do. He was speechless, and the sudden tension left him weak-kneed and slightly nauseous.

Whitedeer's bulky frame was dark and motionless. He, too, was silent, waiting for Will to speak. Finally Whitedeer asked, "May I talk with you?"

Will was instantly relieved by the calmness of Whitedeer's voice, and he replied without thinking, "Yes … come in … please."

When they were inside, Whitedeer spoke again. "I've come to talk to you and the owner of the property, Mr. Green. I wanted to tell you that I did not remove the boards from his barn."

"Yes … Mr. Whitedeer," Will replied. "I found out later who really took them, and I apologize to you for having accused you of that."

It was not a good feeling for Will to be standing in a darkened room with a man of Demus Whitedeer's reputation, and so he turned slightly and motioned toward the kitchen. "Can we go into the kitchen," he asked. "I have a fire started, and I'm going to put on some coffee."

Without answering Whitedeer followed Will into the kitchen and stood by the table while Will lit a lantern.

By the lantern's light, Will could see Whitedeer's features. He had the high cheek bones of his father and the dark skin and wide nose of his mother's race. His hair was black and curly, and it fell loosely past his shoulders. He was an imposing figure.

Will pulled out a chair for Whitedeer, and the two men sat. Will began spinning the story of the bear attack and how he was weakened by the loss of blood. He told about Makepeace's heroic killing of the bear and how he too had been injured.

Whitedeer was attentive as Will explained that he was now the owner of the property. He further explained that Makepeace was gone and would probably not return.

"I heard that Green had strangled a bear when I went to the Mast store in Valle Crucis," Whitedeer said. "They were making him out to be a living legend."

"Would you like some coffee, Mr. Whitedeer?" Will asked.

"Thank you, sir ..."

"My name is Will Parker. Please, just call me Will."

"Thank you, Will, and you must call me Demus," Whitedeer said. "I will have coffee with you another time. The snow is about to fly and I must go."

Whitedeer stood and reached in his coat. "I know that you don't have a cow yet, so I brought you a quart of milk. It will go well with your coffee," he said.

Whitedeer sat the jar of milk on the table and turned to leave.

"Thank you," Will said. "Thank you very much for the milk and for coming. I hope to see you again."

"And I hope to see you again too," Whitedeer replied, and with no further word, he walked through the front room and out the door.

As soon as Whitedeer left, Will dropped into a chair and put his head on the table. Only then did he realize how bad he felt. He wondered if the need for food or his weakened condition could be responsible for his sudden debility, but he soon concluded that the shock of Demus Whitedeer's unexpected visit was to blame.

As he sat waiting for his fire to heat the stove, he thought back over the previous minutes. He had been feeling well, preparing his supper, there was a knock on the door, and when he opened it, he came face to face with the most reviled man in the valley—a man with whom he had exchanged threats!

The man spoke politely, came in and made a clarifying statement about not having taken boards from the barn, sat with him briefly, gave him a gift of a quart of milk, and calmly left. And if this wasn't enough, he used just about the most refined and eloquent English he had ever heard!

He wondered how this man could be so feared and despised. He decided he would find out.

———

The silence of dawn was broken by the muted clatter of wagon wheels on the drive. Will turned in bed and raised his head to listen.

"A wagon," he thought. "Now who could be coming at this time of day?"

He got out of bed and pulled back the curtain to reveal a landscape covered in snow, and the source of the racket—Uncle Roamer.

Roamer stopped his mule near Will's front porch, put a bundle under his arm, and climbed down off the wagon. He gingerly made his way up the snow covered steps and walked right in the front door. Dawg ambled over to greet him.

"*Will*," he hollered, "*hit's me…Roamer. Why ain't ye up an' stirrin' yet?*"

"I'm stirrin'," Will answered. "Didn't sleep very well last night."

"I'uz worried 'bout ye," Roamer said, "bein' in bed 'is time o' day."

"I'm okay," Will said. "How about startin' a fire in the kitchen and stokin' up the parlor stove while I'm getting dressed. How much snow did we get?"

"Oh, jest a skifflin … three … four inches. Hit'll be gone by dark. Sweetie sent ye some more grub," he called out as he busied himself getting the fire started. "She's a-frettin' 'er self silly, thinkin' ye gonna starve t' death up 'ere. Won't listen t' me 'bout ye bein' a growed man—no, sir, Mister! Thinks she's got t' nanny ever'body. Say, where'd ye git th' milk?"

"Neighbor brought it."

"Preacher Babb?" Roamer asked. "I recon he's got two cows bein' 'is wife bakes s' much an' all."

"No," Will called out. "Demus Whitedeer brought it."

A crash came from the kitchen as Roamer dropped his armload of stove wood.

Will hurried in with shaving soap on his face to see what caused the racket and found Roamer pie-eyed, picking up the wood.

"Did you say *Demus Whitedeer*?" Roamer asked. "Demus wuz here? In 'is house?"

"He was, indeed," Will replied. "We had a nice visit, Demus and I, but let me ask, Uncle Roamer, why's he so disliked? He's really a very nice fellow."

"Why! He's a savage, jest lack 'is daddy," Roamer said indignantly, "an' 'is mama wuz a ignernt slave! Worst kind o' folks!"

"Have you ever talked to him?"

"I don't go nowhur near 'im! 'Fraid I'd git m' throat cut," Roamer replied.

"Well, I've got some more finding-out to do," Will said, "but if he's the kind of person I think he is, this community is in for a surprise."

Roamer soon left in a huff, and Will went about the business of starting the day. After he had eaten and fixed breakfast for Dawg, he pulled on his coat, grabbed the water bucket, and headed out the back door to get what he hoped would be his last bucket of water before the indoor spring house was hooked up.

On the back steps, he stood and looked out at the spring snow that had fallen the night before. The ground was bathed in white and sparkled with the light of the morning sun. It seemed that every branch of every tree was reaching for the earth under its icy load. He marveled at how quiet and still the earth lay, waiting for the sun to restore the browns and greens of the yard and the forest.

Down the hill the river rushed over rounded boulders that were covered in white. He looked forward to summer when he could sleep to the music of those rippling currents.

In spite of the beauty that lay before him, Will was soon brought back to the realization that there was work to be done. He descended the steps and took his first step into the soft blanket of white. "I hate to spoil it," he thought out loud, and then he saw that it was already spoiled.

Coming around the house from the direction of the road was a set of footprints—small footprints. They led to the bedroom window and then tailed off across the yard and around behind the smoke house.

"Roamer?" he said to himself. But these prints were too small for even Roamer's diminutive frame.

He placed the bucket on the ground and circled around the yard to the side of the smoke house opposite the trail of prints. When he reached the back of the building, he peeked around the corner, and sure enough, there was Sonny Day peeking around the other corner toward the house.

The snow was soft and fluffy enough to make no sound when Will walked on it, so he moved very slowly and carefully until he could reach out and grab Sonny by the collar.

Sonny let out a shriek that set Dawg to barking. He fought against Will's grip and tried to run as he yelled, "*Et me doh! Et me doh!*"

"I'll let you go," Will said, "but first you have some explaining to do. Why are you here sneaking around my house?"

"*I didn't teal anytaing!*" he cried. "*I wanna doh home!*"

"I'll let you go home," Will answered, "but I am going to talk to your daddy."

"*My daddy dawn,*" the boy cried, and he jerked away from Will's grip and tore off across the yard toward the road.

Will watched as Sonny ran toward the river, across the bridge, and out of sight. *These unexpected visits are gonna do me in*, he thought to himself.

———

By late afternoon the snow had mostly melted, and Will had running water in the indoor spring house and the kitchen sink. James

Plumlee had returned the horses, saying that plowing was done and that the Plowsharers would be back later to harrow the field and plant corn and hay. To top things off and show his thanks for the use of the horses, he brought a cherry pie from his wife and a chocolate cake from his brother's wife. How could life be better!

It had been a good day. Work had been done, and neighbors had reached out again, but he couldn't stop thinking about Demus Whitedeer and Sonny Day. "How strange," he thought. On the one hand, there was Demus, the dark, mysterious man who was in fact a genteel intellectual, and on the other hand there was Sonny Day, the fragile child of innocent years who was a holy terror! Both, he decided, were fertile fields waiting for the plowman.

———

Sunday dawned as a glorious day. Will lay in bed past his normal time for getting up and savored his new surroundings.

The bed was harder than he was accustomed to, but he noticed that his back seemed to be benefiting from the firmness. He was a little annoyed that his bedroom window faced the south and let in the morning sun, but he wondered if that feature too wasn't to his advantage—with him being a gentleman-farmer now.

The most favorable amenity though was the sound of the river that could be heard throughout the night even with the windows closed. It had sung him to sleep like a lullaby.

Then his mind wandered back to Sonny Day and the burden of his speech impediment. He knew the agony a child goes through when he is shackled with that encumbrance. He remembered a classmate who spent his early years speaking as Sonny did, and he recalled the many times the lad was teased mercilessly by the other children. There must be some way to help Sonny.

He would have stayed in bed much later had it not been for Dawg, who decided that he needed to go outside. Since he was up, he started a kitchen fire and got the coffee pot ready to go.

That morning he took advantage of his new luxury in the kitchen. Instead of walking to the river for water, he simply turned the tap in the kitchen sink and filled his coffee pot. How, he wondered, did he live without that convenience in Charlotte?

A look out the window revealed that the snow was gone, replaced by bare ground with some icy patches. The road seemed clear and dry, and he decided he would fulfill his promise to Preacher Burden and attend church.

His clock, which he had set on Friday by the sound of the school bell, showed the time to be 9:05. Figuring his travel time to the church, he determined that his preparation could be leisurely.

By 10:15 the horses were hitched to the wagon and he was on the way out the South Road. Matthew Day's home soon came into view, but there was no apparent activity there.

He rolled along until he came to West Road, and when he looked down toward Preacher Babb's house, he saw a woman walking with a boy in tow. It was Sonny and his mom on the way to the Baptist church. "I hope he learns something," he muttered to himself. The horses looked back at him as if they understood.

The yard of the Methodist church was cluttered with wagons when Will arrived, and the last of the men were putting out their smokes and entering the building. The silence of the scene belied the fact that the church was filled with members about to begin the boisterous practice of country worship.

When Will entered, Preacher Burden was standing to give the announcements. He instinctively threw up his hand in greeting when he saw Will, and every face turned to see the object of the preacher's greeting.

An old gentleman who was seated on the Elder's bench at the rear of the church jumped up to show Will to an empty seat and then returned to his place of honor. Preacher Burden waited patiently until the movement had ceased before he began.

"Oh ... praise the Lord this morning for a beautiful day and especially for bringing us an honored newcomer, Mr. Will Parker," he announced. "Now you've all heard about him ... and I want you to greet him when the service ends, but I want you to know that there will be *no fighting* over who will have him to Sunday dinner, 'cause he's comin' home with *me!*"

A trickle of laughter circulated through the crowd, and a group of young girls whispered and giggled

"Next Sunday," the preacher continued, "there will be open season on Mr. Parker, but I hope you'll keep your fighting over who gets to feed him restricted to the church yard."

Again all heads turned toward Will, and the laughter intensified.

The service was a profound departure from the Episcopal service that Will grew up attending. The music was loud and spirited. Since there were no hymnals, it was led by a choir member who sang each line, which in turn was repeated by the congregation. All voices sang the melody except for a few of the men who favored the bass part.

Preacher Burden delivered a profound and animated sermon punctuated by shouts of "amen" and "praise the Lord" from the Elder's bench. Scripture and prayer were interspersed generously through the service.

When the final "amen" was sounded, Will decided that the country church was going to take some getting used to.

At 2:00, after thanking his hosts for Sunday dinner, Will started for home. The meal had been all that country cooking could be, and the preacher and Naomi had lifted his spirits with their conversation. Rachel had retreated back into herself, and her only discussion with Will had been centered on whether or not Goober had been in touch since he left.

On the way home, Will took the North road. When he got to Roamer's house, there was no sign of activity. He concluded that they must still be at church having their dinner on the grounds.

When Demus Whitedeer's farm came into view, Will caught a glimpse of Demus going into his house. He considered stopping until he remembered that at home he had the cake and pie James Plumlee had brought.

Since Demus had given him the milk, he decided he would go home and return with half of the cake.

Back at Demus's house, Will knocked on the front door with the cake and Demus's empty milk jar in hand. Demus answered his knock holding a book and smiled when he saw who his visitor was.

"Welcome, Will! Come in," he said. "I'm glad you came."

When Will entered the house, he felt as though he had stepped into a library. All four walls of the front room were lined with book-laden shelves from the floor to the ceiling. A peek into the other rooms revealed the same.

"Come back to the kitchen where it's warm," Demus said. "I'll fix some coffee."

"I brought some cake to go with it," Will said, "and I brought back the milk jar along with my thanks."

"Cake! Now that's an extravagance I seldom have," Demus exclaimed as he filled the coffee pot with water.

"Demus, do you mind if I ask you a personal question?" Will inquired as he took a seat at the table.

"I suppose not."

"Your English is flawless!" he said. "How did you grow up in this remote place and learn such refined English grammar?"

Demus emitted a deep, resonant laugh, and a smile stretched across his face. "It's very simple," he replied. "My father was a Cherokee. He was educated in the missionary school before he came here. The priest and the monks who taught him were very strict. They didn't allow the students to speak Cherokee, and they drilled them in the proper use of the English language. Father learned well.

"Then when he was taken in by Seth Leggery, his education continued. Grandfather Leggery was a well educated man who owned thousands of books ... the books you see here in my house. He taught father, and when I was old enough, he taught me. I've read all his books at least once...some of them several times ... and with the spare money I get selling ginseng, I buy more."

Will looked through a stack of books on the kitchen table, recognizing some and asking questions about others. The title of one, *Robert, the Black American Hermit,* caught his eye.

"There's something else I've wondered," he said. "I know you're a very private person. Why did you come to see me?"

Demus turned from the stove and faced Will. "Well, I must say that my privacy, for the most part, is not by choice. You see, I've never been accepted by the community because my father was an Indian and my mother was a Negro slave. When you're not accepted by those around you, you become a private person by default."

"Now … to answer your question," he said. "When you came to my house about the rails and plow, you called me 'Mr. Whitedeer.' That was the first time in my life that I had heard those two words used together. I could tell by the way you approached me that you were a good man…a decent man. You gave a measure of kindness to me, and by coming to see you I was giving a measure of kindness back."

Demus turned to the stove and checked the fire in the fire box before he continued. "I'd like to explain that when I threatened you, it was because I was afraid … being confronted by two men, and knowing that I was in the wrong."

He went on to say that he thought Makepeace's farm had been abandoned and that he took the plow and rails thinking that no one would know or care. "When you came to my house," he explained, "I panicked. I am sorry. That is why I returned the plow and rails as soon as I could."

"And you plowed the garden plot," Will said.

"It was the least I could do."

By that time the water was coming to a boil and the smell of coffee was rising.

"I wondered too," Will said, "how you've managed to exist by yourself with no friends?"

"Oh, I have hundreds of friends," Demus answered with a laugh. "I have Chaucer and Shakespeare. I have poet friends like Byron, Shelly, and

Keats. I have new friends like Dickens, Thoreau, and Twain. They keep me company."

"But you can't talk with them like we're doing," Will argued.

"Sadly … that's true," Demus replied.

"May I ask about your mother?"

"Mother was born at Grandfather's home in Virginia," Demus said. "She grew up working in his family's house, and although she wasn't educated, she picked up some culture by … osmosis, you might say. She supported my learning as best she could, and later in life, I was privileged to teach her and the other servants to read and write."

"What are you reading now?" Will asked.

Demus picked up his book from the table and held it up for Will to see. "It is a book about my father's culture," Demus replied. "It tells how the missionary teachers taught the Cherokee children to speak English."

Demus sat down at the table and leafed through the book. "You may or may not know that the Cherokee language uses many sounds that are not used in English," he said as he found a page of reference. "The missionary teachers devised a way of breaking English words down into syllables, and syllables down into what they called 'utterances'… the very basic particles of speech. According to this book, my father learned English by overcoming the pattern of Cherokee utterances, much as a child with a speech impediment would learn to overcome his artificial utterances. Very interesting reading," he stated as he closed the book.

Demus looked up to see Will sitting with a look of amazement on his face. "Did I say something wrong?" he asked.

"No, I think you said something very right," Will replied. "Do you know a boy named Sonny Day?"

"Can't say that I've had the pleasure," Demus said with a chuckle.

"Would you like to meet him?"

Demus laughed his deep, rumbling laugh. "With a name like 'Sonny Day'," he replied, "how could I resist?"

Twenty-Two

ALICE

While Will was recuperating at Roamer's house, Makepeace had been mending at Dr. Noren's clinic in Burley. When Thursday, the day of his expected release rolled around, Dr. Noren was having a busy day. He started his morning with two surgeries followed by a birthing on the edge of town.

As the doctor ran out the door on his way to deliver the baby, he passed Makepeace and Glenn Neil in the front room and said, "I vill be back soon to examine you, Mr. Green. You vill yust have to vait."

Glenn Neil had a finger raised and was about to comment, but before he could speak, Dr. Noren was out the door and gone.

Makepeace was finally examined, given a clean bill of health, and released in the early afternoon. His prognosis was good. Full healing would occur in about six weeks. He was instructed to keep his cast dry and to use the new aspirin powder as needed for pain.

Since the hour was late, Neil decided that they would not be able to see any landowners that day, so they moved Makepeace into the inn and started making plans for Friday.

"First thing we should do," Neil said, "is go to the livery stable and check on that horse and surrey of yours. You won't mind us using 'em to track down those land owners, will you?"

"I don't mind a bit," Makepeace said, "but *you* should! We show up with a decent horse a-pullin' a surrey, an' 'em farmers is gonna set ye packin'."

Neil squirmed in his seat. "What should we do?" he asked.

"We need t' find us a mule an' a rickety ol' farm wagon," Makepeace declared. "Go rollin' up 'ere lookin' lack one o' them."

Neil looked puzzled. "Are you sure that's necessary?" he asked.

"Ye gonna haf t' trus' me on 'at," Makepeace answered. "'At's whut yer payin' me fer, ain't it?

"Now," Makepeace continued, "nex' thing we gonna haf t' do is t'git ye some decent clothes ... some overalls ... an' some work boots."

"What?" Neil was disbelieving. "I'm not going out to *plow*! I'm going out to buy land! I'll wear what I always wear."

"An' th' seat o' ye suit britches'll bear some farmer's footprint!" Makepeace declared. "Now ye gonna haf t' listen t' me on 'is an' trus' whut I tell ye. *You* know cotton mills, an' *I* know mountain farmers!"

"Okay," Neil sighed. "Let's go to the store and see what we can find."

As they walked down the street, Glenn Neil took in the scenery and pulled in deep breaths of fresh air. He couldn't seem to get enough of the mountain atmosphere.

He noted the crystal-clear sky and commented on its blueness. He stopped to feel the bark of an oak tree and look into its heights at the buds that were about to burst into green. As they passed a neatly kept yard, he marveled at the jonquils pushing up through the dark soil. "How," he asked, "could anyone not want to stay here forever?"

"Ain't no theaters in Burley," Goober mumbled under his breath.

The general store was quite large for a town the size of Burley. Neil wondered why, and Makepeace explained that not only did it service the needs of the locals, but it sold wholesale to other stores around the region like Burden's.

The store had anything a person could want and then some. A sign by the entrance proclaimed, "ALL YOUR NEEDS—FROM CRADLES TO COFFINS". And it was true. The cradles were on the left by the front door, and the coffins were stacked on end across the back wall.

Men's clothing was in a room off to the right, and the selection consisted mainly of hats, work boots, flannel shirts, long johns, and overalls—mountains of overalls.

Neil joined a farmer who was intent on finding his size and started looking through the selection himself. Makepeace wandered up behind the two, and as he did, he noted that Neil and the farmer were about the same size.

He tapped the farmer on the shoulder and said, "Say, Mister, whut size boots do ye wear?"

The farmer gave Makepeace a stern look and responded, "'Leven an' a ha'f. Whut's it to ye?"

"Thought we might work out a deal," Makepeace said. "See, m' friend here needs some boots 'at's broke in good … an' 'e needs some overalls with th' shine wore off …"

"Now see here," Neil demanded.

"Ye got t' trus' me on 'is," Makepeace said. "Can you wear a 'leven an' a ha'f boot?"

"Yes, but …"

Makepeace turned back to the farmer. "I figgered whut I'd do is t' trade ye a new pair o' overalls and a new pair o' boots fer whut ye got on."

Neil stood silently and listened, and the farmer looked puzzled.

"You mean t' tell me you gonna gi' me a new pair o' boots an' a new pair o' overalls fer whut I'm a-wearin'? the farmer asked.

"'At's 'bout th' size of it!"

"Got y'self a deal," the farmer said, and he sat down on the floor and started pulling off his boots.

Friday dawned as a warm day in Burley as it had in Avery Cove, but there, too, change was in the air. In the west beyond the mountains, the skies were gray, and the wind was starting to blow.

Neil met Makepeace in the dining room at 6:00 a.m. for breakfast. He was wearing his overalls, which were freshly washed and dried.

"'Em overalls looks good on ye," Goober said after he had wished his boss a good morning.

"You know," Neil replied, "they feel good too! Gives a man a sense of freedom … you know, not having a belt squeezing him around the middle. I might give up the suit and start wearing overalls all the time."

"I kin jest see ye a-meetin' with President Cleveland a-wearin' 'em overalls an' boots," Makepeace said. "Ye'd prob'ly have 'im a-wearin' 'em 'fore long."

After breakfast, it was time to find transportation. The livery stable had an old wagon, but they didn't have a mule. What they did have was an old swaybacked mare named "Sis" that Makepeace thought would work even better than a mule. "A'ter all," he told Neil, "we want a looker, not a strong puller."

Neil had been thinking and had decided that he wanted to go back to see Smithfield, the man who raised sheep and had kicked him off his property. He thought the thing to do was to keep his mouth shut and let Makepeace do the talking. Makepeace hardily agreed.

And so, with Sis harnessed to the wagon, the two men set off northward toward the Smithfield farm.

It was midmorning when they arrived, and Smithfield was walking toward his house, having just finishing his morning chores. He paused when he saw the wagon approach and set his water bucket on the ground.

"*Mornin!*" he hollered when the wagon was close enough for his voice to be heard.

Smithfield was a gnarled old man, tall and thin, with snow-white hair showing around the brim of his hat. He wore the traditional shepherd's canvas coat that reached below his knees. It was stained and stiff with blood from the springtime ritual of lambing. Neil was seeing firsthand that raising sheep was not a suit-and-tie line of work.

The house was like many others in the valley, a white frame structure with a porch, surrounded by the normal complement of outbuildings. A rope swing hanging from an oak tree in the yard and some scattered toys gave evidence that a child lived there.

Will climbed the porch steps, dodging toys as he went, and made his way to the front door. His knock was firm but not aggressive.

In a few moments, the door opened slightly and Sonny's mother peeked through the opening.

"Mrs. Day?" Will inquired.

There was a pause before she answered, "Yes."

"My name is Will Parker ... your new neighbor. I'm living across the river in the Green place. Can I talk to Mr. Day?"

There was another pause before she answered. "What do you want to see him about?"

"It's about Sonny, Mrs. Day. Is Mr. Day at home?"

"Is Sonny in trouble?"

"Not anything bad. Mostly mischief."

"Can't you tell me about it?" she asked.

Will was perplexed. He had always thought that this kind of thing should be handled man to man. "I'll just come back another time," he answered. "Will you tell Mr. Day I was here?"

It was only then that Will noticed the frightened look in her eyes. He felt embarrassed that he had surprised her and had then stood on her porch and broached such a sensitive issue. The door slowly closed with him standing there, and if she had answered his final question, he didn't hear it.

Back at home, he went about the business of laying out his garden. Good Friday, the day of planting, was just around the corner, and he wanted to be ready to put his vegetables in the ground.

He had laid off the rows for sweet corn and green beans and was preparing to choose a place for tomatoes when he saw Mrs. Day coming up the road with Sonny in tow.

She looked much different than before. Her hair was neatly brushed and dropped uncovered over her shoulders. She was wearing a blue house dress and a white knit sweater, and she walked assuredly, comfortable now in her appearance.

As she approached, Will noticed that she carried a package in the hand that was not clamped onto Sonny's arm. She walked up and held the package out toward him.

"Mr. Parker, I believe you said. ... I brought you some bread to welcome you to the valley. I'm sorry that I didn't know we had new neighbors."

"Yes, it is Parker," Will replied as he reached out for the package. "Will Parker. Just call me Will, and thank you very much for the bread. I can smell it through the wrapper."

She came straight to the point. "May I talk to you about Sonny?" she asked.

The look in her eyes somehow told Will that it would be all right to discuss Sonny with her, and he invited her to sit with him on the porch.

As they walked toward the steps, Will looked back at the boy and said, "Sonny, do you like dogs?"

He could tell that Sonny was frightened. He walked with his shoulders drawn up around his neck, and he looked up with anxious eyes. "Tome ob um," he answered.

"Can I bring out my dog and get you to play with him while I talk to your mother?" Will asked.

Sonny dropped his shoulders a bit and nodded yes.

When they were on the porch, Will opened the front door and Dawg ran directly to the boy. Sonny drew back a little and then laughed when he saw that Dawg was playful.

"Please sit down, Mrs. Day," Will said. "Sonny, take Dawg out in the yard and throw a stick to him. He loves that."

As soon as Sonny and Dawg were in the yard, Will sat in a rocker across from Mrs. Day.

"Is Mrs. Parker going to join us?" Mrs. Day asked.

Her question caught Will off guard, and he laughed nervously. "Oh! Mrs. Day," he replied. "There is no Mrs. Parker. ... Just Dawg and me. We are the entire Parker family."

"I'm sorry," she said. "I just assumed…"

"No apology necessary," Will answered, and he rocked back, still chuckling.

Mrs. Day twisted uncomfortably in her rocker, embarrassed over her false assumption. "Mr. Parker," she began.

"It's Will."

"Will, I have some explaining to do. Please bear with me. … I've gone through some rough times." She put her hand to her face and looked away while Will brought his rocking to a halt.

When she had composed herself, she continued. "Will, Matthew … my husband is dead. He was killed last September in a logging accident."

The words shot through Will like a bullet. His heart pounded, and he felt his face turn red. "I'm … I'm sorry," was all he could utter.

"When you came to my house, and I didn't know you, I didn't tell you because I was alone …"

"I understand," Will managed to say.

"I didn't mean to be rude, but a woman by herself …"

"Mrs. Day, you don't need to explain. I feel awful about coming unannounced and raising a complaint about Sonny when I didn't even know you. … I am so … sorry."

"As for Sonny," she continued, "he was always a spirited child, but since Matthew's death … I can't control him." She put her hands to her face and cried silently. "Sometimes he will leave and be gone all day. If I punish him, he just runs away again."

"How does he do in school?" Will asked.

She pulled a handkerchief out of her sleeve and wiped her eyes. "He hasn't been to school since Matthew died," she said. "Miss Pack has been giving me things for him to work on, and I've been teaching him at home."

"Miss Pack … Is that the teacher's name?"

"Yes … but Sonny has always had a hard time at school because of his speech problem. He was constantly in trouble."

Will sat forward and put his elbows on his knees. After he thought for a moment, he said, "Mrs. Day, Sonny reminds me of a boy I went to school with, and I think I know what he's going through. I wonder if you would let me work with him and see if I can help him."

"I'd be grateful if you'd try," she said, and a look of relief crossed her face for an instant. "What did you have in mind?"

"Well, to start with, he can help me put back the boards he took off my barn."

Her eyes flashed instantly to the barn and focused on the gaping hole. "Sonny did *that?*" she asked.

"Took 'em and made a hut up by the river."

"What else has he done?"

"Shot Goober Green *and* me with a slingshot."

Both of Mrs. Day's hands covered her mouth as she gasped. "Are you hurt?" she asked.

Will laughed. "It wasn't quite as bad as the bear attack."

She gasped again. "I heard about that at church. Did Sonny have anything to do that? "

"No, of course not," Will replied quickly, and he laughed to ease the tension that they both felt.

In spite of the stress of the hour, Mrs. Day followed Will's lead and let a smile appear on her face. Will got the impression by her look that a smile was a rare treat for her, and he hoped that some help for Sonny would bring more.

With her purpose fulfilled, Mrs. Day stood and thanked Will, explaining that she had chores to do and must leave.

As they shook hands, Will chanced bringing up his main concern.

"Mrs. Day," he said, "if there were a way to help Sonny with his speech problem, would you agree to me trying?"

"Oh, yes," she quickly replied. "I'd be grateful for *anything* you could do for him."

"It would involve him working with another person who lives here in the valley … someone you don't know."

"If you know the person, I'm sure it would be all right," she said. Her eyes danced back and forth as the prospects of help ran through her mind. "When can you start?" she asked.

"Let's take things one step at a time," Will said. "Let me get to know Sonny and, hopefully, gain his trust, and then we'll try to get the other issues worked out. Now … when can he come to work?"

"When do you want him?"

"How about two hours a day after his chores and schoolwork are done? We'll begin with some fun things, and after we get to know each other, we'll start getting some work done."

"Oh … Mr. Parker," she whispered, and she hurried down the steps to where Sonny was playing.

Kneeling where he stood, she took Sonny by the hands and talked to him as he looked into her eyes. In a moment, Sonny nodded to his mother and glanced up at Will, smiling. After a few more words from his mother, he waved goodbye to Will, hugged Dawg, and trotted off toward home ahead of his mom.

Will watched as Sonny ran up the road, kicking stones as he went. He watched Mrs. Day as she followed, wiping tears from her eyes, but going home with a quickened step.

It had been a good day.

Twenty-Three

THE SALES PITCH

G lenn Neil was up and crackin' on Sunday morning at 6:00 a.m. He had allowed himself to sleep late since the service at Mr. Smithfield's church didn't start until 11:00 o'clock.

He put on his robe and scurried across the hall to bang on Makepeace Green's door. "*Green,*" he hollered as he banged. "*Get up and get ready to go!*"

Makepeace was up, but he wasn't crackin'. He had spent most of the night worrying about how he would approach the group of mountain farmers about selling their land—the land for which their grandfathers and great-grandfathers had fought with the Indians. He could see himself covered with tar and feathers, running from a mob that would have his hide! The vision was not a pretty sight.

"I'm up, Mr. Neil," he said. "Whut time is it, anyway?"

"It's time to get going," Neil answered.

For Makepeace, everything had to be perfect, so when he opened his door and saw that Mr. Neil was wearing his suit, he was distressed.

"Why are ye wearin' 'at suit o' clothes?" he enquired.

"I always dress like this for church," Neil answered.

"Ye wanna live up 'ere an' raise sheeps?"

"Okay, now what?" Neil wanted to know.

Makepeace ticked off his instructions on his fingers. "Overalls ... white shirt, no collar ... boots ... hankerchief hangin' out in ye back pocket ... no suit ... no tie ... none o' them fancy shoes."

"You have this all figured out, don't you, Green?"

"Yes, sir. I know hillbillies!"

"You know how to get insolent too," Neil said in a syrupy voice.

Makepeace stuck his chest out with pride. "I been a-tryin'," he answered.

Neil did wear his suit to breakfast, but when he went back to his room to get ready to leave, he changed into the uniform Makepeace had prescribed. He even found a red handkerchief that he let dangle from his right rear pocket.

As they walked to the livery stable, they found that Friday night's snow was mostly gone. All that remained was the dingy refuse kicked up by wagon wheels and small patches on the north side of buildings. The jonquils that were pushing their heads up in the gardens were not even aware that a late snow had tried to cover them.

The air was fresh and clean. No coal smoke stained the sky and the wood smoke that took its place perfumed the air like a fragrant incense.

When they got to the livery, they found Sis ready to go, thankful for the opportunity to get some exercise, and before long she was harnessed to the wagon.

Although breakfast and the walk to the livery had been leisurely, there was an abundance of time left before church services. It was still before 9:00 o'clock when Sis exited the livery stable yard.

"You plannin' t' go t' Sunday school?" Makepeace asked as he turned Sis toward the north-bound road.

"Not today," Neil answered. "I've got something I want you to see. Head up the road past the church and on past Smithfield's place."

"Pastureland?"

"Nope, a spot I've picked out for my house."

"Ye ain't even bought any land yet, an' ye already movin' in!"

Neil didn't answer, but when Makepeace glanced over, he found the big man deep in thought. If he could have read Neil's mind, he would have found the story of a man who was bored with industry and wealth—a man who longed for simpler things. He would have found a man who wanted to be what his father had been as a boy in the Grampians of Scotland.

The road climbed and Sis strained under the load of the wagon. They passed the church and the Smithfield farm, rolling through the hills until they finally reached the end of the road.

Stretched out before them were chains of mountains that rippled into the distance like crumpled fabric. The highest of the peaks were still capped with snow, but below the white caps the slopes displayed the light green shades of spring that darkened and then shifted to blue in the distance.

When the wagon stopped, Neil finally spoke. "This is where I'll build my home," he said. He climbed down to walk to the highest spot and gaze to the north.

Even though he had grown up in the glory of the hills, Makepeace was impressed. He stood and looked, imagining what it would be like to live in an idyllic spot like that. In Avery Cove the view was only up. Here it was out and beyond, into Virginia and Tennessee.

When a few minutes had passed, Neil pulled out his watch and saw that it was time to go. As he walked back to the wagon, he pledged to return with workers and wagon loads of building supplies.

———

The clatter of the wagon ceased when Makepeace pulled up beside the church. It was only then that the boisterous singing of the congregation could be heard. Services had begun.

When they entered, the singing continued, and heads turned row by row to see the strangers. To show their welcome, the congregation sang the final verse with spirit.

Let us love our God supremely,
Let us love each other too.
Let us love and pray for sinners
Till our God makes all things new:

Then he'll call us home to heaven.
At his table we'll sit down.
Christ will gird himself, and serve us
With sweet manna all around.

Perhaps it was by coincidence that the preacher chose for his Scripture reading 1 Samuel 17:34-37; or perhaps he knew that the legendary Goober
Green was going to be in attendance. Either way it was the ideal text for
the day. As he read, the congregation listened in awe and snuck glances at
Makepeace.

> 34 And David said to Saul, Thy servant kept his father's sheep, and
> there came a lion, and a bear, and took a lamb out of the flock:
> 35And I went out after him, and smote him, and delivered it out
> of his mouth: and when he arose against me, I caught him by his
> beard, and smote him, and slew him.
> 36Thy servant slew both the lion and the bear: and the uncircum-
> sized Philistine shall be as one of them, seeing he hath defied the
> armies of the living God.
> 37David said moreover, The Lord that delivered me out of the paw
> of the lion, and out of the paw of the bear, he will deliver me out of
> the hand of the Philistine. And Saul said unto David, Go, and the
> Lord be with thee.

When the preacher finished his reading, he closed The Book and looked out
over the congregation.

"Now ... we don't have any lions here in Watauga County—least I ain't
seen any ... but we do have *bears*! Any o' you chil'ren ever seen a *bear*?" he
asked as he pointed to a group of kids on the front row.

The children looked up with mouths open and shook their heads *yes* in
unison.

"Any o' you chil'ren think you could go out and catch a bear by his beard
and kill him?"

All the children and some of the adults vigorously shook their heads *no*.

Then the preacher raised his voice to the rafters. *"I'm here to tell you that there ain't a man alive that could kill a bear with his bare hands ..."* Then he whispered, "... unless *God* was with him."

"I hope t' my never," Makepeace muttered, and he hunkered down in the pew in an attempt to fend off glances that were cast his way. It was obvious that they knew who he was.

Glenn Neil sat with his arms folded across the bib of his overalls, his attention riveted on the preacher.

The preacher continued, whipping the congregation into a frenzy as he described the weakness of man and the power of God. He told how a small, weak man with the power of God in him could have the strength to overcome any man or any animal.

He never mentioned Makepeace by name. As far as anyone could tell, he never even looked directly at him, but every person there knew who the man with the power of God inside him was. He was the little man hunkered down in the pew.

When the service concluded, the congregation descended on Makepeace like a swarm of locust. Little children climbed through the forest of legs to be able to touch the bear killer.

"I wanna shake 'at man's han'," someone bellowed.

"Tell us how ye done it," another person hollered.

"I hear he's a-gonna give a speech," someone else announced. "Let th' man tawk!"

Makepeace was mortified!

Mr. Smithfield ran to the pulpit and banged his hands on the surface. "Hesh up!" he shouted. "Hesh up! He's gonna tawk, I tell ye! You ladies go on outside an' put th' dinner baskets out whilst Mr. Green tawks to th' men folk. You younguns go on out w' ye mamas."

Within a minute, the ladies and children were in the churchyard and the men were in their seats. There was a muted buzz as the men put their heads together and whispered excitedly.

Smithfield escorted Makepeace to the podium and banged the pulpit again. "Now, men," he said, "'is here is Goober Green ... but he goes by Makepeace now... an' he's th' man ye all been a-hearin' 'bout. Now as I tol' most of ye, him an' his frien' here has a business proposition they want t' lay out fer ye. An' I know ye all gonna listen real good. So here's Mr. Green."

Makepeace's confidence wavered as he looked out over the crowd of men. He examined their faces trying to determine their openness, and for the most part he liked what he saw.

"I wanna thank ye fer letting me come t' see ye today," he said softly. "Me an' Mr. Neil here brung ye some good news 'bout a way ye kin make some money an' live a little easier at th' same time."

Someone in the audience spoke up. "Thought ye was gonna tell us 'bout that bar."

"Tell ye whut … soon as business is over, we'll go outside an' talk 'bout 'at very thing, but fer rat now, 'et's tawk 'bout sheeps.

"Now I ain't no business man, but I think I'm a purdy good judge o' character. I kin look a man in th' eye an' tell ye if he's a good man or a crook! Th' man 'at come wi' me t'day … Mr. Neil here … is a *good* man … an' ye kin take th' word o' Goober Makepeace Green that he ain't no *crook*."

Every eye was fixed upon Makepeace's face. Every man there was trying to look through his eyes and into his mind. Every man there wanted to bask in the glory of the one who was both brave and wise—the one who walked with God and killed bears.

"Mr. Glenn Neil is jest one o' us," Makepeace said as he pointed toward his boss. "He buttons th' straps on 'is overalls one at a time jest lack you an' me. He's a man 'at loves th' hills an' takes care o' th' land. Only difference in him an' most o' us is God put a few more coins in 'is purse. He's gonna talk to ye now … an' I want ye t' listen. I want ye t' listen real careful!"

And then Makepeace sat down.

On Tuesday morning, Will scurried about the house after breakfast getting things in order. He was still trying to arrange the house in a familiar fashion and develop a routine that he could live by. While he worked, he planned his day.

Roamer hadn't been back since he left in a huff the previous Saturday, so it was time, he decided, for "Mohammad to go to the mountain." While he was there, he could see if there were any odd jobs that needed to be done.

Then, since his milk supply was long gone, he decided, too, that he would go by Demus Whitedeer's house to visit and hopefully work out a deal to buy milk on a regular basis.

The mist was hanging heavy over the valley that morning, brought by the dampness of the snow melt and the warming temperatures. It was so heavy in fact that it gave an even more distant sound to the school bell when it rang at 8:00 o'clock. He was growing used to the sound, and he wondered how he would do without it when summer vacation came. Perhaps by then, he thought, his body would be on Avery Cove time. By then, too, he might have his clock regulated.

Don and Molly appeared out of the mist when Will called, anxious for a trip outside the fence. They held still as they were harnessed to the wagon and were soon on their way out North Road.

Demus was outside doing his morning chores when the wagon came rattling down the road. He stopped and watched, admiring the movement as the horses danced in front of the wagon. Will was a welcome sight.

"Mornin', Demus," Will called out as he entered the yard.

"Good morning, Will. What brings you out?"

"Came to talk business."

"Fair enough. What's on your mind?"

Will climbed down off the wagon and stretched his legs. "I mainly wanted to see what a hard working man does this time o' day."

Demus sounded his deep laugh. "This one just milks the cow and feeds the chickens."

"Ah-ha!" Will declared. "You said the magic word!"

"Which one of *those* words is magic?" Demus asked.

"Milk!" Will replied. "I wanted to see if we could make a deal for me to buy milk on a regular basis … that is, if you have some to spare."

"I almost always have some spoil," Demus said. "Tell me what you need."

"Couple of quarts ... twice a week. In Charlotte, the going rate was two cents a quart."

Demus whistled. "That would buy some extra books! Sounds good to me!"

"You mentioned chickens, too," Will said. "Would you have any laying hens you want to sell?"

"About all I could give up right now is an old brood hen that's sitting on six eggs. If you're patient, you could have laying hens in a few months." Then Demus rubbed his head and looked toward his hen house. "Maybe I could throw in another hen that's laying now."

"How much?"

"How about twenty cents for the lot?"

"That's a done deal!" Will exclaimed. "I'll pick 'em up on the way back from Roamer's."

———

Roamer was bent over his cold frames checking has tobacco plants and Sweetie was sweeping the porch when Will pulled into the yard.

Sweetie propped her broom and smoothed her apron before she came down the steps to meet Will. "Law, Honey," she said. "I been worried 'bout you. I feared some animal drug ye off an' et ye!" She flashed her toothless smile as she came to greet him.

"Wal look whut a buzzard dropped outta th' sky," Roamer chirped. "You're a sight fer old eyes."

"I thought I better come and start paying you back for all the food," Will said. "What needs to be done?"

"Roamer's been a-frettin' over 'em terbackie plants ... an' I ain't been able t' git no stove wood split," Sweetie offered.

"Speakin' o' terbackie," Roamer added, "I could use some he'p a-puttin' 'em plants in th' ground in a week er so. I can't hardly bend over at m' middle no more."

"Aunt Sweetie, point me to the wood pile, and Uncle Roamer, consider your plants in the ground."

By the time Sweetie's wood box was filled, she had the midday meal cooked. Will got a meal of polk salat, fried fat back, pickled peppers, and corn bread.

The polk salat was a new experience for Will. Sweetie explained that a "mess o' polk salat" was eaten in the spring both as a taste treat and as a spring tonic. She told how she had gathered the tender young growth of the poisonous wild polk plant, boiled it in "several waters" to remove the "pizen," and then fried it up in bacon grease.

Will had to admit that it was delicious, even though he wondered what it would do to his digestive tract. Despite the risk, he had seconds on everything.

After lunch he went to the stable and cleaned the mule's stall and put down straw. Then he carried in three buckets of water for Sweetie.

When the fire in the kitchen stove had died down, he emptied the ashes and put them in the ash bin to be used for making soap.

He remembered that Roamer had said the meat supply was getting low, so he went to the wagon and got his rifle, walked off into the woods, and came back shortly with two fat squirrels.

"I been a-hankerin' fer some squirrel stew!" Roamer exclaimed.

As Will was leaving, Roamer perked up and said, "I'uz 'bout t' fergit … Preacher Babb said t' tell ye they's a spacial council meetin' 'is Thursday. Wanted t' make sure you wuz 'ere."

"Wonder what that's all about," Will said.

"Didn't say. Jest said hit wuz spacial."

On the way home, Will stopped at Demus Whitedeer's house to pick up the chickens and the nest of eggs. Demus loaned him the box that the hen was nesting in, and they wrapped the hens in burlap with their heads sticking out.

While Will was putting the hens in the wagon, Demus went to his spring house and got two quarts of milk that was fresh from that morning.

"I'll bring the jars back and get two more quarts on Friday, if that's alright," Will said. Then he reached in his pocket and handed Demus twenty-five cents. "Keep the penny change for the good service," he told him as he climbed up on the wagon.

"I'm gonna like doing business with you," Demus replied with a chuckle.

When Will got home around 4:00 o'clock, he found Sonny in the yard playing with Dawg. He had totally forgotten that Sonny was coming.

He watched the boy as he pulled the wagon up into the yard, and the boy he saw was not the same Sonny he had known before. The old Sonny was a frightened, confused kid, bent on getting into trouble. This boy seemed happy and secure—at least for now. Maybe there *was* some hope for him.

Will parked the wagon, climbed down, and tousled Sonny's hair. "Sonny, there's not much time left today," he told the boy. "Why don't you come back tomorrow, and I promise I'll be here."

"Mama want you t' tome t' tupper."

"She wants me to come to supper? Today?"

"Dat right."

"Are you sure?"

"Dat what tee taid."

"Let's see if I have this right," Will said. "Your mama wants me to come to supper ... today ... and that's what she said?"

"Dat right."

Will squatted down and looked the boy in the eye. "Well ... I hope you have that straight, Sonny, cause if I go over there for supper and she's not expecting me, I'll be embarrassed."

"Wealy ... dat what tee taid. Tan Dawg tome too?"

"No, Dawg can't come. Maybe some other time. Now, while you're playing, I'm going to put my chickens in the hen house. Then I'm going to go in, put my milk in the spring house, and clean up for supper. It's not often I get invited to a meal by one of Dawg's buddies."

The day was waning when Will and Sonny finally left for supper. It was the time of day that Will found so different in Avery Cove.

In Charlotte when the sun set behind the horizon, darkness came; but in Avery Cove, the sun would set behind the high western mountain and there would still be about an hour of light left. The long period of sunless radiance would give a shimmering effect to the surroundings and cast eerie shadows.

When Sonny's house came into view, every window seemed to be filled with light. A column of smoke rose from the kitchen chimney, and Will was sure he could smell the fragrance of bread.

As Will parked the wagon in the yard and set the brake, he noticed another thing. The toys that had cluttered the yard and the porch steps were gone and the yard had been swept clean. "Maybe I am expected," he thought.

As he and Sonny started up the steps, the door opened and Mrs. Day appeared. "You've come!" she said. "I was afraid that Sonny had gotten your invitation mixed up. He mixes things up sometimes."

"No, he did fine," Will told her. "I must admit though, he didn't have to beg. I'm not much of a cook."

"Well, it's ready … such as it is … and I hope you're hungry."

Will crossed the porch and entered the front room. The house was neat and clean and was furnished with items not normally found in the remote mountains. It looked more like a town home with its upholstered sofa and chairs. All of the other furniture seemed to be store bought, too.

"You have a nice home," Will said. "It looks like you picked up rooms in the city and moved them here."

"That's sorta what we did … Matthew and I. We moved here from Chattanooga right after we were married, and we brought some heirlooms from both of our families. Matthew inherited the farm from his grandfather. He had loved the valley since he was a boy, so moving here was a natural thing for him."

"And how about you? Was it natural for you too?"

"Oh, no! I hated it at first ... being from the city. I was so homesick! But I've grown to love it ... even without Matthew."

While Mrs. Day talked, she moved from the stove to the table carrying bowls and dishes of food, finishing up with a roasted chicken.

Seeing the meal laid out in festive fashion, with Sonny eying the food, had Will a flashback. For a moment he was carried to his mother's table in Charlotte. For his mother, every meal was a festive occasion with meat, bread, vegetables, and dessert. There was always dessert.

"You've gone to a lot of trouble, Mrs. Day," Will said.

"Not really," she replied. "I feel like you are the one that's gone to a lot of trouble ... reacting to Sonny the way you have. He's talked about nothing but you and your dog since we came to your house. You're a godsend, Mr. Parker."

"I thought you were going to call me Will."

"Okay, I'll call you Will if you'll call me Alice."

When she looked at Will and spoke her name, a small spark of something other than neighborly admiration jumped between them. It was something that neither of them expected or even wanted, and both were caught off guard.

Alice turned away abruptly and busied herself fumbling around for some unknown thing.

Will sat uncomfortably before reaching over and tousling Sonny's hair. "You look hungry," he said.

"I want tome o' dat ticken!" Sonny replied. The look on his face was convincing.

"Ah-ha!" Alice exclaimed as she turned and held up a serving spoon. "Here it is." It could just as well have been a fork, or a knife, or a ball of yarn. The tension of the moment was broken.

The conversation throughout supper was light and cheerful. Will asked Sonny his age, and he said that he was ten years old. "Well, awmote ten," he admitted.

Both Will and Alice included him in the discussion of topics such as the weather, gardening, and school work. For an almost ten year old with a speech impediment, he held his own pretty well.

He voiced his approval of the recent snow and expressed his willingness to help grow some popcorn. School work though was another matter. When that topic was raised, he asked to be excused from the table.

"You know, Sonny," Will said, "if you're going to be my helper, you'll need to have an education. I'll be asking you to do things that require reading and numbers and things that you learn in your school books. Wouldn't it be worth some study to be able to come and help me on the farm and play with Dawg?"

Sonny didn't answer. He just grinned and skipped off to his room.

"It's just as well that he left," Alice remarked when Sonny was out of earshot. "I wanted a chance to talk about him anyway."

"Alice, I think Sonny will be all right," Will told her. "I see a glint of light in his eyes that shows his mind is working full speed. He has so much energy and too little way to use it, and I've been thinking about things he could do for both of us."

"Like what?"

"First off, what would you think about him going hunting with me?"

"After what happened to *you?*"

"Well, you'll have to admit that was a very rare occurrence, and I'll assure you that I'd take extra care with him along."

"Such as ..."

"I thought I'd get another adult ... a seasoned hunter ... to go with us."

Alice put her elbows on the table and stared toward Sonny's room. "He's never been around guns much," she said. "His father wasn't a hunter. We ate a lot of chicken and pen-raised pork."

"I'll teach him," Will insisted. "I had to learn, and I learned the right way."

She stared toward Sonny's room again, this time in deep thought, before she turned back to Will. "Okay, you can take him," she replied as she shook a finger in his face, "but you'd better take good care of him. He's all I have in this world!"

Will took the warning seriously. He saw in Alice Day's eyes the same look that Glenn Neil had when he warned Makepeace that he would nail his skin to the front door of the mill.

"He'll come back a happy and healthy hunter!" he told her. "I guarantee it!"

The conversation continued with Will telling Alice about Charlotte, his grandfather's farm, and the realization of his dream to live in the mountains.

She told him about Chattanooga, her city upbringing, and the horror she felt when she saw the rigors of mountain life. Then she recalled how her love for the valley had grown when she saw the fruit of her and Matthew's labor.

She told about their first harvest and how the people from the church had come to help them gather in the corn and hay. She told how the women had taught her to preserve vegetables and how the men had taught Matthew how to slaughter the pigs and cure the meat.

She told Will that she and Matthew were married two days after her sixteenth birthday and left for Avery Cove the next week. In ten months, she said, Sonny was born.

Will's mind went into motion, adding sixteen and nine to make twenty-five. She was twenty-five years old—an older woman! Then as Alice continued talking, his mind was busy telling himself that he shouldn't be making such calculations concerning a recent widow whom he barely knew. It just wasn't proper!

"Will?" she said, breaking his train of thought. "Did you hear me?"

"What?"

"I said when are you going hunting?"

"I'm sorry, Alice," he answered. "Friday, I guess. I must be tired. What time is it anyway?"

She turned and glanced toward the mantle. "Ten thirty-five."

Will jumped to his feet. "You can't be serious," he said. "I had no idea it was that late! I'm keeping you up ... and Sonny ..."

"It's okay ... really!" she said assuringly. "Will ... I haven't had such a wonderful time since ..." Her smile turned to a look of melancholy before changing again to a look of simple contentment.

"Can I look in on Sonny before I leave?" Will asked.

"Sure. He'll want to say goodnight."

He walked to Sonny's door and peeked in. The boy was sleeping—lying on top of his covers, slightly curled up. The little scamp with the slingshot was peacefully still. Beside him was a book Miss Pack had sent home for him to study, his finger marking a page, and on his face was his mother's look of simple contentment.

Twenty-Four

ANKYLOGLOSSIA

Early Wednesday morning Will went to the chicken house to see how his hens were doing. The brood hen was happily sitting on her eggs with her head held high, ready to fight off intruders. The other hen was pacing the floor, anxious to get out into the sunlight.

The fence around the chicken yard turned out to be in worse condition than he had first thought. Holes had eroded in the dirt along the bottom of the fencing, and the wire itself was so rusty that he feared it would collapse under a strong wind. It was clear that the fencing would have to be replaced, especially with biddies about to hatch.

A couple of days earlier Will had found some cracked corn in the barn. He threw out a double handful on the floor of the hen house, gave the birds some fresh water, and promised them that by day's end they would have access to the outside world. They seemed to understand and clucked their approval.

When the chores were done and he and Dawg had eaten breakfast, Will hitched the horses to the wagon and headed out for Burden's. He had thought about the things he needed to buy, and as he rode along he reviewed his list: chicken wire, staples to hold the wire, a turnbuckle for the gate, laying mash, a bone for Dawg, a box of ammunition for the rifle, and a large box of salt. With his list committed to memory, he allowed his mind to move on to other things.

He had been so tired at the end of the previous day that even thoughts of Alice were blotted out by the need for sleep. Now, after a good night's sleep, and with the drone of the wagon wheels and the song of the birds providing the proper atmosphere, he allowed himself to reflect on what had occurred between them.

The feeling that came over him the night before was nothing new. He had experienced a similar feeling as a teen in Charlotte when he was introduced to the visiting cousin of a friend. Her name was Victoria Elizabeth Malfort. She was a tall, willowy girl with dark hair and eyes who spoke with a slight British accent and carried the fragrance of lavender in her hair.

When they first met they chanced to look into each other's eyes, and the same spark he had felt with Alice had jumped between them; but alas, the spark was extinguished when Victoria left for home the next day, never to return. Soon after that his friend moved out west, and all hope of seeing Victoria again was lost.

While there were similarities between Victoria and Alice, there were also vast differences. The physical differences were great, but as he wisely thought, they were the least important. Alice was pretty and cultured, while Victoria was elegant and sophisticated. Victoria was just entering womanhood, and Alice was as mature as her twenty-five years would allow. Victoria had the aura of Europe surrounding her, while Alice was taking on the gentle aura of the mountains.

All of those things were secondary to Will—mere trappings of the surface. There were more important things to consider. Alice was a widow of only a few months. Perhaps it wasn't proper, especially in mountain culture, for him to be seeing her. He had to consider too that her momentary attraction to him might be just that—momentary. He reckoned that for her, it could just be a passing fascination that would never return.

And then there was Sonny, who would come with Alice as a package deal. He was growing fond of Sonny, but he couldn't imagine being the parent of a nine-year-old boy, especially one with a penchant for trouble.

Chicken wire, staples to hold the wire, a turnbuckle for the gate, a speech impediment, laying mash, three mouths to feed—a tangle of thoughts were running through his brain, colliding with each other into a jumbled stream of consciousness.

"*Will!*"

What is the proper time to court a widow? Don't forget a bone for Dawg. Maybe two boxes of salt.

"*Will! Are you asleep?*" A voice was calling. "*Will.*"

Will snapped out of his daze and looked to his left to see Demus walking across his yard toward the road. He brought the wagon to a stop and threw up his hand absentmindedly.

"For a minute I thought you were asleep," Demus said as he walked up to the wagon. "Are you all right?"

"Demus, what is the proper time to wait before asking a widow if you can come calling?"

"*What?*" Demus said laughing his deep, resonant laugh. "You're asking *me*—a confirmed bachelor? Why on earth would you ask me a thing like that?"

"It was just a thought that came to me."

"It does seem that I read somewhere that a year was about right," Demus said. "Maybe it was Jane Austin that touched on that. That does go back a ways though, doesn't it? It's probably not that long now. It could be two weeks as far as I know," and the deep laugh started up again.

"Demus, how would you like to have some fresh pork?"

"How did we get off on that subject?"

"I wondered if you might want to go hunting Friday."

"I could arrange that."

"Would you mind if Sonny Day came along?"

"He's an experienced hunter?"

"He's never been hunting before."

"Sounds to me like he would fit right in," Demus said, and his laugh rolled out like thunder.

"Tell you what," Will said, "I'm going to Burden's to get some chicken wire and I'll stop on the way back. We'll talk about the details then."

"Sonny Day!" Demus declared as he chuckled. "Can't wait to meet *him!*"

Will clicked the horses into motion, and with a wave to Demus, he continued down the road. On this leg of the journey his thoughts shifted to hunting.

It was his intention to go back to the spot where the bear attack happened and start the hunt there. When he pictured the place, butterflies filled his stomach and his hands trembled. He wondered what he would do if he got a pig in his sights and his hands began to shake. It was good that Demus would be along, he decided. Maybe Demus would be his rescuer this time, slapping some sense into him if he panicked.

All was quiet when he reached Roamer's house. He pulled into the yard, set the brake on the wagon, and made his way toward the porch. Smoke was curling up from the kitchen chimney, but that was the only sign that anyone was there.

A knock on the door brought Sweetie with her toothless smile. "Law, Honey," she said, "ever' time I see ye I jest git th' all-overs. Whut has brung ye out t'day? Do ye need some food t' tide ye over?"

"No," Will replied, "I just wanted to see if you could still use some fresh pork. I'm going hunting Friday."

"Law, we kin always use fresh pork," she said. "Roamer likes sausage an' liver mush, ham, shoulder, fat back ..."

"Where is Roamer anyway?" Will asked. "I wanted to see about borrowing his .22 rifle for the Day boy to use."

Sweetie's expression turned serious. "He ain't here," she said.

"Will he be back soon?"

"Hit's hard t' say."

"Aunt Sweetie, is everything all right? Where is Uncle Roamer?"

Sweetie sidled over to Will and grabbed his arm. She looked all around as if she wanted to make sure no one was listening. Then she drew up close and whispered, "Roamer's up at 'is secret place on th' side o' th' mountain."

"His secret place?"

"Th' place whur 'e does 'is doin's," she whispered.

"I guess he wouldn't want to be disturbed then."

Sweetie got a strange look in her eyes. "Oh, no!" she said. "An' even if 'e did, you'd never find 'im ... no, sir ... never in a million yars!"

Will looked out toward the road and remembered his hens that were shut up in the chicken house. "I tell you what, Aunt Sweetie," he said, "I'll stop on the way back from Burden's and see if he's back from his ..." Will lowered his voice to a whisper. "... secret place."

Sweetie formed her lips into a perfect little circle, and with wide, serious eyes she nodded her approval.

When Will arrived at Burden's store, he found the normal hub of activity. There was a group caucusing on the front porch, embroiled in a heated discussion about the roads, while inside there was a more amiable gathering centered on the pies at the Baptist gathering the previous Sunday.

Preacher Burden forced himself away from the pie meeting to pull Will to the side. "Son, did you get word about the special meeting?" he asked.

"Preacher Babb told Roamer to let me know," Will answered, "but he didn't say what it was about."

"*Preacher!*" Doc French hollered as he came in the door.

"Over here, Doc," the preacher answered.

"Did my supplies come on the freight wagon?"

"Sure did! Excuse me, Will," the preacher said. "I'll get Naomi to help you while I try to get the old saw-bones satisfied."

In a moment Naomi appeared out of the back room looking frazzled.

"Will!" she said, "you're looking well ... not a thing like that pitiful soul I helped nurse back to health."

"You're looking well yourself," Will replied, "but you look like you're under stress! What's going on?"

"It's that Morse code, Will!" she said as she threw her hands in the air. "The preacher and Rachel and I are learning to operate the telegraph, and I hate it! I'm so glad you came in so I can get away from that clicker!"

It hadn't dawned on Will that Avery Cove was about to enter the modern age with telegraph service. Next would be the telephone if somehow that miracle happened, and there would be no hiding—not even in Avery Cove.

"When will the telegraph be working?" Will asked.

Naomi looked toward the back room to make sure the preacher wasn't around. "I'll tell *you*," she said softly. "That's one thing on the agenda for the special meeting. It'll be up and running in a few days. Preacher's going to announce it *and* the electricity tomorrow night!"

"Big doin's," Will said softly.

"The biggest!"

Will recited his list to Naomi, and she went about the task of getting his order together.

When Doc reappeared from the back room, Will took the opportunity to pull him aside and ask, "Doc, are you familiar with Sonny Day's speech problem?"

"Yeah," he answered. "He was born tongue-tied. There's a fancy name for it, but I can't remember it. It's a condition where the bottom of the tongue is closely joined to the floor of the mouth."

"Can it be fixed?" Will asked.

"Well, it's *been* fixed," Doc answered. "Kind of accidentally, you might say. When he was about five, he had a stick in his mouth and fell, and it tore the area loose. Matthew brought him to me and he was bleeding like a butchered hog and screaming, and I checked him out. Wasn't much I could do, but his tongue is free now. There are doctors in the big cities that do the same thing that stick did and charge a lot of money."

"Well, why does he still have the speech problem?"

"Habit, I guess. … That's the way he learned to talk. … It's sort of imprinted in his brain."

"Could he be taught to speak correctly?"

"Possibly … but not probably. There are doctors at some universities that are working with speech … but not around here. I wouldn't know where to begin." Doc looked away and rubbed his chin. "I feel sorry for the boy," he said.

———

Before long Will was back on the road with his chicken wire, staples to hold the wire, a turnbuckle for the gate, laying mash, a bone for Dawg, a box of ammunition for his rifle, and a large box of salt. In addition to his original order he had added another box of salt and a box of .22 caliber ammunition in case he could get Roamer to loan him his rifle.

As he rode along, his mind shifted from one thing to another—Alice to hunting—hunting to Sonny—and back to Alice again. He kept telling himself that dwelling on thoughts of her was premature if not unhealthy. He had spent less than five hours in her presence, which he knew was not enough time to form an opinion of her, much less get to know her.

The same was true of Sonny, he reasoned. He had seen him as a troubled child, determined to rain havoc, and a detriment to a relationship with his mother; but considering the loss of his father and his speech impediment, perhaps he really wasn't doing too badly.

The sights and places that were growing familiar to Will clicked by until he finally came to Roamer's house. Roamer was in the yard, kneeling at his cold frames, working with his tobacco plants. He watched the old man even as he turned into the yard and was almost to him before he raised up.

"*Ye skeert me!*" Roamer hollered when Will had stopped the horses. "I didn't hear ye a-comin'."

Will climbed down from the wagon. "You weren't here when I came by earlier."

Roamer slowly rose to his feet and brushed the dirt from the knees of his overalls. "Wal, with th' weather a-warmin' up, I figgered on takin' a walk up th' mountain. Me an' th' mule."

"Find anything interesting?"

"Yep. Ever'thing was right whur I lef' it in th' fall. Only difference is hit's a whole lot further up 'ere than hit used t' be."

"Maybe if the tobacco crop does well this year, you won't have to make those trips up the mountain."

For a moment Roamer seemed lost in thought, ruminating Will's notion. "'At's fer a truth," he said. "'At's fer a truth!"

"Well, the reason I came by was to see if I could borrow your .22 rifle to teach Sonny Day to shoot. I'm going hunting with him Friday. ... Gonna bring you some pork when I return the rifle."

Roamer pulled off his hat and slapped his leg with it. "*I'm fer that!*" he hollered, and he hurried off toward the house.

Soon, Will was back on the road with the rifle by his side and a box of food from Sweetie, including an apple pie, in the wagon bed.

———

Demus and Will sat to talk on the rock wall in Demus's yard. "Let me tell you about Sonny Day," Will said.

"I'm all ears."

"Sonny's a troubled lad. I came to know him when he shot Makepeace Green and me both with a slingshot. He lost his father a few months ago ..."

"I heard about that at the Mast store," Demus interjected.

"... and he has a speech impediment. Doc says he was born tongue-tied."

"Ankyloglossia," Demus said.

"*What?*"

"Ankyloglossia. That's the medical term."

Will straightened up and looked at Demus with his head tilted. "How did you know that?"

"Grandfather had a house servant named Romulus who was tongue-tied. They said that he was a good worker but he was hard to understand. Grandfather spent a lot of time working with him and helped him a lot."

"Whatever happened to him? Is he still around?"

"No, as soon as he learned to talk, he ran away. No one ever saw him again."

"Do you know how your grandfather helped him?"

Demus thought for a moment. "No, but I have one of Grandfather's books somewhere that describes the condition and the treatment."

"That's incredible!" Will said. "Can I read the book?"

"Sure ... if you can read French," Demus chuckled.

"I can't read French!" Will exclaimed. "I doubt there's anyone in the valley that can."

"I can."

"You read *French*? What else am I going to find out about you?"

"You'll probably find out sooner or later that I also read Latin, Greek, Spanish, Italian, and German ... and a little Russian ... I'm *struggling* with Russian."

"Good Lord!" Will said. "And in Avery Cove!" He then went on to explain that he had thought up the hunting trip when he heard about the way Demus's father learned English from the missionaries. "I thought you might be able to help the boy because of your reading on that subject," he said. "Now that I've heard about Romulus, I'm convinced that you're the man that can help the boy."

Demus looked away with a serious expression on his face. "I'm not a doctor, Will."

"Will you just *try*?"

Demus thought some more before he answered, and as he thought, the expression on his face lightened. "I'll try," he said, "if you'll take that sling-shot away from him," and his laugh rolled out like thunder.

Will was hungry when he got home, and he knew just what he wanted. When the horses were put out to pasture and the food Sweetie had sent was put away, he cut himself a big slice of the apple pie.

Will had grown to love Avery Cove, and the people were growing on him, but the thing he was learning to love the most was the local cooking. Everything he tasted was rich in butter and salt, cinnamon and sugar. Everything he was eating was fattening, and it was showing in the way his clothes were fitting. He was telling himself that if he didn't get his full energy back and start working some full days soon, he would be as large as one of Laddie Green's barns.

He took a bite of pie, stared off into space, and wondered, "Would Alice Day like me if I was fat?" He was back to that again, and he was enjoying thinking of her when the front door opened and Sonny ran in.

"I tome to work!" Sonny called out as he ran in.

"That's good," Will answered, "because there's plenty to do. Have you finished your school work?"

"Uh-huh."

"Did you do your chores, all of them?"

"Uh-huh."

"Did you eat a piece of pie?"

"Huh?"

"Pie ... all my workers have to be pie eaters!"

A big smile broke out over Sonny's face, and he sat down at the table while Will cut a slice of pie and placed it in front of him.

"We have a lot to do today," Will said. "First, we have to put up new wire around the chicken house ..."

Sonny looked up as he shoveled pie into his mouth.

"... and then, since we're going hunting tomorrow ..."

Sonny stopped chewing and his eyes got as big as water buckets.

"... I'm going to teach you how to shoot."

"*A dun?*"

"That's right, a .22 rifle."

Sonny shoved the last piece of pie into his mouth and swallowed it down. "*A weal dun?*"

Will chuckled. "Yes, a real gun."

The chicken wire went up in a snap. Sonny pulled it tight from the end while Will hammered the staples into the posts. Then they screwed the turn-buckle onto the gate, and Will let Sonny adjust it until the gate no longer dragged the ground.

A walk-around inspection revealed no gaps in the wire, so Will got a shovel and supervised as Sonny filled the holes under the fence. As he worked, the boy reveled in his worth.

The time for the test had come. Will went in the fence, threw out some laying mash, and opened the door to the hen house. In a few seconds the laying hen came to the door and stuck her head outside. She looked around, and sensing no danger, she carefully stepped into the yard and began pecking at the ground. In a moment the brood hen stuck her head out the door, looked around, and satisfied that all was well, returned to her nest.

"Tan we toot de dun now?" Sonny asked.

"I think you've earned that," Will replied. He went to the house, returning with Roamer's rifle.

It occurred to Will as he left the house that he had taken on an awesome responsibility. He was about to introduce a firearm to a youngster, who a few days earlier, had no compunction about shooting people with a slingshot. For his sake and for the sake of the valley he would have to proceed with caution. He took Sonny to the porch steps and sat him down.

"Sonny," he said, "if you shot someone with your slingshot, you could hurt that person badly. If you hit someone in the eye, it could blind that person. Do you understand?"

"Uh-huh."

"Will you promise me that you will never shoot anyone with your slingshot again?"

Sonny vigorously shook his head yes.

"On the other hand, if you shot someone with this rifle, it could kill that person. Do you understand that?"

Sonny's eyes got large, and he shook his head yes again.

"Will you promise me that you will never even point a gun at another person ... even if it isn't loaded?"

The boy's countenance was grim. Perhaps he was remembering how his father had died and how final and serious death was. The corners of his mouth turned down and his lip quivered. "I pwomut," he said.

Will reached over and tousled his hair. "I think you're man enough to learn the rules," he said, "but I'm going to tell you what my grandfather told me. If you get careless, I'll take the gun away until you're old enough to be careful."

Sonny straightened up, sniffled, and nodded his head yes. He had been given a portion of responsibility, and he had accepted it.

Then Will showed him how to hold and carry the gun with the barrel pointed down and away from others. He told him how he should know what was beyond his target. He gave him a lesson on how to operate the bolt and safety switch, and warned him to keep his finger away from the trigger until he was ready to fire.

Will's shooting range was an area behind his house that had a dirt bank as a backdrop. The next step was to go there and teach Sonny how to aim and fire.

Will went first. He chambered a round and fired at a target he had set up, hitting the bull's-eye. The pop of the small caliber bullet amused Sonny and he begged for a turn. "Et me toot it! Et me toot it!" he said.

Will showed Sonny the sights and told him how to align the front sight in the groove of the rear sight, and then he placed the rifle on Sonny's shoulder and showed him a proper stance. With his finger over Sonny's, he squeezed back on the trigger and the gun popped off another round. "*I tot it!*" the boy bellowed.

"You may have shot it, but you didn't hit the target," Will said.

He let Sonny try it again, this time with no help, and he hit the second circle from the center.

By the time Sonny had fired about ten rounds, he was consistently around the bull's-eye.

With his first shooting lesson under his belt, Will took Sonny back to the steps and sat him down again. "Tomorrow," he said, "we're going to start putting the barn back together. If you work hard, we'll have another shooting lesson, and then on Friday, we'll go hunting for pigs."

"*Can I toot a pig?*"

"No, your rifle isn't big enough for pig hunting, but you can learn. I have a friend who's going with us, and we'll teach you how to hunt. If you learn well, I'll move you up to a larger gun and you can shoot a pig another time.

"Now," Will said, "why don't you go on home and see if your mother needs any help. Tell her that I'll come by tomorrow on my way to the council meeting and tell her about Friday."

"*Aw wight!*" Sonny hollered and ran a few steps toward the road, but then he stopped. He ran back and threw his arms around Will's neck. "Pank you, Will," he said, and then he ran off toward home.

Alice was expecting Will when he stopped by on his way to the council meeting. She was wearing a fresh spring dress, even though the temperature was still a little cool, and her hair was put up in the "city" style. She politely asked him to eat, but he declined, saying he hoped she would ask him again another time.

She was thrilled about the progress he had made with Sonny, telling him how Sonny had recited the rules of handling a gun to her. She said she hadn't seen him so excited since the Christmas before his father had died.

Will told her how hard Sonny was working and how attentive he had been. He assured her again that the primary concern of the hunt would be Sonny's safety.

"If it's possible," he told her, "I'd like to get an early start tomorrow. So have him come as early as he can get his chores done."

She agreed.

On that visit there were no sparks between them—no awkward eye contact—but there was an indescribable feeling of comfort that they shared. Will knew that in time the sparks might come again but for now, he was satisfied with just getting to know her and Sonny.

When Will arrived at the Baptist church, only Doc, Preacher Babb, and Preacher Burden were there.

"At least one more person's on time," Preacher Babb said when Will walked in.

"Howdy, Will," Doc said. "How you keepin'?"

"Not bad, thanks to you."

"Don't you mean in *spite* o' him?" Preacher Burden asked.

Will grinned.

"Brother Will, this is going to be a monumental meeting!" Preacher Babb said. "Despite being a Methodist, you've brought good fortune to this valley."

"From what I suspect, good fortune was already on the way when I got here," Will answered.

"Before I forget it," Preacher Burden interjected, "you have some mail. Thought you'd like to have it."

The preacher handed Will two letters—one from Esther and the other in the unmistakable handwriting of Makepeace Green. Will went to sit on the front pew, and while the other's carried on with their foolishness, he opened Esther's letter.

My Dearest Brother,

How I miss you. How I miss Charlotte. How I <u>hate</u> Wilmington!

Every day I realize more and more what a mistake it was to move to this God-forsaken place. In the winter, the cold, wet Atlantic wind cuts through my body like a knife. In the warm months, the heat is oppressive, and the burrs and sand fleas are a curse.

My students are mostly the children of fishermen. When I came here, I thought I could make a difference in their lives, but their parents want the boys to be fishermen, too, keeping them out of school to work on the boats. The girls have no value to their parents other than to work in the home until the age of about fifteen, and then they are given up to marriage. Education for the girls is considered foolish.

Oh, please, please, Will, tell me that I can come and spend the summer with you in the cool of the mountains. Please write to me soon and tell me I can come. How fortunate you are to live where you are happy and the people are good.

Please forgive my rant. I was so happy to hear that you are healing from your injuries. I would credit the wonderful people there and the magic of the mountains for your quick recovery.

Now that I am in a place where I have no family or friends, my mind wanders back to our grandparents who were so happy living where the laurel blooms, heat is unknown, and the hawks ride the winds that rush up the slopes of the hills.

Please tell me soon that I can come to visit and recover.
Your loving sister,
Esther

Will put the letter back in its envelope and put that in his pocket. He was so shaken by his sister's distress that he sat unmoving, numb to his surroundings.

The other members of the council were arriving, milling about, and talking. When Preacher Babb came to the front to call the meeting to order and saw Will's anguish, he motioned for Preacher Burden to come to his aid.

The preacher came forward and sat on the bench next to Will and whispered, "Son, what's wrong? Did you receive bad news?"

Will glanced briefly at the preacher before looking forward again. "No, not really. I was just thinking about my sister. We were very close before she moved away, and I miss her."

"Let's come to order," Preacher Babb said as he banged his gavel on the pulpit. "Let me remind you men who have forgotten your manners that the hat rack is at the back of the room and this still is a church." He paused as a few of the men removed their hats and hung them on the nails driven in the back wall.

"Now I've got some old business we need to handle. Our road-work day was snowed out and we need to get the holes filled before we lose somebody in a wash, so I'm going to declare Saturday as road-work day."

A wave of mumbles moved through the crowd as comments were exchanged.

"Brother Will, I wonder if you'd loan us those horses of yours to pull Karl Badger's road grader. Brother Eli's oxen move so slow that the road can wash out on the startin' end while they're finishing up on the other end!"

"They'd appreciate the work," Will said.

"O' course, I'll have Brother Billy Babb's Baptist Bible Buddies out to-tin' water for y'all … and the animals too."

"All in favor? … That looks like everybody. *Approved!*"

"Now … Brother Eli is a-chompin' at the bits to bring up some new business, so without further ado, I'll turn the floor over to my fellow preacher."

Preacher Burden walked to the pulpit and looked out over the council as though he were about to launch into a sermon. When he was satisfied that he had the attention of the crowd, a smile stretched across his face. "Gentlemen," he said, "I have three bits of *wonderful* news!" When he had said that, he paused and looked at each member of the group for effect.

"Number one … At 8:00 tomorrow morning, the long awaited *telegraph* will be *operational!* Messages can be sent and received at the store!"

A murmur moved through the group as the men realized that they were becoming a part of the modern age.

"Number two … A week from Saturday you and everyone in the valley are invited to my store at 10:00 sharp for the lighting of the first electric light in Avery Cove. If anyone wants to hook up and have lights of his own, there'll be a member of the line crew there to tell you about it."

Paul Thiggery jumped to his feet and pointed a finger in the air. "I declare, I still ain't in favor o' that 'lectricity!"

Instantly, Caldwell Turpin jumped to his feet and turned to face Thiggery. "*Then jest stay in th' dark, Paul!*" he shouted.

"*Men … men!* I thought we got this settled at the last meeting," Preacher Burden declared. "Paul, I'd recommend that you come and at least talk to the man that's puttin' up the wires. … Let him explain how it works. I guarantee that nobody's going to force you to light up, and I guarantee that the valley won't burn down!"

Thiggery sat abruptly and crossed his arms over the bib of his overalls. He still looked determined, but at least he was silent.

Preacher Burden pulled down on his suspenders and cleared his throat. "Now, men, I've saved the most important thing for last," he said, and he rose up as tall as his stubby frame would allow to look out over the group.

"We've all been concerned about what would happen since our teacher, Miss Pack, decided to leave and go to college next year."

The preacher's words sent a shock wave through Will's body. There would be an opening for a teacher!

"I am happy to announce tonight that I have found her replacement!"

Will's heart sank. As quickly as the door had opened for Esther, it had slammed shut.

"I have secured the services of *Mr.* Peter Paul Lamb, who has graduated *two years* of Teacher College, and is teaching this year in Celo."

"Why's he leavin', Preacher?" someone asked.

"School's shuttin' down. Not enough students."

"Is he a God-fearin' man, Brother Eli?" Preacher Babb asked.

"Yes he is, Brother Billy. Says in his letter here that before he came to Celo he taught a Sunday school class of boys for three years in Raleigh."

"Must be a Baptist," Preacher Babb said.

"We can convert him!" Preacher Burden shot back, and the Methodists in the group laughed and slapped their knees.

"Now, to help me out, what with the new power and telegraph and all, and to let us get to know him, he's going to move on up here in June and work in the store till school starts. He'll be boarding at my house until he can find him a place of his own. Any questions?"

Preacher Burden searched the faces in the crowd and found, with the exception of Paul Thiggery, a happy and satisfied group. "No questions ... so I'll turn the meeting back over to Brother Billy."

Preacher Babb came back to the pulpit, asked the group to stand, and led in prayer. "Heavenly Father, bless the people of Avery Cove as they work on Saturday and keep 'em safe from harm. Thank You for sending us a new teacher for our younguns. Calm the fears of them that mistrust e-lec-tricity, and may all the news that comes over our new telegraph be *good*! Amen ... and *dismissed*!"

Twenty-Five

Sonny Meets Demus

When the called meeting of the Avery Cove council ended, Will made his way down the front steps of the Baptist church and started his walk home. Although the meeting had been brief, the temperature had dropped several degrees while he was inside. He pulled the collar of his coat up around his ears, thrust his hands deep into his pockets, and quickened his pace as he walked out into the darkening evening.

Esther's letter was in the inside pocket of his coat, but the words spoke to him as if he were reading them off the page. "Every day I realize more and more what a mistake it was to move to this God-forsaken place. Oh please, please, Will, tell me that I can come and spend the summer with you in the cool of the mountains." He knew exactly what his reply to her would be, and so he set his mind on other things that were less important at that time but still pressing.

He thought about Sonny and the hunt that would take place the next day. He thought about chickens and bears and pigs. He dwelled briefly on Demus Whitedeer, the telegraph, and Roamer and Sweetie. And then with the cold northern wind blowing in his face and darkness enveloping him, he thought of Alice.

When a dim, yellow light appeared ahead on the left, Will realized that he was about to pass Alice's home. He sensed from the faintness of the glow that it came from a single lamp. He imagined that Alice and Sonny were seated on the big upholstered sofa in the front room, talking and listening as mother and son. He wondered if they spoke of him and, if they did, what they might say. He searched the glow for a clue and found none. Too soon its dim output was faded and gone, leaving the stars as his only light.

As he approached his house, the sound of the river grew, and before long the timbers of the bridge were beneath his feet. In an instant the tangle of thought left his head, replaced by visions of the mountain water rushing to the sea. He imagined that it would someday reach the ocean, find it unappealing as his sister had, and rise upward to the clouds where it would drift once again to the mountains and fall as rain. Ah, if Esther could only come that easily!

Once his head finally rested on his pillow, the tangled stream of consciousness was back, hammering his brain with fragments of thought. There were the usual pieces of cerebral clutter—Sonny's speech impediment—Demus and his hoard of books—chicken wire—staples to hold the wire—Roamer's secret place—Alice's hair in the "city" style—Morse code—"Can I toot a pig?"—"Every day I realize more and more what a mistake it was to move to this God-forsaken place"—Karl Badger's road grader—and it continued, flowing endlessly. But beneath it all was something that wouldn't surface— something he could not remember. He fought to recall it, and as he tried to dig it from the depths of his mind, he fell asleep.

———

As the clock was striking three, Will awoke with a start and sat up in bed. "The letter from Makepeace!" he said out loud. "I forgot the letter!"

When Will's feet hit the floor, Dawg came running to see what all the commotion was about. "It's all right, Dawg," he said. "There's something I need to do, and then we'll go back to sleep."

By the light of a lamp, he wrapped himself in a blanket and searched through his pockets. The letter was tucked away in the left rear pocket of his trousers. He opened it and grinned as he began to read.

Dear Will

    This is Makepeace writting to you. I am in Burley but I will be leeving soon to go back to Charlott reel soon for Mr. Neil has bought all of the land that he wanted to by and he says it is all because of me and he give me my bonus in cash money. It is the most money that I have ever saw. I am woried for I have not still herd from Judy Ruth and I fear that something has come betweene me and her. My hart will be broke if she don't like me any more. I hope you will writ a letter to me reel soon to tell me of how you are doing and Uncle Roamer and Aint Sweetie.
Your freind Makepeace Green Make.

A burden had been lifted. The forgotten thing had surfaced, and for now, the stream of consciousness had ceased. "Make" was okay, even if his heart was to be temporarily broken, he had a feeling of peace about Esther since he knew where she would spend the summer, and there was a place growing in his heart for Alice and her scamp of a boy. With his mind at ease, he went back to bed and was soon asleep.

The next sound he heard was the rumble of small feet running up the stairs, across the porch, and through the front door. Sonny had arrived with the dawn. Dawg sang out an enthusiastic greeting, and with all the clamor there was nothing Will could do but rise and shine.

"Aren't you a little early?" he called out to Sonny.

"No," Sonny answered.

"Have you had breakfast?" Will asked as he entered the parlor.

"No."

"Are you hungry?"

"Uh-huh."

"Do you know how to build a fire?"

"I make pires por mama."

"Well how about stoking up the fire in here, and then get a fire started in the kitchen stove. Do you like pancakes?"

A big grin crossed Sonny's face. "*Uh huh*," he exclaimed as his head bobbed up and down.

Will watched as the boy scurried about, putting sticks of wood in the parlor stove and opening the damper. When he was satisfied that Sonny could handle the fire-making duty, Will retreated to the bedroom to start getting dressed.

As he was pulling on his boots, Will heard the clatter of wood being loaded into the kitchen stove, and then he heard the front door open and the voice of Demus Whitedeer.

"Will ... are you up?"

"Come on in, Demus," Will answered. "I'm gettin' dressed."

"I brought your milk."

"Take it in the kitchen and get your money out of the change lying on the table. I'll be right there."

It wasn't until Will said the word "kitchen" that he remembered that Sonny was there, and that Sonny and Demus hadn't met. He grabbed his shirt and hurried into the kitchen to find Demus and Sonny staring at each other.

"Well ... you must be Sonny Day," Demus said in his most resonant voice.

Sonny ran to Will and circled around behind him where he thought he would be safe from the dark-skinned man.

"Sonny, I want you to meet Demus Whitedeer," Will said as he took hold of Sonny and tried to bring him out from behind his back.

"Id he a nidder?" Sonny asked softly.

Demus tilted his head to the side and looked at Sonny in wonder. A slight smile came across his face. Will felt his face turn red with embarrassment.

"Sonny, Mr. Whitedeer is my friend. We say 'Negro'. "

"It's all right," Demus said. "I've heard it all my life."

For the first time, Will came to the realization that Sonny had never seen a Negro or even an Indian, for that matter. Demus lived on the North Road, and Sonny used the South Road to get everywhere he went. Even though they lived less than two miles apart, Sonny and Demus had never crossed paths.

Will sat Sonny at the table and sat down beside him. "Sonny," he said, "Demus's father was a proud Cherokee Indian and his mother was a Negro who grew up in slavery right here in Avery Cove. Demus got the very best characteristics of his mother and his father and of the man he called his grandfather, and he's a proud man himself."

Will looked up at Demus, who had a gentle smile on his face. "I want you to know that Mr. Whitedeer here is one of the most intelligent and well-read men I have ever known, and he is becoming one of the best friends I've ever had. You and I both can learn a lot from him if we just watch and listen when we're around him."

"Id he a weal Indun?"

"Yes."

"*Wow!*" Sonny exclaimed as he looked up at a smiling Demus.

"Tan I be a weal Indun too?"

"You know," Demus said, "maybe you *can* be a real Indian if you really want to be. I'll tell you what … I'll think about a way a fellow who wasn't born an Indian can become one, and I'll let you know."

"*Wow!*" Sonny exclaimed again. "Tan I toot a bow an' awo?"

"Well," Demus said as he rubbed his chin, "that's an art I never learned myself … but I'll teach you the things my father taught me. He was born into the Wolf clan. They're the only clan that can hunt wolves, and they're the clan that the war chiefs come from."

"*Wow!*" Sonny exclaimed once more. "Tan I be a wuff tan?"

"Well, you have to be born into a clan," Demus said as he paced the floor. "I guess what we would have to do is think up a clan just for you … you being an outsider and all."

"*Wow!* Wha' tan I be?"

"Let's see," Demus said, "there are seven Cherokee clans … and several of 'em are named after animals. I think I'll watch you and see which animal would be best to name your clan for."

"*Wow!*"

"Demus, are you hungry?" Will asked as he began stirring the batter for Sonny's pancakes.

"I've already eaten," Demus replied, "but I'll eat a few pancakes. Indians are always hungry … aren't they, Sonny?"

Sonny looked at Demus and shook his head vigorously up and down. "Dat *right!*" he said emphatically.

———◆———

Makepeace's pace quickened when Sarah's Cafe came into view. He had spent a sleepless night, his restlessness fueled by the apprehension of the first day back at the mill and his desire to see his beloved Judy Ruth. Nothing could stop him now. He had cash in his pocket, love in his heart, and a job working for a man who respected him!

The cafe was empty when he entered, and he wondered if he had stumbled into some sort of practical joke. Had they heard that he was returning and hurried to hide behind Sarah's counter?

The front door closed with a bang, and Sarah appeared from the back room tying her apron. "Goober ... Goober Green!" she said. "You're back! Where's Will?"

"Howdy, Sarah. Will decided t' stay in Avery Cove, so hit's jest me. Whur is ever'body?"

"Honey, don't you know what time it is? The rest of the bachelor boys are probably not even up yet. What are you doin' out so early?"

"Couldn't sleep. Prob'ly jest nervous 'bout bein' back t' work. Anxious t' see m' girlfrien' too."

"I see," Sarah said as she checked the fire in her stove. "I heard you and Will might swap houses. So Will decided to stay in the mountains?"

"Yep."

Sarah picked up a handful of bacon and started laying strips in the frying pan. "Gonna break a lot o' hearts. A bunch of girls had their eye on him. What you gonna have today, Goober ... the usual, two *chicken* eggs with all the trimmin's?"

"'At sounds good, Sarah, but I don't go by Goober no more. Folks is callin' me by my real name now ... Makepeace."

Sarah struck her spatula against the edge of the frying pan and turned to look her customer in the eye. "Makepeace?" she inquired.

"'At's right …'cept ye can call me 'Make' fer short. 'At's whut Will calls me."

Sarah turned back to the stove and adjusted her bacon in the frying pan. "Then Make it'll be!" she declared.

"How's ever'body doin'?" Makepeace asked.

"Everybody's fine … Make," Sarah said. "Pearl'll be in shortly, and then the bachelor boys'll start staggerin' in."

"They all still workin' at th' mill?"

"They're all still workin'," Sarah replied, "except for Tommy Lee Jones. He up and got married while you were gone and moved to Gastonia."

Makepeace slapped the counter and howled, "*Tommy Lee Jones got married*? Who'd marry 'at slacker?"

Sarah slipped her spatula under a row of bacon and flipped the strips in the pan. "Don't know her," she said, "but I heard Pearl say it was some little hussy named Judy Ruth Roach."

———

The morning mist had lifted, but the trail beside the river was still damp and slippery. Molly had to choose her steps carefully as she followed the three hunters up the slope toward the chestnut grove.

For Will, the trip to the hunting grounds was much like it was the fateful day he was attacked by the bear. The weather was cold and damp, and like before, he was filled with nervous energy.

This time though there were some big differences. Before, the sky had been visible through the bare, overhanging limbs. This time, there was a canopy of green above making the trail dark and ominous. Will wondered as he walked if the sound of the river was covering the murmur of wild animals waiting to pounce on them. Fear was settling in on him, and he wondered if he would be able to continue.

As if he had sensed Will's anxiety, Demus moved up beside him and pointed upward toward the trees that enveloped them. "Isn't this wonderful?" he asked. "When I'm in a place like this I feel like I'm enveloped in peace and security. If I could, I'd pick up my house and carry it up the mountain to a spot like this ... leave the heat of the valley behind."

The words were reassuring, but more comforting still was the fact that Demus Whitedeer's bulk was between him and danger.

Sonny had been given the job of leading Molly up the trail, and Will and Demus had almost forgotten about him until he spoke out. "Id it mutt furder?" he asked.

Will turned and looked back at the boy. "What did you say, Sonny?"

"I taid, id ... it ... mutt ... furder?"

"It's not much further," Will answered. "Are you getting tired?"

"Tome," Sonny replied.

Demus was watching Sonny intently as he had since they met, trying to find the areas of speech that were most difficult for the boy. With a quickened pace he moved close to Will and lowered his voice. "It's the 'sss' sound he's having the most trouble with, isn't it?"

"So it would seem," Will said.

"I think that if we can help him with the 'sss' sound, that would be a good start."

"I hope you're right," Will replied.

Soon, the trail ended and they were at the place where Will and Makepeace had left Molly on the day of the bear attack. With Molly tied to a tree, they began pushing their way through the undergrowth and away from the river. When the sound of the river had become a muted whisper, the gully appeared.

The place was quiet. This time there were no sounds of animals moving through the undergrowth. The wind was still, and the only sign of life was the occasional chirp of a bird.

Will chambered a round of ammunition into his rifle and motioned for Sonny to come up next to him. "Sonny, we're not far from where the pigs should be," he said. "You stay right here behind me and keep quiet."

"Aw wight," Sonny whispered.

With Will leading the way, followed by Sonny, and Demus bringing up the rear, the hunters moved to the right along the edge of the gully and up the hill still further away from the river. Eventually the gully was only a depression on the forest floor and they were nearing the top of a ridge. All around them were the empty, spiny husks of chestnuts and the massive trunks of the trees that had shed them.

Demus moved up, motioned for Sonny and Will to stop, and looked around to get his bearings. As they were talking about the best route to take, they heard from the other side of the ridge the grunts and squeals of a group of pigs.

"Down!" Demus said quietly, and they all fell to the forest floor. Demus pulled Sonny to the middle between Will and himself and listened intently. "They're over the ridge to the left," he said. "Let's crawl to the top of the ridge and see if we can see them. Sonny, you keep back a little bit and stay quiet. Will, when we see them, you choose one on the right and I'll choose one on the left, and we'll fire at the same time. We'll probably just get one shot each before they scatter, so make it a good one."

The three crawled along on their stomachs dodging rocks and chestnut burrs until they were on the top of the ridge. There before them was a group of pigs—two sows, a huge boar, and about seven shoats, all foraging on the forest floor.

"Will, do you have one picked out?" Demus whispered.

"I have one in my sights," Will whispered back.

"So do I," Demus said. "We'll shoot on three. One … two …"

And then "*thwap*" went Sonny's slingshot, and the big boar squealed in pain, turned, and charged toward them.

"*Good Lord, fire!*" Will screamed, and six rifle shots quickly rang out.

The boar fell in his tracks and twitched a few times before becoming still. Four of the shoats fell dead, and the rest of the group scattered into the undergrowth.

Demus rose to his knees and surveyed the scene. "*Saints preserve us!*" he exclaimed. Then he turned to Will. "I thought you were going to take that boy's slingshot away from him! We could have been *killed*!"

Will was lying with his face on the ground. "I had no *idea* he'd do that!" he said. Then he raised up and looked at all the pigs lying dead. "But then ... we would have only gotten two if Sonny hadn't gotten things started by shootin' that boar."

"I tot a pig!" Sonny shouted. *"I tot a pig!"*

———

It was still early in the day when the hunting party got back to Will's house with the four shoats. Will set the big black pot to boiling, and Demus made quick work of dressing the little pigs. Before long the hot water had removed the hair from the pigs' bodies, and the meat had been processed.

"How would you feel about taking Roamer's pig to him?" Will asked Demus.

"How do you think *he* would feel about it?" Demus asked in return.

"I think that if you showed up at Roamer's house with a fresh, young pig already dressed out, you'd make another friend," Will said. "You could take Molly to carry the meat and return Roamer's rifle at the same time. If you'll do that, Sonny and I will take a pig to his house."

Demus walked over to the water bucket near the fire and thrust his hands into the water. He picked up the bar of lye soap lying on a tree root and began to lather up his hands and arms. Will could see deep thought in Demus's eyes, and he imagined him struggling with the prospects of having to face Roamer and Sweetie, who had shunned him all his life. He could see on his face the look of sorrow, resentment, and a touch of fear. He had seen Demus's reaction to fear when he was confronted about the plow, and he wondered if he had made a mistake by putting him in what could be another fearful situation.

Finally, Demus took a towel off the clothes line and dried his face and hands. "Well," he said, "I've already faced an angry boar today. Maybe I could borrow Sonny's sling shot ..."

"Sorry," Will said. "That's what I used to start the fire."

The talk about the slingshot gave Sonny an idea. "Mitter Whitedeer, tan I be in duh pig tan?" he asked.

"The pig clan?" Demus replied. "I have something better in mind for you. I saw you crawling on your belly when we were stalking those pigs, and you got along pretty well. Reminded me of a snake! I think we should make you the first member of the snake clan."

"Wow! Duh nake tan?"

"That's right. You could be the first … pass it down for generations. Do you think you can learn to make a snake sound?" Demus asked.

"Wha tound dud a nake make?"

"A snake hisses," Demus said, "like this … sss. Can you do that?"

"Tttuh"

"Pull the corners of your mouth back like this … and make the air whistle between your tongue and the roof of your mouth … sss."

"Tttuh"

"You keep practicing. You'll also have to learn to make your tongue go in and out of your mouth like a snake does."

Sonny watched intently as Demus pierced the air with his tongue. He tried, but his own tongue wouldn't respond.

"Tell you what," Demus said, "grab your tongue with your fingers and pull it out … stretch it. Keep doing that, and practice the sss sound, and when you can do it, Will and I will initiate you into the snake clan."

"Wow!" Sonny exclaimed in amazement.

———

The sun was falling toward the southwest when Demus approached Roamer's house riding Molly. Molly walked comfortably under the weight of Demus, a fine young pig, and Roamer's .22 rifle.

The real weight was on Demus's broad shoulders. It was the weight of scorn and rejection he always felt when he had to face one of the valley residents. He had made up his mind that he would deliver the pig and the rifle and leave straight away, hopefully without incident.

Roamer was on his knees, tending his tobacco plants, when Demus rode up and stopped. It wasn't until Demus was sliding off the horse's back that Roamer realized he was there. He turned with a start, jumped to his feet, and grabbed a shovel that was lying beside him.

"*Whut do you want?*" he asked excitedly.

"I'm sorry I startled you, Mr. Robinson," Demus replied. "Will sent me."

"Will sent ye? Whut fer?"

"Will and I went hunting today, and I brought you and Mrs. Robinson a pig. Will said you wanted one."

Roamer twisted his head around and looked at the sack draped over Molly's back. "A pig, ye say? ... Ye brung me a pig?"

"Yes, sir, a fine, young shoat. I brought you the liver too, and the liver from my pig. I never acquired the taste for liver."

Roamer cautiously laid his shovel down and eased toward the horse. "Ye brung me two livers ... an' a whole pig?"

"Yes, sir," Demus said, looking somewhat relieved, "and if you'll allow me, I'll help you get it ready to go to the smoke house or your ice cave."

Roamer circled closer to the horse, and his eyes darted back and forth between Demus and the sack on the horse's back. "*Sweetie ... come 'ere!*" he hollered. "*Come see whut 'is man brung us!*"

Sweetie came out on the porch carrying a broom and started down the steps with her eyes glued on the dark man in her yard. Her mouth made a little round circle, and her tongue darted around between her gums. "*Whut's he a-doin 'ere?*" she snarled.

"'Is 'ere's our neighbor, Nicodemus Whitedeer," Roamer said excitedly. "He's brung us a pig w' two livers!"

"I ain't never saw a pig w' two livers!" Sweetie declared.

Roamer raised his arm upward in a commanding position with his finger pointed toward the sky. "Well, this-un's got two, an' you're gonna cook um fer supper! I want mine biled … an' I want ye t' cook up a loin, too … 'at is, if Mr. Whitedeer'll jine us!"

———

M akepeace Green was a pitiful sight as he walked down the steps of Inverness Mill at the end of his shift. His heart was empty, and the mill seemed empty too since Judy Ruth was not there. To make things worse, his new boss—Will's replacement—had scolded him for being distracted. He wished he were back at Avery Cove where life was simpler.

When he got to the road and turned right, he decided that he would go by the company store and pick up a couple of things he needed. He didn't have much of an appetite, but he did need a spool of blue thread, to sew on a button, and a pound of coffee.

The distraction for which he had been scolded at work persisted as he entered the store, and he walked right by the storekeeper and a young girl who were stocking shelves near the front door.

"Green, you're back!" the storekeeper said. "I have something you ordered."

"Uh … a spool o' blue thread an' a pound o' coffee," Makepeace answered.

"Did you hear me, Green? I got in those handkerchiefs you ordered."

The storekeeper's declaration finally jolted Makepeace into an awareness of his surroundings, and he turned to face him and the pretty young girl behind the counter. "I ordered hanker-chiefs?" he asked.

"Before you left," the storekeeper said, and he reached under the counter and produced a flat, square box. He laid it on the counter and opened it, revealing three white handkerchiefs bordered with delicate lace. On the corner of each, the initials J R R had been embroidered.

Once again Makepeace was jolted, this time by the memory of having ordered the handkerchiefs for Judy Ruth Roach's birthday.

"Is something wrong?" the storekeeper asked, having seen the look on Makepeace's face.

"I … don't need 'em now," Makepeace said. "They was fer my girl-friend … 'cept she ain't my girlfriend no more." He closed the box and handed it back to the storekeeper. "Could ye take 'em back?"

"I could if they weren't embroidered," the storekeeper said.

For a moment Makepeace stood and looked at the box. "I reccon I can send um to m' Aunt Sweetie," he said. "She don't read, an' she wouldn't know whut J R R means."

For the first time the pretty young girl spoke up. "Did you say, J R R?" she asked softly. "Why, those are *my* initials!"

"I'm sorry, Goober," the storekeeper said. "I want you to meet Janie Rose Rainey. She just came to work here in the store. Miss Rainey," he said as he turned to the girl, "how about you taking care of Mr. Green while I help the folks that just came in. Goober, I hope you understand about the handkerchiefs."

"Oh, 'at's fine! Jest fine!" he said as the storekeeper walked away, "'cept I go by Makepeace now. 'At's my real name … Makepeace."

"Makepeace?" Janie Rose giggled. "I like formal soundin' names, and it's a fine, upstandin' name, too. It sounds almost like poetry."

"Well!" Makepeace declared, his confidence building. "Janie Rose Rainey! 'At's a fine name, too. Why, hit sounds almos' like a song!"

Janie Rose put her hand to her mouth and giggled as she cast a girlish look across the counter at Makepeace.

"Tell ye whut," Makepeace said almost giddily, "why don't I give 'em hanker-chiefs to *you*, seein' as how they got your letters on 'em …'at is o' course, if ye don't think ye boyfriend'd get mad."

Janie Rose put her hand to her mouth and giggled again, blushing a bright crimson. "Why, I ain't got a boyfriend."

"I hope to my never!" Makepeace said as he leaned forward on the counter, confidence rising from him like steam. "Well, how about me a-walkin' you home after work so's I can tote them hanker-chiefs fer ye!"

"I get off in fifteen minutes!" Janie Rose giggled.

S aturday. Road work day. Will didn't know what to expect, but since his horses would be pulling Karl Badger's road grader, he knew he'd better get an early start. While the sun was still behind the eastern ridge, he pulled himself up on Don's back, took Molly's reins, and started down the North Road toward Avery Cove's center of commerce.

The horses moved easily through the cold morning air. They seemed to enjoy plowing through the mist that floated above the damp places, and as they trotted along, the tufts of hair around their ankles gathered droplets of water and scattered them like rain drops.

Will loved this time of day. It was the time before his mind became cluttered with thoughts of things that needed to be done. It was the time he could reflect on the previous day and be thankful—or sorrowful—for the things had happened.

Today was a thankful day. His larder was laden with pork, salted and drying, waiting to be smoked. He thought of the strides that had been made with Sonny and the new speech skill the boy was learning. He thought about Demus and how he was learning to accept others as friends. And he thought about Alice and how much fun she was to be near.

So deep in thought was Will that he almost rode past Demus again. Demus was standing in the road holding a shovel when Will looked up and saw him almost within arm's reach.

"I'm beginning to think you're trying to avoid me," Demus said.

"Sorry, Demus. I was thinking. Where you goin' with the shovel?"

"Going to do my road work."

"Want a ride?"

"No, I work alone. It's always been understood that I fill the holes on the west road. I get over there and get done before the road grader comes along."

"Wanna go fishin' this afternoon?"

Demus took off his hat and rubbed his forehead. "That's mighty tempting," he said, "but I promised Roamer I'd split some hickory for him this afternoon. We're getting ready to smoke his pig."

Will nearly fell off the horse. "You and Roamer are getting along?" he asked, trying not to show surprise.

"I guess you could say so," Demus replied. "Mrs. Robinson was a little slower to come around, but before I left she'd quit shaking her broom at me ... even cooked supper for me and thanked me for coming."

Will wanted to hear more, but the sun was rising and he felt he must go. He wished Demus well and continued down the road.

His mind then turned to a piece of paper he had in his pocket. On it was the text of two telegrams he would send when he got to Burden's Store.

My Dear Esther: Your room is waiting. I'll meet your train in Burley and welcome you to Paradise. Tell me when you can leave and I will send ticket. Letter to follow.
Will

Dear Make: Congratulations. Knew you could do it.
Regarding JRR- All will be for the best. Letter to follow
Will

He thought as he rode about the wondrous telegraph. Someone at the store would click the key, and someone in Wilmington or Charlotte would write down his message and deliver it to the person for whom it was intended. Before the day was out, his messages would be received hundreds of miles away. In Charlotte he had taken the wonder of the telegraph for granted. Here in Avery Cove it was new and miraculous.

There was a group of men gathered on the porch of the store when Will rode up, and they were paying particular interest to the ceiling above their heads. Oscar Levee, Preacher Babb, and James Plumlee stood motionless, their faces pointed upward. Each firmly gripped the straps of his overalls while Caldwell Turpin pointed toward the object of their attention, a sparkling Edison light bulb. As Will walked by, Caldwell was explaining that in just one week the bulb would come to life in a grand and glorious ceremony that would bring electricity to the valley. "Ain't it a wonder?" Caldwell was saying.

Inside Preacher Burden was holding court with several other men who were waiting to get started with road work. "Here's our teamster now," the preacher said. "I guess we better get started fillin' holes."

"Before we do can I get you to send a couple of telegrams?" Will asked.

"The preacher straightened up, and his eyes got large. "Telegrams? You want to send some telegrams?" he asked excitedly. "Oh my! *Naomi … Rachel … Get out here! We got our first telegram customer!*"

Twenty-Six

Sonny Says, "Sssss"

The midnight that separated May and June was heralded by thunder rolling down the mountains west of the valley. Will awoke and lay still, waiting for the drumming of rain on the roof. He had come to expect—even accept—the rains that came almost daily in the mountains, knowing that they would soak into the soil and push his crops to the surface.

When morning dawned he pulled on his boots and overalls and walked outside to see cloudless skies above the misty fields. Every leaf of every tree and every blade of grass had been scrubbed clean and covered with dew. Spring was truly there.

The months of April and May had passed quickly. His wounded body had healed, and he was strengthened by the physical labor of patching up his house and outbuildings. His property was returning to a cared-for state.

Near the middle of May he had harrowed his fields and planted his hay and feed corn. The preparation work that had been done earlier by the Plowsharers had paid off. The remnants of the previous year's crop had been turned back into the soil where they decayed quickly into the black dirt of the hills. Now, on the first day of June, those black fields were covered with green sprouts.

His garden too was showing signs of life. Peas and sweet corn were sprouting and would soon be followed by okra, squash, green beans, cabbage, and all the other gifts of the earth that were to come. The tomato plants that Roamer had given him were thriving and already looking upward for a place to climb.

He had been busy with other things as well. Esther's room was clean and polished, awaiting her arrival, and Roamer's tobacco plants and Alice's garden were planted, thanks to his help.

And then there was Sonny. Will had spent countless hours giving the boy attention and direction. He had taught him how to plow, plant, chop, hammer, and saw; but more than that, he had taught him how to trust.

Demus too had spent time with the boy, and both had benefited. While Sonny was struggling with his language skills, Demus was patient. He coaxed and cajoled, reminding Sonny that initiation into the snake clan would be the prize for learning. Demus's prize for teaching was companionship.

As he stood in the front yard of his home looking toward the east, across the road, beyond the barn, and on to the mountains that framed the valley, Will considered all he had accomplished. He turned and faced the house and the outbuildings that were now patched, scrubbed, and painted, waiting for Esther to come. What a difference a few short weeks had made!

A wave of anxiety rushed over him. Esther would be there soon! He was anxious to introduce her to all the people of the valley for whom he had grown so fond. He smiled as he wondered what on earth she would think of Roamer and Sweetie, but his mood was more serious as he wondered if she would see Demus Whitedeer through understanding eyes.

He reminded himself that she had accepted Makepeace readily and without reservation, but then Makepeace was hard *not* to like. Here she would be surrounded by the likes of Caldwell Turpin, Jasper Jeter, and Paul Thiggery. She had never been around people of this sort and could be in for some culture shock.

But surely she would be impressed with the Burden family—the hub around which the valley revolved—and Doc French could carry on an intelligent conversation. Her acceptance of all his new-found friends was important, but he was mostly concerned about what she would think of Alice.

He thought Esther would instantly like Alice, she being a woman near her own age who had enjoyed a similar upbringing. He could see them talking about the things young women—unmarried women—talk about. He hoped they would become friends, but what would she think about Alice as a potential love interest for her brother—this slightly older widow with a mischievous son? And would it really matter what Esther thought? How he hoped that question wouldn't have to be answered!

There would be no school bell today. The first day of June marked the beginning of summer vacation for the kids in the valley and for Esther and her students as well. Esther had promised that she would send a telegram on the first day school was out and give her travel plans—plans he was anxious to receive.

Knowing Esther as he did, Will imagined that she had risen with the sun and hurried to the telegraph office with her neatly written note for the telegrapher. It was probably in the hands of Preacher Burden by now, he reasoned, and the excitement welled up in him like the promise of Christmas.

He made quick work of his chores, had a hasty breakfast, and hitched Don and Molly to the wagon. They danced in place as Will climbed on the seat, and soon they were turning onto the road and across the bridge toward Alice's house.

Will had started making it a practice to check with Alice to see if she needed anything from the store. Usually she didn't, but it gave him an excuse to see her. She was eager to see him as well, and she was becoming good at thinking up small things for him to do such as hammering a nail or checking her hens for lice. He wondered if she was feigning dependence, but it really didn't matter.

On this trip he was greeted at the door by Alice with her flour sifter in hand—that is to say, the sifter in one hand and the handle in the other. "I'm so glad to see you," she said. "The handle on my sifter is broken, and I wonder if you'd fix it for me?"

"Is that the only reason you're glad to see me?" he asked.

"I'll never tell," she answered.

"You know if I fix your sifter, you'll have to bake me a cake," he explained.

"Do a good job and I'll give you something even better," she replied.

"And what could be better than one of your cakes?"

"You'll see."

The handle was missing a pin that held it to the metal body of the sifter. Will began a search through Alice's tool box looking for a replacement, and as he looked, he asked, "Where's Sonny? I didn't see him outside."

"One of the hens got out, and the last I saw of him, he was chasing her up through the woods," she answered.

"I guess I'd better check your fence while I'm here," Will said.

"You come in pretty handy," she stated with satisfaction in her voice.

Will found a small nail that fit the hole in the handle perfectly. He drove it home, nipped it off with a pair of cutters, and braded it over with a tack hammer.

Satisfied with his repair, he handed it back to Alice, who turned the crank and beamed with delight as the wire beaters rubbed against the metal screen.

Then before Will knew what was happening, she put her arms around his neck and kissed him on the cheek. "Now ... wasn't that better than a cake?" she asked.

Will's answer wasn't vocal. He put his arms around her and pulled her close to return her kiss ... and then came the unmistakable sound of Sonny running up the porch steps.

They broke away from each other's embrace just as Sonny ran in the door. Both were in a state of shock at what was happening and a state of dismay that it had to end, but Sonny was not to be denied his attention.

"*Will!*" he shouted. "*Are you doein' to de tore?*"

"Sure am," Will replied, still trying to pull himself together. "Wanna come along?"

"*Tan I, Mama?*" he asked excitedly.

"Did you catch the hen?"

"*Uh-huh.*"

"Well calm down then. Don't you have something to say to Will?"

"*Tan I hab tome tandy at de tore?*"

"That's not what I meant," Alice said. "You need to calm down and tell Will the things you told me this morning."

Sonny couldn't contain himself. The thoughts of getting a piece of candy at the store were flooding his brain. He ran out the door, jumped up on the wagon seat, and started bouncing up and down.

"I'd better go before he breaks the wagon seat," Will said.

"You don't mind taking him?" Alice asked.

"No!" Will said emphatically. "That means I'll get to come back by here on the way home."

———

The ride to the store was punctuated by Sonny's nonstop chatter. He told Will about the hen that got out and the chase through the woods. He vented his excitement about his school work being over for the summer. He explained how Miss Pack had given him a private test and passed him up to the fourth grade. And then he went on and on telling Will about how he would be able to spend more time with him over the summer.

Will had grown accustomed to Sonny's speech impediment and could understand everything the boy had to say. He wondered though if Sonny would ever speak normally—if he would ever be able to fit in with the other children. As he rode along with Sonny's banter in the background, he asked himself if he and Demus were wasting their time trying to get him to speak as other children did. For now, the answer would have to be no! It was not a waste of time.

Preacher Burden was on the porch of the store as Will approached. He turned quickly and ran inside, returning in a few moments with a piece of paper that he held high in the air for Will to see.

"*Telegram!*" the preacher hollered as Will pulled up and set the brake on the wagon. "*Just came in ... and not to worry ... It's good news!*"

"That's what I came for," Will said as he climbed down.

He crossed the yard and went up the steps of the porch with Sonny close by his side.

"Hot off the wire," the preacher said as he handed the telegram to Will.

Will stood and read the telegram as Sonny pulled closer to him under the gaze of two old men sitting on the porch in chairs. While Will was reading, one of the men sharpened his pocket knife on a small slip stone, and the other cut a chew of tobacco from a large black twist.

Finally Will folded the paper and put it in his pocket. "I guess you know already, Preacher," he said, "but my sister's coming to spend the summer. She'll leave Wilmington on the train day after tomorrow, and I'll pick her up in Burley on Saturday."

"Ain't that somethin'!" the preacher declared. "The new teacher's supposed to get here about that time too."

Will looked away and stared at nothing in particular. "Yep … that's somethin', all right," he said, and he turned and went in the store with Sonny clinging to his shirt.

Doc French and James Plumlee were sitting in ladder-back chairs talking when Will and Sonny came in. James stood and walked off toward the post office as Will approached, and Doc leaned his chair back against the big pot-bellied stove that had been given the summer off.

"Will!" Doc said, as if he were happy to get a different person to talk to. "How's my favorite bear-attack customer?"

"Better every day," Will replied. "Especially good today. My sister's coming to spend the summer."

"It's about time we got another pretty lady in the valley," Doc said. "I assume she's pretty since she's your sister. And how's my friend Sonny?" he said as he pulled Sonny close to his side. "I swear, boy, every time I see you, you've grown an inch. Are you glad summer's here?"

Sonny lowered his head and shuffled his feet. "Yes, sir," he said softly.

Doc leaned his chair back against the stove and looked reflective, as if he were about to make a comment. Then he brought his chair back down on all four legs and took Sonny by the arm. "Sonny … what did you say?" he asked as he looked at the boy in wonder.

"I sssaid 'yes, sir,' " Sonny replied, still looking downward.

Will fought to hold back a "whoop." "Sonny, go get yourself two pieces of candy from Preacher Burden. No, make it three!" he said.

As soon as Sonny's face was pressed against glass of the candy counter, Doc leaned forward and lowered his voice to Will. "What's goin' on with *that*?" he asked. "The boy talked as normal as anybody!"

"I'm as shocked as you are," Will said, a look of amazement painting his face. "He jabbered all the way down here like he always has … then when we got here and he calmed down …"

"Have you been working with him?" Doc asked.

Will continued staring at Sonny as he selected his candy. "No, Demus has," he said offhandedly.

Doc looked shocked. "Did you say '*Demus*'… as in *Demus Whitedeer*?" he asked as he leaned forward some more.

"Yeah … he had a book in his collection that described Sonny's condition and the treatment. He even knew the scientific name for it."

"Whitedeer has a *book*?" Doc asked. "Did you read it?"

Will pulled the other chair around and sat down where he could keep an eye on Sonny. "No, I didn't read it," he said. "It was written in French."

Doc slid to the very front edge of his chair. "Whitedeer reads *French*?"

"And Latin, and Greek, and Italian, and German, and I don't know what all," Will said.

Doc sat up straight and slapped his knees. "Well, as Goober Green would say, 'I *hope to my never!*' "he declared.

———

While he was on his lunch break, Makepeace left the mill, ran across the road, and bounded into the Inverness company store. He looked around at an empty room, not seeing a single sign of life until he saw the top of Janie Rose Rainey's head sticking up from behind the main counter.

"Janie Rose … I see you a-hidin' back 'ere," he said. "Come out … come out … whur-ever ye are, or I'm a-gonna jump 'at counter an' git ye!"

Janie Rose let out a squeal and giggled as she raised up and peeked across the counter at Makepeace, who was crouched like a cat inching toward her.

"How did you know I was here?" she asked, still giggling.

"I seen ye purdy little head a-stickin' up lack a flower," Makepeace said. "I think I'll jest pluck 'at flower."

Makepeace crouched down again with his fingers out like claws and inched toward Janie Rose as she squealed and giggled.

"*Cut that out! This is a place of business!*" the storekeeper bellowed as he came out of the back room. "Grow up, you two! You act like teenagers!"

Janie Rose stood and smoothed her dress. "Well, I *am* a teenager," she declared.

"*Well he ain't!*" the storekeeper bellowed as he pointed at Makepeace. "*He's a grown man, and he ort to start actin' like one!* By the way, Make," he said, his voice returning to normal, "the freight man delivered a crate for you today."

"Fer me? A crate? I ain't ordered nothin'."

The storekeeper lifted the crate from the floor and set it on the counter. "Didn't say you ordered anything," he said. "It's addressed to you in care of Inverness Company Store, Charlotte, North Carolina. Now … are you gonna open it, or keep us in suspense?"

The playful look had left Makepeace's face. "Whut in tarnation could it be?" He tilted the crate one direction then another, examining it from every angle.

"Are you gonna open it, or keep us in suspense?" the storekeeper repeated.

"Well … let me have somethin' t' pry with, an' I'll open 'er up."

The crate was a wooden box about eighteen inches square, sealed tightly with nails. Sure enough, the label read:

Mr. Makepeace Green
c/o Inverness Company Store
Charlotte, North Carolina

Makepeace took the pry bar the storekeeper gave him and started removing the lid from the crate. Janie Rose moved back a step and grimaced as the nails squawked under the force of the tool.

When the lid was finally off, Makepeace reached in and removed a black, furry bundle that had been carefully folded and tied with twine.

"Whut … in th' world …?" he uttered as he began to unfold it on the counter.

"There's a letter inside," the storekeeper said as he removed a piece of paper. "I'll read it for you … 'Dear Makepeace,' " he read as he looked down his nose and through his glasses. "'This is the hide of the bear you strangled. Jasper Jeter tanned it for you just as he promised, and I am sending it with thanks on behalf of the whole valley for ridding us of this creature and saving Will's life. Never in the history of this region has there been such an act of courage as yours. You will forever be in our hearts and in our memory. Sincerely, Preacher Eli Burden'."

A stony silence fell over the store as Makepeace ran his hands over the soft fur. Finally, Janie Rose inched forward and then lunged—wrapping her arms around Makepeace's neck. The storekeeper carefully folded the letter, put it back in the crate, and walked away, giving Makepeace and Janie Rose their privacy.

The secret that Makepeace and Glenn Neil had so carefully guarded was out.

———

"Let's see …" Preacher Burden said as he waved his pencil above a piece of paper, " that was one stick of peppermint … one licorice whip…one jaw breaker … a can of saddle soap … and a sack of layin' mash!"

His pencil moved quickly over the paper. "That'll be thirty-seven cents! Cash or charge?"

"I think I might have that much," Will said as he plunged his hand deep into his pocket. "Might as well keep up to date."

"Much obliged!" the preacher sang out before he lowered his voice. "Say … don't mean to pry, but did I overhear you and Doc talking about Nicodemus Whitedeer?"

"Yep!"

"I haven't seen him in *ages*. I was startin' t' wonder if he was still around these parts."

"He's still around! It's a shame you haven't seen him."

"He's such a *loner*," the preacher said. "I don't see how he gets along without buyin' anything. Looks like he'd at least need some salt or somethin' every now and then."

"He goes over to Valle Crucis to get his staples," Will replied. "Says folks over there accept him. Folks around here are missing a lot because of that. He's sure been a good friend to Sonny and me!"

Will gave the can of saddle soap to Sonny and threw the sack of laying mash over his shoulder. "Come on, Sonny," he said. "Let's go feed the chickens. See you Sunday, Preacher!"

The preacher threw up his hand distractedly and watched as Will and Sonny left. "Yeah … Will … see ya Sunday."

When Will and Sonny were back on the wagon seat, Will sat forward with his elbows on his knees and bent his head in Sonny's direction. "*Sonny!*" he said proudly. "I didn't want to make a big deal of it in there, but I just about flipped over when you said 'yess, ssir' to Doc French! Was that what your mother wanted you to tell me … that you had learned to do that?"

"Uh-huh."

"You can say 'yes' now."

Sonny grinned. "Yes."

"Don't you think we'd better go by and see Demus?"

Sonny's grin expanded "Yes, I guess so," he said ever so plainly.

———◆———

As Will's wagon was pulling away, Preacher Burton and Doc walked out on the porch of the store for a breath of air.

"Here, Doc," the preacher said. "Have a licorice whip." The preacher held out a long, twisted rope of candy that was the color of tar, and he stuck another strip in his own mouth.

"Don't mind if I do," Doc answered. "You know, my mama wouldn't let me have this stuff when I was a boy ... said it would rot my teeth."

"Maybe she was right. You still have all your teeth, don't you?"

"Most of 'em ... but you know," he said reflectively, "I think I'd rather have licorice than teeth. ... I'd forgotten how good this stuff is."

"Doc ... what do you think about this Demus Whitedeer thing?"

Doc walked to a rocker and sat down. "I was gonna ask you the same thing. All I know is the man that raised him was a good man. Different ... but good."

"Maybe we should reach out to him," the preacher said as he plopped down in a rocker beside Doc.

"Is that the preacher talking ... or the store keeper?"

The preacher paused, looking fretful. "Well, either way I'd feel better."

The two men sat silently chewing their licorice and rocking as a two-horse phaeton appeared, coming from the direction of Burley.

When it got closer, Doc spoke up. "Who is *that*, Preacher?"

"Never seen him before in my life."

"He's making good time!"

"Those aren't plow horses ... and he ain't no farmer, that's for sure," the preacher said as he stood up from his rocker.

The phaeton pulled into the yard of the store, and the horses stopped with a snort and pawed the ground. The driver pulled the brake and jumped down with a thud.

He was a large man—not as much in height as in girth, but not short either—about five-eleven and 260 lbs, the preacher guessed. He had a head of dark hair that made him look as though he was wearing a hat even though he had a large black Stetson in his hand. He glowed with the light of confidence and success, and Avery Cove hadn't seen many men like this!

He crossed the few steps between the phaeton and the porch and put his foot up on the bottom step. "Good morning, gentlemen," he said. "I'm looking for Preacher Burden."

"Well! Good morning to you too, Sir. I'm Preacher Burden."

The stranger extended his hand upward and shook the preacher's hand. "I wonder if you would be so kind as to give me a few minutes in private?" he asked.

"I suppose so. Forgive me, sir," the preacher said. "This is Doc French, our community physician."

"Well! I've heard *that* name!" the stranger said emphatically, and he stuck out his hand to Doc. "I'd like to include you in the conversation, too ... if you'd be so kind."

Doc looked at the man searchingly and nodded, shaking his hand without comment.

"I have a little office in the back of the store where we can talk," the preacher said. "If you'll follow me, we'll sit down there for a chat."

The preacher led the trio through the store and into the back room where an office had been partitioned off. He entered the room and proudly reached up to switch on an electric light. "Have a seat, sir ... you too, Doc. Let's see what's going on."

The stranger laid his hat on the preacher's desk and remained standing. "Gentlemen, my name is Glenn Neil. I'm a friend of Will Parker and Makepeace Green."

"You're the mill owner!" the preacher declared.

"That's right, and I hope you'll forgive me for not introducing myself earlier," he said as he took a seat, "but I'd like for my trip here to remain confidential for now."

"Whatever you say, sir. I'll have to say your timing is good if you want confidentiality. You missed Will Parker by about five minutes!"

"Well, for now, I'm glad I missed him, and I think you'll understand why once you've heard me out. Anyway ... back in December I told Makepeace Green ... he was Goober back then ... that I'd like to look into raising some sheep and open a small woolen mill up here."

"Well, with all due respect," the preacher said, "this really isn't sheep country, sir."

"Goober ... I guess I really should say 'Makepeace' ... made that very clear, much to my disappointment, so I went up above Burley where the folks are used to sheep, and with his help, I bought some property."

"Then you're all set up?" Doc asked.

"Not exactly, Dr French. Since that time I've gone up east and gotten educated."

"Do tell!" the preacher said.

Neil shifted in his chair and leaned forward. "You see, I had it in my mind all along that I wanted a totally electric mill like my cotton mills. I wanted *my* mill to be more modern than any woolen mill in the world. State of the art! But I was wrong! I saw that fine wool has to be handled the old-fashioned way ... worked slowly, don't you see. You can't turn it out like you do canvas. What I want to do is go back to a water-powered mill like they have up east ... and there's not a decent river on my property at Burley."

"So weaving fine wool is more like art work," Doc said.

Neil almost jumped out of his chair. "*Exactly!*" he shouted.

"And where do we fit in?" the preacher asked.

"Well, Makepeace talked me out of Avery Cove because of the roads and the lack of electricity, and the lack of workers. He was right at the time. Your roads are horrible. ... I'll get back to that in a minute, but you have electricity now," and he pointed up at the bulb hanging from the ceiling. "And even though I want a water-powered mill, I want light bulbs! And since I talked to Makepeace, you've gotten telegraph, and phones are on the way!"

"Let's get back to those roads," the preacher said. "We fight these roads like the plague."

"I've checked, and if you had just one small industry and a few more people up here to justify it, the state would take over your roads and maintain them ... all the way into Burley!"

"You mean we wouldn't have to fill pot holes anymore?" the preacher asked.

"That's right! The state would grade them, fill the holes, and eventually put down gravel!"

"Oh lord! My head's a-spinnin'," the preacher said.

"Mine too!" said Doc. "But that leaves the question of the workers."

"Well that's the most beautiful part," Neil said. "When I went up east I discovered that all the workers in the finest woolen mills are straight from Scotland. They love America, but just like my daddy, they miss the highlands. They'd jump at the chance to come to a place like this to work, and they're good people ... good citizens ... hard workers!"

Preacher Burden stood and walked around the room with his hands on the small of his back. He seemed to be searching for the words he wanted to use. "Mr. Neil, you had me jumpin' there for a minute ... but I think ... and I'm sure that Doc here would agree ... well, you see, I've heard about those mill villages. I just really don't think that would fit in up here."

"Preacher Burden, Dr. French, mill villages are good in their place, but I agree. Putting a mill village in a setting like this would be like putting a cat house in a church yard ... if you'll excuse the simile."

Doc and the preacher perked up.

"Preacher Burden, Makepeace tells me you have a substantial holding of property in the area. I'd like to spread my workers out on farms all over the valley. I think that's the only way they'd be happy, and it would mean that if you're willing, you could sell some of those farms at a handsome profit."

The preacher's eyes got large. "You don't say!"

"I *do* say!"

"Well my head really *is* spinnin' now," the preacher declared, "and I'll tell you what ... we need to talk some more about what you'll be needing in the way of property. Any of those folks Methodists?"

"I think I've heard that a lot of 'em are Presbyterians, but you seem to be the kind of man that could convert them ... so to speak," Neil said with a grin.

Doc raised his hand and waved his finger in the air as he chose his words. "Seems to me that when Goober ... Makepeace was telling me about how he was going to help you find property over in Burley, he said you wanted to retire to the mountains. You gonna live over there ... or over here?"

"If the rest of this valley is as beautiful as the little I've seen, I don't think you could tear me away from here. If we can come to an agreement on a mutual need, and we have mutual goals in mind, I'd like to come back in a few weeks and look around."

Preacher Burden jumped to his feet and motioned to Neil. "Come out back here. I want to show you somethin'."

The preacher's round body nearly floated as he wound his way through the back of the store with Neil and Doc behind. When he got to the back door he threw it open and held his arm out toward the west. "Take a look at that view," he said to Neil. "They don't have anything like that over in Burley."

He paused as Glenn Neil took in the scenery—the mountains in the distance and the crystal-clear river on his left. "Now you see that notch in the mountains straight ahead?" the preacher asked Neil. "Right below that notch is where Will Parker lives.

"Now if you'll look to your right, you'll see a little finger of hillside that sort of juts out into the valley. The road rises and goes over it where you see that big rock stickin' out. Right there is the prettiest spot in Avery Cove! You can see all the way around the valley, and there's a beautiful view of the river! What we'll do is cut a road a few hundred yards up the side of the hill, clear out the trees, and build you any kind of house you want ... wood, stone, brick ... solid gold if you want it. I happen to own that property and you can have it for a song!"

"You don't say!" said Neil.

"I *do* say!

"Well it sounds like we have mutual needs and goals," Neil said as he continued to gaze.

"I'm in," Doc said. "We need some new blood in the valley."

Preacher Burden's eyes were wide, and they darted back and forth as though they were seeing the future. "Look, Mr. Neil," he said, "those fancy horses of yours need some rest before they go back to Burley. Why don't you spend the night with me? My wife and daughter will fix you a welcome-to-the-valley meal ... Doc, you're invited too ... and we'll sit and discuss where you want your mill, and what kind of land you think your workers would find desirable, and then we'll see ..."

"Preacher Burden," Neil said as he gazed toward the finger of hillside, "I'd be delighted!"

Twenty-Seven

A Clandestine Visit

"Mrs. Burden, that was an outstanding meal! *Outstanding!*" Glenn Neil leaned back in his chair. "Preacher, I hope you know how lucky you are to have not one, but *two* good cooks sharing your home."

Rachel and Naomi blushed slightly and smiled at Neil.

"That's not by luck." the preacher said. "That's by the grace of God."

Neil touched his linen napkin to the corners of his mouth and laid it on the table next to his plate. "That was the finest roast beef I've ever put in my mouth," he said.

"You wanna know why?" Preacher Burden asked. "Well, I'll tell you why! That's genuine *Angus* beef. Your daddy would have known that breed, him being from Scotland and all, and I, Mr. Neil, have one of the first herds of Angus cattle in the United States of America!"

Preacher Burden stood and proudly patted himself on the chest. "You see, Mr. Neil …"

"Call me Glenn," Neil said.

The preacher sat back down and cleared his throat. "You see, Glenn, this is the perfect place to raise Angus cattle. We've got good grass, perfect weather, and clean water just like they do where these cows' daddy and mamas came from. Why, if those cows had been blindfolded on their way across the ocean, they'd *swear* they were still in Scotland! That's why this is cattle country and not sheep country."

Neil and Doc French nodded in agreement.

"Raising beef cattle up here isn't a big challenge, but now we *do* have a challenge when it comes to getting the cows to market," the preacher said. "We can sell 'em if we can get 'em down the mountain without half of 'em breakin' a leg."

The preacher stood again and pushed his chair back. "Now, if you can get our roads improved the way you say you can, we'll have a straight shot to the trains in Burley."

"I hope you'll keep that in mind when you start pricing out your land to my mill workers," Neil said. "That is, if I decide to come."

"Those abandoned houses with their garden plots and outbuildings don't have a lot of value to me," the preacher said. "It's the fields and pastures I want. It seems to me we have a match made in heaven, what with you needing houses and me needing open land."

Neil and Doc nodded in agreement again.

"Look, gentlemen," the preacher said, "why don't we go sit out on the porch where it's cool? I'll get Rachel to bring us some coffee."

The sun had set behind Will's house, and the valley was beginning to take on the shimmering glow of twilight as the men walked out onto the porch. The preacher and Doc settled in rockers, and Neil walked to the porch railing to gaze at the finger of land jutting out into the valley beyond Karl Badger's house.

"This is my favorite time of day," Doc said as he settled back in his rocker.

"And mine," said the preacher, "and th' crickets and tree frogs must like it too. ...That's a happy song they're singin'."

The talking ceased. All three men listened as the frogs and crickets sang, with the distant sound of the river providing the accompaniment.

Finally, the preacher spoke up. "What do you see, Glenn?"

Neil's gaze remained steady as he looked toward the northwest. "I was looking at that finger of land with a view that you pointed out," he answered.

"I remember my father telling me about a place in Scotland not far from Fa'side Castle where he would go when he was a boy. It was on a finger of land that jutted out into the Firth of Forth, and he said the view was spectacular! He said he would sit and watch the ships come and go. … He said it was there that he first dreamed of coming to America."

The encroaching darkness was robbing Neil of his view, so he came to sit with the others. "If I owned that piece of land, I'd call it 'Fa'side," he said, "because I'd be able to see my own dreams from up there."

"And if you built a home there, would you call it Fa'side Castle?" Doc asked.

"It wouldn't have battlements or towers," Neil said, "but it would be a castle to me."

Several moments of silence went by before Neil spoke again. "Preacher, if I bought that land, could I have some field and pasture land to go with it?"

"There's room above the road for a good-sized garden and pasture," the preacher said, "and you could have the original fields in the bottom land below the road. Why … you're not thinkin' about puttin' sheep down there, are you?"

"No," Neil replied, "no sheep. I'd just like enough room for all contingencies."

"Glenn, if this works out, I'll find you all the field and pasture land you need."

"It has to work out," Neil said with determination.

The preacher stopped rocking and leaned forward. "*Has* to work out?" he asked. "Mr. Neil … do you already have an investment in this valley?"

Neil slowly got up and walked to the edge of the porch again. "Yes, Preacher, I do," he said, "but it's not an investment in land. … It's an investment in a young man named Will Parker."

Neil turned and faced the preacher and Doc. The look on his face was gentle—almost soft. "Gentlemen, my wife and I were never fortunate enough to have children. As a matter of fact, neither of us has any family left at all. Will Parker and his sister, Esther, are the closest thing we'll ever have to children."

He took a step forward and a look of solemnity came over him. "Now, Doc," he said, "you're a physician … and Preacher, you're a minister of the Gospel, so I'm going to place the burden of professional confidentiality on you both. Will and his sister are my only heirs. When my wife and I are gone, they'll get everything I have."

"Oh, my!" Preacher Burden said.

Doc sat motionless, looking shocked.

Neil's mood then brightened. "But, if he's going to inherit a fortune from my wife and me, I'm going to be close enough to him to see to it that he looks after us in our old age!"

"That's the spirit!" Doc said.

"And I know he'd like to have us near to him even though he won't know about the inheritance. … So that's the reason I didn't want to see Will today," Neil said. "My wife and I are about all he and his sister have for family too. I didn't want him to get his hopes up about me coming here until I was pretty sure I would."

"So … are you pretty sure now?" the preacher asked.

"If we can find a place on the river to build a mill … it's a done deal," Neil said.

The preacher jumped to his feet and thrust his right hand out to Neil. "Then consider it done! I'll show you the place tomorrow morning!"

Will's wagon rolled slowly down North Road toward Demus Whitedeer's house. The horses walked with care in the total darkness that had just fallen. Alice sat on the seat beside Will, and Sonny sat on the rear of the wagon bed with his legs dangling down. It was a solemn occasion, and when they spoke, it was in muted tones.

Against Alice's better judgment, the three were on their way to Demus Whitedeer's house for the ceremony that would make Sonny a member of the Cherokee Indian tribe, and the one and only member of the snake clan.

It was Sonny's reward for learning the "sss" sound and partially overcoming his speech impediment.

As Demus' house came into view, they could see a bonfire in the yard, lighting the scene. The fire gave off a ghostly light that caused strange shadows to dance around Demus's house and yard.

Alice slid closer to Will, allowing her arm to touch his, and she spoke softly. "Will, are you sure this is a good idea? Everyone says this man is no more than a savage. I worry about Sonny being involved with him."

"Alice, Demus is the one that made such a difference in Sonny's speech. He's a good man. He's no more a savage than Preacher Burden or your Preacher Babb! Besides, I have a feeling that he's gone to a lot of trouble for Sonny's ceremony."

"Why does Sonny have to be an Indian anyway?" Alice asked.

"Things like that are important to a boy his age," Will replied, "and you know yourself how hard he's worked to reach this goal."

He leaned slightly toward Alice and let his arm press more firmly against hers. "You trust me, don't you?"

Alice gave him a little shove. "Oh Will … you know I trust you … but this is *spooky*. Why couldn't he have at least done it in the daylight?"

Two people were already seated on a log by the fire when Will's wagon pulled into Demus' yard. When the wagon came to a stop, one of them looked in their direction.

"Well look whut th' buzzards dropped outta th' sky!" It was Roamer's voice coming from out of the dim light. "'Cept o' course fer you, Alice … an' 'at boy o' yourn."

"Roamer, I wish you'd jest shet up 'at foolishness," Sweetie said. "'Is here is a solemn occasion accordin' t' Demus!"

Will and Alice took a seat on the log and quietly exchanged pleasantries with Roamer and Sweetie, while Sonny entertained himself by throwing twigs on the fire.

As soon as the adults had finished their greetings and had settled in their places, Demus appeared out of the shadows beyond the fire's light. He was wearing buckskin trousers and an open, beaded vest that revealed his dark arms and chest. Around his brow was a beaded band that held two feathers above the back of his head, and across his nose and cheeks there were two stripes of white paint.

When he had the attention of the gathering, he stepped forward into the light, raised his arms and face toward the sky, and in his most mighty voice shouted, "MUMBO JUMBO! ABRACADABRA!"

"*I hope to my never!*" Roamer exclaimed.

"Shet up, Roamer," Sweetie whispered.

Sonny froze in place, his eyes enlarged to better see the dark image, and in a soft voice he uttered, "Wow!"

Demus walked around the fire and placed a blanket on the ground next to Sonny and instructed him to sit on the blanket and remain silent. When Sonny was seated, Demus circled back around the fire and stood, raising his arms and face to the sky again.

"*Oh, Great Spirit ... look upon this solemn gathering ... as we induct the brave, Sonny Day ... into the snake clan ... and into the Cherokee Nation!*"

With that, Demus reached into a pouch that was hanging at his waist and took a pinch of gun powder, throwing it on the fire. WOOSH! ... For an instant, the fire jumped skyward, scattering sparks into the air. Even though Sonny had been instructed to remain silent, he couldn't control himself. "*Wow!*" he said again.

Demus glared down at Sonny before he raised his arms and face again to continue.

"*Oh, spirit of the snake ... look with favor on the brave, Sonny Day ... and allow him to take your name as the sign of his clan!*"

Another pinch of gunpowder hit the fire, and the sparks flew upward. Sonny lost control again and slid backward, away from the fire.

"*The snake is a powerful creature,*" Demus intoned. "*He is a mighty hunter ... but respectful of man.*"

More gunpowder ... more sparks.

"*He is a hard worker and obeys his mother... He learns his lessons well!*"

Gunpowder ... sparks.

Alice slid closer to Will, and Will put his arm around her waist. She slid closer still.

Roamer and Sweetie were transfixed by the ceremony and sat with their eyes glued to Demus.

Demus then circled back around the fire and stood in front of Sonny. He kneeled and tied a piece of twine around Sonny's head and stuck a chicken feather in the back. He placed his right hand on Sonny's head and raised his left hand skyward.

"*Sonny, the brave,*" he said, "*like the snake, you are respectful of man ... you are a mighty hunter ... and you have learned your lessons well. You obey your mother!*" He paused and gave Alice a sideways look. Alice smiled and let out a nervous giggle.

"*Therefore ... as chief Indian of Avery Cove,*" he continued, "*I do hereby establish ... and induct you into the snake clan ... an honor which you may pass down to your descendents in perpetuity!*"

Sonny glanced around to make sure his mother was taking all of this in, and she gave him a little wave.

Demus then stood and hit the fire with a most generous pinch of gunpowder.

"*Lord have mercy!*" Roamer exclaimed as the sparks lit the sky.

Demus glanced at Roamer, placed his right hand back on Sonny's head, and raised his left hand skyward again. "*And now brave Sonny ... seeing as how you are a member of the snake clan ... and knowing that you will never again shoot anyone with your slingshot ... I hereby ... as chief Indian of Avery Cove ... induct you into the Cherokee Nation ... as a full-fledged member ... with all the rights and privileges of a regular Indian!*"

Demus then bent down and whispered in Sonny's ear. Sonny stood, and he and Demus bowed to the assemblage.

"Ladies and gentlemen," he announced, "*I present to you Sonny Day, assistant chief Indian of the entire valley of Avery Cove. Please give him a round of applause!*"

The audience stood and applauded with vigor. Alice took a handkerchief from her sleeve and wiped a tear from her eye.

"'At's th' most solemnest thing I have saw since Sweetie was babatized," Roamer said as he clapped his hands.

"Hit give me a case o' th' allovers!" Sweetie added.

When the ovation had ended, Alice pulled Sonny to her and hugged him, telling him how proud she was of him. Then she went to Demus and took his hand. "Mr. Whitedeer," she said, "it's such a pleasure to finally meet you. How can I ever thank you for all you've done for Sonny?"

"The pleasure is mine, I assure you, Mrs. Day, and I would be honored if you would let me continue to work with Sonny. He is, after all, my Indian brother." A smile crossed his face, and his booming laugh rolled out into the darkness.

"Tan I tome see Demus tomorrow?" Sonny asked.

"You see," Demus said, "we still have a lot of work to do."

———

A chilling breeze was blowing from the mountain as Will's wagon rolled west from Demus' house. Alice pulled her sweater tightly around her shoulders and braced against the wind.

"Will," she said, breaking the silence, "why didn't you tell me that Mr. Whitedeer wasn't a savage?"

"*What?* I did tell you! You wouldn't listen!"

"You didn't tell me forcefully enough!" Alice argued.

"Did you want me to hit you over the head?"

Alice thought silently before she answered. "No … you wouldn't do that."

Will turned and looked back into the wagon bed. Sonny had curled up on some hay and was sound asleep. He motioned for Alice to look at her sleeping Indian.

Alice looked back to see Sonny lying on the hay in his normal sleeping position. "I can't believe the change that's come over him," she said.

"We've all changed," Will said. "A lot has happened."

Alice thought silently again before she turned to Will. "It's happening too quickly, Will."

Will turned and looked at her. "You mean … us?"

"Yes, us," Alice said haltingly. "I don't want to fall in love with you yet, Will."

This time Will was silent as he searched for the right words. "I'm afraid it's too late for me," he finally said, "but I understand ... and you're right. I won't rush you."

The wagon crossed the bridge over the river and continued to roll slowly toward Alice's house. Both Alice and Will were quiet in their thoughts until Will finally spoke. "Alice, can we at least work together to keep Sonny on track?"

Alice took a deep breath and released it, freeing the tension bottled up inside her. "I'd like that," she replied. "I'd like that very much."

———

The first light of Thursday morning fell on Preacher Burden and Glenn Neil as they pulled their wagons out of the preacher's yard and turned to the right. The preacher's buggy led the way followed by Neil's sleek phaeton. They went the short distance to the store, turned left, and headed out the road toward Burley.

When they pulled into the yard of Caldwell Turpin's mill and stopped, Neil called out, "Is this what you wanted me to see?"

The preacher climbed down from his buggy and motioned to Neil. "Come around here below the mill and I'll show you the spot."

The two men walked to the lower side of the mill and the preacher pointed across the river. "Now over there is where you could put your mill," he said. "You could put your water wheel right there below Caldwell's."

"I suppose you own that land?"

"Lock, stock and barrel," the preacher said proudly.

"Well, preacher, I hate to tell you this, but there isn't enough flat land there to build a mill! Why ... even a *modest* woolen mill would be three or four times the size of your store."

"Well, I know you'd have to cut some trees ..."

"But look back there behind the trees. There isn't forty feet of flat land before you come to that hill side."

The preacher craned his neck and looked across the river. "Oh my!" he moaned. "You mean you couldn't fit your mill over there?"

"Not unless you can make that hillside disappear," Neil said. "Isn't there anything else close by where there's some flat land beside falling water?"

The preacher removed his hat and rubbed his head as he thought. "Come to think of it, back before I came here, there was a grist mill on the river up where Will lives."

"Is the land flat, and are there rapids?"

"Well, yes," the preacher said. "There's flat land on Will's side of the river and on the other side too ... plenty of it. And the river runs fast along there. It wouldn't take more than two hundred feet of headrace to supply a good sized water wheel."

Neil put his hands on his hips and looked around. Disappointment clouded his face. "I'd have to see it," he said, "but I can't go up there today. I can't run the risk of Will seeing me. I suppose you own the land across from Will's property too?"

"Why no, I don't happen to own that particular piece of land," the preacher said apologetically. "I tried to buy it some time back but I couldn't find the owner. Came to the conclusion that it was hopeless. It probably belongs to some speculator now."

"Have the taxes been paid?"

"Faithfully! The tax office said the identification of the owner was clouded, but the tax payments came out of a bank in Asheville."

Both men were clearly disappointed. Preacher Burden had failed to sell his useless piece of land, and Neil had hit a roadblock in the construction of his mill.

But as they were walking back to their wagons, the preacher had an idea. "You know, Glenn, Will's going to Burley tomorrow to pick up his sister. If you stay over, I'll take you up to look at that spot as soon as he's on his way; then you can leave here on Saturday."

Neil rubbed his chin and thought for a moment. "That's not a bad idea," he said, "but I'll have to keep you busy on that telegraph key of yours."

"Oh my ... then times-a-wastin'!" the preacher said. "Let's get to work!"

Before the sun was up over the eastern mountain, Preacher Burden had set up an office at his home for Neil Glenn, and he had organized the day in his mind. Naomi would run the store and post office as long as need be, he would man the telegraph key, and Rachel would be Neil's secretary, ferrying messages back and forth from the house to the store.

The preacher and Naomi had no more than opened the store when Rachel was through the door with the first communication that Neil wanted sent. It was to Mr. Massey, the superintendent at Inverness Mill, and it read, "Tied up with new project. Must postpone meeting until Friday next week. Glenn Neil."

When Rachel returned home she made a pot of coffee for Neil and picked up the text of two more telegrams he wanted sent. One was to the livery stable in Burley saying that he was delayed, that the horses and coach were satisfactory, and that he would be in on Saturday to buy them. The other was to the foreman of the crew building his new mill in Concord advising him that he had decided to go with the revised plans for the office space.

After she had delivered those to her father, she returned to the house with a bottle of Carter's midnight-blue ink for Neil and picked up the text of the final telegram Neil would send before lunch. It was addressed to The Honorable Jasper Walker, Presiding Judge, North Carolina Western District Court, Asheville, N. C. It read, "Dear Pinky, Need name and address of land owner south side of Avery River, western end of Avery Cove N.C. across river from Will Parker property. Send to me c/o sending office listed above. Thanks, Glenn N."

"*Pinky?*" the preacher exclaimed when he read Neil's message. "Oh my! Well, they say it's not *what* you know ... it's *who* you know!"

By mid afternoon Neil had received a reply from Massey at Inverness Mill and two messages from the construction foreman in Concord. Then around five o'clock in the afternoon Rachel delivered a reply from The Honorable "Pinky" Walker. It read, "Glenn, owner is attorney Daniel Taylor, 420 Mission Street, Asheville. Probably inherited from previous owner Jeremiah Taylor. Grandfather perhaps. Pinky"

"Do you want to send a reply?" Rachel asked when Neil had finished reading the message.

"No, I think I might make a detour through Asheville and see this Taylor fellow face to face," Neil replied. "I'd like to see my old pal Pinky anyway."

———

The preacher was up before dawn the next morning, but he wasn't the first one up. When he noticed that the front door was partially open, he walked out on the porch to find Neil looking toward the spot he called Fa'side, waiting for the first glints of sunlight to fall on it.

"Got your eye on that parcel of land, I see," the preacher said.

"I'll have my eye on it for sure as soon as the sun strikes it," Neil replied.

"What are you gonna do if you end up without a place to put your mill?"

Neil took a deep breath and blew it out. "Well, if I can strike a deal with you on that high ground ... I might just build a house up there anyway. Maybe I'll become a pig farmer ... or a moonshiner."

The preacher laughed a hoarse belly laugh. "You'd last about fifteen minutes as a pig farmer. You ever smelled a big pig farm?"

"Can't say as I have," Neil answered.

"And we already have a moonshiner in the valley ... Roamer Robinson, Goober's ... Makepeace's uncle. He pretty much has that business sewn up."

"Has a good product, does he?"

"Now, Glenn ... you're asking the preacher! I only use it medicinally with a little honey, and I hold my nose when I take it."

"Well then, I guess I'd just have to try to work out a deal with Will ... trade him his farm for Fa'side and put the mill where his house is."

"You don't own Fa'side yet," the preacher said.

"And I've probably worked myself into a corner lettin' you know how much I want it. What's your price?"

"Well! So we're gettin' down to business," the preacher said as he took a seat on the porch railing. "Now if you want the field land down below the road along with the hill-side property, that would be the entire parcel as it was originally laid out ... a quarter of a section ... a hundred and sixty acres."

The preacher stood and walked a few steps before turning and coming back to sit. "Now, Glenn, that's prime land ... best in the valley as far as pretty goes ... and the fields and pasture are as good as there is up here."

"Looks sorta rocky from here," Neil said.

"Oh, there's just that one big rock sticking out kinda like a guide post," the preacher said. "That land is so fertile, you'd have to throw your seed and jump back to keep from gettin' swallowed up by the sprouts!"

"So how much?"

"Let's see ... hundred-sixty acres prime land ... fertile fields and pasture ... best view in North Carolina ... You know," the preacher said, "I'm just about to talk myself outta sellin' that quarter section. I might just move up there myself."

"How much," Neil said impatiently.

The preacher turned to Neil and placed a finger in the air. "Twenty-four-hundred!" he said quickly.

Neil gulped. "*Twenty-four hundred?* You can't be serious! I can buy land in Charlotte for that and have the convenience of city living!"

"Ah! But the city doesn't have a view...or clean, cool air."

The preacher stood and walked a few steps, thinking as he went. "But then ... if you want to live in the city ..."

"*Sixteen-hundred dollars!*" Glenn declared. "That's ten dollars an acre for land that's going to need lots of improvements! There probably isn't even any fencing, is there?"

"Well, no, no fencing except that Paul Thiggery's fence is already there on one side...but there's water up there ... springs ... and a branch for livestock. And the fields—they back right up to the river. Why a man could sit up there and look down on his crops literally *jumpin'* out of the soil!

But then again, if it's the money that's botherin' you, I've got some other spots …"

"*Two thousand!*" Neil declared, putting his hands to his face. "For land I haven't even walked!"

"*Sold!*" the preacher shouted. "And guaranteed. We'll walk it when we go up to see that place across the river from Will's."

Neil settled back on the rail and chuckled. "Preacher," he said, "do you realize we just bought and sold a parcel of land dressed in our night shirts?"

"Oh my … *oh my!*" the preacher said. "We better get dressed before the ladies get up!"

———

The big rock at Fa'side was glistening in the sun as the Preacher and Neil walked to the store. Each had a large biscuit filled with ham and eggs in one hand and a mug of coffee in the other. They talked between bites of food as they went.

"You think Will will be by the store early on his way to Burley?" Neil asked.

"I'm sure he will. He's an early riser," the preacher answered. "Anxious, too. He must be close to his sister, the way he carried on when he found out she was coming for the summer."

"You think he'll come *in* the store or just speak on his way by?"

"Oh, he'll check on his mail. He has a letter from Goober … Makepeace. Hope he'll read it out loud."

Neil swallowed a bite of his biscuit before he spoke again. "I'll watch out for him and hide in the back when he comes. It'll be strange seeing him and not even speaking … but I'll make up for it later."

"You can let him know you're here, can't you, now that you've decided to come for sure."

"I won't hold him up," Neil replied. "I'll be back when Esther's settled in."

When they got to the store, the preacher unlocked the front door and entered to ceremoniously pull the cords attached to his electric light bulbs. "Just like in the city," he proclaimed to Neil.

"Can I use your phone?" Neil asked with a grin.

"Won't be long before I can answer that question '*yes*'!" the preacher said boldly, and he grabbed a broom and walked out to the porch.

The preacher was sweeping and Neil was gazing out the window when Will's wagon appeared, coming slowly down the road. Will had fastened a framework of boughs bent over the bed of the wagon and had stretched canvas over them to create his own small version of a Conestoga.

"That's my boy!" Neil said to himself when he saw Will's creation. "He'll be high and dry under that Inverness canvas!"

As soon as Will pulled up in the store yard and set his brake, Preacher Burden propped his broom against a post and hollered, "Will! Come on in. I have a letter for you from Goober ... Makepeace."

Neil took one last look and scurried to the back room.

"You got everything ready for your sister?" the preacher asked as Will was coming up the steps.

"I sure hope so," Will said. "I want everything to be just right. She needs a break from Wilmington."

Will stomped the dust off his feet and entered the store behind the preacher.

"Will, please tell her that I sure wish I'd known that she was so unhappy in Wilmington. I would have tried my best to talk her into leavin' that dreadful place and comin' to teach in our little school."

"Things always work out for the best, Preacher. I'm sure that Peter Paul Lamb was meant to come here for some purpose ... some purpose we may not even be aware of now."

The preacher leaned up against a barrel and reflected on Will's statement. "Appreciate you sayin' that, Will," he said.

"Didn't you say that I have a letter from Makepeace?" Will asked.

"Oh my, yes," the preacher replied, snapping back to reality. He hurried around the counter, went directly to Will's box, and pulled out the envelope.

"I hope the boy's okay," the preacher said. "I worry about him being there in that big city alone … him bein' a country boy and all. There's lots of temptation for a country boy in the city."

"There's lots of temptation for a city boy in the country too … or a country boy in the country," Will said as he took the letter. "Or a city boy in the city," he added as he tore it open.

"Let's see … it says … *'Dear Will, this is Makepeace Green writing to you. Have I got news for you. I am getting'* … Well how about that!" Will said. He let his hands fall to his sides, and he took on a look of disbelief. When he brought the letter back to his eyes he continued reading. *"'I am getting marred'* … I think he means married … *'to Janie Rose Rainey that I told you about when I told you about Judy Ruth running off with Tommy Lee Jones to get … married. Her daddy even said it was okay and her mother.'*"

"I can't believe it!" the preacher said.

"'Please tell Uncle Roamer and Aunt Sweetie and Preacher Burden too' … That's you, Preacher … *'that I am getting married to Janie Rose Rainey and tell Mr. Jeter that when Janie Rose seen that bear skin that I kilt is when she knowed I was a real man. So thank him for sending it. I will let you know when we are … married and I will bring Janie Rose to meet you all, except … she says she knows you Will and used to moon over you till she met me she says.'* And he signed it, *'Your friend Makepeace Green but you can call me Make.'*"

Glenn Neil had heard it all from his hiding place in the back of the store, and ideas raced through his mind. "I've got to do something for that boy," he thought, "and his Janie Rose Rainey."

Will was continuing to scan the letter with a puzzled look on his face. "He says that she knows me and used to *moon* over me until she met him! I've never known a Janie Rainey! I'd remember that. That's one of those names like 'Sonny Day' that you just don't forget!"

The preacher scratched his head. "Well, it'll probably come back to you eventually. In the meantime, I wouldn't mention it to the boy. He might think you still have feelings for his intended."

"I just hope I recognize her when I see her," Will said. "I'd hate to think that a total stranger was moonin' over me and I didn't even know it."

Will folded the letter and put it in his pocket. "Anyway, Preacher, give me three cents' worth of cheese, three cents' worth of crackers, and a can of those sardines. It's a long trip into Burley."

Twenty-Eight

SUMMER WITH ESTHER

Preacher Burden and Glenn Neil stood at the window and watched as Will's wagon went over the hill and out of sight on its way to Burley.

"Godspeed," the preacher said softly but loud enough for God to hear. It was more than a cliché to the preacher. It was a heartfelt prayer.

"You must know why I feel so strongly for that boy," Neil said.

"Glenn, I must confess, there was a time when I pictured Will as my son-in-law ... but the *chemistry* just wasn't there! I'm beginning to wonder if my Rachel will ever find someone she can relate to. I may die without ever knowing the joy of holding a precious grandchild in my arms."

As the preacher was finishing his statement, Rachel started up the porch steps, and all talk of chemistry and grandchildren ceased.

"I'm here, Daddy," Rachel announced as she entered the store. She immediately went behind the post office counter, removed her bonnet, and set her basket on the floor.

"Mr. Neil and I may be gone until after lunch," the preacher said. "Is your mama gonna come help you?"

"She'll be along as soon as breakfast is cleaned up," Rachel answered.

"The freight wagon will be here early this afternoon. You and your mama be sure to check everything. Last time they shorted us a hoop of cheese."

The preacher put on his hat and motioned for Neil to follow. "Probably ate it on the way back to Burley," he muttered as he started out the door.

"Oh, by the way, Rachel," he said just before he shut the door, "Will got a letter from Goober Green. He's gettin' married!"

Rachel didn't reply, but a veil of sadness fell over her face. She turned her back to her father and began fumbling with the outgoing mail.

The air, the temperature, and the feel of the morning breeze were all familiar to Preacher Burden. The smells of the valley—fresh pine, wood smoke, and newly plowed soil—rested in his nostrils, but to Glenn Neil, these things were new. He was invigorated—intoxicated even—by the sight, sounds, and smell of the valley. All thought of Inverness Mill, Concord, Pinky Walker, and a thousand other things that cluttered his mind were reduced to triviality as he walked along the road with the preacher.

"We'll take my buggy," the preacher said as they neared the barn. "We'd attract too much attention in that rig of yours. We'll make a loop of the entire valley so you can see your place, the mill site, and a lot of the abandoned places that are for sale. Course, I'll point out places of interest along the way ... show you where Will lives and so forth."

"Are the people here pretty tolerant of newcomers?" Neil asked as they picked up speed.

"No."

"*Really?*"

"Well, newcomers ... such as you, for instance ... are accepted when the folks see that I or Preacher Babb accept 'em. It's not like we're the wise sages up here or anything like that, it's just that they've come to look at us as sort of ... measuring sticks. They've got too much to do to be sittin' around trying to figure out if somebody's a good person or not."

"I'm glad I've got you fooled then," Neil said.

The preacher gave Neil a glancing look and grinned. "Well, who knows ... you may not fool Preacher Babb!"

Soon the preacher pointed out his first place of interest. "Now here on your left is where our blacksmith, Karl Badger, lives." Then he pointed beyond the house. "That's his shop out back there. Good man."

"What's that coming up in his field?" Neil asked.

"Corn and hay. Most everybody grows corn and hay for their animals."

"Nice vegetable garden."

"Everybody up here has a nice garden."

After they had passed two abandoned homesteads and the old Tribble place, the road started to rise toward Neil's Fa'side.

When the preacher stopped his buggy at the crest of the hill, he pointed out the boundaries of the property both on the mountain and in the bottom land.

Neil got down and walked up the slope of the mountain toward the spot where he pictured his home would sit. The preacher followed from a distance, giving him some privacy.

Finally, about a hundred yards from the road, Neil stopped and looked down on the valley. He studied the scene for about a minute; then he walked toward the east about a hundred feet and surveyed the valley again.

After he had looked in all directions and had smelled the air to his satisfaction, he began to gather rocks and place them in a pile. "This is where my house will sit," he said, "and I want my front porch to face due south to soak up the winter sun."

Back at the buggy, the preacher pointed out the two churches, the school house, and other points of interest. He told how from that vantage point one could see weather approaching from the west, and he explained how that side of the mountain was protected from the howling north winds of winter. "Honest to goodness," he said, "I wish I could just pick up my house and store and move 'em up here."

When they were back underway, Roamer and Sweetie's house, more abandoned properties, and Demus Whitedeer's house passed in succession until finally Will's property came into view.

"Look at that barn!" Neil said. "It looks like a scene in the Swiss Alps. Just look at the form and the attention to detail!"

"Goober's ... Makepeace's daddy built that barn along with a lot of the other barns and houses in the valley," the preacher stated. "But you see all that fretwork and gingerbread up in the eves and around the windows and doors? Guess who did all that!"

"I'd say the man that did that was straight from Europe," Neil replied.

The preacher laughed a satisfied kind of laugh. "Goober did all that when he was about fifteen years old. Drew the designs out on butcher paper, transferred them to the lumber, and cut them out with a coping saw. He learned a lot about carpentry before his daddy died."

Neil was astonished. "Then why didn't he become a carpenter?"

"Because people were moving out of here on an almost weekly basis. Nothing was being built. Besides, Goober was always wantin' to try something new. I think that's why he did so well in the mill and then when he helped you buy that property at Burley. He considered those things a challenge."

The buggy continued on slowly past Will's house and over the bridge.

"Well … here we are," the preacher declared as he stopped the buggy again. "This is the place! Does that look like enough level ground to build your mill on?"

Neil hopped down and walked a few steps off the road. "This looks ideal. *Ideal!* And the river rises just about right. Like you said, a headrace a couple hundred feet long would be plenty." He pointed to some stone pillars along the river bank. "Those look like the supports for the race that was here before."

He looked around in all directions and smelled the air. Then he walked back to the buggy and pulled himself up on the seat. "You know, Preacher, I've been thinking. A building about the size and shape of Will's barn would be just about right for my woolen mill. I like that old-world look too—with the fancy trim in the eves and around the windows." He paused as he thought and rubbed his chin. "You know anybody that might take on the challenge of building a structure like that?"

———

Will's wagon lumbered slowly down the road beside the Avery River on its way to Burley. It dodged potholes and ruts washed out by the spring rains and finally came to the valley where the road and the course of the river parted ways.

When the horses had drunk from the river, Will proceeded to the flat, grassy area where, as a newcomer to the land, he had spent the night with Goober and Preacher Burden. He unhitched the horses and gave them their temporary freedom.

The spot had changed from the wintry place where he had slept in March. Then, there were patches of snow under barren trees. Now, the trees and fields were dressed in their spring coat of green, and flowers abounded.

After he had feasted on the glorious sight of that remote valley, he turned to other things. The trip had given him time to think. He had asked his mind to dwell on pleasant things like his sister's arrival, and in so doing, he had avoided thoughts of Alice; but as hard as he tried, he couldn't keep her totally out of his mind.

He knew why she felt as she did about their relationship. He knew that it was fitting and proper that she should mourn for Matthew and take time to reflect on their life together. He knew how important it was for Sonny to remember his father. He knew that when the time had arrived for them to continue their courtship, they would have a mutual awareness of its coming. All these things he knew, but his heart still ached for her.

On the practical side, he worried about how he would entertain Esther now. Much of what he had planned for her centered on Alice, and now he feared those plans were in jeopardy. He wanted his time with Esther but feared that she would be bored being around him constantly. If familiarity breeds contempt, he thought, then Esther just might become contemptuous before many days had passed. Likewise, he didn't want her to feel that she had to work beside him in the garden and in the fields. He wanted her to be on the plane of an honored guest.

The horses grazing in the meadow reminded Will that he was hungry. He retrieved his canteen, his package of cheese and crackers, and his can of sardines from the wagon and spread a piece of canvas on the ground. With the sun overhead to warm him and a steady breeze to keep the insects away, he began to enjoy his feast.

About halfway through his third cheese cracker, he heard what he thought at first was a rumble of thunder. Quickly though, he realized that the "thunder" was the sound of horses' hooves and wagon wheels coming from the direction of Burley. When it appeared from behind a grove of trees amid a cloud of dust, he saw that it was the big freight wagon that delivered goods to Burden's.

He recognized the driver whom he had seen before. He was the tall skinny man who was always so friendly. He was dressed as usual in denim pants, a plaid shirt, and denim vest. He wore a black cap perched precariously on the back of his head, and a gap-toothed smile dominated his face. His appearance would not have been remarkable though, had it not been in such great contrast to the man seated beside him.

His passenger was a young man, fair of complexion, dressed in a cream-colored suit. He was slender in build, and although he was seated, it was obvious that he was tall. He wore a derby hat that matched the color of his suit, and beneath the rim of his derby was a fringe of neatly trimmed, blond hair.

As the wagon passed, headed for the water of the river, the driver threw up his hand, grinned, and shouted a greeting. The passenger, on the other hand, sat sternly upright and only stared as if to say, "My, you're a shabby looking soul."

It wasn't until the wagon was down at the river that Will said to himself, "I sure hope that wasn't Peter Paul Lamb!"

———————

Demus and Sonny sat on the rock wall in Demus's front yard ready for a lesson in elocution. Demus was back to his normal farm attire, and the white stripes on his face had been washed away. Sonny was proudly wearing the chicken feathers on the back of his head— the sign that he was the assistant chief Indian of Avery Cove.

"That was some ceremony, wasn't it?" Demus asked.

Sonny nodded enthusiastically. "*Uh-huh!*"

"Don't forget to say 'yes,' " Demus reminded him.

"*Yes!*"

"You want to continue working on your speech, don't you?"

"Sure."

"Would you like to go back to school in the fall?"

Sonny's chin fell. "Miss Pack is dawn."

Demus put his hand on Sonny's shoulder. "Will said there'll be a new teacher next year ... a Mr. Lamb. You may like a male teacher."

"Day'll still make pun ob me," Sonny said, his chin still resting on his chest.

"Suppose we work hard on your speech for the rest of the summer. By the time school starts you just might be speaking as normally as any of them."

"Dhey'll still make pun ob me. Dhey'll tall me Toudy Day."

"Cloudy Day?"

"Yes."

"You're going to have to develop thicker skin, Sonny. Unfortunately, everybody is teased about something. Just think about the way people make fun of me!"

"You stay *away* pom um *too!*"

The words cut Demus like a knife. He *had* been staying away from those who treated him badly just as Sonny had.

"Tell you what, Sonny, I'll take what you said as a challenge. If you can go back to school, I can work on getting along with the people around here better."

Sonny thought for a moment and then nodded his head.

"And I thought of something else," Demus said. "Isn't 'Sonny' just a nickname?"

Sonny's curiosity was raised. His eyes widened as he nodded.

"What is your real name?" Demus asked.

"Daniel."

"That's a good, strong name!" Demus said. "Daniel Day! I remember a story about Daniel in the lions' den. Why don't you ask your mother if you can start using that name?"

Sonny's eyes darted to and fro as he thought about the possibility, and a slight smile appeared on his face.

"And now," Demus continued, "I think it's time we started working on some new sounds."

W ill stood on the platform of the depot under gray, threatening skies. Since his only other trip to Burley had been under a cover of clouds, he wondered if Burley was always that dark and dismal; still, though everything around him was gloomy, the little spot where he stood was bright with the promise of Esther's coming.

It was six a.m. according to the depot clock—an hour and five minutes before Esther's train was scheduled to arrive. He could have been sleeping, but the anticipation of seeing his sister had pulled him from his bed at the Burley Lodge and brought him there to wait.

He paced back and forth along the platform alone, stopping occasionally to read the notices posted on the station wall beneath the eaves. He studied the skies for a clue about the weather while the telegraph clicked in the background.

He wondered what Esther was doing at that moment. He imagined that she had just left her compartment after a night of sleep and was on her way to the dining car for breakfast. He imagined that through her eyes he could see the mountains rolling by in all their splendor. He could see miles of trees and farm land parading past the window of the dining car, and he could feel her excitement.

And while he was in that town that somehow linked him to his past in Charlotte, he remembered those friends and acquaintances he had left behind.

He thought of Sarah, who stood over her stove day after day, cooking for him and the impish bachelor boys. He thought of the ever stoic waitress, Pearl, who would bring his food and then magically disappear. He remembered Prissy, the shallow-as-a-puddle waitress, who worked as hard at husband hunting as she did waiting tables. He thought of the folks at the mill who had labored in the same rut as he, but who, unlike himself, would never escape.

And he couldn't help but think about Makepeace and his soon-to-be bride, Janie Rose. What happiness they must be experiencing! Then there was Hattie Jackson, the former slave, who toiled over her washboard for nickels and dimes and still maintained a sense of humor. He even thought about Traveler and how lucky he was to have Makepeace as his master.

"Waitin' fer a train?" a voice said.

Will turned and saw the station master leaning out of the ticket window. "Waiting for the seven-o-five," he answered.

"Ye pickin' up somebody or goin' someplace?"

"I'm waiting for my sister. She's coming up from Wilmington."

"That's a good place t' be comin' from," the station master declared. "Went there once. Didn't like it."

"That's how my sister feels."

"It's gonna be a while. Want to wait in here? Have some coffee?"

Will looked back up at the sky. The clouds seemed to be darkening. "Well, if I stay out here, I'm gonna get wet, so I'd be much obliged."

The coffee wasn't particularly good, but it was hot and it cleared the cobwebs from Will's head. After he had filled his cup for the second time, he was awake enough to ask the station master what took him to Wilmington.

"The war," he replied.

"Were you stationed at one of the forts?"

"Nope. Went down thar with a group on a supply mission. Took four big guns from th' foundry t' Fort Fisher."

He then went on to tell how his group had reached Wilmington on New Year's Eve in 1864 and had spent the next two days unloading and positioning their cargo.

"That was th' coldest I ever been in my life!" he declared. "Th' wind was a-howlin' off th' water, and we didn't have enough t' wear ... it bein' near th' end o' th' war."

He told about their struggle to move the heavy guns from the wagons up to their mounts, and how one of the men was killed when a chain broke, and the gun it was holding fell and crushed him.

"We took a beatin' down thar deliverin' them guns," he said, "but it wa'n't nothin' compared to th' beatin' them men took when th' fort fell t' th' Yankees a couple o' weeks later."

It may have been years since the station master had released his burden of the memories of that painful time, and he talked freely about the war, his discharge, and his return to Burley.

Then, as if on cue, just as he was recalling his reunion with his mother and sisters, a train whistle sounded in the distance and echoed across the hills.

Rain was falling by then—not in torrents, but in a fine mist that just settled on everything it touched and soaked in slowly. That wasn't enough to stop Will though. He thanked the station master for the coffee and the company and went out on the platform to wait. He wanted to see the first signs of smoke as the train neared the town.

Esther was sitting by a window when the train pulled in, but when she caught a glimpse of Will, she jumped up and bolted forward toward the door.

The train stopped and the conductor opened the door and placed the step on the platform. Esther sprang off the train and ran speechless to Will's embrace. The reunion of the station master and his sisters could not have been sweeter.

Preacher Burden rested his hand on the high front wheel of Glenn Neil's phaeton as Neil climbed up on the seat. "Glenn, I hope you have a good trip back to Burley. Looks like it might rain."

"I've been wet before," Neil answered. "At least it's warm. Now you get those papers to me as soon as possible, and I'll start getting some plans made for the house."

"They'll be to you as quick as the mail can get 'em up here from Burley for me to sign," the preacher declared.

He stepped back from the rig as Neil took up the reins. "I been thinking," he said. "You'll probably pass Will between here and Burley. How you gonna handle that?"

"I thought about that too. I'm gonna pull the top up over me and put my slicker on. He won't know this rig, and he probably won't pay me any attention."

"Well, if he does recognize you, it won't be the end of the world."

"You're right," Neil said. "Thank Naomi and Rachel for me again, won't you, and thanks to you to for your hospitality."

He popped the horses with the reins and was on his way. His destination was due east, but as he turned onto the road, he twisted in his seat and gazed northwest toward Fa'side.

———————

The town of Burley crept past as Will and Esther rolled west toward Goober's mountain guide post. Esther's head turned to the right and to the left as she took in the new surroundings.

"You've been awfully quiet," Will said as they came to the edge of town.

"Just taking it all in," Esther replied.

"So ... what do you think so far?"

"Is it always gloomy like this?"

"No, we had a clear day in March."

Esther grabbed Will's arm and slid close to him. "I've been waiting for the real Will to appear," she said. "I've missed your teasing."

"Who's teasing?" he asked.

Esther laughed. "I can read you like a book! Besides, your letters spoke of warm, sunny days."

"To be honest with you, we usually get our rain in the afternoon, and then it usually lasts only an hour or so. It's not normal for us to have rain on special days like this."

"Is this canvas covering one of your inventions?" she asked, looking up at the covering above her.

"You'll be glad we have it if the rain gets worse," Will said. "We can move back in the bed and sit high and dry on that hay."

"You've thought of everything!"

"That's right, and now that we're out of town, I have some big news for you."

"*Really?* Why did you have to wait?"

"I didn't want you squealing in town. Somebody may have thought I was kidnapping you!"

"*You're getting married!*" she screamed.

"No, not *me*. I got a letter from Makepeace yesterday. *He's* getting married."

Esther put her hand to her mouth and let out a little squeal. "*You're teasing!*" she squawked. "Like he'd say, *I hope to my never!* Is he marrying anyone I know?"

"I'm glad you asked! Her name is Janie Rose Rainey, and he says that she knows me. He said she used to moon over me. Do you remember a girl by that name?"

"No, I think I'd remember a name like Janie Rainey."

"That's what I said."

"Well, since we're talking about affairs of the heart, how about you and your lady friend, Alice? How are things going with her?"

Will didn't know how to answer, so he sat silently, trying to think of a reply.

"Did I bring up an unpleasant subject?" Esther asked.

"Oh, Esther," Will said with a sigh. "It's a very pleasant subject … but she wants to slow our relationship down for now, and that's unpleasant."

"What happened, Will?" Esther asked softly.

"Well, you have to understand that her husband has been dead less than a year … a whole lot less than a year to be exact … and she needs time to grieve. I love her, Esther, and I think that in time she'll love me too … but I have to respect her wishes."

Esther laid her head on Will's shoulder. "You're a good man, Brother. I hope I find a man like you someday," she said.

They passed the grassy spot where Will had first met Preacher Burden, and they continued up the mountain. It was surprising how much faster the trip went since they were not following the preacher's lumbering oxen.

When they reached the top, Will stopped, and as Preacher Burden had done, he pointed out the gap in the far hill where the river and the road ran. For the first time that day, the sun broke briefly through the clouds, and Esther drank in the view.

After the horses had rested, the trip continued. With the light wagon and nothing to slow them down, Don and Molly made good time. At the bottom of the mountain, Will pulled over in the pasture near the convergence of the rivers and set Don and Molly free to graze and rest.

"This is where we camped the night before I arrived at Avery Cove," Will told Esther. "We'll stay long enough to eat our lunch and then we'll be on our way."

"Are you going to shoot a bar for us to eat?" Esther asked.

"Sorry, but bars are tough this time of year," Will answered. "You'll have to settle for the ham biscuits and cake the lady at the lodge packed for us."

Just then, the rain that had held off so beautifully for so long began falling again. Will and Esther moved up under the canvas cover and seated themselves on Esther's trunk.

As Will was opening the package of food, Esther asked him, "Do you remember the fort we built when we were kids … the one with the pine-bough roof?"

"Yes, and I remember us getting caught in there in a rain storm with lightning popping all around."

"Exactly!"

"Pine boughs don't shed water like Inverness canvas."

Esther laughed out loud. "Exactly! We got soaked and scared out of our wits!"

Laughter and the drumming of rain on the canvas blended into a song as Will and Esther remembered scenes of their childhood—the fort, the swimming hole, the measles, their school—each remembrance bringing laughter.

"Will, I just realized that I've laughed more this morning than I have in the past year," Esther said.

"I'm gonna *keep* you laughing too!" Will replied.

The rain had slowed to a gentle patter when Will heard another sound. It was the wet clop of horses' hooves and the rumble of wheels, coming from the direction of Avery Cove and getting louder. He and Esther moved to the back of the wagon bed and looked out, expecting to greet a fellow traveler making a rest stop.

Instead, they saw a sleek phaeton pulled by two spirited horses pass by at high speed. The top was pulled up over the driver who appeared only briefly as a large, shadowy figure. He didn't acknowledge their calls of greeting.

"Would you look at that!" Will exclaimed. "That's some rig to be coming out of Avery Cove! Probably some drummer trying to sell Preacher Burden something."

"He sure was rude!" Esther said. "He could have at least waved!"

E sther's introduction to Avery Cove was just like everyone else's—that first glimpse of Turpin's Mill. There it sat on the left, its wheel turning at a steady pace.

In the yard sat the wagons of those who had come to get their week's supply of corn meal ground. The horses and mules stood in silence, while their owners joked and gossiped inside the mill.

As they rode by, Esther sat quietly, seemingly unimpressed.

"You're quiet again," Will said.

"I expected more ... open space."

Will chuckled.

When the wagon reached the crest of the hill and the valley opened up before them, Esther put her hand to her mouth and took a deep breath.

"Is that what you expected?" Will asked.

"Oh ... it's more," Esther answered. "It's more. There's Preacher Burden's store, and across the river there is Doctor French's house, and over to the right is the blacksmith's house, and directly ahead at the end of the valley is your house, and ..."

"Whoa!" Will said. "I'm supposed to be the tour guide."

"But it's just as you described it," Esther said. "Are you going to take me up North Road so I can see where Roamer and Demus live, or are you going to take me up South Road so I can see where Alice lives?"

"Well, since you're the tour guide, which way do *you* want to go?"

Esther thought before she answered. "Let's go up the North Road. We can see Alice tomorrow. I'd like to be dressed a little nicer when I meet her."

Will shook his head and moaned. "This isn't going to be like the contest you had with that prudish friend of yours in high school, is it ... always trying to see who can out-dress the other?"

"Nooo, I just want to make a good first impression for my future sister-in-law!"

"*Esther!*"

"Now, Will, you have to trust me. Women know these things. I can see the pattern."

"Sis, *you* have to trust *me*," Will said. "Right now, I'm the furthest thing from her mind. I don't want you trying to stir things up either!"

Smoke was rising from the kitchen chimneys of the houses along the way, and no one was in sight—a sure-fire indication that supper time was near. Will began to wonder what he would fix for his and Esther's supper. He hoped that the chickens had been productive and that Sonny had remembered to gather his eggs.

"Are you hungry?" he asked Esther.

"I wasn't going to say anything," she answered, "but I'm starved."

"How does bacon and eggs sound?"

"Scrambled, with crispy bacon?"

"Cooked to order!"

"Sounds like heaven."

By the time the roof of Will's barn came into view, the sun was falling behind the tops of the trees on the western ridge. The barn's cedar shingles, bleached almost white by the sun, shimmered under the fading light.

"That must be your barn ahead," Esther said. As the house came into view she added, "And there's your house. I'd know it anywhere."

Will drove up into the yard and unloaded Esther's trunk, valise, and hat box before taking the wagon and horses to the barn.

While she waited, Esther walked about the yard looking at the trees and flowers, and as most newcomers did, she took in great volumes of the sweet smelling air.

When they had made their way to the porch, they found a note on the door. Will read it, smiled, and handed it to Esther. "It's for you," he said.

> *Dear Esther,*
>
> *Welcome to Avery Cove. I hope your stay is pleasant and restful.*
>
> *Knowing that you would arrive late in the day, Sonny and I have left a light supper in the spring house for you and Will.. I would like to have you over for a proper meal as soon as possible, so that I can get to know you.*
>
> *Again, welcome to our valley.*
> *Sincerely,*
> *Alice Day*

Esther handed the note back to Will and gave him a devilish smile.

"It doesn't sound to me like you're the furthest thing from her mind," she said. "Now, let's go see what kind of cook she is."

On the kitchen table was a loaf of bread wrapped in a linen cloth and a black walnut cake under a glass dome.

In the spring box there was a large crockery butter churn covered with another linen cloth. Esther uncovered it and began removing layers of food. On top was a plate of fried chicken. Beneath the chicken was a bowl of potato salad, and beneath that was a bowl of green beans and squash cooked with bacon. On the bottom was a covered dish of deviled eggs and an assortment of pickles.

"Some *light* supper," Esther said. "There's enough food here to last a week. It's just not right!"

"What's not right about it, Sis?" Will asked.

Esther turned toward him, poked out her lip, and tilted her head.

"If I stay here the entire summer," she said dejectedly, "by the time I leave I'll be as big as your barn."

Twenty-Nine

DEMUS GOES TO CHURCH

Mamie Peeley's feet moved slowly and steadily, treading the pedals of the old pump organ at Avery Cove Baptist Church. Up and down they went, drawing in the flower-scented air that exited the organ as a fervent love song. The women in the packed congregation dabbed their eyes with lacey handkerchiefs, and men sat uncomfortably, wishing they were working in the fields instead of attending a wedding.

Will stood before the congregation in his freshly-pressed suit with his best man, Preacher Burden, by his side. Their eyes were fixed on the door that stood closed and unmoving at the rear of the sanctuary.

Will wasn't concentrating on Mamie Peeley's playing, but as she began a new piece, he recognized it as one she had already played. He couldn't look at his watch, but he knew the hour was late.

Suddenly, the door swung open, and the silhouette of Preacher Billy Babb appeared, framed in the doorway by the light of the summer afternoon. Without hesitation he walked to the front of the sanctuary with his black string tie bouncing up and down and stopped where Will was standing.

"Brother Will," he said as he placed his hands on Will's shoulders, "I'm sorry to have to tell you this, but Sister Alice has decided to cancel the wedding. She and little Sonny have left to go back to Chattanooga. She wanted me to tell you that she is deeply, deeply sorry."

A flurry of movement went through the congregation as the lacey handkerchiefs came out to be used again. The men squirmed in their starched overalls and exchanged puzzled looks.

Disbelief washed over Will's face as he stood trembling. His face sparkled under a mix of sweat and tears.

"What do you mean?" he demanded, and he searched Preacher Babb's face for a hint of reason. "She just ran off … leaving me to stand here like a fool? I must be dreaming!"

"I know it's a shock," Preacher Babb said, "but these things are usually for the best. I just think that she never really got over Matthew's death. She probably never will, so if I were you, Brother Will, I'd simply forget her and let this time pass into the graveyard of memories."

"*I've got to go after her!*" Will shouted, and he made a move toward the door. "Preacher Burden, you'll go with me, won't you?" he asked, turning and pleading with his best man.

"Now hold on there," Preacher Babb said. "Preacher Burden is about to get real busy! I'm happy to announce that there's *still* going to be a wedding, and *he'll* be doin' the officiating for this one!"

Preacher Babb's face glowed with happiness, and his teeth shown like the white keys on Mrs. Peeley's organ.

"Will," he announced, "I'm pleased to tell you that your lovely sister, Esther has decided to take advantage of this wonderful turnout and be married herself!"

Mrs. Peeley, who had been taking in the proceedings from the stool of her organ, rotated herself and began pumping with both feet and pulling out stops with both hands. Then when the organ bellows were fully charged, she launched into a rousing rendition of a wedding march.

Suddenly, Esther and her groom appeared in the doorway of the church. She was wearing a flowing white gown with a long train, and her smile beamed through her veil. She had never looked lovelier.

For a moment Will's personal tragedy faded as he shared his sister's happiness and marveled at her beauty—and then, his eyes focused on the groom.

Esther was holding the arm of a young man, fair of complexion, dressed in a cream colored suit. He was tall and slender in build. He wore a derby hat that matched the color of his suit, and beneath the rim of his derby was a fringe of neatly trimmed, blond hair.

The groom's eyes were fixed on Will, and there was a look of disdain on his face.

Will fell to his knees!

"*Esther!*" He screamed! "*Not him! Not Peter Paul Lamb! Esther ... No! ... No! ... No!*"

Guided by the light of dawn, Esther ran through the door of Will's bedroom and threw herself on his bed. As she had done so many times when he was a boy, she put her arms around him and pulled him close.

"*Will! Wake up! You're dreaming!*" she said frantically. "It's all right ... I'm with you now."

For a moment, Will was back in Charlotte. He was four years old and was being held and comforted by his mother. The growing up, the loss of his parents, the move away from Charlotte, and the bear attack were forgotten—locked outside the shield of his sister's embrace—and all was well.

When just a moment had passed and the cloud of sleep was lifted, Will pulled away from Esther's embrace and sat up in bed.

"Oh, Esther," he said, "that must have been the worst nightmare I've ever had!"

"Want to tell me about it?" Esther asked gently.

"I need some coffee first," he replied.

"Tell you what, if you'll build a fire while I get dressed, I'll start earning my keep by cooking you some breakfast. Then I want to hear about this Peter Paul Lamb person."

"You've got a deal," Will said, his voice still shaking.

———

L ater that morning when Will and Esther arrived at the Methodist Church, the singing had already started.

"I see some things never change," Esther said as Will brought the wagon to a stop. "I have *never* known you to get to church on time!"

"I was ready to leave a full ten minutes before you were!" Will moaned.

"You wanted me to look presentable, didn't you?" Esther asked.

And "presentable" she was! Downright lovely if the truth were to be known. Will hadn't really looked closely at his sister that morning, but now that his attention was drawn to her, he saw a beautiful woman, confident and flawlessly dressed. He thought of his dream of her on the arm of Peter Paul Lamb, and he hoped that Mr. Lamb would not be in attendance that morning. He didn't want to have to deal with that!

The singing was ending just as they entered the church, and Preacher Burden was standing to make his announcements. He smiled broadly and nodded when he saw Esther.

"My friends," he said, "we are blessed this morning with *another* new face. Our brother, Will Parker, has brought his sister, Esther. who is visiting for the summer, and I know you're gonna make her feel at home!"

Esther and Will made their way down the aisle, and a place was made for them on the third row of the left side. A murmur went through the crowd and all eyes were on Esther as they took their seats. Then, just as Will's back-side touched the bench, the person in front of him turned around, and he was eye to eye with Peter Paul Lamb.

Lamb's steely look at Will was but a flash before he turned his gaze briefly to Esther. He smiled a toothy sort of smile and slowly turned his head back toward the front. Will could feel his head about to explode.

"Now, my friends," Preacher Burden continued, "and especially you children, we're very fortunate this morning to have our new school teacher, Mr. Peter Paul Lamb, with us, and at the close of the service I want you to introduce yourselves to him and get to know him. Boys and girls, he'll be working in the store this summer, learning our little community, and if you want to get on his good side and become the teacher's pet, then you come around and butter him up a little."

A wave of nervous laughter floated through the congregation.

"And too," the preacher continued, "y'all know what a blessin' Will Parker has been to us. Why, it's just like he's always been a part of our community, and in the short time he's been here, he's earned the respect of every soul in the valley. While I haven't had the opportunity to meet and talk to his lovely sister, I just *know* that while she's here, we'll learn to love her as much as we love her brother!"

Will glanced over at Esther. She was blushing a crimson red.

"And now," the preacher continued, "since we've gotten our introducin' out of the way … I want you to get your Bibles out and turn to the tenth chapter of Luke. We're gonna read the 25th through the 37th verses."

Preacher Burden paused as the sound of turning pages filled the room. Will had forgotten his Bible and was forced to look at the only thing directly in front of him—the back of Peter Paul Lamb's blond head sitting atop the collar of his cream colored suit. "At least," he thought as he stared, "he's not wearing that cream colored derby, and at least, I can't see the sneer on his face!"

When Preacher Burden was satisfied that most of the congregation had found the tenth chapter of Luke, his eyes fell upon his own Bible and he prepared to read. At just that very moment, he and his pulpit were flooded with light as the church door opened, letting in the morning brilliance. For an instant he was blinded by the brightness that shone as radiantly as the sun itself. It was as if God had sent it to get the attention of the good preacher, and when his eyes focused, he was shocked at what he saw. There, entering the church, was the imposing figure of Nicodemus Whitedeer.

When the members saw the preacher's reaction, they turned almost as one body to see what had brought the look of astonishment to his face. From the choir, Naomi and Rachel gasped and put their hands to their mouths.

"Whut's he a-doin here?" someone near Will muttered.

"He better not be bringin' no trouble," someone else said.

Will immediately stood and faced his friend, and as he did, he saw him as he had never seen him before. He was wearing a white shirt and collar and a black string tie. The legs of his dark gray trousers were tucked into his polished black boots, as was the fashion of the day, and his hair was pulled back and tied into a pony tail. It was obvious that he had dressed as best he could out of respect for the church and those gathered there. The thing most different about his appearance though was his countenance. The expression on his face was that of a frightened child. He seemed to be about ready to turn and run as Will walked toward him with his hand extended.

When Will reached his friend, he took him by the arm and led him down the aisle to where he had been sitting. To the amazement of the preacher and the others gathered there, Esther slid over and Demus took his place between her and Will.

"Preacher," Will said as he looked up toward the pulpit, "you had the honor of introducing Esther and Mr. Lamb. Would you allow me the honor of introducing Mr. Whitedeer?"

The preacher, who was still in a state of distress, uttered a high pitched sound and nodded in the affirmative.

Will stood and turned to the congregation.

"My friends," he said, "a few months ago I came to live in your community. For whatever reason ... you quickly accepted me and took me in. When I was injured, you gave me healing ... and while I was healing, you gave me food and labored for me. But most of all ... during these few months, you have given me something of even greater value ... your friendship."

Will paused to look into the faces of those to whom he was speaking. Every eye was on him.

"One of the first people I met in the valley was this man seated here beside my sister, Demus Whitedeer. I can tell you that our first meeting was not very pleasant ... not because of anything he did, but because of the way I approached him, having heard of his reputation. I thought he had taken something from me ... stolen it. As it turned out, he hadn't. I approached him sternly and he was stern in return. We backed away from each other before we came to blows, but I went home hoping I would never have to see him again. Soon after that I met another stern resident of the valley ... a bear ..."

A ripple of laughter moved through the congregation breaking the tension a little.

"... and as you know, I was gravely injured. When I returned home to heal ... the *very first person* at my door was Demus Whitedeer. He had come to try to make amends for our unpleasant encounter ... even though it was my fault. He explained to me that when I had approached him, he was frightened. This big, imposing man was frightened of *me* and the way I had acted … and *he* wanted to make things right. Can you imagine that?"

Will looked into the faces of the congregation and then glanced back at Preacher Burden, who was sitting with his elbows on his knees listening intently.

"Since then, we have become close friends, Demus and I, and I've come to know him as he *really* is."

Will turned and looked at the preacher, who was still listening intently.

"Preacher," he said, "with all the education you have … college, seminary, and all … you may be interested to know that Demus Whitedeer is probably the most educated man I've ever known. He has a library of books that would rival many cities, and he speaks several foreign languages …yet, with all that, he has never tried to be superior to me in any way. He has never been boastful because he's wiser than me, and you know what? I've never heard him say one ill thing about anyone in this valley … even though there have been plenty of people here who have treated him poorly. The only way I have ever seen him use his learning other than for his own enjoyment is to help a young boy…Sonny Day, with his speech problem. He's spent countless hours with Sonny, and they're making genuine progress. Isn't it a *shame* that we haven't known him well enough to take advantage of his wisdom … and isn't a *shame* that he hasn't been able to take advantage of the wonderful things each person here has to offer!"

He took a deep breath and turned back to the congregation. Many in the group were looking down at their laps, their heads lowered in shame. He glanced over at Esther, who was dabbing her eyes with a handkerchief.

"I'm reminded of a story in the Bible," Will said. "It's about a man who was robbed and beaten, lying on the side of the road about to die. People came along and looked at him and passed him by. They had better things to do. If I remember correctly … one of them was even a *preacher*! Then this Samaritan came along, and he stopped and took care of the stranger and treated his wounds and found a place for him to stay while he healed up. Even *paid* for it! He stopped and helped this man ... even though he was a different sort of person. I wonder how many good Samaritans there are here today."

"*Preach!*" someone on the Elders bench shouted.

"*Amen!*" someone else shouted.

"No, I'm not preaching to *you*," Will continued. "I've got to confess that as I've been talking, I've realized I was preaching to myself. I have to confess that I came to church this morning thinking badly about a certain person I don't even know ... and before I leave today, I'm going to shake that person's hand and try to get to know him."

Will turned back toward Preacher Burden, and as he prepared to take his seat, he said, "Preacher, I apologize for taking so much of your sermon time. If you keep the folks late today they can blame me."

A wave of laughter moved over the group, and Will noticed that even Peter Paul Lamb was joining in the merriment.

Preacher Burden stood and walked to the pulpit, visibly shaken. He looked out over the congregation that was now smiling and happy, and he lifted up his Bible.

"My friends," he said softly, "if you will look at the verses of Scripture I asked you to find ... you will see that they tell the story of the good Samaritan ... the one Will was telling you about." He cleared his throat and continued in a low voice. "My sermon this morning was to be on that very subject ... and I want you know I spent many hours in preparation ... but Brother Will here has stolen my thunder. He has preached a sermon better than any I could have prepared ... and he did it in about a *tenth* of the time it would have taken *me!*"

Another chorus of laughter erupted, and Peter Paul Lamb laughed so hard that he shook.

"And so ... the only thing I'll add to what he said is this ... Mr. Whitedeer ... we're happy that you have honored us this morning by coming to worship in our church. We have a lot to make up to you ... and I *pledge* to you that we will try our best to be your friend ... and we want you to come and be a regular part of our fellowship."

He then looked Demus squarely in the eye and wagged his finger as he said, "And don't you go visitin' the Baptists ... we have the best cooks right here!"

———

D on and Molly walked slowly out of the church yard and turned up East Road ahead of Will's wagon. On the seat sat Will and Esther while Demus sat on a wooden box in the wagon's bed.

"Appreciate the ride home," Demus said, "and I especially appreciate the kind words you had to say."

"My pleasure," Will replied. "You know, we have dinner on the grounds on the first and third Sundays. The bachelors set up tables and chairs and aren't expected to bring food."

"I can get used to that," Demus said. "But I just have to ask, should I call you 'Preacher Parker' now?"

"I'd just as soon you didn't!"

"It sent shivers up my spine," Esther said. "I mean the way you talked about the good Samaritan when it was going to be the Preacher's sermon ... that was unreal!"

The wagon rolled along for several hundred feet before anyone spoke again. Finally, Will broke the silence.

"Did you see the way Rachel Burden was hanging on to Peter Paul Lamb after church?"

"Exactly!" Esther answered.

"In my humble opinion, that was the best part of the day!" Will said.

"You've got to be kidding," Esther replied. "What was so good about that? Has she been chasing after you or something? Are you glad she's sparing you and latching onto someone else?"

"Pretty ... addle pated ... Esther!" Will said. "Haven't you picked up on the fact that I've been scared to death that Lamb might take a liking to you?"

"Getting a little protective in your old age, aren't you?" Esther asked. "Don't you think I can take care of myself? Huh? I bet I can still beat you up!"

Esther slid over closer to Will and began boxing his arm while she giggled.

"Wait a minute! Hold on there," Demus interjected. "If you two are going to fight, I'll get out and walk!"

Esther giggled louder.

"Don't pay us any attention, Demus," Will said. "This is our brother and sister act. You'd better get used to it."

Demus settled back down on his wooden box and chuckled a satisfied laugh. It seemed, he thought to himself, that a laugh on a regular basis was something else he was going to have to get used to.

About that time they came to the North Road, and Will turned the horses to the left and headed toward Demus's house.

"By the way," Will said, "I've been wondering how we got to church before you did, and we didn't pass you on the road."

Demus took a deep breath and let it out.

"I got to church probably an hour before you did, Will," he said, "and I hid around back trying to get up enough nerve to go in. I started home two or three times before I decided to come inside."

"But you finally did!"

"Yes, and how glad I am!"

"This could be a life-changing experience for you, Demus. ...Why did you decide to do it?"

"Daniel shamed me into it. I told him he was going to have to develop a thicker skin, and he more or less told me that I was going to have to do the same ... stop keeping to myself so much."

"That's very good, but who is Daniel?" Will asked.

"Daniel *Day*! *Sonny*! He wants to be called *Daniel* now."

"Oh man!" Will said. "I was having a hard enough time learning to call Goober 'Goob', and then 'Makepeace', and then he wanted me to call him 'Make'. Now, I'm gonna to have to learn a new name for Sonny!"

"Life isn't fair, is it?" Esther said. "I think I'll change my name to … to 'Genevieve'!"

"Well, as Goober would say, *I hope to my never!*" Will replied.

Esther took on a thoughtful look. "Getting back to the school teacher … you were talking about him when you said you came to church thinking badly about someone … weren't you?"

"Yes."

"Did you shake his hand?"

"Yes."

"And?"

"And actually, he was pretty nice. I think the way he looks at people is just his way of covering up his insecurities."

"He needs to get himself a pair of overalls," Demus said. "That would cover his insecurities!"

Esther laughed. "And a straw hat instead of that derby!"

The sun was high overhead as the wagon inched up the road, but no one was in a hurry, even though it was dinner time. It had been a good day, and everyone was comfortable with their newfound happiness. Esther had escaped the dungeon called "Wilmington" and could rest in the ease of paradise, even if it were only for the summer. Demus had been released from the prison of his solitude where he had dwelt since the death of his "grandfather." He was finally basking in the friendship of others. Will was glorying in his new home, the company of Esther, and his fledgling sense of worth, with only his unrequited love for Alice standing in the way of total contentment.

So on they rode—talking and laughing—prying into each other's deepest thoughts—each mining the gold from the other's nature, until a wagon appeared in the distance.

"Demus," Will called out, "isn't that Roamer and Sweetie coming toward us?"

Demus raised up off his box and craned his neck. "Yes … I believe it is," he replied.

Esther adjusted her bonnet and tucked in a strand of wayward hair. "Oh, goodie!" she said, "I finally get to meet them."

Roamer's mule and Will's horses eyed each other as they passed slightly before the wagons stopped side by side. Roamer squinted in the sun and lolled his tongue around in his toothless mouth before he greeted the unlikely trio.

"Wal, lookie here!" he said. "'Is here's a handsome group! I believe we have fin'ly got t' see Will's sister that we have been a-waitin fer so anxious! An' she's about as purdy a young woman as I have ever saw …ain't she Sweetie?"

"Oh *yas!*" Sweetie said. "An' who's 'at dandy a-sittin on th' wood box? Shorely hit ain't Demus … dressed up lack a dog's dinner. I 'most didn't realize 'im fixed up lack 'at!"

"Sweetie and Roamer Robinson, I want you to meet my sister, Esther. Esther, these are my good friends, the Robinsons. And yes," Will added, "that *is* Demus in the wagon in all his glory. I'll have you know he went to *church* this morning … and made a *hit!*"

"I hope to my never!" Roamer declared.

"We were going to come see you this afternoon," Will said. "I want Esther to get to know you."

"Wal you jest turn 'at wagon 'round an' come back to th' house an' have dinner w' Roamer an' me," Sweetie demanded. "I've got a stew a-simmerin' on th' stove, an' I'll open up some jars t' go with it! Demus, you an' Will can split me some far wood whilst me an' Esther git t' know one another!"

"Exactly! And thank you!" Esther said.

"Yes, exactly!" Demus added.

———◆———

It was about 3:00 p.m. when Will and Esther dropped Demus off at his house and continued on toward home. Esther hadn't stopped talking about Sweetie's stew, the ingredients of which Sweetie refused to discuss. Esther had described it as both "scrumptious" and "exotic" and was diligently trying to guess the elements that made it so unique.

"The way the meat was spiced made it hard to tell if it was pork or chicken," she stated.

"I'm not sure I want to know what it was," Will said. "It may have been muskrat, or rattle snake, or possum. They're Roamer's favorites."

"*Oh, Will, surely not!*" Esther said. "*I may just throw up!*"

"Well, would it really matter, Esther? You've been saying it was good."

Esther slid to the far side of the wagon seat, crossed her arms, and looked away from her brother.

"You've ruined my day, Will," she said. "I may never eat again ... and here Mrs. Robinson has filled that box in back with jars of ... food."

Will laughed his "wicked brother laugh" as he bounced on the seat.

"Don't worry," he said. "Roamer said it was chicken, and that her secret flavoring was sarvice berry preserves. I even saw a jar of sarvice berries in the box."

"I'm going to *throttle* you before the summer is over, Will Parker!" Esther growled.

As Will's house came into view, he could see Sonny sitting on the front steps petting Dawg.

"Looks like you're going to get to meet Sonny," he said to Esther.

"Oh, Will," she mused, "my future nephew has come to see me!"

"Don't start that," Will replied. "You'll notice that his mother isn't with him. She probably sent Sonny over here to get him out of the house so some gentleman caller could come courtin'."

Esther was learning that nothing she could say would allay Will's fear of losing Alice, so she remained silent for that moment.

When the rumble of the wagon wheels finally attracted Sonny's attention, he looked up to see Will and Esther coming up the road. Sonny jumped up and ran a few steps before he stopped to stare at the extra person on the wagon seat. Then his run continued as a trot, his gaze still glued upon Esther. He had known that Esther was coming, but he didn't seem prepared to finally see her.

"*Hello, Sonny!*" Will hollered when he was within hearing range.

The boy's pace quickened a little when he heard the call, and soon he was trotting alongside the wagon, silent but grinning, eyes still fixed upon Will's lovely sister.

"Hop on," Will said. "We'll give you a ride."

Sonny hopped aboard and settled down on the pile of hay.

"Be careful of the box," Will said. "It has jars in it. Now, I want you to meet my sister, Esther, from Wilmington. Esther, this is my friend and co-worker, Sonny … or are folks calling you 'Daniel' now?"

"Mama said it's aw-wight."

Esther turned and looked at the star-struck boy.

"Daniel, I've been looking forward to meeting you," she said. "I've heard a lot of good things about you."

Daniel nodded his head but didn't reply. He was looking at the most beautiful woman he had ever seen besides his mother.

"Esther is a school teacher," Will said.

Daniel nodded again.

"Mama wants you to tome t' supper," he said in Will's direction.

Esther giggled her sister giggle and cut her eyes over at Will.

"*What?*" Will said, turning all the way around to look in Daniel's eyes. "Are you sure about that?"

"Uh-huh."

"What's your mama doin' right now? Will asked. "

"Tookin' supper," the boy replied.

Esther fumbled with her bonnet as she and Will rolled down the road toward Alice's house. She had torn her dress as she climbed up on the big farm wagon, and she was fit to be tied.

"Will, I think you'd better just turn around and take me home so I can change," she said. "I can't be seen looking like this!"

Will stopped the wagon in the road and looked Esther up and down. She was as elegant as anything he had ever seen, he thought—much too elegant to be riding on a farm wagon.

"Now, Esther," he said, "we're not going back. There's nothing wrong with the way you look. If you want to know the truth, you look beautiful."

He reached down and examined the hem of her dress. "This is nothing more than a conversation starter," he said as he examined it. "You and Alice can have fun mending it."

"*Oh* ... I want everything to be just right," she said.

"Well, I'm sure Alice is just as nervous as you are. She's kinda persnickety herself, and if you go in all tensed up, she's going to tense up too; then both of you will be uncomfortable. Now ... take a deep breath, smile, and relax. Her house is just ahead."

The smell of food met them before the house came into view. Fresh bread and sweet potatoes were the dominant aromas, and roasted chicken with rosemary soon followed.

"She's a good cook," Will said.

"What else?" Esther asked.

"She's a good mother ... a good housekeeper ... a good listener ..."

"Someone you might spend your life with?"

"Yes ... at least, she was."

"She will be again, Will." Esther said gently. "Women know these things."

Daniel saw them coming. He had been watching from his perch in the sycamore tree, and when he was sure it was them, he slid down the rope, and ran toward the house.

"He reminds me of the boys in my class," Esther said. "Does he ever *walk* anywhere?"

"Nope. He's like a little fox, darting about with his nose to the ground ... looking for something to get into."

"Watch him!" Esther declared. "He's gaining on the house ... He's up the steps ... He's through the door ... *Oh, the door! He just about knocked it off the hinges!* He's a handful, Brother."

"You should have known him before I took his slingshot away."

In moments, Daniel was back out the door, running toward the wagon, and his mother was standing on the porch, waving a greeting.

Seeing her gave Will the feeling of warmth he always got when he saw her. Their separation could be for days or for a few hours, and seeing her again was like falling in love once more. For awhile he could see that look in her eyes, but lately, it had been hidden behind a curtain of sadness.

When the wagon stopped, Alice immediately went to Esther's side and reached up, offering her hand. After Esther was down, they embraced as sisters might, looking deeply into each other's eyes and talking softly. The bond between them was instantaneous.

"Please come in and sit with me while I finish our supper," Alice said, and she and Esther walked arm in arm up the steps to the house.

"Hel-lo, Alice," Will called from the wagon seat. "May I come in too?"

Alice wheeled around and put her hand to her mouth.

"Oh, hello, Will!" she cooed. "Of course you can come in. I have a wobbly chair that needs fixing … and then if you've a mind to, you can check the fence around the chicken house."

Will shrugged his shoulders and turned to Daniel, who was standing by the wagon. "How 'bout it buddy, are *you* glad to see me?" he asked.

Thirty

A MENACING CREATURE

"Knee-high by the fourth of July!" The well-worn bromide that came by way of his grandfather had rattled around inside Will's head for days, and it resonated on a positive note as he walked his corn field on the first day of July. Not only did his crop measure up to his grandfather's height standard, but the stalks were full, healthy, and emerald green as well.

The corn however was not the only thing growing in Will's corn field. The weeds were growing like—well—*weeds,* thinking they had just as much right to be there as the corn! Will wasn't worried though. He was anxiously awaiting delivery of his new McCormick riding cultivator that was due at Burden's any day, and he knew that when it came and was harnessed to his horses, the weed's hours would be numbered. Alice, Demus, and Roamer were anxious too, having been told he would cultivate their fields as well, saving them hours of back-breaking work with the hoe.

So he walked the rows, kicking stones and clods of dirt, occasionally picking up an arrowhead, and basking in the early morning sun until a voice called out from the road.

"*Yo thar, Will!*"

It was R. Z. Ross, a member of his church, sitting atop his mule at the edge of the field. Will threw up his hand and walked the row briskly until he reached him.

"Mornin', R. Z.," he said.

"Howdy thar, Will," R. Z. replied. "'At corn looks t' be a rat good crop!"

"Lookin' like it, R. Z.," Will answered. "What brings you up this way?"

R. Z. got down off the mule and hiked up his trousers.

"I wuz jest a-goin' 'round axtin' folks if they got any goats, er foals, er calves, er other small animals penned up outdoors."

"Not me," Will said. "What's up?"

"Wal, some creature kilt one o' my goats last night! Tore hit's throat out an' ate both hind quarters!"

"Wolf, you think?"

"Ain't no woof could'a eat half a goat!"

"Bear, maybe?"

"Could'a been a bar, I reckon. Didn't leave no tracks. Tell ye what though, hit's tasted a farm animal, an' hit'll be back … if not my place … summers else."

"I'll be watching out, R. Z.," Will said as his neighbor was hoisting himself back up on the mule. "Let you know if I see anything."

He walked from the field and up the road toward his barn, watching as R. Z. headed off toward Demus Whitedeer's house to spread the news. "Funny," he thought. "In Charlotte we had a newspaper. Up here the folks take turns being the town crier." There were some things Will missed about the city. The newspaper was one of them.

The cultivator wasn't the only new thing Will had bought. Since Esther had found it so hard to get up on the big farm wagon, he had made up his mind that he would get some sort of small carriage for transportation and a gentle horse to pull it. He missed Traveler and the surrey, but he had come to the conclusion that a surrey wasn't really suited to the mountain roads.

After looking around and talking to neighbors, he decided to buy a spring-seat buckboard and replace the back seat bench with a wooden box to carry various small items. Along with the buckboard he purchased a gentle, young mare named Judy. Then he had Karl Badger install an iron framework around the seat and box over which he stretched a canvas cover. All in all it turned out to be a neat and efficient runabout. Several of the valley residents had even tried to buy it from him.

Esther quickly learned to hitch up the rig and drive it by herself. Soon she and Alice were visiting on an almost daily basis and going back and forth to Burden's.

Things were changing for Sonny too. Those close to him were, for the most part, calling him "Daniel," and he was living up to his grown-up name. He was working in his own little garden growing popcorn, watermelons, and pumpkins. In addition he had been working hard with Demus learning the "ca" and "th" sounds and was able to use them if he concentrated hard enough.

The mare, Judy, wasn't the only new animal on the farm. Will's chicken flock was up to eight and would soon increase again thanks to a proud young rooster that happened to show up one day. Will and Esther had been shocked awake at dawn one June morning by the rooster's crow, and when Will went out to investigate, he found the bird circling the chicken pen, trying to get in. He had simply opened the door to the pen and the rooster had walked inside. He had quickly made friends with the brood hen, and before long she was sitting on six more eggs. With the pullets from his first brood maturing, Will knew it wouldn't be long before he had a steady supply of eggs and fryers.

And so, with a growing farm, a good crop, and happy people surrounding him, Will found that the only cloud above his head was his uncertain future with Alice. While her friendship with Esther had grown and flourished, Alice was still aloof as far as he was concerned. She was happy and most gracious to accept his offers of help when it concerned Daniel or her farm, but her gaze was distant and unemotional.

Yet, while the dark cloud of uncertainty was hanging above Will, unbeknownst to him it was hanging above Esther too. She watched in silence as Will's love for Alice went unanswered, and she quietly grieved for him. She used every opportunity to talk to Alice about Will, his virtues, his goals, and her sisterly love for him. She was his gentle advocate—his promoter—and by her sisterly cunning, his cupid.

With a list of projects coursing through his brain, Will was approaching his barn, prepared to fork hay and clean stalls, when Demus appeared out of nowhere.

"You snuck up on me," Will said to his friend. "Are you practicing your Indian stalking skills?"

"Oh *no!*" Demus replied. "If I were, you wouldn't be seeing me now!" and he laughed his hearty laugh. "It's about time to see how the chestnut crop is developing, and I thought you might want to come along."

"Maybe bag a few boomers on the way?" Will asked.

"Some squirrel stew would be good," Demus said. "How about tomorrow?"

"Squirrel stew would be good for supper. How about this afternoon?" Will answered as he opened the barn door.

Demus removed his hat and pushed his hair back from his forehead.

"If it's all the same to you, Will, let's go tomorrow. I didn't sleep very well last night."

"Conscience bothering you?"

"Don't have one," Demus quipped, and then his look became serious. "I woke up twice last night and couldn't go back to sleep. Both times I could have *sworn* I heard a woman scream! I started to come up here and check on you and Esther, but it wasn't a sound like I thought Esther would make. It was an eerie, *haunting* kind of sound."

Demus removed his hat again and looked toward the hills as if he were searching for the source of the terrible cry.

"If I hear it again, I'm going to go look for it," he said. "I have to see if it's from the hills ... or in my head." He put his hat back on and walked away toward the road. "See you tomorrow," he muttered.

———◆———

The next morning dawned to the crow of the rooster, who, in addition to his duties as the brood hen's consort, had accepted responsibility of announcing each new day.

Will awoke refreshed on the rooster's first call. His sleep had gone un-interrupted, thanks to the sound of the river and the exhaustion that comes from a hard day's work. He hoped as he stretched himself awake that Demus had slept equally as well, and that the screams he had heard the night before were simply caused by—as Ebenezer Scrooge had conjectured—"an undi-gested bit of beef," or a "blot of mustard."

He hoped too, as he did each morning that Alice and Daniel were well and content, knowing that it wouldn't be long before he would find out. Daniel arrived early most mornings looking for adventure and for Will's companionship. Although his mother cooked him a good breakfast, the growing boy usually ate another breakfast with Will and Esther. Esther ap-proved and always encouraged it in an attempt to get to know him better.

Pots and dishes clanged and clattered as Will shaved, and before he had rinsed the last of the soap from his face, Esther's kitchen sounds were joined by the rumble of Daniel's feet on the porch.

"*Will ... Esther!*" he hollered as he burst through the door.

"*What's up?*" Will hollered back from the bed room.

"Are you hungry?" Esther asked from the kitchen.

Will's question went unanswered as Daniel ran into the kitchen.

"Hab you got oatmeal?" he wanted to know.

"I can fix it," Esther said. "Would you like it cooked with a little cinnamon?"

"Yes! And sugar and milk!"

"You're spoiled!" Will said as he entered the kitchen.

"'At's what Mama says."

"*That's* what Mama says," Will replied.

Daniel concentrated. "Ttthat's ... that's ... that's."

Esther placed her big wooden spoon in the pot of oatmeal and went over and gave Daniel a hug.

"I'm proud of you, Daniel," she said. "I hope I have a boy just like you someday."

"Wow!"

Will chuckled at Daniel's remark as he pulled out a chair and sat down at the table.

"Say, Daniel, Demus and I are going to go up the mountain and check the chestnut crop today … maybe hunt a few squirrels. You want to come along?"

"Wow! Tan I shoot your rifle?"

"*Can* I shoot your rifle?"

Daniel took on a look of total concentration.

"Can … can … can I shoot your rifle?"

"I don't see how I could say no," Will answered.

By the time the stove was hot and Daniel's oatmeal was ready, Demus had arrived. He brought Will's milk and, as a bonus, a wheel of butter. "That's for being such a good milk customer," he told Will.

Esther reacted by saying, "Oh, goodie! Now I can make a pound cake!"

Between spoonfuls of oatmeal and gulps of milk, Daniel told Demus, "Will said I … can shoot the Winchester rifle."

Demus looked at Daniel and beamed with pride. In the few months he had known him, the boy had transformed from Sonny—a withdrawn, troubled lad with a crippling speech impediment, to Daniel—a confident, reliable, well-spoken young man.

———◆———

The hour was still early as Will, Demus, and Daniel prepared for their trek into the back woods. A mist hung over the center of the valley marking the course of the river, and the sun was still behind the eastern mountains. Even though Demus had wanted to explore the mountain side behind his farm, it was finally decided that they would go up the river behind Will's house since it was closer and the trail was better. Will and Demus began the walk with Daniel following behind on Demus's mule.

As they started up the road toward the river trail, Will turned to Demus. "Say, did you hear any more screams last night?"

"No," Demus answered, "not last night. I'm beginning to think I was dreaming."

"Me and Mama heard screams last night," Daniel said.

Will and Demus stopped in their tracks and looked back at the boy sitting up on the mule.

"Are you sure, Daniel?" Will asked. "Are you sure *you* weren't just dreaming?"

"It was 'fore we went to bed," Daniel answered.

Demus and Will exchanged glances.

"What did it sound like?" Demus asked.

"Mama said it wad a mountain wion. It wad s-spooky!"

"What made your mother think it was a mountain lion?" Demus asked. "There haven't been any mountain lions around here in *my* lifetime!"

"Mama said when she wad a little girl a circus come and s-stayed near her house. She s-said they had a big mountain wion in a cage, and that's how it s-sounded in the night."

"Do you think it's possible that we could have a mountain lion in the valley?" Will asked Demus.

Demus removed his hat and pushed his hair back.

"Well, I suppose it's possible," he said. "I read somewhere that there are plenty of mountain lions, or cougars, or panthers ... whatever you want to call them in Florida and out west, and even though there haven't been any around here in years, I guess there could have been some close by."

"And you think that could be what killed R. Z.'s goat?"

"It stands to reason," Demus concluded.

Will's eyes searched the mountain side as if he expected to see one of the creatures looking back.

"You won't see one unless he wants you to see him," Demus said. "They're perhaps the most elusive animals that have ever been in these parts. The Cherokee people thought they were the spirits of dead warriors."

The walk continued in silence, each of them on guard for the unexpected. When they got to the river, they turned and started up the trail. The thick summer foliage closed in around them, and with no sunlight to filter through the trees, it was almost totally dark.

"I don't like this," Will told Demus.

"If you're worried about a panther attack, don't be," Demus said. "He would be more frightened of you than you are of him."

"And how do you know that?"

Demus chuckled. "He can see in the dark, Will. He'll see that Winchester you're carrying."

"And what if it's not a 'he'? What if it's a female?"

"She'll see how ugly you are," Demus replied, and he laughed his big, booming laugh.

The sun was finally up and the surroundings were a little brighter when they reached the end of the trail. Demus tied his mule to a bush, and Daniel slid down.

"I guess I don't have to tell you that it's not panthers we need to worry about," Demus said.

"Pigs?" Will asked.

"That's right," Demus answered, "They can ruin your day ... and we can't afford to shoot any of them this time of year. A pig would spoil before we could get it home."

"As little as they've been hunted, we can come back in the fall and get a smoke-house full," Will said.

"When can I s-shoot your rifle?" Daniel asked.

"We'll check the chestnuts first," Will replied. "Then we'll see if we can find some squirrels."

"There's a big grove of hickory trees just north of the chestnuts," Demus said. "We can probably find some there."

After a steep, winding climb, they came to the place where they had found the pigs in the spring. The tops of the majestic chestnuts soared above the ridge, and it was clear, even from there, that the crop of nuts would be good. On every branch, above the slim, glossy leaves, the lighter colored, spiny nut casings were growing profusely.

The climb up the ridge left the trio winded, so they settled down on the forest floor for a rest.

Demus removed his hat and lifted his arm up toward the tops of the trees. "That's a pretty sight," he said. "If they're doing well here, they'll be doing well on my property."

"It means a lot to you, doesn't it?" Will asked.

"That's tax payments, and books, and coffee, and sugar growing up there on those trees," Demus replied.

"How about when we have a poor crop? What happens then?"

"I just have to hunt ginseng a little harder," Demus answered.

Daniel couldn't stand it any longer. "When can I shoot your rifle, Will?" he asked.

Demus chuckled a hearty laugh. "Come on, Snake Man," he said. "Let's go find some hickory trees."

The trio continued on to their right below the crest of the ridge and down a slope. They were still on Will's property, but they were in an area where Will had not been before. Soon they crossed a small branch and started up another rise. Before them were the hickory trees mixed with other deciduous varieties— locust, white oak, and a few poplar. The hickory trees were small in comparison to the chestnuts, but their fruit appeared to be closer to maturity. Sure enough, when they stopped to look around, they heard movement in the branches above.

"Squirrels?" Will asked Demus.

"Yes. They've seen us and they're hiding now … but give them a few minutes and they'll get brave and come out."

"Can I shoot now?" Daniel asked impatiently.

Will moved up close beside the boy and handed him the big rifle.

"Now, Daniel," he said softly, "shooting this gun isn't like shooting Roamer's .22. This one has a kick! Now … be sure to shoot to the west because these bullets carry a long way. They could reach your house."

"Wow!"

Will showed Daniel how to work the lever and instructed him to chamber a round only when he was ready to shoot. Then everybody settled back and waited for the squirrels to start moving again.

Soon, a flurry of movement started in the tree tops. Demus pointed to a squirrel that had come out on a branch and was sitting still. Daniel looked down at the Winchester and examined it as he slowly worked the lever, chambering a round.

"Aim for his head," Will said softly, fully expecting Daniel to fire, be knocked to the ground, and give up on shooting the big gun.

Daniel pulled the gun up slowly to his shoulder and leaned into the stock. He took aim and quickly fired. The recoil turned him slightly, but he stood his ground.

Instantly, the squirrel flew off the limb and fell to the forest floor.

"*You hit him!*" Demus shouted.

"*I did it!*" Daniel shouted.

Suddenly the trees were full of movement as squirrels ran for cover. They went in all directions, flying through the branches like a swarm of locust.

"Go get the one you shot," Will said. "Let's see if he has warbles. If he doesn't, you can try for another one."

Daniel quickly returned holding his squirrel by the tail. Its head had been cleanly severed. Will ran his hands over the animal's skin feeling for warbles, the larvae of the bot fly that often burrows under the skin of squirrels in the summer.

"This one's clean," Will said.

"Can I shoot again?" Daniel asked.

"Remember the rules," Will answered. "Know where you're shooting. There are seven more rounds in the magazine, and if you don't make any mistakes, and you can use those up."

Will and Demus watched as Daniel crept through the woods, stalking one squirrel after another. He chose his shots carefully, trying to take only head shots since the high-powered rifle was so destructive. After he had hunted for about an hour, he had fired all eight rounds and had eight squirrels.

On the way back down the mountain, Daniel took the lead on the mule, and Will and Demus followed along behind.

"He has a good eye and a steady hand!" Demus said as they were talking about Daniel's hunting skill.

"I'm going to have to see about getting him a .22 rifle though," Will said. "Those .44 rounds are expensive and a bit of an overkill for squirrels."

Daniel decided on his own that he would give his mother two squirrels to make a stew, that he would give Will and Demus two each, and that he would send two to the Robinsons. The idea that he would share with the Robinsons made Will especially proud.

Back at Will's house the squirrels were dressed and Dawg was treated to some of the inside delicacies. Demus went on his way with good thoughts about the chestnut crop and the squirrels for the Robinsons and himself.

Will stoked up the fire in the kitchen stove and put his squirrels on a slow simmer. Then he and Daniel hitched up the farm wagon and drove off toward Daniel's house.

"That was quite a morning we had, wasn't it?" Will asked as they bumped along.

"Yep!"

"I'm proud of you for a lot of things," Will said, "but I want you to know that I'm especially proud of you for sharing your squirrels with the Robinsons."

Daniel sat silently and looked ahead. Finally he said, "Well ... they're gettin' old. I reckon dey need help sometimes."

"We all need help sometimes," Will replied. "A lot of people helped me when I was hurt ... Doc French and the Burdens ... the Plowsharers from your church ... even you helped me when I was getting better. Then Demus and I tried to help you some."

"I know."

"Seems like everybody in the valley looks out after one another."

The wagon rolled on slowly, nearing Daniel's house.

"I'm glad your mother has people to help her out," Will said. "She has Esther, and Preacher Babb, and the Plowsharers, and a lot of the ladies around the valley ... and of course, you ... especially you."

"But none of them folks is who Mama needs the most."

"Really?" Will said, turning to the boy. "Who did I leave out?"

"You," Daniel said softly.

Will slowly pulled back on the horse's reins and brought the wagon to a stop. Daniel looked over to see him staring ahead with no emotion, as if in a trance.

"What's wrong, Will," Daniel asked. "Are you okay?"

"I'm okay."

"Did I say sompin' wrong?"

"No ... but you say your mama needs *me*?"

"She talks about you all th' time. She says 'tuff like, 'I should ast Will,' or, 'You should ast Will ... he'll know,' or, 'I wish Will wad here now.' And sometimes when I tell her about taings you do or say, she'll cwy. She don't know I see her ... but I do. She gets lonesome like when Esther goes home and she don't have a grownup person to talk to ... and she'll talk about when you used to come ober more."

Will looked deeply into Daniel's eyes. "Daniel, your mother loved your daddy and she misses him. I want you and your mother to always remember him because he loved you too. She needs time to get over him leaving, and someday ... even though she'll always miss him ... she won't hurt so bad."

He put his arm around Daniel's shoulder and pulled him close. "In the meantime, I'll be here for you ... and if your mama needs me. ... I'll be there for her too. Okay?"

Daniel pursed his lips, looked away, and nodded.

———◆———

When Daniel's house came in view, Alice and Esther were sitting on the front porch. Daniel's exuberance got the best of him, and he bounded off the wagon with his squirrels and ran as fast as he could to meet his mother.

Will could see him as he ran up the steps to show his mother his prize. They hugged, and then both looked toward Will and waved.

Will's pulse quickened a little when he saw Alice and thought about the things Daniel had told him. Maybe there *was* hope for their relationship. Maybe she *was* ready to explore their future. If time alone wasn't the answer, maybe Esther's encouragement was the spark that would relight the flame.

When the wagon came to a stop in the yard, Will called out, "That's some hunter you have there, Alice! Did he tell you how many squirrels he got?"

"Oh, my!" Alice answered. "He said he got *eight*! We heard a lot of shooting."

"Eight booms … eight boomers," Will said proudly. "And Sis, there are two simmering on the stove at home. Daniel's talk about stew made me want some."

"Then I'd better go see what we have in the garden that I can add to it," Esther said as she started down the porch steps. On the way by she gave Will a little wink.

As Esther was leaving, Alice asked Sonny to check on the eggs and feed the chickens, and she invited Will in for a cup of water.

"Will, I need to talk to you," Alice said when they were inside. She pulled out a chair for him at the kitchen table and sat down in another. When Will was seated she took a deep breath and blew it out toward a strand of hair that had fallen across her forehead.

"Did Sonny tell you that we heard a mountain lion last night?" she asked.

"Yes. Are you sure that's what it was?"

"What Sonny didn't know is that after he went to bed, I saw it out near the chicken house. It was *huge*, Will!"

Will leaned back from the table and made a whistling sound as he exhaled. "What about your chickens?"

"They were in their house on the roost, and I guess they didn't know what was prowling around outside. Thank goodness they didn't make any sound or it would have probably gone after them."

Will leaned forward and put his elbows on the table. For a moment he was deep in thought. "These animals don't usually come this close to civilization," he said, "so I'm led to believe that this is either a very brave cat ... or one that's unable to hunt in the wild anymore. Either way ... it would probably be best if you and Daniel ... Sonny didn't go out after dark until the cat's ... gone."

"That's scary, Will."

"Do you even have a gun in the house?"

"We have Matthew's old flintlock on the wall in the bedroom."

"Can I look at it?"

"Sure," Alice said.

Alice led Will back to the bedroom and pointed to the rifle hanging on the wall. "Matthew used to keep it loaded," she said.

Will took it down off its rack and pulled the ramrod from beneath the barrel. He shoved it down the barrel and when it reached the bottom, the depth notches indicated that it was loaded. After he had put the ramrod back beneath the barrel, he lifted the lid on the flash pan and saw that it held powder.

"It's primed and loaded," he said. "Don't let Daniel handle it."

"His daddy was *adamant* about that!"

Will pointed the weapon at the floor and placed his thumb on the hammer.

"If you ever need to fire it, pull the hammer all the way back and just pull the trigger. Don't worry about hitting your target because you won't ... but the sound would chase off the devil himself!"

"I'm sorry, but that doesn't make me feel a whole lot safer," Alice said.

"I know," Will answered sympathetically as he put the rifle back up on its rack. "I tell you what ... how about me letting you keep Dawg over here at night until this is all resolved. He'd probably enjoy staying with Daniel ... and I think we'd all feel better."

Alice's shoulders relaxed as she blew at the strand of hair on her forehead again.

"Now that *does* make me feel better," she said. "Maybe I'll be able to sleep tonight"

"Good!" Will said as he walked from the room. "Now how about that drink of water?"

While Will was drinking his water they sat and talked about securing the chicken house and where Dawg would sleep. When he finished his water he put the cup on the table.

"I'd better go and get my work done," he said. "Send Daniel over this afternoon and Dawg can come back with him to spend the night."

He started to leave, but Alice stopped him.

"Will."

"Yes," he said turning back to her.

"Thank you."

Will tilted his head and thought before he answered. "I really haven't done that much, and what I have done … I've enjoyed."

"What I meant was … thanks for being patient with me. You couldn't have enjoyed that."

"I understand what you're going through," Will said. "I've seen Daniel working his way through it, too."

"I'll get better, Will."

"I know that for a fact," Will said, and he turned and left.

——————

Will had a lot to think about on the way home, and for the first time in several weeks he was able to think about Alice without a cloud hanging over his head. He knew then that he could concentrate on his crops, his garden, and the threat of the mountain lion.

As he neared the bridge he was met by R. Z. Ross riding his mule.

"*Howdy, R. Z.,*" he hollered.

"*Yo thar, Will,*" R. Z. hollered back. "I been a-lookin' fer ye. Ye sister said I'd find ye over 'is way."

They stopped in the road, and R. Z. got down and hiked up his trousers.

"How you keepin', R. Z.?" Will asked.

"Fair as fer common, I reckon."

"You had any more trouble over to your place?"

"Nothin' more'n my rumatiz! I'm a-puttin' my goats up in th' barn at night fum here on."

"Say, R. Z. … Alice Day said she saw a mountain lion in her yard last night. Said it was a big one."

"A *mountain lion! Do tell!* Well … I been a-goin' 'round tellin' folks th' preacher had a calf kilt over in Hogg's pasture las' night. An' they's several people has tol' me they heared somethin' a-screamin' 'round the valley. 'at injun friend o' yourn was one of 'em."

Will looked off at the mountain ridge behind his house. "Looks like we gonna have to do something, R. Z."

"'At's another reason I come. Th' preacher said they's a spacial meetin' o' ever'body in th' valley Thursday night at the Meth'dist church, an' fer all th' men-folk t' be thar."

"I'll be there, R. Z.," Will said.

R.Z. climbed up on his mule, gave her a little nudge with his heels, and continued on his way.

Will watched him go and thought to himself, "If R. Z. is going to be the town crier, the council really needs to buy him a bell!"

A cool, invisible vapor was rising from the river as the wagon crossed the bridge. The contrast in its temperature and that of the surrounding air gave Will a pleasant little chill—so pleasant in fact that he decided he would return when his day's work was done for a dip in the water. "What a pleasant thought, and why haven't I done that before?" ran through his brain and was repeating itself as a refrain when he looked ahead and saw an unfamiliar sight in his yard. There in the shade of a tree sat a sleek phaeton coach hitched to two magnificent horses.

Thirty-One

Happy Birthday, Brother

The closer Will got to his house, the more agitated he became. Here some drummer, that same drummer he had seen on the road to Burley, had invaded his home and was probably hard at work trying to sell Esther something. *What could it be?* he wondered. *It would have to be something expensive for the salesman to be driving a coach like that,* he decided.

But what if it wasn't a drummer? Suppose it was a lawyer there to serve a subpoena, or a government man who had come to tell him there was a mistake, and the property wasn't really his. Whatever it was, he thought, it could come to no good end!

"No hurry," he thought. He would put his wagon in the barn and the horses in the pasture, and then he would confront the scoundrel and send him on his way—him and his fancy coach! A few minutes earlier he had been hungry. Trekking through the woods does that to a man. He had been ready to have a quick dinner and then get to work, but now the hunger was gone, replaced by a knot in his stomach.

The fancy horses gave him a look as he crossed the yard and started up the steps. It was a look much like Peter Paul Lamb could give. He resented it from Lamb, even more from a pair of horses, and now he was about to face an obnoxious salesman. He swung the door open, walked in, and came face to face with Glenn Neil.

Will's knees almost buckled! Anger, replaced by surprise, nearly sent him into shock. He was frozen in place and speechless.

"Aren't you going to say anything?" Neil asked, grinning from ear to ear.

"I'm … I'm …"

Esther stood at the kitchen door laughing. "What's the matter, Will? Cat got your tongue?"

When Will had partially regained his composure, he went to the big man and gave him a hug.

"Mr. Neil," he said. "I'm … I'm …"

"You're glad to see me! You're overwhelmed! You're wondering what the old man is doing here! There! I said it for you."

"It's just that I came in here prepared to throw out some pushy sales-man," Will stammered, still red-faced and weak-kneed, "and found the man … who has been like a father to me!"

"Now cut that out," Neil said. "I might get teary-eyed."

Will backed away so he could see Neil. He scanned each line of the big man's face, trying to make sure he wasn't an apparition.

"Esther, did you know about this?" he asked, turning to his sister.

"No … I had about the same reaction you did," she said.

He turned back to Neil. "Well, why are you here? How long can you stay? How did you even find me?" he stammered, getting excited again.

"I'm here to check on business, I can stay a couple of days, and Preacher Burden showed me where you live back the first week of June."

"Then it was *you* I saw on the road when I was bringing Esther up from Burley!"

"Yes, it was me, and I'll be telling you all about it. Your lovely sister has asked me to have dinner, and she said that if I'll stay for supper, I can have some squirrel stew! In between, I'd like to follow you around the farm and go wading in that river of yours."

"I'd like nothing better," Will said.

While Esther was cooking dinner, Will and Neil put Neil's horses in the pasture and talked mostly about Inverness and the little that Neil knew about Makepeace's bride-to-be.

Neil said he had met Janie Rose in the company store. Will questioned him about her, and Neil said that she was pretty but looked awfully young to him. "Of course," he said, "I don't consider myself to be a good judge of a woman's age. Any woman under thirty looks like a child to me."

Then Neil got wound up on the textile industry. Will got the impression that the industry was booming and that his former boss was knee deep in cotton canvas. Neil also said enough about the construction of his new mill to make Will wonder how he would take so much valuable time coming to see him. He wondered, but he didn't pry. He simply let Neil talk.

———

When dinner was done Neil thanked his hosts, pushed back from the table, and disappeared into Will's bedroom with a bundle he had brought. In minutes he reappeared wearing his boots and overalls.

The surprise caught Esther off guard. She put her hands to her face and squealed. Will did a double take and threw his hands in the air.

"*Whoa!*" he exclaimed. "*Look at the gentleman farmer!*"

Neil posed, modeling his outfit. "Ain't this somethin'?" he said. "This is my new look!"

"So you were serious about following me around the farm?" Will asked.

Neil struck another pose. "Never been seriouser!" he answered.

———

The sun was well on its way toward the western horizon when Will and Neil finished their chores. The day had been hot, even if by mountain standards, and Neil was sweating profusely.

"I'm about to burn up," he told Will as he propped his hoe against the side of the barn. "How about that wade in the river?"

"How about a *swim?*" Will asked.

"It would have to be a skinny dip," Neil said. "I don't have a swimmin' suit. Do you know a private spot?"

"Sure. There's a hole down by the bridge, and it can't be seen from the house. And one good thing about living on the end of the road is nobody passes by."

Will and Neil undressed under the bridge, waded into the cool water, and moved to a deep hole about ten feet below the span. The two men sank into the river and allowed the flow to wash away their cares along with the dirt.

"Been a long time since I went skinny dipping in a river," Neil said.

"Me too," Will replied.

"Will, my boy, it's plain to see why you wanted to move away up here. You know ... I've been watching the folks that live in the valley. Some of the most contented people I've ever seen."

"That's right."

"Not a care in the world."

"Oh ... they have cares, Mr. Neil. They're just different kinds of cares ... like, right now, they're worrying about a mountain lion that's running around killing stock. They worry over whether it'll be chestnuts or ginseng that'll pay their taxes. They worry over their crops ... and whether or not the old folks down the road have enough fire wood. They worry about the roads getting washed out enough to slow 'em down gettin' to church. Then, they worry about what they should take to dinner on the grounds ... green beans or ham biscuits. Usually end up takin' both."

Neil chuckled. "Green beans or ham biscuits!"

"But I can also tell you what they don't worry about," Will continued. "They don't worry about getting to work before the clock turns over. They're usually there already. They don't worry about having enough to eat, because everybody shares. ... And even though they want their younguns to learn to read and write, they don't worry about 'em learning trigonometry."

He bobbed up and down as he watched the wind blow his hay growing on the bank of the river. What a beautiful sight it was from that angle, he thought.

"You know what I've been worried about, Will?" Neil asked.

"I'd think a man of your means wouldn't have a care in the world."

"I've been worried that I won't find enough workers to run my new mill without having to hire children. I've been worried that the price of cotton will go up and I'll lose hundreds of thousands of dollars on my government contract. Been worried, too, that they might not even *renew* that contract … and I'll be scrapping around, trying to find somebody else to buy my canvas."

Will didn't know what to say. He had never thought about the pressures on a titan of industry.

"And I worry about not seeing my wife … and that I'm working my-self into an early grave … and that's really why I'm here, Will. I think you should know that I've …"

The words were just about to come out of his mouth. He was just about to tell Will why he had been sneaking around the valley, when they heard horse hooves and carriage wheels.

"Somebody's coming, Mr. Neil," Will said. "Be still and maybe they won't see us."

In seconds Doc French's buggy was on the bridge, and suddenly it stopped.

"*Will! Is that you in the water?*" Doc called out.

And then, "*Are you having a swim, Will?*" Alice called out as she leaned across Doc.

"Good Lord!" Will said to Neil. "It's Alice! Stay under water."

"*Can you do the backstroke, Will?*" Alice shouted as she started to climb down from the buggy.

Just then, Daniel ran up on the bridge and looked over the edge.

"*Hey, Will!*"

"*Alice! Mr. Neil is down here!*" Will barked.

"*Oh, wonderful! I get to meet him!*"

"*Alice!*" Will screamed. "*This … is … not … a … good …time!*"

"Get in the buggy, Alice," Doc said firmly. "We'll see 'em at the house."

It suddenly dawned on Alice what was going on. She covered her face with her hands and ran back around the buggy.

"*Sonny*," she hollered. "*Get ... off ... the edge ... of ... that ... bridge!*"

———

Will and Neil didn't have much to say as they were getting dressed. Each was wondering how he was going to face Alice, and Will was particularly curious about where Alice and Doc were going.

Finally, as they walked up the road, Neil spoke. "The water in that river sure is clear."

"I was thinking the same thing," Will said.

"Do you think it's ... uh ... clear enough ..."

"I was wondering the same thing!"

About that time Will spotted Preacher Burden's buggy coming from the other direction, and it turned into his yard. Then he saw Roamer's wagon sitting in the yard along with Doc's buggy. Several people, including Demus, were milling around under the trees.

"Something strange is going on," Will said. "Mr. Neil, do you have any idea what all those people are doing at my house?"

"I promise you, son, I don't have a clue."

Will picked up the pace and studied the scene as he walked, trying to make sense of it. Someone had fashioned a table under the trees using sawhorses and lumber, and the table was laden with food. As Will and Neil approached, the group began to clap and cheer—everyone except Alice, who buried her face in her hands and turned away slightly.

"*Here come the bathing beauties*," Doc announced.

"Will someone please tell me what's going on?" Will said in mock desperation.

Esther came forward and hugged her brother. "Will, have you forgotten?" she asked.

"I must have," he replied. "It looks like everybody knows what's going on but me."

"Happy birthday, Brother," she said.

And for the second time that day, Will was weak-kneed and speechless.

———

"Alice, I want you to meet Mr. Glenn Neil. Mr. Neil, this is Alice Day and her son Daniel. And if you hear someone mention 'Sonny,' that would be Daniel's nickname."

Alice blushed a crimson red and put her hand to her forehead. When she started to speak, Neil interrupted her.

"Now, young lady, before you say a word, I want to offer my most sincere apologies to you."

He raised his left hand and put his right hand over his heart. "I'm a grown man who's supposed to be in a responsible position, and I should have known better than to put you and Will in an embarrassing situation like that. Will you please forgive me?"

He had bent his knees to get closer to Alice's level and was trying to look her in the eye.

"Oh, Mr. Neil," she said, finally looking up at him. "I feel so *stupid*. I'll tell you what ... I'll forgive you if you'll forgive me. Okay?"

"*That's a deal!*" Neil bellowed, and he grabbed Alice and gave her a big hug.

"Now, Daniel," he said, "Will tells me you're a crack shot. I want to go huntin' with you someday ... hire you to give me some shootin' lessons!"

"Wow!" was all Daniel could utter as he looked up at the big man.

Next, Will introduced Neil to Demus, and after they had talked for a few minutes, Neil pulled Will to the side and whispered, "Son, that man's a genius! He told me things about Grover Cleveland that I never knew. I want to talk to him some more ... pick his brain!"

"And now," Will finally said, "I've saved the very best for last," and he introduced Neil to the Robinsons.

"So you're th' feller 'at took my nephew, Goober an' treated 'im s' good!" Roamer said. Then he lowered his voice to a whisper. "I want ye t' come by my place an' let me give ye a li'l' somethin' spacial 'at'll warm ye insides."

"Roamer, I wish you'd hesh up 'at foolishness," Sweetie said as she dealt Roamer a blow with her elbow. "Mr. Neild don't want none o' yer doin's!" Then she curtsied to Neil and softly said, "Hit's a plasure t' meet ye, Mr. Neild, and I thank ye fer bein' s' good t' Goober!"

"Well, now I can see why Goober is such a wonderful man, coming from a wonderful family like this!" Neil declared. "I'll tell you now … that's quite a nephew you have there!"

"Will," Esther called from the table, "we're going to spread blankets for everybody to sit on, but could you get two chairs from the house for the Robinsons?"

Will raised a finger of compliance and started for the house.

"I'll help you, birthday boy," Alice called out.

When they got inside, Alice made a detour into Esther's room and returned with a package. It was wrapped with brown paper and tied with red yarn.

"Will," she said, "Esther said not to bring presents, but I already had something for you."

Will was about to get weak-kneed again. He took the package tied up with red yarn and examined it.

"Can I open it now?" he asked.

"It's not much, but you can if you want to."

Nervous fingers worked at the yarn bow until the paper opened, revealing a hand-sewn shirt of bleached white linen.

"Esther let me use one of your shirts for a pattern. I hope it fits," she said.

He held it up to his chest and the shoulders matched his.

And there was more. Beneath the shirt was a hand-stitched quilt made of bits and pieces of cloth, some of which he recognized as remnants of her dresses and Daniel's shirts.

"I was worried about you staying warm this winter," she said as he examined it. "It's called a 'Joseph's-coat quilt'."

"Oh my, Alice!" he said looking at her. "All along I thought ..."

"Well you were wrong," she said softly.

———

Naomi Burden was serving up slices of her coconut layer cake for desert when Preacher Burden stood and banged a spoon against his cup.

"Folks ... folks ... cut out your foolishness for just a minute and listen up," he said.

When the noise subsided, he continued. "That was some of the best squirrel stew I have ever eaten, and I want to thank Sonny Day for providing the squirrels; and I want to thank Esther, and Alice, and Nicodemus, and the Robinsons for cooking 'em up with those delicious vegetables; and I want to thank my precious wife, Naomi, for suggesting that they mix 'em all up into one grand and glorious concoction t' bring all those flavors together; and I want to thank Will for gettin' a year older so we could gather here tonight and celebrate."

"*Preach!*" Roamer shouted.

The preacher held up his hands and shook his head.

"No, I'm gonna hush now, but before I do, I wanna call on a man that's come a long way to be here this evening. ... He didn't even know it was Will's birthday ... but he came anyway."

Then the preacher got serious and struck a dramatic pose.

"Doc and I met Mr. Glenn Neil just about a month ago ... and he laid out a plan to us that just blew my mind to *smithereens!* Now, he asked me if he could tell you folks ... you people who are Will Parker's best friends ... about his plan. So I'm gonna ask him to stand up here now where ever'body can see him and tell you about the future of Avery Cove!"

Will was baffled. He turned and looked back at Esther, who shrugged her shoulders and shook her head. The preacher sat down with Doc, and they exchanged smiles and whispers, giving Will a little encouragement that nothing bad was about to happen.

Glenn Neil stood and walked to the center of the group. Even in his overalls he was an impressive man. He hesitated before he spoke, and the concentration on his face would have led one to believe that this was the most important speech of his life. Finally, he turned to Will.

"Will, I've been trying all day to find just the right way to tell you what I've been up to. ... I wanted to tell you *first* since you're the one that led me to this place ... but something was always coming up to *stop* me. I hope you won't mind me speaking directly to you in front of all these folks. I understand you're close to all of 'em."

He paced in a circle before he stopped in front of Will again.

"Truth of the matter is, I'm gettin' tired ... and I want to settle down. ... Don't want to *die* yet, but I do want to rest in peace!"

"*A-men*," Roamer shouted, and he got an elbow in the ribs from Sweetie.

"So what I did was buy a little piece of heaven from Preacher Burden down the road there, and I'm gonna build myself a house and settle down with my wife. Get out of the rat-race!"

A murmur went through the small group. Will looked back at Esther again, and she was wide-eyed and had her hand over her mouth.

"I'm gonna want my wife ... to take cookin' lessons from you ladies, and I'm gonna take farmin' lessons from you, Will ... and shootin' lessons from Daniel over there!"

Alice gave Daniel a nudge, and he grinned from ear to ear.

"And I'm gonna hang around Burden's store and trade stories with the local folks ... try to soak up some o' their wisdom!"

"Yeah, and you'll end up as addled as we are," Doc said.

Neil paused and smiled as the group laughed, then he turned back to Will, who had taken on a look of pure amazement.

"Will, my boy, I hope you don't mind, but I've also bought that piece of land across the river from you where the old mill used to be. I'm gonna build my life-long dream, a tiny, little, water-driven woolen mill!"

"My word!" Will said out loud.

"I don't want you to worry, though. There won't be any looms runnin' all night long coverin' up the sound of the river. We're going to get the job done in one shift."

Will looked around at the others and nodded.

"There'll be some Scottish families moving in from up east to turn my wool into cloth, and they'll be a nice addition to your community ... I guarantee it!"

Roamer sidled up to Sweetie and whispered in her ear, "Wonder if 'em folks can learn me t' make Scotch whiskey?"

Then Neil turned to the Robinsons.

"Mr. and Mrs. Robinson!"

"'At's Roamer an' Sweetie, Mr. Neild," Sweetie said.

"Well then ... Roamer and Sweetie ... and you just call me 'Glenn' ... this will be of *special* interest to you. I want a comfortable, well-built house, and I want my mill to look a lot like the fine barns in the valley ... to blend in ... so I've hired a person I can trust to come and oversee the construction. This winter, your nephew, Goober, will be moving back to Avery Cove, and he'll be here for at least a year."

Roamer and Sweetie grabbed on to each other and held tight as if they feared they might fall off the earth. They began to weep, and Sweetie clasped her hands beneath her chin and looked to heaven.

"Oh, *thank* ye, Lord ... *thank* ye! Did ye hear? *Goober's* a-comin' home!"

"And he asked me to tell you that he's bringing his bride, Janie Rose!"

"*Hallelujah!*" Roamer shouted, and his body shook with emotion.

"And he says that if you have room, they'd like to stay with you until he can find a place of his own."

It was almost more than Roamer and Sweetie could bear. Doc and Preacher Burden went over and comforted them as they cried and rejoiced, and then the preacher addressed the group again.

"Now folks," he said, "let's just keep this under our hats until our meetin' tomorrow night. I'm gonna tell the folks all about Mr. Neil's plan, and he'll be there to answer questions."

"I think we ort t' sing *Fer He's a Jolly Good Feller*," Sweetie declared, waving her hand in the air, "an' I think we ort t' sing it fer Will an' fer Mr. Neild too!"

And they did.

The Baptist church was almost full when Preacher Burden, Will, and Glenn Neil arrived. When they walked in, the noise level went from a roar to a gentle hum.

"'At's him 'ere," someone said.

"Why, he don't *look* like no city slicker," someone else responded.

"I gotta give 'im credit fer gittin' Goober Green back up 'ere," another man said.

Preacher Burden went directly to Preacher Babb, shaking his head on the way.

"Sorry we held things up, Brother Billy, but we found another dead calf on the way up here," he said.

"You think it happened last night?"

"Must have. I was up by there yesterday."

"Well, we'd better get started. We've got a lot to go over."

Preacher Babb went to the pulpit and slapped his hand on the surface.

"*Let's come t' order!*" he shouted. "*Brother Olie, you and Brother James get yer hats off.*"

When the crowd came to order, Preacher Babb called on Preacher Burden to lead in prayer. The instant his brother sounded the "amen," Preacher Babb slammed his hand on the pulpit and continued.

"We got a lot of stuff to talk about … the most pressing of which is this animal that's killing stock."

"*Hit's a painter!*" James Plumlee shouted.

"Prob'ly is, Brother James," Preacher Babb said, "but Mrs. Day is the only one that's seen it … and that was at night. If it *is* a panther, we really *do* have a problem. They're sneaky ... and nobody around here has dogs trained to hunt 'em."

"*I got a Winchester rifle trained t' hunt 'em!*" someone shouted.

"*Well gooood luck!*" somebody else hollered. "*Ye got t' see 'em first 'fore ye can shoot 'em!*"

"All right, men, come to order!" Preacher Babb demanded as he slapped the pulpit. "What we need are good suggestions as to what we can do to get rid of this creature. Has anybody got one?"

Will stood up slightly and raised his hand.

"*Chair recognizes Brother Will Parker.*"

"Thank you, Preacher Babb," Will said. "I think R. Z. Ross had a good idea when he came by to see me. He's putting his stock up at night ... a little extra work, but it seems it would be worth the effort."

"'At's right," R. Z. said.

"*My barn ain't big enough fer eighteen cows an' four horses an' two goats!*" someone shouted.

"But this panther hasn't been going after large stock," Will said. "So far all it's taken are goats and calves. I think it would be worth a try for everybody to put up their small animals and secure their chicken houses for a while. Maybe if there aren't any animals to eat around here, he'll go somewhere else. ... Let the folks in Burley or over in Tennessee worry about him. Now, he showed up here all of a sudden ... maybe if he doesn't have anything to eat, he'll suddenly leave."

Paul Thiggery jumped to his feet and pointed a finger in the air. "*I declare,*" he said, "*I think we ort to band t'gether an' go find 'at creature an' see to it that nothin' else is kilt!*"

"You're *crazy, Paul!*" Caldwell Turpin hollered. "*Ye can't jest go 'round shootin' up the woods in th' dark!*"

"*Men ... men!*" Preacher Babb shouted as he pounded his hand on the pulpit. "Brother Caldwell's right. If we go out huntin' this thing at night, one of *us* is gonna get killed. Do I hear a motion we do like Brother Will said, and at least *try* puttin' up our small animals at night?"

"*Motion!*"

"*Second!*"

"*All in favor? . . . Passed!*" and the preacher slapped the pulpit. "Now, let's press on! At this time I want to recognize my fellow pastor, Brother Eli Burden."

"*Preach!*" One of the Methodists shouted.

"Hush up, Lucas," Preacher Burden said as he walked to the pulpit. "If you'd stay awake in church, you'd hear all the preachin' you could stand!" and he stepped up on the podium.

When the laughter subsided, Preacher Burden studied the crowd, as was his practice, and leaned into the pulpit.

"I've brought you folks some good news tonight," he said with a measure of drama. Then he studied the crowd some more. "We have here tonight a man who'll soon be our neighbor ... a man that will bring a wealth of benefits to our valley ... *a man that will bring a better way of life to each ... and ... every ... person ... here!*" The preacher was pounding the pulpit to drive home his point, and his face was turning red.

"*We already know all 'at, Preacher!*" somebody shouted. "*Roamer Robinson tol' us.*"

The preacher's jaw dropped.

"You mean ... he told you about Mr. Neil?

"*Yep!*"

"And that he's gonna build a house and a woolen mill?"

"'*At's right!*"

"And the Scottish people movin' in?"

"*Yep, an' we're all fer it! An' 'e tol' us 'bout Goober Green comin' back an' buyin' timber from us t' build th' house an' mill, and he said Mr. Neil tol' 'im that the state wuz gonna take over th' roads an' keep 'em scrapped! We're shore fer that ... Whut we wanna know is ... can we go ahead an' change th' name o' th' valley t' Green Cove 'fore Goober gits here!*"

A mighty cheer went up in the little church as the men jumped to their feet. Preacher Burden stood back and looked, not knowing what to do, so Preacher Babb came forward and regained order by pounding repeatedly on the pulpit.

"*Hush up that yellin'!*" he demanded. "*This is th' house of God!*"

The reminder about where they were brought the noise down to a manageable level, so Preacher Babb continued. "I thought we settled this 'Green Cove' business a long time ago!"

"*Wa'n't never settled a-tall*" Ansel Falwell said. "*Think we ort t' vote on it!*"

When the noise level came up again, Preacher Babb turned to Preacher Burden. "What do you think I ought to do, Brother Eli?"

"I'd say open it up for discussion ... and then call on Will to give his opinion. I'm not gonna jump into *that* fray again!"

Preacher Babb turned back to the pulpit and slapped his hand on the surface. "*The chair will now open the subject for discussion and call on Brother Will for his opinion.*"

The look on Will's face was that of a reluctant witness. He had a strong conviction about the issue, but it was in opposition to most folks there. He could only hope that his argument was one that would persuade the gathering rather than more fully divide it. He stood and faced the crowd.

"Makepeace ... Goober grew up here among you people, and you know him well. Doc, you delivered him, and later you saved his life when he was choking to death. Preacher Babb, you baptized him in the Avery River. Uncle Roamer, you and Aunt Sweetie became his parents when his real parents died. I'll bet that there's not a soul here that hasn't touched his life in one way or another."

The men cast glances at each other. Some nodded.

"When he was 'Goober' he took a lot of good-natured teasing from just about everybody. He couldn't seem to get past being the little rooster that everybody picked on, so he moved away to make a fresh start...but I'll venture to say there isn't a person here that didn't miss him! Then, when he came back and did a really heroic thing ... you wanted to acknowledge that! What a wonderful thing! What a simply *marvelous* thing to want to do!"

The men reacted with nods and a few "amens".

"Now ...I'm going to tell you why naming this valley 'Green Cove' would be wrong way to honor him."

A murmur went through the crowd as heads turned and whispers were exchanged.

"It would be wrong because Makepeace wouldn't *want* you to do it. Simply put ... he'd be embarrassed by it!"

Ansel Falwell jumped to his feet and shook his finger in the air. "Young feller, I don't think ye understand. All we want t' do is thank 'im fer savin' a man's life!"

"I *do* understand, Mr. Falwell," Will said calmly. "It was my life he saved."

Ansel started to respond, but he thought better of it. He sat down, put his elbows on his knees and looked at the floor.

"Can I say something?" Glenn Neil asked as he raised his hand.

"Chair recognizes our distinguished visitor, Mr. Neil," Preacher Babb said.

Neil stood and looked around.

"You folks don't know me from Methuselah," he said, "but I got to be friends with Mr. Green when he worked in my mill in Charlotte, and I became very close to him when he went over to Burley and helped me buy some land a while back. Very good man ... very humble man. Having talked to him quite a bit, I'd have to agree with Will here that naming this valley after him wouldn't be right. It would be like hanging a burden around his neck. I'm afraid it would be something he'd feel like he had to continually live up to! Now, I commend you for wanting to honor him ... but maybe there's a better way. What I'd like for you to consider is allowing me try to come up with something that would be a little easier for him to swallow. If you'll do that, I'll ask the two ministers to work with me to make it something special."

Neil looked around the room into the faces of the men who weren't staring at the floor, then he continued. "Now please remember that Will was the one most impacted by what Mr. Green did. I hope you'll honor him as well by respecting *his* opinion."

Neil sat down and another wave of whispers moved through the crowd.

"How does that sound, Ansel?" Preacher Babb asked. "You willin' to see what Mr. Neil can come up with?"

All eyes turned to Ansel, who raised his head and mumbled, "Long as you an' 'em others is a-goin' in with 'im, I reccon I'm willin'."

"You want to put that in the form of a motion?" Preacher Babb asked.

"I reccon I'll motion it," Ansel said.

"*Second!*" someone shouted.

"*All in favor? Passed!*" And Preacher Babb slapped the pulpit.

"*I want Brother Neil t' tell us 'bout them roads!*" someone shouted.

Neil looked to Preacher Babb for direction and then stood.

"Well, gentlemen ... I contacted the state road department, and they pledged that if there was a small industry and a few more people in Avery Cove, they would take over all the roads in the valley as well as the road to Burley ... and that they would improve them and maintain them on your behalf. You'll never have to fill another pot hole!"

The women who were sitting at home waiting for their husbands must have wondered what had happened at that moment, because a cheer went up in the little church that could be heard all over the valley. Glenn Neil had worked his magic again and demonstrated why he was a titan of industry.

And despite the ruckus in the house of God, Preacher Babb let the cheering continue. He just knew that God in heaven must be cheering along with them.

Thirty-Two

A Scream in the Night

W ill had searched the house over, and the *Old Farmer's Almanac* was not to be found. The nail by the back door where it usually hung now held one of Esther's aprons.

"Esther, have you seen the almanac?" he called out from the kitchen.

"Sorry … it's in my room," she answered. "I'll get it."

In a moment, Esther came into the kitchen, thumbing through the well-worn book.

"Looking up a treatment for the gout?" Will asked.

"No, as a matter of fact, I was reading about making you some peach preserves. I'm wondering though if it would be worth the effort with those little hard, knobby peaches you have on your tree."

Esther sat down at the table and lay the book in front of her. She tilted her head and assumed a thoughtful pose.

"You know," she said, "that's the only thing I can think of that's better in Wilmington."

"What's better in Wilmington?"

"Peaches … those and fresh seafood, of course! Everything else on earth is better here."

Esther had been talking a lot about Wilmington for several days. The summer was winding down, and in three short weeks she would be leaving

Avery Cove to return to the coast. Will could see a change in her mood at certain times of the day. Her happy disposition was ebbing away as she thought about having to leave.

"By the way, what do you need the almanac for?" she asked.

"Wanted to look up the dog days of summer … see when they end."

Esther leafed through the book and stopped to read silently. Finally, she announced, "Says here they end the eleventh of August."

"Another week!" Will declared. "I hope that'll end the hot weather for this year."

"It won't in Wilmington," Esther said glumly. "We'll have hot days and hot nights through October."

"What are your plans for tomorrow?" Will asked, changing the subject.

"More canning. I'm going to pick up Aunt Sweetie, and we're going to Alice's and spend the day putting up vegetables with her. Aunt Sweetie is going to teach us how to make kraut." She got up from the table and gave Will a little bump as she walked by. "You're gonna get fat over the winter, Brother," she said. "The root cellar's filling up fast. At least there'll still be plenty left when I get back next spring."

"Don't know what I would have done without you this summer, Sis," Will said. "I can't see *me* doing all that canning."

Esther was right. The root cellar *was* filling up fast. The shelves were already lined with jars of corn, beans, peas, squash, several kinds of preserved tomatoes, fruits and berries, jams, jellies, and juices. Then there were the jars of pickles, relishes, and vegetable soup sitting above the bins that had been cleaned out for the potatoes, turnips, and apples that were yet to be harvested. Nobody would go hungry that winter!

———

The bell on the door at Burden's store jingled as James Plumlee entered. Preacher Burden looked up from the post office counter and greeted him.

"Mornin', James," he said. "You come to jaw, or can I sell you somethin'?"

"Wife needs more jars," James said. "Twelve quarts and twelve pints … an' two dozen o' them screw-on lids."

"Looks like there'll be good eatin' over at the Plumlee house this winter," the preacher said.

"Fair to middlin'," James replied, "dependin' on how th' hogs do."

James walked over and looked over the selection of pocket knives while the preacher was counting out the jar lids. "Say, Preacher," he said as he looked, "reckon 'em Scotland people are church folk?"

The preacher straightened up and gave James a look. "Neil says he thinks they're mostly Presbyterians."

"Ye think they'll want their own church house?"

The preacher thought before be answered. "That would be all right, I guess. There's room in the valley for a Presbyterian church … or they can join up with us. They aren't too different from Methodists or Baptists as I understand it. I've got to read up on 'em before they get here."

"Least they ain't *Jews*, ner *Cath'lics*, ner them people 'at worships *cows*" James declared. "Wouldn't want *them* t' git a foot hold 'round here!"

"Yeah, that would be unfortunate," the preacher replied. "That would be most unfortunate."

———

As soon as breakfast was cleaned up, Will walked Esther down to the barn and helped her hitch Judy to the buckboard. When she was on her way, he turned his attention to his new project—modifications to the barn.

The barn had been built with eight animal stalls, which was more stalls than he needed, even if he bought a cow or two sometime in the future. What he did need was space for his new cultivator, the seed drill, and the buckboard. His project was to tear out the front two stalls and level the ground to make more room for his rolling equipment. This sort of work required more muscle than carpentry skill, so it was just the kind of thing he could do with Daniel's help.

He was prying off his first plank of lumber when he heard Dawg barking in the distance. Before long Dawg ran into the barn with Daniel on his heels.

"Hey, Dawg," Will said. "Who's your buddy there?"

"It's dust me," Daniel announced.

"Are you ready to work?"

"Yep."

"Finished all your chores at home?"

"Yep."

Will laid down his pry bar. "How's Dawg doin'? Is he still satisfied to sleep on your porch?"

"He stays with me now."

"In your *room*?

"In my bed!"

"In your *bed* ? You're going to spoil him rotten! What does your mama think about him sleeping with you?"

"She said it makes her peel safe to have 'im in the house. Guess what!"

Will picked up his pry bar and forced the point under another plank. "What?" he asked.

"I sold six watermelons to Preacher Burden for *furty cents.* "

"*Thirty cents*!" Will declared. "What are you going to do with all that money?"

"You won't tell?"

"No, I won't tell."

"I'm gonna buy Mama a Christmas present."

The thought of Christmas and a .22 rifle for Daniel popped into Will's mind.

"And what would you ask for for Christmas, if you could have anything in the whole world?" he asked.

Daniel turned his back and took a step toward the door. Will lay down the pry bar again and put on his serious face. He had learned to know when something was troubling the boy.

"Come on and tell me, Daniel," Will said. "We've always been able to tell each other things, haven't we?"

Daniel kept his face toward the door and looked at the dirt he was standing on. "I know my daddy can't come back …" he said, "… so I'd wike to come stay with you."

Will felt the warmth in his cheeks that came when his face turned red.

"You know, Daniel, your mama needs you real bad right now," he said as gently as he could. "Why … you're the man of the house … your mama's protector! Are you and your mama not gettin' along right now?" he asked.

"We get along pine …" Daniel said. "… I want her to be with you too."

Will was broadsided by Daniel's remark. He went over and sat down on his cultivator and rubbed the back of his neck.

"Daniel … I don't know exactly what to say about that right now," he said. "I really appreciate you telling me that … but I want you to do me a favor and not say anything like that to your mama."

"Why not?"

"Because she doesn't need to think about stuff like that right now. She's too busy getting ready for winter … and looking after you … and she's too busy remembering your daddy."

He got up and walked over to the boy and put his hands on his shoulders. "Tell you what," he said, "… how about we just keep this conversation between us men … not worry your mother with it. Okay?"

Daniel didn't answer, but he nodded.

"And one thing more," Will said. "I want you to know that I love you too."

———————

After supper that evening, Will hitched Judy to the buckboard, and he and Esther headed out to see Demus. Esther carried a stack of books she was returning, and Will carried the burden of his conversation with Daniel. Esther was talkative, telling Will about the novel she had just read, and Will was silent, not really hearing her.

"You're quiet this evening, Will," Esther said. "Are you feeling all right?"

"I'm fine," he said. "Just have a lot on my mind." Then he told her about asking Daniel what he would like for Christmas and Daniel's reply.

"What did you tell him?" Esther asked.

"I really don't know," he said somberly. "I said something like 'we should just keep this between us and not to bother his mama with it' or something like that, and I told him that I love him ... I think that was what he was sort of telling me. I hope I said the right thing."

"I wasn't going to tell you about this," Esther said tentatively, "but a few days ago we were riding over to Aunt Sweetie's, and out of the blue, Alice said, 'I think that in the spring I'm going to ask Will if we can get a rig for me to use in case he's using this one.' Honest Will, she didn't even realize what that sounded like! And then yesterday she said, 'I think Will and I should get a cow,' and when she realized what she had said, she got all flustered and said, 'I mean ... I think *I* should get a cow.' If I didn't know better, I'd think she was having thoughts of her own."

"I wonder why we haven't seen Demus lately," Will said.

"You think you're pretty good at changing the subject, don't you?" Esther replied.

"You're awfully chipper this evening," Will said. "What perked you up?"

"Oh, nothing maybe ... but I got a letter today from a girl I taught with last year. She was going to a teacher college this fall, but she may not be able to come up with the money. She wanted to know if she could stay with me this winter and look for a job."

"That sounds good!"

"It sounds *wonderful*! It would mean that I wouldn't have to go home to an empty house. I would actually have an *adult* to talk to." Esther took a deep breath and blew it out. "I'm not going to get my hopes up though."

"Preacher Burden said there's a new teacher college over in Cullowhee," Will said. "Said Rachel had talked about going over there to look at the place ... and he said they were giving grants to students to get the school started. You think your friend would be interested in coming up here to go to school?"

"Not Blanche! She has saltwater in her veins. She'd never leave the coast." Esther thought for a minute as she clicked her shoe on the foot board. "Maybe I should go over there myself and see about getting some more schooling. I might even meet a nice teacher-boy while I'm there!"

"Well, in the words of Goober Green …" Will muttered.

"I know," Esther blurted out, "I hope to my never!"

When Demus's house came into view, there was a thick column of smoke rising from his kitchen chimney. As they got closer, they could see that he had his doors and windows open, letting in some cooler air.

Demus greeted them at the door with a makeshift apron tied around his waist. He held a dish cloth in one hand and a large wooden spoon in the other.

"You're just in time," he said. "I'm about to cap the last of my canning for the day."

"I hadn't thought about you doing canning," Esther said. "If I had, I would have included you in our canning group … Alice, Aunt Sweetie, and me."

"I've always managed to get it done by myself. Besides," he said, "your group probably wouldn't appreciate the spices us Asian people use," and his big laugh rolled out like thunder.

Will followed Demus back in the kitchen and sat at the table while Demus tightened the lids on the last of his jars.

"You've been scarce lately," Will said.

"Indeed I have. It's that busy time of year," Demus replied. "I've been putting up food for winter … and last week I went hunting over into Tennessee and got a deer ..,. put up thirty-six jars of dried venison. Then I helped Roamer Robinson some, as I know you have. Busy! But there'll be time for fishing and reading after the first killing frost."

"Didn't run into the mountain lion while you were hunting, did you?"

"No, but I heard him a couple of nights ago, and he sounds hungry. I'm tired of having to put my pigs up at night."

"*Demus*," Esther called out from the parlor, "do you have any Nathaniel Hawthorne books?"

"My bedroom ... by the window ... top shelf."

"Thanks."

"Are you looking for novels or short stories?" Demus asked.

"I really don't know that much about him," Esther answered as she walked into the kitchen.

"You've read *The Scarlet Letter*?"

"Yes."

"Then I'd recommend *The Marble Fawn* if you want a novel ... and *A Wonder Book for Girls and Boys* would be good for your students."

"Say! Do you have any of those *Yellow Kid* picture books that just came out?" Will asked.

Demus drew back and frowned. "You've got to be kidding!" he exclaimed.

M akepeace slid down off Traveler's back, tied him to the picket fence, and bounded up the steps of Janie Rose Rainey's house. Mrs. Rainey met him at the door and invited him into the parlor.

"Come on in, Makepeace," she said. "She's freshenin' up. She'll be out in a minute."

Makepeace jerked his hat off and began twisting it into a knot.

"Thank ye, ma'am," he replied. "I'll jest sit an' wait, if ye don't mind."

"Have ye eaten yet?" Mrs. Rainey asked.

"Oh, yes'm!" Makepeace answered. "I took m' supper at Sarah's."

"Wouldn't want my future son-in-law to go hungry," Mrs. Rainey sang as she left the room.

"Oh, no ma'am, I ain't hungry a bit ...'cept I might could eat some pie later on."

By that time Mrs. Rainey had cleared the parlor, and the comment about pie went unheard.

Before Makepeace could re-examine all the portraits hanging on the parlor walls, Janie Rose appeared from her room, floating on a cloud of loveliness. She was wearing a soft pink dress with short puffy sleeves, and her hair was put up and tied with a pink bow. Her eyes sparkled, her cheeks and lips had a soft red glow, and she had the faint fragrance of lilacs hovering around her.

"Hello, Makey," she said. Her face tilted down and a little to the side, but her eyes remained focused on Makepeace.

Makepeace jumped to his feet.

"Ohhh, Janie Rose," he moaned. "You look s' purdy!"

"I was hopin' you'd like m' dress," she said. "I bought it 'cause I thought you would."

"Oh, Janie Rose," Makepeace groaned, "was we suppose t' go out tonight? I mean … you're dressed up purdy as a apple blossom."

"No, Makey, I jest dressed up for you. Now go on an' sit on the sofa, an' I'm gonna sit next to you."

Makepeace untwisted his hat and lay it on the end table. Then he took a seat on the sofa and swallowed hard. Janie Rose sat next to him, pulled her feet up underneath herself, and snuggled up close to Makepeace.

"Are you comfortable?" she asked.

"Ohhh, yes, Janie Rose," Makepeace said, his voice beginning to tremble, "but how 'bout yer mama an' daddy?"

Just then the back door closed, and Janie Rose slid a little closer. "They just left to go visit the Coxes. I guess we're by ourselves now."

"Ohhh, Janie Rose!"

"Makey … I want t' ask you somethin'," Janie Rose said.

"Well …" Makepeace sputtered.

"Why can't we go on and git married now? I don't want us to have to wait till Optober."

"You mean … *now*?"

Janie Rose ran a finger down Makepeace's cheek and sent a shiver up his spine.

"Tomorrow's Saturday," she said. "If we got married tomorrow, we'd have all day Sunday for our … honeymoon."

"Ohhh, Janie Rose!" Makepeace moaned.

"We could run off after work and go to a Justice of the Peace … and be back at your house 'fore Mama even knew I was gone."

"Your daddy ud *kill* me, Janie Rose."

"He'd get over it real quick … besides, he don't like gettin' dressed up and goin' to weddin's anyhow."

"Oh Lord!" Makepeace moaned. He started to squirm, and a cold sweat broke out on his forehead. "The house is a mess … an' I've got t' change th' sheets … an'…"

"If we was married, I'd do all those things for you," Janie Rose crooned, "and we'd have more time to ourselves 'fore we moved in with your Aunt Sweetie and Uncle Roamer."

Janie Rose slid even closer to Makepeace and blew in his ear.

"Ohhh, Janie *Rose,*" Makepeace gasped. "I don't know whut t' say."

"Then jest say yes, Makey."

"Ohhh, Janie *Rose,*" he said, his voice almost trembling out of control, "do ye think ye could git off work a little early t'morrow?"

———

Will and Esther sat on the front porch listening to the crickets' serenade. Will was in a rocker with his feet on the porch rail and his hands clasped behind his head, and Esther was seizing the last rays of the sun as she read a book.

"This is the time of day that Grandpa referred to as 'in the gloamin','" Will said.

"I remember," Esther said, putting her book aside. "He would sit and rock at twilight, and Grandma would knit. She could even knit in the dark."

"I wonder what Grandpa would think of my farm?" Will asked.

"Oh, Will … he'd think it's *wonderful!* I couldn't help but notice that your garden is laid off just like his used to be … and your corn rows are as straight as an arrow … and he'd *marvel* at the horses, and the cultivator, and the other things you've added."

"And Alice?"

"He'd love her ... but Grandma would gather her up and not let her go! She and Grandma sew and knit the very same way ... and they both have that feisty little spirit ... and Will, don't you know how much Daniel is like you were at his age?"

"He does love the things I loved when I was ten."

First one frog and then another joined the crickets, and the sun finally gave out for the day.

"Have you decided what to tell Blanche?" Will asked.

"That didn't take long to decide!" Esther replied. "I'm going to send a telegram tomorrow and tell her where the key is ... tell her to be moved in by the time I get back! Then I'll write her and tell her about the new school in Cullowhee ... but I hope she'll stay in Wilmington with me."

Will nodded his approval, but Esther couldn't see him. She settled back though, knowing she was doing the right thing.

"What are you gonna do tomorrow?" she asked.

"Uh ... Demus helped Daniel make some fish traps and I'm gonna help him set them in the river."

"Fish fry tomorrow night?"

"Maybe Sunday night ... What are you gonna do tomorrow?"

Will could hear Esther's little hum as she thought it over.

"I might just gather up my skirt and get in the river with you and Daniel," she said.

———

Alice lay in bed waiting for sleep to come, and as she waited she thought about her day. In her mind she pictured Sweetie and her toothless smile. She recited Sweetie's lesson on making kraut and repeated it over and over again, trying to make sure it would be forever imprinted in her brain.

"Now ye take ye cabbage heads an' ye cut 'em up with ye knife into pieces 'bout thick as a sliver dollar ... like 'is! Ye cut out them hard cores now ... but don't ye throw 'em out, ye hear? I'll give 'em t' th' hogs!

"Then ye put some o' ye cabbages ... jest a few inches' worth ... in ye crock an' put 'bout a thimble full o' picklin' salt on 'em and mix 'em up w' ye hands. See th' salt a-startin' to draw out th' waters?

"Now! Put some more of 'em in ye crock ... jest a few more inches' worth ... an' add some more salt an' mix 'em up w' ye hands real good. See how them waters is a-comin out o' th' cabbages? 'At's good!

"Now! Keep on a-addin' cabbages an' salt till ye git up 'bout four inches from the rim o' ye crock. ... Ye gonna have 'bout five heads o' cabbage an' 'bout three-quarters of a cup o' salt in 'ere when ye done. Law ... look how much waters 'at salt has already drawed off! ... Some people adds a pinch o' sugar 'long bout here ... but I don't. ... Then, ye put some plates on th' top to mash 'em down an' squeeze th' waters out.

"Now! Here's th' tricky part. We gonna cover up th' crock with a rag an' tie it off, an' we gonna put it on th' shelf in th' spring house whur hit won't git too cold ner too hot. Ye git it *too* cold, an' hit won't work off!

"An' ye let it ferment fer 'bout three er four weeks till hit stops a-bubblin, an' then hit's ready t' jar up! An' 'at's how ye make kraut!"

"I hope it works," Alice thought as she drifted off. "If it spoils, I've wasted five heads of cabbage and a lot of time ... but then ... it was fun."

In the back bedroom, Daniel was lying in his bed waiting for sleep to come too. His thoughts were about the speech lesson Demus had given him while they were making fish traps. He moved his tongue around in his mouth the way Demus had taught, and when he thought it was in just the right position, he would make a soft sound, repeating it until he got it just right.

"I'm *astounded* at the progress you've made, Snake Man," Demus had told him. "The chief of the Cherokee Nation would be very proud of you too! If you keep up your good work, you can go back to school speaking like any other boy."

"Speaking like any other boy ... speaking like any ... other ... boy ..."

And at about the same instant his mother drifted off into dreamland, he did as well.

At twenty minutes past one a.m., the night was filled with a horrible scream! Alice was jolted from her sleep and sat up in bed, afraid that what she had heard was not a nightmare. Daniel woke up, rolled over on his side, and watched as Dawg jumped out of bed and ran to the window.

"*Sonny!*" Alice called out. "*Did you hear that noise?*"

Dawg stood at the window twitching and whining, his night-seeing eyes glued to the chicken house.

"*What was it, Mama?*" Daniel called out. He eased out of bed and ran to her room.

Alice was sitting on her bed, her robe already on, putting on her slippers.

"Light a lantern," she said. "I think that panther is back."

While Daniel was lighting the lantern, a crash came from the direction of the chicken house, and the chickens erupted in panic.

Alice ran out on the porch and looked around the corner toward the chicken house and saw a gaping hole in the fence. A dark being was crouched at the small opening the chickens used to get into their shelter.

"*Mama,*" Daniel cried, "*don't doh out there! Dit back inside!*"

As he stood at the door with the lantern, begging his mother to come in, Dawg ran past him, down the stairs, and around the house toward the intruder.

"*Dawg!*" Alice screamed. "*Get back here! Get back on this porch!*"

She made a move toward the steps, and all at once the air was filled with violent screams and cries. Dawg's yelps were of panic, and pain, and anger, and they built and faded with each moment.

Alice grabbed the lantern from Daniel and ran down the steps yelling and screaming at the top of her lungs, begging the melee to stop, pleading with Dawg to come to her.

Every emotion that Daniel had ever known surged through his system. He ran back into the house knowing the only thing he could do—the only chance he had—he ran in his mother's room and jerked the flintlock rifle off the wall.

"Don't ever touch that rifle!" his father had told him more than once, and more than once he had promised his father that he never would, but now the vow was broken. He made a run for the door, and as he went, he felt the spirit of his father urging him on.

"*Run, Sonny! Your mama needs you! Run, boy!*"

When Daniel reached the porch, the sound of the fight had ended. The only sound he could hear was his mother crying.

"*Mama...Mama,*" he called out.

"*Don't move, Sonny,*" she screamed. "*It's up the sycamore tree. It's right above me!*"

Sonny looked out at his climbing tree, and from about eight feet up, two glowing, yellow eyes looked back. They were like the eyes of the devil himself—fiery and piercing.

His mother was crying softly—the crickets were singing their song—and he was pulling back the hammer—and aiming—aiming between the two piercing, yellow eyes.

The gun exploded with a roar like a mighty artillery piece—louder by ten than Will's .44. The recoil sent Daniel across the porch and crashed him against a rocker. There was a thump in the yard, and his mother screamed a long, shrill scream that echoed and bounced across the valley with the gun's report.

When he had righted himself, Daniel moved cautiously down the steps and toward his mother, crying as he went, not knowing what to expect.

He reached her, and she was standing above the lifeless body of the enormous cat. The light of her lantern reflected in its still-open eyes.

"Go get Will," she said softly. "Dawg is hurt."

———◆———

Will had heard the first scream of the cat. It was faint, but it had awakened him, and he sensed that it was coming from Alice's direction. He had gotten out of bed and had pulled on his pants and boots. He had stuck his Colt revolver in his waist band and walked out of the house.

When he got to the road he heard the melee as Dawg and the cat tangled. When the flintlock sounded he knew exactly what it was, and then he heard another scream that was different from that of the cat. That scream, he knew, was Alice.

He set off in a run across the bridge, kicking rocks as he went but managing to stay upright. Adrenalin propelled him. He ran quickly and effortlessly through the darkness.

When he met Daniel, the boy was crying. He was out of breath and bruised from a fall on the road. Will picked him up and continued to run, not knowing what he would find, because Daniel was unable to tell him.

Preacher Babb was already at Alice's house when he got there. He was sitting on the ground comforting her, and she was still reeling from her ordeal.

He rushed to her and was holding her in his arms before he saw the beast lying by her lantern.

"Are you all right?" he asked. "What on earth have you been through?"

"I'm alright now ... but Dawg's hurt. He's in the chicken yard."

When Will reached Dawg, he was motionless but panting. A long, deep gash crossed his shoulder and ran several inches down his front leg. He was covered with blood, but it looked like the worst of the bleeding had stopped. By that time two more men had arrived. Artis and James Plumlee had rolled up on James' wagon carrying lanterns and rifles. James was gripping his rifle with both hands and his lantern was dangling from his right wrist.

"Whut's goin' on?" James asked.

"Whut was 'at mighty boom an' all 'at hollerin'?" Artis wanted to know.

When Preacher Babb motioned to the cat and the two men saw it, they both jumped back and readied their rifles.

"*Good Lord!*" Artis exclaimed. "*Look at th' size o' 'at animal!*"

"*Did you shoot 'im, Preacher?*" James asked as he eased forward and looked the beast.

"I didn't shoot him. ... Sonny did," the preacher said. "Shot him right out of that Zacchaeus tree."

"*'At youngun shot him?*" James asked. "*Whut did he use ... a cannon? Hit might near blowed off th' top o' hits head!*"

"Whur is 'at boy anyhow?" Artis asked.

The preacher pointed toward the house. "He ran off inside."

From out of the shadows, Will appeared carrying Dawg.

"Mr. Plumlee ... I need to get my dog down to Doc's," he said with some urgency. "Will you take me in your wagon?"

"Looks lack 'e needs it!" James said. "Course I will!"

"I'll go with you," Alice said softly to Will. "You need me right now more than Sonny does." Then she turned to Preacher Babb. "Preacher, will you take care of Sonny while I'm gone?" she asked.

"Don't you worry, Alice," he said. "Artis and I'll see to his every need."

———

Doc stood over Dawg, his robe hanging loosely around him. His hair was wild, and sleep was still in his eyes.

"He's in shock, Will," he said. "Fear and blood loss." He gently lifted Dawg's head and looked into his eyes. "But look here!" he said. "You still have that sparkle in your eyes though, don't you, boy?"

Doc gently lay Dawg's head back down on the table and began to examine his shoulder wound. He pulled back the skin on his shoulder and looked deep inside. Alice turned away and buried her face in her hands.

"See this muscle here, Will, and this one?" he said. "They're torn and need stitching ... and there's a nerve that runs down the side of this one. ... Doesn't look like it's damaged. . . . Hope not. The main thing though," he said as he raised up and looked at Will, "the bleeding has stopped."

He bent down again and examined the rest of Dawg's body and looked in his mouth.

"Look here, Will," he said. "He lost a canine tooth! I just bet if you look at that cat real close, you'll find it buried in him somewhere. This old boy really put up a fight. I guess you noticed that all his wounds are on the front part of his body. Looks like he stood toe to toe with th' creature. ... Yep, he's hurt bad ... but I think ... can't guarantee it, but I think he's gonna be just fine!"

Alice moaned, and great convulsive sobs came from deep in her chest. Will turned and grabbed her just as her knees began to buckle.

"It's all right now," he told her as he held her. "You're all right, ... Dawg's all right, ... and that little man of yours is all right. Matter of fact," he said as he rocked her back and forth, "the whole valley's all right now."

Thirty-Three

Another New Hero

Esther stood over Will's bed with her hands flailing the air. "*And I just slept through it?*" she shouted.

Will had just told Esther what had happened the night before, and he wasn't gentle in the way he told her. She had awakened him at seven a.m. on Saturday morning, thinking something must be wrong for him to be sleeping so late.

"I thought you must be *dead!*" she told him.

"I didn't get home until almost five o'clock," he said tersely.

"Well, why didn't you wake me up?"

"Esther! I didn't even know anything was wrong until I got to the road, and then things started getting a little bit urgent!"

Esther wheeled around and stomped toward the door. "Well, I'm going to check on Alice! You can lie in bed for the rest of the day for all I care!"

As soon as Esther was out of the room, Will swung his legs over the side of the bed and sat for a moment with his elbows on his knees and his face in his hands. Finally, he pulled himself to an upright position and looked around for his boots.

"Give me time to get cleaned up a little," he called out to Esther, "and I'll go with you. Goodness knows I won't get back to sleep now anyway."

There were daily chores that needed to be done. The chickens and the horses needed to be fed; the garden needed to be checked and vegetables picked; there was housework that needed to be finished; but chores along with sleep would have to wait. Esther had made up her mind!

As they pulled out of the barnyard onto the road, Esther's questions began. She was particularly interested in Alice and Daniel and wanted to know if Doc French had checked them out.

Will said that he hadn't, but that he didn't think it was necessary. "I was with Alice and all that was wrong with her was a bad case of nerves," he explained.

"As for Daniel, he had a skinned knee and elbow where he had fallen, and a bruised shoulder from the recoil of the flintlock. That's just normal wear and tear on an active boy," he said.

"Can't you go any faster?" Esther asked.

"And why do you want to go faster?" Will asked in return.

"I just can't imagine poor Alice at home alone with a bruised up child after all that happened to her. She must feel so all alone. She's probably coiled up in a corner waiting for another panther to leap through the window. Oh, please, Will," she begged. "Go just a little faster!"

When the house came into view, it was obvious that Alice and Daniel were not alone. Several wagons and saddle horses littered the yard. One group of men was gathered at Roamer Robinson's wagon where a quart jar was being passed around. On the other side of the yard, Preacher Babb and Demus were squatting down close together having a serious discussion; but the largest group of men along with some boys had gathered under the sycamore tree. They were standing over the body of the panther, talking and gesturing.

"Looks like word got out," Will said. "News travels like a rifle shot in the valley."

Before his wagon was in the yard, Will was met by Jasper Jeter.

"Will," he said, "wonder if ye could git that Day boy t' come out o' th' house. I wanna talk to 'im 'bout tannin' 'at painter's skin fer 'im like I did 'at bar skin fer Goober. Ain't never tanned a painter skin b'fore, an' 'at un's a beauty!"

"Well Jasper," Will answered, "I'd hate to disturb the boy, but I'd say he'd appreciate it. Why don't you go ahead and do that? I'll see to it that he knows what you're doing."

As Will was turning into the yard, a cheer went up from Roamer Robinson's group followed closely by cheers and applause from the group under the sycamore. Preacher Babb and Demus stood and turned toward the house. Daniel was standing on the porch with a bewildered look on his face.

"*Thar 'e is!*" someone shouted.

"*Come on out here, boy, and tell us 'bout shootin' 'at creature!*" someone else shouted.

When some of the boys started running toward the porch, Daniel retreated into the house. The door slammed, and through the window, he could be seen running toward his mother's bedroom.

"I hope he doesn't start withdrawing like Makepeace did," Will said. "He has enough problems without adding that to his list."

When Will and Esther got to the front door, Alice cracked it, peeked out, and invited them in. She was in her housecoat, and her hair was wrapped up in a piece of cloth. Esther lost no time in embracing her.

"What can I do?" Esther asked as she held Alice close.

"You've already done it," Alice answered. "You came."

Esther loosened her embrace, stepped back, and raised her voice. "Can you believe that Will let me sleep through all of that?" she asked.

"At least *he* didn't sleep through it," Alice said, and she reached out and touched Will's arm. "He was my shelter in the storm last night," she said to Esther, but as she spoke to Esther, she was looking at Will.

All of a sudden, Daniel burst through the bedroom door carrying the flintlock. "*Mama,*" he said excitedly, "*can I show them boys my gun?*"

Alice put her hand to her face and turned to Will.

"I'll go with him," Will said. "I think it would be good for Daniel to do that."

When Will and Daniel stepped out onto the porch, the cheers started again, and once more the boys ran toward him, with most of the men coming too. This time Daniel stood his ground and greeted his admirers.

"Sonny," one of the boys said as they pushed and shoved to get close, "did you really shoot that painter lack 'em men said ye did, er did somebody else really shoot 'im?"

"I shot him right between the eyes!" Daniel said. "It wad easy as pie!"

"*Gaw!*" one of the boys said. "Ye shot 'im with 'at ol' gun?"

"Ain't nothin' wrong wid this old gun," Daniel said. "It's all in knowin' how to shoot it!"

"Hey, Sonny, why ain't ye talkin' funny like ye used to?" someone else asked.

Daniel threw his chest out and looked around at the group. "Cause Demus Whitedeer, chief Indian of Avery Cove, an' me hab been workin' on my talkin' an' his socializin', and that's a fact!"

"*Gaw!*" several boys said in unison.

"Did 'e teach ye t' shoot a bow?" someone asked.

"We don't fool with them things!" Daniel answered with confidence. "We just shoot big-bore guns!"

"*Gaw!*" they said again.

"Sonny, ye wanna play Indians?" one of the boys asked.

"Can't right now ... maybe later," he answered. "Me and Will have got to go down t' Doc French's and check on my dog."

He looked up at Will with hope in his eyes, and Will nodded yes.

———

"Sonny the dragon slayer!" Doc said when he opened the door. "Dawg and I have been hoping you'd come. Glad to see your mother and Will and Esther, too."

Doc held the door while the group entered and he motioned toward the hallway. "Come on in and we'll go back to my dog hospital, and you can visit the patient."

Doc led the party back to his own bedroom where Dawg was lying in the corner on an old blanket. He lifted his head and wagged his tail when he saw Daniel.

"How's he doing, Doc?" Will asked.

"Can he come home?" Sonny wanted to know, and he knelt down and patted Dawg's head.

"He's doing fine," Doc said. "He actually got up and limped outside to do his business a while ago. … Then he came back in and drank some water … but it wore him out. Preacher Burden brought some calf's liver over, and I'm gonna see if I can get him to eat it. If he'll eat and build up his strength, I think he can go home in a few days. Now … how are you four doing?"

"About like you," Alice said. "We need sleep, but this is more important for Daniel. Now that he's seen Dawg, he'll probably go home and take a long nap."

"He's not the only one," Will said, yawning.

Will rose before dawn on Sunday morning after a sound, uninterrupted night's sleep.

The day before was a blur. After the group left Doc French's office, he had gone by Burden's store so Esther could send her telegram to Blanch. While they were there, Daniel had seen more admirers, Preacher Burden gave him a sack full of candy for killing the beast that had haunted his cattle, and his hand had been shaken by at least a half dozen men.

Now, as he puttered around the house, Will wondered how the events of the previous day would impact him and those close to him. Daniel would most certainly be the one who would see the most change. Not only was he now accepted by his peers, he was admired by them! Will considered that Daniel's newfound popularity would probably mean he would see less of him, but maybe, he reasoned, that would not be all bad. The boy needed to be doing things with other boys during his formative years.

Alice, too, would be affected. Now her Sonny would go back to school, and she would be freed of her teaching responsibility. More importantly though, she would be freed from seeing Daniel grow up without friends his own age.

While Will was out gathering vegetables and collecting his meager supply of eggs, Esther got up and started preparing breakfast. With the chicken flock still growing to a more productive size, she resorted to her old standby— oatmeal, coffee, and a slice of grilled bread with a smattering of butter. This, on a Sunday morning, would tide them over until the mid-day meal of fresh vegetables and cornbread.

Esther was quiet during breakfast. It seemed she was back to her gloomy mood about having to return to Wilmington. When she had finished her oatmeal, she took a deep breath and looked up at Will.

"I'm thinking about going back to Wilmington early," she said.

"Are you serious?" Will asked. "I thought you were happy here."

"That's just the problem," Esther said. "If I wait till the last minute, I'll be so dejected when I get back that I may not be able to function. Maybe Blanche and I can cheer each other up."

Will got up and poured a second cup of coffee and sat down again.

"Well, Esther," he said, "if you think that's what you need … I'll take you to Burley."

Esther stood and put her hand on Will's hand.

"It's just a thought, Brother. I'll let you know," she said. "I'm going to get ready for church."

———

For the first time in anyone's memory, Will would be early for church! The stars and planets had aligned in such a way that his and Esther's preparations went smoothly, and the ride down the road was going amazingly well.

Since Judy had seen an abundance of work over the past week, Will had decided to harness Don and Molly to the wagon and give them some exercise. They were showing their appreciation by maintaining a brisk gate.

When they passed Alice's house, all was quiet, but a column of smoke was rising from the kitchen chimney. Will commented that he could smell bacon frying.

Things were quiet, too, when they passed the Plumlee brothers' houses. When Will observed the calm settings, he couldn't help but compare that peaceful morning to early Saturday morning when the Plumlee brothers pulled up at Alice's house with their rifles and lanterns. What a difference a day could make!

After they had passed the Levees' house, they saw a commotion in the road ahead. Approaching them was an oxen-drawn wagon, and the driver was frantically popping a whip above the heads of his beasts.

"Will! That looks like Preacher Burden!" Esther said.

"Can't be!" Will replied. "The preacher wouldn't be out here this hour on a Sunday morning."

But he was! Preacher Burden was standing on the footboard of his wagon desperately urging his oxen along with a whip. Even from a distance Will could tell the preacher was beside himself. As Will's wagon approached him, the preacher pulled his wagon to a stop, sat down, and tried to catch his breath. Will pulled up beside him and jumped down onto the road.

"Preacher," he called out. "Where are you going? What's wrong?"

The preacher cut his eyes over at Will. He was breathless and looked desperate.

"Will," he gasped. "I'm glad I found you. I … need your help."

Will climbed up on the seat of the preacher's wagon and took the whip from the preacher's hand while Esther looked on helplessly.

"Tell me what's wrong," Will said calmly.

"It's Rachel, Will … she's … run away … I've got to go to Burley … and find her," he whimpered, and he turned his face away in anguish. "I was hopin' you'd go with me. I don't think … I could make it on my own."

Will turned to Esther who had a blank look on her face.

"Do you think you can drive Don and Molly to the preacher's house and let me drive the preacher's wagon?" he asked.

Esther nodded and took up the reins, looking bewildered.

Will turned the oxen around in the road and started the lumbering trip back toward Preacher Burden's house. He was silent as he worked the beasts, but he was thinking as he went that the situation must be serious. He had never imagined that this pillar of strength—the pastor who dealt with the grief and loss of others on a regular basis—could be lowered to such depths of despair.

When they were well on their way, the preacher began to regain his composure.

"Will," he said as he wiped his eyes, "since you're willing to help me, I guess I better tell you what has happened."

"Thank you," Will said.

"The truth of the matter is, Rachel has run off with ... Peter Paul Lamb. She left a note saying they were going to get ... married. They took my buggy. Said I could pick it up at the livery stable in Burley."

"O, my!" Will said. "I thought you liked Peter Paul ... and you know, daughters *do* eventually get married. I'm sure everything will work out all right."

"I *did* like him ... but I don't anymore," the preacher said angrily, "and I'm going to Burley and *stop* Rachel before she makes a foolish mistake!"

The preacher began to cry again, and Will held his questions. All he could do, he felt, was to help and encourage someone who had helped and encouraged him.

"One thing more," the preacher blubbered. "Don't say anything to Esther about why Rachel ran off. If I can find her and bring her back, maybe you'll be the only person other than her mother and me to know about this."

"Okay," Will said.

———

Will and Preacher Burden left for Burley on Will's wagon, and Esther caught a ride to the Baptist church with Doc French. Her plans were to meet up with Alice and Daniel and stay with them until Will got back—whenever that might be.

Preacher Burden was solemn, and he was silent until they had passed Caldwell Turpin's mill.

"They got a big head start on us, Will," he said as they started down the grade.

"What time did they leave?" Will asked.

"I have no idea," the preacher replied. "Naomi and I were sound asleep when she snuck out?"

"When *they* snuck out?"

"Peter Paul didn't leave from my house, Will," the preacher said. "I made him leave my house Saturday evening, and I don't know where he went from there. Naomi loaned him my buggy to move his things, and he didn't return it. I figure he came back in the night and spirited Rachel away."

Nothing more was said for several minutes. Will worked at keeping the wagon out of pot holes, and the preacher stared off silently into the trees that grew up to the road's edge. Finally, when the road leveled and smoothed out a bit, Will spoke up.

"Preacher, you don't have to say any more if you don't want to, but I think there must be a lot more to this than you're telling me."

The preacher made a little whimpering sound before he answered.

"Oh, Will," he said, and he paused to blow his nose. "Rachel and Peter Paul came to Naomi and me Saturday evening and said they wanted to get married. At first, Naomi and I were pleased. ... Seemed like a good match. They're about the same age ... they seemed to love each other ... they had similar interests ... and Peter Paul seemed to be a good, God-fearin' boy."

"So what happened? Was Rachel ... I mean did they have to get..."

"O, no! Nothing like that ... worse!" and he began to cry again. "I told 'em I would be happy to marry 'em, and that's when all *Hades* broke loose!"

"Preacher, you're not making sense."

"They said they didn't *want* me to marry 'em, Will," the preacher bawled. "They wanted a ... *priest* to marry 'em! *A priest, Will! ... Peter Paul Lamb turned out to be a Cath'lic! ... A papist! ... Prays to Mary and some so-called saints ... and he's draggin' Rachel down that road! She's joinin' up with him!*"

"So that's what this is all about!" Will thought to himself.

"Can't you go any faster?" the preacher asked.

———

I t was late afternoon when they got to Burley. The business part of town was deserted, and the only activity was around the Baptist church where folks were gathering for an evening service.

Their first stop was the livery stable where they found the preacher's buggy parked under a shed and his horse in one of the stalls. The livery operator was nowhere to be found. They found empty stalls, and feed and water for Don and Molly. Will left his wagon in the yard.

Their second stop was at the Burley Lodge. After the preacher had re-peatedly banged the bell at the front desk, a clerk appeared with a napkin tucked under his chin and told him that he hadn't seen anyone matching the descriptions of Rachel and Peter Paul. When the preacher asked about any trains leaving town, the clerk said one had left around three p.m.

"Let's go to the depot, Will," the preacher said dejectedly.

The station master turned out to be the same one Will had talked to when he came down to pick up Esther. Will reintroduced himself and Preacher Burden, and the station master readily remembered him as the fel-low who brought back memories of Wilmington.

"How's ye sister?" the station master asked. "She like it better up 'ere than she did down on th' coast?"

Will thanked him for asking, told him that Esther was fine, and assured him that she loved the mountains as much as she hated Wilmington.

"I knowed she would," the station master said.

"Sir," the preacher said as he stepped up beside Will, "I wonder if you could help us out. We're looking for a couple that may have left on your train that pulled out around three o'clock ... an attractive, young couple travelin' light."

"Now let's see," the station master said as he rubbed his chin and looked upward. "There was this one couple. ... early twenties, I reckon. ... she was purdy ... thin ... dark hair. He was a blond-headed feller ... wearin' a cream-colored suit ... an'... I remember he was a-wearin' a cream-colored derby!"

"Oh, Lord!" the preacher said. "And they left out on the train?"

"Yes'r, shore did. Bought tickets fer Washin'ton D.C.!"

The preacher's countenance fell like a rock, so much so that Will moved in close to him, afraid that he might collapse.

"Mister," he said softly to the station master, "I'm Preacher Burden, the telegraph operator in Avery Cove. Can you send a message to my wife at the office there? She'll be at the store first thing in the morning."

"Why shore, Preacher Burden! I key you folks all the time. What do you want me to say?"

"Just say, 'Too late ... she's gone,'... and sign it Eli."

"Well all right," the station master said with concern in his voice. "I'll get it out first thing in th' mornin'. By th' way, I have another message t' forward t' your station in th' mornin'. It's to a ... Will Parker."

"That's me!" Will said.

"Well happy day!" the station master said. "I'll give it to ye now, an' save th' trouble o' sendin' it!" He shuffled some paper on his desk and pulled out a yellow note pad. "It says: 'Me and Janie Rose run off Saturday and got married. Never happier. Makepeace'."

"Hallelujah!" Will shouted, and his arms shot up in the air. "I can't *wait* to tell Roamer and Sweetie! Isn't that *great*, Preacher?"

Preacher Burden didn't answer. He sat down on a chair and cried silently.

"I wish I knew what's going on," Esther said to Alice. "I just can't get over the way Preacher Burden was carrying on. You would have thought that Rachel had died!"

"You don't think that she's gone and gotten herself ..." and she looked over to make sure Daniel wasn't looking before she patted her belly.

"You never know," Alice whispered. "Ol' Peter Paul Lamb may be hiding out in the hills right now, waiting for the preacher's shotgun to rust."

"Wonder if they'll get the little one a cream-colored derby?" Esther whispered back with a grin.

"I sure hope they don't, if it's a girl!" Alice giggled.

"Exactly!" Esther said, and then the smile slowly left her face. "I just hope Will's all right," she said with a serious tone.

Alice didn't answer. She just walked over to the window and looked down the road.

The next morning Will and the preacher left the lodge and walked to the livery stable. The preacher was quiet and forlorn. They were greeted at shed by the livery owner.

"'At your buggy?" the livery man asked.

"Yes, it is," Preacher Burden said. "If you'll get my horse and those two Clydesdales we left, I'll pay you and we'll be on our way."

"Can't do that!" the livery man said.

The preacher bristled. "Why not?" he asked.

"Cause ye got a wheel 'bout t' fall off 'at buggy. 'Em younguns was lucky they made it here."

"Can you *fix* it?" the preacher asked.

"Can t'morrow."

"In heaven's name ... why tomorrow?" the preacher asked indignantly.

"Cause th' smithy ain't here t'day. 'At's why, mister!"

"Wait a minute," Will said. "Do you think we could get the buggy on my wagon?"

The livery man walked around behind Will's wagon and looked, glancing back and forth between the wagon and the buggy.

"If ye'll git 'at canvas cover off 'ere, I think we might git th' buggy on sideways. ... Let th' wheels hang off on either side. We can take off th' horse shafts an' lay th' top down, an' ye ort t' scrape by long as th' road don't git too narrow."

Before long, the buggy was loaded up, and the odd-looking sight was headed up the mountain with the preacher's horse bringing up the rear.

"Rides a little smoother with a load," Will said as they bumped along the road.

"Will, I don't know how I'll ever thank you," the preacher said. "I wouldn't have made it without your strong support."

"We all need a little help and comfort now and then," Will answered.

"There's *one* thing though that neither you nor or anyone else will be able to help me with."

"I can't imagine what that would be!"

"I don't know how I'm going to be able to face the community."

"The community will fall over themselves supporting you," Will said. "You've been there for them through thick and thin."

"But a preacher is supposed to be above reproach, Will. He's supposed to be able to at *least* influence his own family in a positive way … keep *them* from strayin'. I've failed in that regard!"

"Preacher, Rachel is a grown woman. There comes a time when you're not *supposed* to control her."

"'Train up a child in the way he should go, and when he is old, he will not depart from it'! That's the Scripture, Will. I failed to train Rachel up in the way she should go."

"But Preacher, are we wise enough to judge whether or not Rachel has 'departed' from your training? Isn't there a chance that this may work out for the best?"

The preacher didn't answer. He turned and gazed out again through the trees that lined the roadway, deep in thought.

After a few minutes he turned back to Will.

"I trusted that boy, Will," he said. "I swallowed his list of credentials hook, line, and sinker. We needed a teacher so bad that I *snapped him* up without checkin' him out. You know in his letter where he said he had been a Sunday school teacher?"

"I remember," Will said.

"I should have checked *that* out! Turns out he taught Sunday school at a Catholic church! Who would have imagined that someone of his faith would apply to a little mountain school like ours ... much less *want* to come?"

"I had a couple of friends in high school who were Catholics ... seemed like real good folks ... strong in their faith. We didn't agree on everything, but we did agree on important things."

"We're talking about our little children, Will. I let 'em down!"

"You did the best you could, Preacher. Good school teachers aren't easy to find."

"How well I know it ... and now we're without one ... three weeks before school starts and we don't have a teacher ..."

For the first time it hit Will! He hadn't even thought of the prospect that Peter Paul Lamb wouldn't be back!

"... and the mamas and daddies in the valley have put their trust in me," the preacher continued.

Will felt his ears turn red as the prospect of a teacher opening slapped him in the face.

"They'll *kill* me, Will! I'm *ruined!*"

"Not if you go out and find another teacher!"

"Be sensible, Will. All the good teachers are tied up by now. I'm not going to find anyone to move to our little community this time of year."

"What if we had someone living in our community ... a qualified, experienced teacher you could talk to ..."

The preacher's jaw dropped, and his eyes became as large as silver dollars.

"You mean ... *surely* not! She wouldn't consider ... *would* she, Will?"

"You'd have to ask her ... use your powers of persuasion ... see if you could tear her away from the fresh seafood and the peaches. You know, the peaches are really good down on the coast."

The preacher was getting excited. For the first time in two days he was thinking about something other than Rachel.

"Oh, *Will*, but would she break her contract? *Surely* she's signed a contract!"

"Maybe she could come up with a person who needs a job ... someone who could take her place."

"Will you talk to her for me, Will?" the preacher begged.

"I'll go with you," Will said, "but you'll have to do the talking. I don't know that much about these things."

The preacher sat upright, breathing deeply through his mouth. His eyes blinked rapidly as thoughts raced through his brain.

"Can't you go any faster, Will?" he asked.

———

W ill's wagon with its unusual load rolled into Avery Cove late Monday afternoon. Preacher Burden became jittery as they approached the store.

"Look at that bunch gathered on my porch," he said. "Looks like a gang of vultures waitin' for me to get back."

"They're your friends, Preacher."

"At least they can help us lift this buggy off. Then we've just *got* to find your sister."

"Wouldn't you rather just wait until in the morning?" Will asked.

"I'd like to talk to her today," the preacher answered. "That way, I *might* get some *sleep* tonight."

When Will and the preacher pulled into the yard of the store, the men on the porch walked down the steps to greet them.

"Howdy, Preacher," one of them said. "Missed ye in church."

"Wonder if you fellows could help Will get my buggy off the wagon?" the preacher asked as he climbed down.

"Don't never 'member you not bein' at church b'fore," someone else said.

The preacher didn't answer. He lumbered up the stairs and into the store where he was met by Naomi and Doc French.

"Preacher," Doc said as he rose from his chair by the stove, "are you all right? I've been worried about you."

"Thanks, Doc," he answered, and he continued to walk through the store toward the back room. "Naomi," he said, lowering his voice, "let me see you in the back."

In a few minutes, the preacher emerged from the back room.

"Doc," he said as he walked toward the front door, "I wonder if you could follow Will and me up to find Esther Parker. We have some school business to talk about."

"Sure … I guess so," Doc said as he stood.

The preacher walked out of the store, down the steps, and climbed back on Will's wagon.

"We'll just leave my horse and buggy here for the time bein'," he said to Will as he took his seat. "Let's go to your house."

"Uh … I think Esther will probably be at Alice Day's," Will said.

"Then go there!" the preacher answered with resolve.

———

Alice Day stood by the window, looking down the road. All at once she shifted. "Esther, here comes Will!" she said. "He has Preacher Burden with him."

Esther stood and walked toward the window.

"And Doc French is coming behind them in his buggy," Alice added.

"Oh goodness," Esther said. "I hope nothing's wrong."

The two women walked out on the porch and watched as the rigs turned up the drive and stopped in the yard. They saw solemn looks on the faces of all the men, but the look on Preacher Burden's face was particularly somber.

No one spoke as the men got down. The preacher led the trio up the steps, and they stopped on the porch.

"Esther … Alice," the preacher said, nodding to the two women. "I guess you can see we're back."

Alice held out her hand toward the preacher and took his arm.

"Preacher Burden, please come in," she said. "Everybody come in," she added.

When they were inside, Alice motioned to the sofa and chairs.

"Everyone … please sit down. I'll put on some coffee."

"Dear Lady, we won't take time for that," the preacher said, "but everybody *do* sit. I need to have a word with … Esther."

Esther looked at the preacher with a surprised look on her face.

"The rest of us can wait outside," Will said, turning toward the door.

"No! *Please* sit … all of you!" the preacher said, and a look of stress came over him. "Sooner or later all of you are gonna know the truth, and I'd like to have some *witnesses* that I at least tried to do the right thing."

Doc French stared into the preacher's face with a look of concern. Will and Alice took a quick look at each other.

The preacher turned to Esther. He gripped the brim of his hat with both hands and squeezed tightly.

"Miss Parker … Esther," he said. "The truth of the matter is … my daughter has run off with Peter Paul Lamb … and by now they're probably married."

"Oh, Preacher Burden," Esther said. "She'll come back to you. You'll see … she'll be back!"

"*No, she won't!*" The preacher roared. His face turned red, and beads of sweat popped out on his forehead.

Doc put his hands on the arms of his chair and almost stood up, but he thought better of it.

"I won't *let* her come back, especially with that … husband of hers. He's of a *foreign faith*. He's a … *Cath'lic!*"

Silence filled the room as the preacher pulled out a handkerchief and wiped his eyes. Alice looked at Will in disbelief.

"That's why I'm comin' to you, Miss Parker … Esther," he said in a calmer voice. "I'm comin' to *beg* … to *plead* with you to please consider stayin' here in our little valley … to teach our children!"

Esther's fingers flew to her face, covering her mouth, and she gasped behind them. Her hands trembled.

The silence of the room continued as the others cut their eyes toward each other. Doc slid forward in his seat.

"It pays $300 a year," the preacher said, still gripping the brim of his hat, "and … and that's the same thing we'd pay a *male* teacher!"

Esther continued to stand wide-eyed and silent, her mouth agape behind her fingers.

"And I'll let you stay in one of my houses … *free!*" the preacher added. "You can take your choice of 'em!"

Esther's eyes turned toward Will, and Will winked. Her eyes turned back toward the preacher.

"I'll find $325.00!" the preacher said.

"*I'll throw in free medical care!*" Doc shouted from the edge of his seat.

"*Atta boy, Doc!*" The preacher hollered, and he tightened the grip on his hat. "*Esther … I'm beggin' … please say you'll do it!*"

"Say it, Esther … say it!" Alice said softly.

Will cleared his throat. "Preacher, Esther could stay with me," he said calmly, "that is, if she even *decided* to stay. That should be worth another $25.00, wouldn't you think?"

"*Three-hundred and fifty!*" the preacher screamed.

Esther couldn't speak, but from behind her hands, her head began to nod—slowly at first and then with intensity. Tears rolled down her face and flowed down her fingers.

The group got up and gathered around Esther and the preacher, thanking them both and celebrating. And while all the attention was focused on them, Alice's hand reached around and rested on Will's back.

Then, amid the celebration, the preacher eased toward the door, his energy spent.

'Doc," he said almost in a whisper, "how 'bout takin' me home."

———

D aniel sat across from his mother with his elbows on the table. His Indian feathers were stuck in the ribbon tied around his head. His hands and face were filthy!

"Why did you want to talk to me, mama?" he asked. "Did I do tomethin' wrong?"

"No, Sonny, you haven't done anything wrong. You've had a good day. I just have a surprise for you, and you'll be the first of the boys to know."

"What is it?"

"Well, you know how Mr. Lamb was going to be your teacher?"

"Yes."

"Well, he's not going to be your teacher anymore."

Daniel had a blank look on his face.

"Why not?" he asked.

"Cause Esther's going to be your teacher now."

"*Esther's going to be my teacher?*" Daniel hollered.

"That's right, but from now on, she'll be 'Miss Parker' to you, Sonny boy!"

Thirty-Four

WILL AND ELLIE BUTCHER

A man gets to know his old ax handle after he's lived with it for a while. He memorizes the size and taper of the stick as it slides through his hand on the down stroke, and it becomes familiar to him—as familiar as the feel of his own hands. A new ax handle always feels strange.

Will stroked a brand new ax handle as he walked down the steps of Burden's store. He examined it with his eyes as well as his hands, trying to get to know it, for it would be a close friend for years to come—a partner in his work.

He was so preoccupied with his new tool that he didn't hear Doc French call to him as approached, so Doc called a second time.

"*Will! Will Parker! You ignorin' me?*"

"Mornin', Doc," Will answered. "You caught me with my mind on something else. What can I do for you?"

"Well, I think it's about time for that old mutt of yours to be dismissed from my hospital. He's eatin' me out of house and home!"

"That's good news for you and me both," Will said. "Especially good for you since I just happen to have a little cash money in my pocket. I reckon we can settle up."

"*Man!*" Doc declared. "I wish all my customers paid like you do! I've hit a regular cash flow jackpot since you came to town."

"It'll be good for Daniel, too," Will said. "I guess Dawg will be staying at his house permanently. After what happened he probably feels a sense of duty over there, and he'll be good company for Alice when Daniel goes back to school."

———————

I n Avery Cove the first day of school always came on the first Monday of September. On the eve of that Monday, Esther was busy going over her roll book.

"Six boys and seven girls," she said in Will's general direction.

Will marked the page in his almanac with his finger and rested it on the arm of his chair.

"I would have thought it would be the other way around," he answered. "You, know ... more boys than girls."

"Preacher Burden says there are a few more school-age boys, but their fathers keep them out to work on the farms. I thought I had left that kind of thinking back in Wilmington."

"Speaking of Wilmington, I wonder how Blanche will cope with the problems you had down there."

"Blanche can deal with it," Esther said. "She grew up there, and she's used to it. At least she can relax now, having a job and my house to live in."

Will laid his almanac on the arm of the chair, got up, and walked over to the window.

"Esther ... how many students will graduate this year?" he asked

"I'll have two boys and two girls in the eighth grade. If things go well, all four will finish."

"You know, Sis," he said. "I was looking at some of those boys in church this morning. A couple of them are pretty big. Think you can keep 'em in line?"

"I won't have any problem with them!" Esther answered confidently.

"So what will you do if they give you a hard time?"

Esther looked up from her papers. "I'll just give 'em 'the look'!"

"The *look?*"

"Exactly! Works every time! You remember Miss Abercrombie in grammar school, don't you?"

"Ah!" Will said, raising a finger. "*That* kind of look! Just be careful you don't injure somebody ... or peel the paint off the walls."

Esther shook her finger directly at Will's face. "Discipline will *not* be a problem in *my* class," she said.

Esther finished writing her name on the chalkboard and turned to face her class.

"Good morning, everyone! I am your teacher, Miss Parker."

She waited for a reply that didn't come before she repeated herself. "*Good morning, everyone! I am your teacher, Miss Parker!*"

"Good morning Miss Parker," the children said in unison.

"Ah! That's so much better," Esther said. "Now, I know a few of you, but I want to know all of you better. I'd like for each of you to stand, give me your name, and tell me something about yourself ... and I think we'll start with ... this young lady right here."

Esther pointed to a tiny little girl sitting at a desk with a larger girl on the front row. The little girl slid down in her seat trying to disappear.

"She's m' sister," the larger girl said. "This here's 'er first day o' school. Her name's Cricket."

There was a stifled snicker in the back of the room that Esther ignored.

"Well then! Let me look in my book," Esther said, and she turned and took her roll book off the desk. "Now, I don't see a 'Cricket' ... but I do see a girl named Sarah Mae who is starting school today. Would Sarah Mae be your real name?"

"'At's her," the larger girl said, "but she jest goes by Cricket."

"Kin she hop an' chirp?" one of the big boys in the back of the room wisecracked, and the other boys exploded into laughter.

"*That'll be enough of that!*" Esther said taking a step toward the back. She put her hands on her waist and gave the boy a mild version of "the look."

"Yes'm," the boy said as the grin left his face.

"Will you tell the class your last name, Cricket?" Esther asked.

"She's awful back'ards," Cricket's sister said, "an' she don't tawk a lot, but 'er last name's Hopper."

The boys in the back of the room erupted into laughter. Esther was about to use her full-fledged "look" when Daniel jumped to his feet.

"*Shut up, Johnny Paul! Shut up Rupert! An' you too, Benny James! Show Esther some respect ... I mean Miss Parker ... an' show Cricket some respect too. You think she needs to hear 'at stuff?*"

The boys' laughter ceased, and Daniel took his seat.

Esther cleared her throat. "Thank you, Daniel," she said, "but I'll take care of this from now on. Now you boys back there ... since you want to be heard, stand up one by one, please, and tell me your names and something about yourselves. We'll start with you, Johnny Paul!"

———————

Daniel and some of the other boys were playing in the school yard when Esther locked the door and left the school. She was happy that the first day was over, but she was even happier with how it had gone.

As she walked down the steps, Johnny Paul and Daniel ran to the little shed where Judy was waiting and began harnessing her to the buckboard.

"You jest watch," Johnny Paul said to Esther. "Me an' Sonny'll hook up 'is ol' horse fer ye. Can't have no lady harnessin' up a horse when they's men-folk aroun'!"

"Why Johnny Paul, what a gentleman you are!" Esther said. "I'll be sure to tell your daddy how nice you've been."

"Me an' Johnny Paul are gonna go see the boys that ain't here today an' try t' get 'em to come back t' school," Daniel said. "That way, we'll hab more men-folk t' take turns takin' care of Judy!"

"Oh, that's great!" Esther said. "Tell them we need all the *men*-folk we can get. Oh, and while you're at it, tell them we're going to be studying some things that they'll really enjoy!"

She stepped up on the buckboard and took the reins.

"Like whut?" Johnny Paul asked.

"Well, I've been thinking about getting some special guests to come talk to the class about history."

"Gaw!" Johnny Paul exclaimed as Esther snapped the reins and pulled away.

She couldn't wait to see Alice. She wanted to share her day with Will too, but he would have to wait until she had told Alice about Daniel coming to her rescue.

Alice couldn't wait either. She was sitting on the porch steps with Dawg by her side when Esther drove up.

"You survived!" Alice said as Esther brought the wagon to a stop.

"Exactly!" Esther said. "I survived, and if you'll ride with me down to Burden's, I'll tell you how a knight in shining armor saved the day for me and a little girl named Cricket."

"Oooo, can't wait!" Alice said as she got up and climbed the steps. "Let me hang my apron up, and we'll be off."

———————

Will crested the hill at Fa'side and started down the slope on the other side, on his way to Burden's. When he got near the old Tribble place, he came upon Ellie Butcher walking toward the store. Ellie looked back when he got near, and he threw up his hand. "Hello, Ellie," he said as he came to a stop beside her.

"Hey, Mr. Parker," she said.

"Ellie, can I give you a ride?"

"'At would be fine, Mr. Parker," she said. "I been a-wantin' t' tawk to ye anyhow."

Will stuck out his hand and helped Ellie up on the seat.

She was a plain, simple girl in her late teens with a pimply face, and she was a little on the heavy side. He saw her at church with her parents every Sunday, but she wasn't the kind of girl that stood out in a crowd, so he had never talked to her.

"Didn't see your daddy at church last Sunday," Will said as Ellie adjusted her skirt and made herself comfortable.

"He wa'n't thar last Sunday," she said. "He can't sit down. He's got a big carbuncle on 'is …"

She stopped before she revealed the location of the boil and put her hand over her mouth. "He's jest got a big carbuncle," she said.

"Well … tell him I asked about him," Will said. "Maybe he should get Doc French to take a look at his … problem."

He paused, thankful that the discussion about Arlie Butcher's boil was over, then he continued. "What did you want to talk to me about, Ellie?" he asked.

"Well, I was a-wonderin' if 'at man 'at's gonna build 'at mill might need somebody t' work up 'ere a-weavin' cloth er anything."

"Are you a weaver, Ellie?" Will asked.

"Me an' Mama spin flax an' weave linen," she answered. "We make a right smart o' our own cloth fer dresses an' sech."

Will rubbed the back of his neck and thought.

"Well, I'll be glad to tell Mr. Neil about you when he comes back," he said, "but you ought to know that there's a lot of difference between weaving linen and the kind of woolen material that Mr. Neil is going to make."

He went on to explain about the Scottish workers who would be moving to the valley and how they had grown up with the tradition of weaving fine wool. He began to tell her in detail about the water-powered machinery including the automatic looms.

When they arrived at Burden's, they continued to sit on the wagon seat as Will described the process of turning dirty wool into world-class woolen fabric. He told about the cleaning and carding, the stages of spinning, dying, drawing in of the warp, and the weaving process. While he sat and talked, he was transported back to Inverness Mill in Charlotte where life wasn't all bad. He was so caught up in his description of mill life that he didn't notice Esther and Alice pulling up into the store yard. He didn't see them as they got down off the buckboard and went into the store, and when they came out, got on the buckboard and left, he was still absorbed in the telling of life in the mill.

Alice was clearly devastated when she saw Will with another woman. Esther was stunned and didn't know what to say, so she said nothing, making things even worse. They were on the way home, almost to East Road, when Alice spoke up.

"Who was that woman, Esther?" she asked, her voice trembling.

"Alice ... I don't know. I'm as shocked as you must be!"

"You don't know her?"

"I've seen her at church. ... She comes with her mother and father, I think ... but Alice ... I have *never* seen Will pay her any attention or heard him mention her in any way ... I just can't imagine ..."

Ellie's father picked her up at the store on his way back from Turpin's mill, and after he finished his business, Will went on his way toward home. On the way he stopped to see Roamer and Sweetie and found them hard at work. Roamer was busy clearing out a stall in the stable for Traveler to use when he got there, and Sweetie was on the porch shaking out a rug from the room Makepeace and Janie Rose would occupy.

"You're already fixing up for Makepeace and Janie Rose?" Will asked Sweetie.

"We gonna be ready fer 'em," Sweetie said. "Hit ain't ever' day that ye boy comes home an' brings a wife."

When Will got home Esther greeted him at the door with her roll book in her hand. She gave him a quick hug and turned to walk toward the kitchen.

"Uh oh," Will said. "I was hoping you'd be a little happier. Did you have a bad day at school?"

"Oh no, school was wonderful," she answered. "Good class ... everyone was there that was supposed to be. I have a precious little first grader named Cricket."

"How did Daniel do?"

"Daniel was my prize student! He came to my rescue when the older boys started to give me a hard time. Then they settled down and got to work. It's going to be a wonderful year. ...*Oh, Will Parker! Who was that woman I saw you with today?*"

Will turned quickly, and Esther was giving him "the look"! She had her hands on her hips and fire in her eyes. His mouth flew open, and he instinctively took a step backwards.

"*Woman? Esther what are you talking about?*"

"*I saw you sitting on your wagon talking to that other woman at Burden's. I saw you ... and don't you deny it!*"

Will closed his eyes and ran his fingers through his hair.

"Esther ... Esther," he said. "That wasn't a woman."

"*It sure wasn't a man!*"

"Esther, that was Ellie Butcher ... Arlie Butcher's girl. She was walking to the store, and I gave her a ride! She asked me about working at Mr. Neil's mill, and I was *trying* to tell her that just because she weaves *linen*, she wouldn't necessarily be qualified to run a woolen loom! She doesn't have enough *sense* to work in a mill anyway!"

Will's face was red, and he had mussed up his hair by running his fingers through it.

"And while we're at it," he continued, "why are you so all-fired upset about seeing me talking to ... *another woman?*"

Esther sat down at the table and started to cry.

"Oh Will, I'm so sorry," she said. "I wasn't upset for me. … I was upset for Alice."

"Why would you be upset for … Oh, no! Alice wasn't *with* you, was she, Esther?"

Esther put her hands over her face and nodded. Will took a seat beside her.

"What did she say?"

"She didn't say anything. She just sat and looked off into space."

"Should I go over there?"

"Let me talk to her, Will. Maybe I can tell her what really happened and she can get over it without any embarrassment. Maybe it'll never be mentioned."

Will got up and walked to the sink. He put his hands on the counter and looked out the window.

"I guess she feels like she's lost whatever she had with me," he said. "At least she had a friend in me … if nothing more … and now, in her mind, that's gone. She must feel like Preacher Burden feels since Rachel left."

Esther sniffled and wiped her nose with her handkerchief.

"I'll straighten things out with Alice," she said. "We'll be laughing about it before long … but there isn't much I can do for Preacher Burden. I talked to him about Rachel when I went in to tell him how school went, and he still hasn't heard from her. He says it's just like she dropped off the face of the earth. He thinks he'll never see her again."

———

The next day Will was anxiously waiting when Esther came home from school. She bounced up the steps humming a tune, and Will greeted her.

"Another good day?" he asked.

"Exactly!" she answered. "Couldn't have been better! We had a new boy today."

"Did you talk to Alice?"

"Yes, I told her what you told me, and she seemed fine with it. She didn't have a lot to say, but you know … she seemed a little distracted … like she had something else on her mind."

"You think I could go over there? She's not going to throw things at me, is she?"

"I think you'll be safe," Esther answered as she patted him on the arm. "Nobody reloaded that old flintlock rifle, did they?" and she bounced into the house, humming as she went.

———◆———

Alice was sweeping her porch when Will drove into her yard. She stopped sweeping and watched as he set the brake on the wagon and climbed down.

"Hello, Alice," he said from the bottom of the stairs.

"Hello Will," she said in return.

She looked tired, he thought, and Esther's comment about her being distracted was right on target. Her look wasn't unpleasant, but she was unsmiling and unemotional.

"Esther had some really good things to say about Daniel," he said from the bottom of the stairs. "She calls him her 'knight in shining armor.' "

"He's my knight, too," Alice said, and she propped her broom against the door casing. "You can come up and sit, if you like."

"I was afraid you might be too busy for a visit. I almost didn't come."

"You're welcome anytime, Will … you know that," she said as they were seated.

"Well … I came to ask you out," Will said. "You know, we never go anywhere. If we see each other, it seems you end up cooking for me … so I want to take you out courting!"

Alice put her hand to her cheek and looked away.

"I don't …" she said before she became silent.

"The Plumlee brothers are having a square dance Saturday night at Artis's barn. Grandpa Plumlee is gonna play fiddle, and there'll be a caller. I understand it's sort of a kickoff for all the harvest parties and corn shuckin's that happen this time of year."

Alice looked toward the road as if she was expecting to see someone coming. She gazed silently for several moments.

"Well … you'll go, won't you?" Will asked. "Daniel can come too, of course."

Alice continued to gaze toward the road. Her hands gripped the arms of her rocker.

"I don't think so this time, Will," she said. "I'm not in a party mood these days. I'm just not in a party mood."

Will leaned forward on his rocker.

"Does it have anything to do with you seeing me with Ellie Butcher? I can explain that."

Alice turned to look at him. Her expression had not changed.

"No, Esther explained about that … but the experience did make me realize how much I care about you, Will … and that realization made me remember Matthew and how much I cared about him."

Will sat back in his rocker.

"I thought you had just about decided to get on with life."

Alice's gaze turned back toward the road.

"I find myself looking down the road, expecting to see Matthew walking home," she said. "He left that morning and walked out of sight, and he never came back. They took him to Doc French … and he stayed there until the funeral. I can't get the vision of him walking away out of my mind."

"Don't you think he would want you to get on with your life?" Will asked gently.

"I picked up the family Bible last night, Will. There in the front, a date jumped out at me. Saturday will be the anniversary of Matthew's death."

Will sank into his rocker and turned his head away.

"Is there anything I can do? Is there anything Esther … or anyone else can do?"

"No, Will. Thank you … but no."

Will sat for a moment before he got up and left. When he looked back, Alice was still in her rocker, gazing down the road.

———————

As September progressed, a change came over the valley. About the middle of the month, along the roadsides and on the edge of clearings, dogwood trees began changing to crimson red. In the vacant fields, golden rod and wild sunflowers were in their glory. Splashes of color were appearing everywhere. The green of the mountains was changing to red where the maples and sourwoods stood. A hint of yellow was replacing the green of the poplars, ashes, and chestnuts.

The corn stalks that had stood like emerald soldiers throughout the summer were taking on the brown shades of fall. They bowed their heads and drooped like old men under their burden of ears.

Fields of hay were falling to the farmers' scythes. The seas of green were being replaced by hills of sheaves, stacked for drying.

The animals, too, had begun to prepare for winter. They were building up their fat supplies and growing their heavy coats for the cold months ahead. The birds that had been plentiful in the summer were leaving, and in their place were some with different songs. Soon they would be gone as well, on their way to warmer places.

———————

It was on a crisp, mid-September morning that Esther stood before her class and checked her roll.

"Hurry to your seats, boys and girls," she said. "We have a special guest with us today."

The children scampered to their seats and sat silently as Esther finished checking all the names. Finally, she laid her roll book on the desk and looked out over the group.

"Johnny Paul and Daniel," she said, "you'll recall that on the first day of school I told you we would be having some guests talk to the class about history."

"Yes'm," Johnny Paul said, and he and Daniel nodded their heads.

"Well, today we're happy to have our first guest come to speak to us!"

The boys and girls looked all around the room, but no one out of the ordinary was there.

"When's 'e gonna git 'ere?" Rupert asked.

"He's here now!" Esther answered. "Who can guess who it is?"

The boys and girls looked at each other and shrugged their shoulders.

"I'll give you a hint. Some of you know our guest … especially if you go to the Methodist Church."

Several hands shot into the air.

"*Hit's Preacher Burden!*" someone shouted.

"No, it's not Preacher Burden. Any other guesses?"

This time, no hands were raised, but the children continued to search the corners of the room for a clue.

"Well … since there are no more guesses, I'll turn the class over to our guest who will introduce himself!" Esther said, and she walked to a chair in the corner and sat down.

The room was silent except for the sounds of the children turning in their seats, trying to find the special visitor. Finally, Cricket jumped to her feet and pointed toward Esther's desk.

"*Look!*" she hollered.

From behind the desk, two feathers standing side by side began to slowly rise. Soon the top of a head appeared, and it was slowly joined by the eyes, face, and body of Nicodemus Whitedeer.

Cricket and most of the other girls squealed and clapped their hands. Several shouts of "gaw" came from the boys.

Demus was wearing his buckskin trousers and beaded vest. The beaded band that held his feathers was around his brow, and across his nose and cheeks he had painted two white stripes. His dark hair was platted into two pigtails that fell across his shoulders.

"Good morning, boys and girls," he boomed with his deep, resonant voice.

The room became ghostly silent.

"My name is Nicodemus Whitedeer, but many know me as 'Demus.' I have lived in this valley my entire life. My father … was a Cherokee Indian, and my mother … was an African slave."

"Gaw," Randall Posey said softly.

"You don't tawk like no Injun," Benny James said.

"Is that right?" Demus said with a curious look. "How do you think Indians talk then?"

"They say stuff like 'how' an' 'ugh' an' stuff like 'at. You tawk like a city man."

Demus chuckled in his rumbling manner.

"As you hear my story today, you'll learn why I talk as I do," he said, "but more importantly, you'll hear the story of my forefathers. I will tell you about the time my people, the Cherokee, were taken from their homes and made to go to another place … a desolate place in the western frontier. I will tell you of The Trail of Tears … or as my people called that journey, '*Nunna daul Isunyi* … The Trail Where They Cried.' "

Demus's eyes focused on the eyes of the children as he told them that in the early 1800's, the Cherokee had adopted in large part the European culture of the white man. "They were not savages!" he said. "They lived in houses and dressed as you do today. Most of the children your age spoke English and went to the mission schools. It was greed for the land of the Cherokee that caused the white men in the 1820s to break their treaties with the Indians and begin pushing them further west."

He told how the government began in the mid 1830s to round up the Cherokee and imprison them in forts until the year 1838, when soldiers forced them to walk to the faraway Indian Territory in the west, beyond the Mississippi River. "That territory is now known by some as '*O-kla-ho-ma*'," he said.

"Four thousand of my people died of starvation, disease, and exposure on that journey," Demus continued, "but many survived, and they and their descendents live there today."

Then he told how his father, a boy of sixteen, escaped the soldiers and hid in the mountains above the valley until he was found and taken in by a kind white man, Seth Leggery. The story unfolded about how his father had married his mother, one of Seth Leggery's slaves. He told the boys and girls that Mr. Leggery had raised his father as a son, and himself as a grandson. He explained that 'Grandfather Leggery' had taught him proper English and encouraged him to read and learn more on his own. He explained further that when Mr. Leggery died, he inherited his house and land.

Then in a low, mysterious voice Demus said, "But my grandfather left me something much more valuable than a house and land."

"Gaw! Whut?" Rupert blurted out.

In the same low, mysterious voice Demus said, "He left me thousands of books and a thirst for knowledge!"

"Whut kind o' books?" one of the girls asked.

"Any kind you could want!" Demus said. "There are books that tell you how to do things, books that make you laugh, books that tell of history, adventure, and faraway lands, stories old and new. Boys, I have a book that tells how to build a log cabin, and make animal traps, and make a bow and arrow! I have books about Daniel Boone and Davy Crockett ... pirates and cowboys!"

"Gaw!" Benny James said.

"And girls, I have books you would enjoy like the 'Little Women' books by Louisa May Alcott. I even have books that tell you how to cook, and sew, and even make yourselves attractive to *boys*!"

The older girls covered their mouths and giggled, and the younger ones squealed and put their heads on their desks.

"I want to read those!" Esther said.

Demus glanced over at Esther and smiled before he continued.

"I haven't told Miss Parker this," he said, "but I am announcing today ... that you children can come with your parents to my home and borrow books to take to your homes to read."

Esther jumped to her feet.

"Oh, Mr. Whitedeer!" she said. "That is the most wonderful thing that could happen to Avery Cove. Children, we have a library!"

———————

Esther left school that day with a little extra bounce in her step. She was seeing her children grow and learn, and since the first day of school, she had added three boys to her roll book. They were behind, but she would work with them to catch up.

Her buckboard turned off East Road and rolled up South Road past farmers working in their fields. Some of their wives were in the yards or on porches taking care of household chores. They had already learned who Miss Parker was, and they waved as she passed. Children too young for school saw her pass as well. They stopped their play and stood and stared as she went by.

When she got to Alice's house, Will was across the road in Alice's corn field. He was stripping the leaves off the stalks and leaving the corn to dry in the sun. When Esther stopped, he walked to the road.

"That looks like a lot of corn for someone who doesn't have any live-stock," Esther said.

"She has a growing boy that likes cornbread and grits and hominy," Will said.

"Shouldn't Daniel be helping you?"

"Daniel will be plenty busy helping me and the Robinsons," Will answered.

"Have you talked to Alice today?"

"I talked to her, but she really didn't talk back. She said 'yes' and 'no' and 'thank you, Will' and that's about all. I'm worried about her, Esther."

"It's still September," Esther said. "Don't be impatient with her."

"I wonder what she would do if I started calling on Ellie Butcher?"

"*Will! You wouldn't!*"

Will took off his hat, wiped his brow on his sleeve, and put his hat back on.

"You're right ... I wouldn't," he said.

Preacher Burden stopped abruptly as he was sorting the mail and examined a letter carefully.

"*Naomi!*" he shouted. "*Come here and look at this!*"

Naomi hurried from the back room and took the letter from the preacher's hand.

"Oh, *finally*, Eli," she said as she opened the envelope. In a strong voice she read out loud.

"Dear Mama and Daddy ... Peter and I are in Washington, D.C. We are happy and well.

"Peter has taken a teaching position at George Washington High School, and I am working part time in a store just a few blocks from the capital building. For the time being, we are living in a rooming house, but we are keeping our eyes open for a place with more space and more privacy. The landlady is nice, but she is very nosy about everything that goes on.

"I am having a hard time getting used to the city. Believe me, it is very different from Avery Cove! There are good and bad things about it, but I will be happy anywhere as long as Peter is there.

"Please try to forgive me for running off as I did, and please forgive Peter as well. We could not live without each other, and leaving was our only option.

"Maybe it is too soon to ask, but would you let us come home to visit at Christmas? I want to see you and share my experiences. If you don't want us to come back so soon, I will understand. I only hope that one day you will accept Peter and me as man and wife.

"Our address is on the envelope. Please let me hear from you. Your loving daughter, Rachel Lamb."

Naomi lay the letter on the counter and placed her hands on the preacher's shoulders.

"Oh, Eli," she said, "please let me write her. Please say you'll let her come."

The preacher swallowed hard and nodded slightly.

"No, Naomi, don't write her," he said. "The mail's too slow Send her a telegram."

Thirty-Five

GOOBER AND HIS BRIDE

On the morning of October the 7th, the first light over the valley re-vealed a frosty landscape. The first heavy frost of autumn had covered the ground and the surrounding mountains with a layer of white.

Will got up on that frosty morning, dressed, and went directly to the kitchen to start the breakfast fire. While the stove was heating, he filled a bowl with cracked corn and walked out the back door on his way to feed the chickens. He had taken only a few steps when he turned and went back inside to get a coat and swap his straw hat for a woolen cap.

"It's *cold!*" he hollered to Esther. "You'd better dress warmly."

Esther went to the window in her room and pulled back the curtain, revealing a frost so heavy that it looked almost like snow. She had known that cold weather was coming, but she hadn't expected it so soon.

Blanch had shipped the winter clothes she had left in Wilmington, but they had not arrived. They were probably sitting on a railroad siding some-where, she imagined, indifferent to the weather. She did have a warm coat though, thanks to a loan from Will. It was too large and not at all stylish, but it would have to do.

Knowing that a fire would have to be built in the stove at the school, she left a few minutes early. Daniel ran out of the house and across the yard when she approached his house, and true to the game they played each morning, he ran alongside the buckboard and jumped on with it still moving.

"Get your homework done?" Esther asked.

"Yep."

"How's your mama this morning?"

Daniel paused before he answered. "'Bout th' same," he said.

"Still quiet?"

"She does all th' stuff she's 'posed to do 'cept laugh an' talk," Daniel answered.

"Well ... we'll just continue to love her and be patient with her, won't we?"

"I reckon," Daniel replied.

———

About the time Esther and Daniel were getting to school, Will was leaving his barn, bound for Burden's store. Don and Molly stepped high in the cold morning air, and clouds of vapor swirled from their nostrils like smoke from a steam engine.

The school bell was ringing in the distance as the morning light peeked over the eastern ridge. The sun's brilliance struck the frosted trees surrounding the valley and made them sparkle like millions of jewels. Will had seen fall colors before, but not in the depth and profusion he was seeing now. It seemed as though the whole world around him was on fire with color.

He stopped to check on Roamer and Sweetie and found her cleaning up after breakfast. She offered him a cup of coffee, and he gladly accepted.

"Where's Roamer? Is he locked in the outhouse?" Will joked.

Sweetie turned quickly from her stove, formed her mouth into a neat little circle, and looked around to make sure no one was listening.

"He lef' out at firs' light," she whispered. "Went up t' see 'bout his doin's. Hit'll be fruitcake time soon, ye know!"

"Fruitcake time?" Will said.

"'At's right! Ever' year Roamer makes up a batch o' 'is spacial doin's fer folks t' soak their fruitcakes in. Uses cherry juice an' elderberry juice in it … but don't ye tell nobody."

She looked around the room again to make doubly sure no one else was listening.

"People comes frum all over th' valley an' far away as Burley t' buy Roamer's fruitcake soak," she whispered, "even teetotalers! Why … Preacher Burden's wife makes out lack she don't know whut's in it … an' she soaks th' preacher's cake with 'bout a *quart* of it! She says hit's whut makes a fruitcake *spacial*!"

And indeed, when Will got to the store, Preacher Burden was acting like he had already been sampling Roamer's fruitcake soak. He was bouncing around the store like a young boy.

"You're mighty spry this morning," Will said. "What's got you so cheerful?"

"Ah, the world's a better place these days," the preacher answered. "There's a nip in the air this morning, there was a good harvest, Rachel's comin' home for Christmas. … It just seems like everything's coming together, you know!"

Then the preacher straightened up and turned abruptly toward the post office counter.

"By the way," he declared, "there's a letter here for you from Makepeace and one for the Robinsons. Wonder if you'd mind takin' them theirs? You'll have to read it to 'em, you know."

"Glad to," Will replied. "Give me mine, and we'll see what he has to say."

Will tore off the end the envelope, blew it open, and pulled the letter out. He read silently and grinned.

"Says he and Janie Rose are coming the second week in November," Will said. "Says Mr. Neil wants him to get an early start harvesting trees. He mentions the letter to Roamer and Sweetie and wants me to make out like they were the first to know he was coming."

"Well then!" the Preacher declared. "We better get busy with that special welcome Neil wanted us to have ready."

"What welcome is that?" Will asked.

"It's a secret, Will. If Caldwell and I time it right, Makepeace and his wife will be the first to see it. Hope you understand!"

"Well, the suspense will kill me," Will declared, "but if it's something Mr. Neil cooked up to settle the issue of not renaming the valley, I'll be glad to wait with everybody else."

Then he looked around the store. "Anyway," he said. "I came to see if my new harness is here yet."

"Freight wagon will be here this afternoon. You want to hang around or come back?"

"I'll deliver the Robinson's letter and come back," Will said. "Maybe Sweetie will take pity on me and give me something to eat."

———

The freight wagon rolled in at two p.m. behind two tired horses. The driver, Will, and the preacher quickly unloaded it, and the driver was soon on his way to Preacher Burden's pasture to swap his horses for two fresh ones.

The Preacher was sorting his new merchandise when two strangers entered the store.

"You Preacher Burden?" the first one asked.

"That's right," the preacher answered.

"I'm here 'bout th' tele-phones," the man said.

The preacher's eyes got big.

"The *telephones*? What about 'em? I never did take that telephone thing seriously, us being so far away from civilization!"

"A crew's down th' road stringin' line. They'll be here in a day er two. Got an order t' run 'em up t' where th' wool mill's gonna be and t' where a Mr. Makepeace Green is gonna be stayin'. I'll need directions, and I'll need t' know who else wants one."

"How about the switchboard?" the preacher asked.

"My papers say *you* get it. That man that ordered the service must be some sort of powerful man! Most *towns* don't have tele-phones yet."

"This ain't no ordinary place," the preacher said, "and most towns don't have a Glenn Neil! Now … let me get my wife out here to look after things, and I'll give you and your friend here a tour of the valley."

"Oh, I'm not with him," the other man said. "I'm with the state road department. I have a crew comin' up here to do some major road work!"

"*My goodness gracious!*" the preacher declared. That Glenn Neil can sure make things happen!"

———————————

About the middle of the morning, just before the children were to be-gin taking a test, Esther went to the back of the room and closed the damper on the pot-bellied stove. It had become a very warm day considering the fact that it was the third week of October.

"Daniel, open a couple of windows, and let in some fresh air," she said as she walked to the front of the room to write her questions on the blackboard.

She had finished writing the questions for the first group and was begin-ning to write the second group of questions, when a strange sound drifted into the room. She paused and turned her ear toward the window. The stu-dents looked around with curious eyes.

Just as Esther was beginning to think her imagination was playing tricks on her, it came again—a long, high-pitched whistle that ended in a lilt and echoed back and forth between the mountains. Cricket slid down in her seat and pulled her head down between her shoulders.

"Whut wuz 'at?" Rupert asked.

Esther paused with her chalk in midair. Her head turned side to side.

"It sounded like a *train*!" she declared.

Could it be, she wondered to herself, *that some atmospheric anomaly had allowed the sound of a train whistle to travel all the way from Burley?* After all, that was the closest a train came to Avery Cove.

But then in the quiet of the room, as the children listened with open mouths and wide eyes, she heard the chugging of a steam engine.

"*A steam tractor!*" she declared to the children. "*There must be a steam tractor in the valley!*"

The children were enthralled! Most of them had never seen or heard either a train or a steam tractor. They sat in their seats mesmerized—amazed that such a wondrous thing could be within earshot.

The whistle sounded again, and this time it was closer. It was coming from the direction of North Road. All at once the boys jumped up as a group and ran for the door.

"*Stop! Come back here!*" Esther shouted, but it was too late. The boys were going to see that machine even if it meant sitting in the corner for a week! "Well come on, girls," she said, "we might as well see it too," and off they ran as a group.

By the time they got to North Road, the tractor had passed, leaving in its wake a freshly smoothed surface. Walking behind was a team of convicts, chained together and dressed in stripped suits, breaking large stones with hammers, and smoothing out the rough spots.

Then a whistle sounded from the east, and another tractor appeared. This one was fitted with a scraper that was cutting a ditch along the side of the road, and it was followed by another team of convicts.

By golly, this was as good as the circus! People from all over the valley were turning out to watch the procession go by. In addition to the tractors and the convicts, there was a supply wagon, a chuck wagon, and a full complement of guards and state workers, all on parade.

In three days they were gone, and Avery Cove had new roads and a school full of children with visions of the outside world in their brains.

———

"Okay, let's give it a try," the phone man said. "Now, if you want to call the store, take this cord here, and plug it into this jack here, and push this switch forward to ring 'em."

"O Lordie!" Naomi said "I'm as nervous as a cat! Eunice, are you gettin' all this? After all, you're gonna be runnin' it by yourself 'til I get home at night."

"I think so, Miz Burden," Eunice answered. "There's more switches and buttons and things here than I've ever seen, but I guess I can learn it."

"Aw, it's easy," the phone man said, and he went over his directions again. He showed them how to call each and every phone in the valley—all eight of them. He showed them again how to start a call and then end it, and he showed them how to call Burley and keep records for the long distance calls.

"Okay now," he said, "Mrs. Burden, call the store and test their line, and then Eunice, I want you to call Mr. Parker and have him ring back and talk to the doctor."

Naomi sat down at the board and put on the headphones. She plugged in a cord, flipped a switch, and waited until the preacher answered.

"*Eli*," she shouted, "*this is Naomi! We're in business, Eli! Yes … yes … yes … you sound like you're right here beside me! Well, I've got to go. I'll call you back later.*" Then she flipped a switch and cautiously unplugged the cord.

"Mrs. Burden, remember, you don't have to holler," the phone man said. "Now Eunice, let's see you try it."

Eunice sat down and put on the headphones. She slowly plugged in a cord and pushed a switch upward twice. She waited a moment and pushed the switch up again. Suddenly, she sat up straight and threw her hands up.

"Oh my *goodness*," she declared, "he's *talkin'* to me! *Will … Will*," she hollered, "*Lord have mercy, can you hear me?*"

She paused and listened before speaking again.

"Yes! It's *wonderful!*" she declared. "The phone man wants us to hang up, and then he wants you to call back and let me switch you to Doc. Can you do that?"

Eunice nodded her head and smiled, and then she looked over the switch board, unplugged a cord and flipped a switch.

"Excellent!" the phone man said.

In seconds, there was a buzz as Will turned the crank on the other end. Eunice chose a cord, plugged it in, flipped a switch, and spoke to Will before connecting him to Doc. When Doc answered, she put her hands in her lap and breathed a sigh of relief.

Before the phone man left, he had both women calling all over the valley and to the operator in Burley. Another step toward the modern age had been taken.

———

November was ushered in with snowfall. It began in the late afternoon on the first Friday of the month and continued off and on throughout the night. By Saturday morning, six inches of wet snow covered the earth. It clung to the few remaining leaves on the trees, and by the time the sun rose, the heavy burden had stripped the trees bare.

Will was looking out the window, drinking a cup of coffee, when the phone rang. In the past two weeks he had talked on the phone quite a bit and was getting to be an old hand at it, but he wasn't quite prepared for this call.

He walked over and took the ear piece off the phone and put it to his ear.

"Will Parker here," he said.

"Glenn Neil on this end," was the reply.

"Mr. Neil! Is that really *you?*" Will said. "Where are you calling from?"

"I'm in Charlotte," Neil answered, "sittin' here with a fellow named Goober Green! Ever heard of him?"

"Makepeace is with you?"

"He's here, and I'll let you talk to him before we hang up, but he's had another name change. He says that since he's coming back up there, he wants to go back to being called 'Goober.' "

"I can't keep up with his names," Will said. "Every time I get used to one, he changes it. I'll have to say, though, that 'Goober' suits him best."

"I agree," Neil said. "Now let's get down to business! Is everything ready for him to come?"

"His aunt and uncle have his room ready, his phone has been put in …
by the way, Roamer won't talk on it, but Sweetie will … and the farmers
around the valley are choosing trees to be cut. There are even several men
who want jobs logging and working on the house and mill. I'd say that
things are *more* than ready."

"That sounds great!" Neil declared. "Goober and his wife are leaving
here today and plan to be there in five days. Since you have phones now,
he'll call his aunt before he leaves Burley. That way, she can have supper
ready for him and his wife.

"Now, before you talk to him," Neil continued, "let me get off business
for a minute. Do you think you could find a place for my wife and me to
bed down if we came up there for Christmas? I want to introduce her to the
place, and I can't think of a better time to do it!"

"*Are you kidding?*" Will said. "Of course we'll find you a place! We'll
make it a Christmas to remember!"

Will turned away from the phone and hollered, "*Esther, the Neils are
coming for Christmas!*"

"Okay then," Neil said, "we'll be there! Now, here's Goober!"

Will waited for Goober to get on the line, grinning all the while. Finally
he heard the familiar voice.

"Will, 'is here's Goober. How ye doin'?"

"Goob! We're great! How's Janie Rose?"

"Will … she's the most wonderfullest thing 'at ever happened t' me!
Married life is jest great! Ye ort t' try it!"

"Oh well, Goob," Will said, "I'm not making much headway right now.
Maybe when you get here my luck will change. By the way," he said, changing
the subject, "you should call your Aunt Sweetie. It would tickle her to death!"

"I'll call 'er right now," Goober said. "I need t' tell 'er 'bout Janie Rose
anyhow. She says she can't eat nothin' greasy fer breakfas' lately. Says hit
makes 'er sick on 'er stomach. Says …"

And the phone went dead.

Will pushed down the earpiece holder and turned the crank. In a moment, Preacher Burden answered the switchboard.

"Is that you, Will?" he asked.

"It's me, Preacher. I was talking to Goober, and we got cut off."

"Goober?"

"He's back to being called 'Goober' again," Will said.

"Oh my goodness!" the preacher said. "I better call Caldwell. We'll have to make some changes."

"Changes in what?" Will asked.

"Son, I might as well go ahead and tell you ... you need to know anyway. The thing for Makepeace ... I mean Goober ... involves a sign at the entrance to the valley."

"Ah!" Will said. "I was hoping it would be something like that ... so let me run this by you. Since Goober will be back in less than a week, how would it be to have to have a lot of people out there by that sign to welcome him home? He's going to call right before he leaves Burley."

"That's a *great* idea!" the preacher said. "We could get the word out when he calls and have everybody out at the sign waitin' for 'em! Now let me go. It's getting late."

"I love a good surprise!" Will said to himself as he hung up the phone.

It wasn't long before Will heard familiar steps on the porch. He glanced out the window and saw footprints in the snow coming from the road and across the yard. All at once Daniel burst through the door with Dawg on his heels, both of them tracking in snow and mud.

"You're gonna have to learn to knock," Will said, "and you're gonna have to clean up the mess you and Dawg just tracked in."

"Sorry," Daniel said as he pulled off his boots. "Is Esther here ... I mean Miss Parker?"

Esther answered from the kitchen. "I'm in here, Daniel, but do you want to see me as 'Esther' or 'Miss Parker'."

"I want to see the Miss Parker one," Daniel said. "I need help with my 'rithmetic."

"How's your mama this morning?" Will asked.

Daniel shrugged his shoulders.

"Grumpy," he said.

"Do you think she'd bite my head off if I went to see her while you get your math lesson?"

"Better you than me," Daniel said.

———

"Come in, Will," Alice said when she opened the door. "I'm glad you came. It's lonely when you're snowed in."

"Wanna build a snowman?" Will asked.

"Not this time," Alice answered. "Have a seat, and I'll get you some coffee."

Alice was already dressed, and she had put her hair up in a style that Will had always liked. She didn't look as tired as he had seen her in recent weeks, but the look on her face was still not happy. He tried to remember her as he had known her when times were better. While she was pouring the coffee and her back was turned, he remembered the impish smile she used to have and he vowed that she would have it again.

"I heard from Mr. Neil today," he said as he sat down. "He and Mrs. Neil are coming for Christmas."

"I look forward to meeting her," Alice replied.

"And I talked to Makepeace on the phone. He wants to be called 'Goober' again. He and Janie Rose are leaving today. They'll be here in about five days."

"That's wonderful," Alice said as she picked up the coffee cups. "Sounds like you and Esther will have a wonderful Christmas."

"How have you been?" he asked her when she had finally sat down.

"I'm getting by," she answered, "due in large part to you … or maybe I should say, 'due wholly to you.'" She paused before she continued. "Will … why haven't you given up on me?"

He wasn't expecting a question like that, and he had to pause and think.

"Remember when Daniel was giving you such a hard time?" he asked.

"Yes."

"Why didn't you give up on him?"

"Because I love him!" she answered without a thought.

Will sat quietly and looked at her, and for a moment she looked back before she finally lowered her eyes.

"I didn't come to make you feel uncomfortable," he said. "I came because Daniel said you're grumpy today. Why were you grumpy with that little imp you love so much?"

Alice took a deep breath, and when she let it out, she managed a slight smile.

"I've been trying to find out what he wants for Christmas," she answered, "and every time I try to talk to him about it, he just clams up."

Will turned his eyes away and sat quietly. Daniel's revelation that he wanted the three of them to be a family burned in his mind.

"Now *you're* doing it," she said. "What are you and Sonny keeping from me?"

"He told me what he wants ... but it's something he can't have," Will said. "Give him adventure books, or a bow and arrows, or a jack knife, or some cowboy boots. Give him an orange and some candy canes! Someday he'll grow up and forget his fantasies."

He got up and walked to the door, and then he turned to look back.

"In the meantime," he said as he opened the door, "why don't you give him back his mother?"

Alice didn't reply, and she didn't look up as he left.

The school bell was ringing the following Monday when Will looked out the window and saw Alice walking toward his house. He watched her as she crossed the yard, dodging patches of snow, and climbed the porch steps. He opened the door before she could knock.

"You must have been expecting me," she said as she entered.

"I was hoping," Will said as he helped her remove her coat. "Let's sit down in the kitchen where it's warm."

They walked back to the kitchen and each took a chair at the table.

"You know why I came, don't you?" Alice asked.

"You probably came to try to pry Daniel's Christmas wish out of me," Will said.

"I don't think I have to," Alice said with resolve. "I think I've known what he wants all along. He wants us to get married, doesn't he?"

Will's heart skipped a beat, and he felt the heat of a blush on his face.

"Yes, Alice, that's what he wants," he managed to say.

Alice took Will's hand and squeezed it.

"I love you, Will Parker," she said, "and I would be proud to be your wife someday ... that is, if you ever get around to asking me."

"You wouldn't bite my head off if I asked?"

Alice laughed the way she used to and squeezed his hand again.

"No, I wouldn't bite your head off!" she said.

Will looked upward and took a deep breath. He hadn't gotten up that morning with plans to propose marriage to someone.

"Well then, Alice Day," he said before he cleared his throat nervously, "I love you too. With all my *heart* I love you. Will you marry me?"

"I know you love me, Will," she answered softly. "I've known it for a long, long time. You've told me in simple ways like checking to see if I need anything from the store, or by fixing things for me, and in more generous ways like plowing my field and harvesting my corn ... and you never expected anything in return. You told me you love me by loving the most precious part of me ... my boy ... even when he wasn't very lovable to anyone except his mama. But most of all, I knew you loved me because you were patient with me when I was down. You never gave up on me.

"So yes, I'll marry you, Will," she said, "but not for Sonny's Christmas present. I hope you understand that I just can't bring myself to do that ... and you know, there are a lot of things to be put in place before we combine two households. But in the spring ... if you'll wait for me ... and not go chasing after Ellie Butcher ... in the spring when the flowers bloom, I'll marry you."

Will let out a deep breath, and his shoulders relaxed.

"And since Goober is coming, don't you forget that this mysterious old girlfriend of yours is his wife now!" she added.

"So I guess Ellie will be the only one with a broken heart," Will said with a grin.

"She'll survive," Alice replied.

———

Will was waiting at the barn when Esther came home from school. He opened the barn door for her and led Judy inside.

While they were walking into the barn, he gave Esther some welcome news.

"You won't have to cook supper or eat my cooking tonight, Sis," he said. "Alice is having us over to her house for supper."

"That's good," Esther said. "I can get my papers graded before we go. What's the occasion anyway?"

"Oh, I told her about the Neils coming for Christmas, and she was excited. She wants to help you with the planning ... you know, cooking, and decorating, and things like that. I think she hopes to make a better impression on Mr. Neil this time. She hasn't gotten over catching him skinny dipping."

"I think Mr. Neil really likes her," Esther said. "You could see it in his eyes when he was around her."

Will led Judy to her stall and hung her harness on the wall by the door. He looked over at Esther, and she was staring at him as he moved about.

"Speaking of eyes," Esther said, "what's that strange look in your eyes today? You look like the cat that swallowed the canary!"

"Not me," Will said. "I don't even like canary!"

———

When Will and Esther arrived at Alice's house, Daniel greeted them at the door and escorted them in. He was dressed in his church clothes and had his hair slicked down—and he smelled of soap! Alice, too, was dressed in her finest. She was wearing a frilly dress under her apron, and her hair was fixed up, but her most important feature was the look of happiness on her face.

Esther reacted with surprise when she entered the house.

"Oh, my, Alice," she said, "I feel underdressed! Will didn't tell me this was a fancy occasion! Are you expecting other guests?"

"No, it's just us, and you look wonderful," Alice replied. "Will looks wonderful too. I just think it's good for Sonny and me to dress up occasionally, and this happened to be one of those times!"

"I feel like a *city* boy or somethin'," Daniel said, "an' my hair feels like it has *glue* on it!"

"Sonny!" Alice said softly as she wagged a finger at him.

Alice had gone all out for supper. She had fixed Will's favorite—roasted chicken with rosemary. She had roasted some potatoes along with the chicken and cooked some of the vegetables she had put up over the summer. For dessert, she had fixed Daniel's favorite—black walnut cake.

"You've been busy!" Esther said as they sat down at the table. "You must have done nothing but cook all day!"

Alice cut her eyes over at Will, and Will fought back a grin.

"Oh yes," Alice said melodramatically, "the servants and I have stood over the hot stove, slaving away since dawn, preparing for a visit from the king and queen!"

She cast her eyes over at Will again, and Will put his hand over his mouth. A faint snicker escaped from his throat, and his face turned red.

"All right you two!" Esther said as she stood. She threw her napkin down on the table and put her hands on her hips.

"A school teacher can tell when somebody's *up* to something ... and you two are *up* to something! Will, you've been running around all afternoon with your head in the clouds, and Alice, you're acting ... more normal than you've acted in weeks! *Too* normal! Now *out* with it! What's going on?"

Alice and Will giggled like children, and Daniel sat dumbfounded, looking at Esther.

"Think we should go ahead?" Will mumbled to Alice.

"I think we'll have to, or Esther's gonna start throwing things," Alice mumbled back.

"Well," Will said as he stood up, "Esther, sit back down." He motioned to her chair, and he waited until she was in her place. "Alice and I have an announcement to make. This morning, I asked her to marry …"

Esther jumped to her feet, and her chair flew across the floor behind her. She screamed at the top of her lungs.

"*I knew it! I knew it!*" she shouted. "*I've been praying for it to happen and I knew it!*"

"Esther, please let me finish," Will said calmly, and he held his hands up toward her as if to hold her back. "I asked her to marry me … and she said, 'Not if you were the last man on earth.' "

Esther stood trembling silently with her hands over her mouth, and Daniel looked back and forth between Will and his mother. He had a look of total confusion on his face.

"I'm mixed up!" he said. "Are y'all gettin' married … or what?"

"Yes, Daniel," Alice said, "we're getting married … but it will be in the spring … when the flowers bloom."

When Thursday came, Preacher Burden waited at his house for Eunice to arrive so he could give her some instructions in person.

"Now, Eunice," he said as she was removing her coat, "this is important! When Goober calls from Burley to tell his aunt that he's on his way up here, you call everybody in the valley that has a phone and tell 'em he's coming."

"Everybody?" she asked.

"Well, you don't have to call Sweetie, of course, 'cause she'll already know! But call Will, Preacher Babb, Doc, Caldwell Turpin, the Levees, and James Plumlee. That's everybody else, isn't it?"

"You don't want me to call the store?"

"*Of course I want you to call the store*!" the preacher hollered. "That goes without sayin'!"

The preacher grabbed his hat and coat and hurried toward the door.

"*Naomi*," he called back over his shoulder. "Get to th' store as soon as you can. Folks are probably waitin'!"

The phone was ringing when the preacher got to the store. When he got the door open, he ran around behind the post office counter and jerked the ear piece off the hanger.

"*That you, Eunice?*" he hollered into the mouthpiece.

"It's me, Preacher. Goober called. They're on their way."

"Well, tell everybody that they should be at the sign by three o'clock … make that two-thirty. When you call the Levees, tell 'em to let R. Z. Ross know. He's gonna ride the valley. Have the Levees tell R. Z. that Will is gonna take all the school children over there in his wagon so R. Z. can tell the parents where their younguns will be. Got that?"

"I got it, Preacher," Eunice said, "and I'll tell you right now, I want you to plan my funeral! You're th' best organizer I've ever saw!"

"Glad to, Eunice," the preacher replied, "but if you're gonna die, how 'bout waitin' till after Christmas. I'm too busy for a funeral 'til after the manger scene at the church comes down!"

By two-fifteen, Preacher Babb had R. Z. stationed on the road between the store and the mill, instructing people to park their wagons so they couldn't be seen as Goober and his bride came up from the other direction. Then he had the folks come up near the sign and get ready to hide when they got a signal from Caldwell who was on the upper floor of the mill acting as the lookout.

The wagon load of children from the school was about the last arrival. Will had filled the bed of the wagon with hay, and the children were having a good old-fashioned hayride. On the seat with Will were Alice on one side and Esther on the other.

"Are you going to tell Goober and Janie Rose about us?" Alice asked as Will stopped the wagon.

"I want him to be the first to know," Will replied. "After all, if it weren't for him, I would have never known you."

The crowd that was completed by the arrival of the children was the largest crowd assembled in Avery Cove in years. Some of them gathered there for the arrival of their conquering hero, the one who had slain a bear to save his friend. Others came to see the return of the prodigal son who had left them to seek his fortune in a sinful, faraway land, but had come back to the open arms of his loved ones. For many of the children though, Goober was a symbol of what a plain mountain boy can gain by breaking free of the bonds of the mountains to prove himself in the greater world.

The crowd was mingling at the mill, laughing and talking, joking and reminiscing, waiting patiently, when Caldwell thrust his upper body out of the second story window and stared down the road.

"Here they come!" he hollered down to the preacher. "Hit's 'em fer shore!"

In seconds, the preacher had folks scrambling. Some went behind the sign, some behind the mill, and others disappeared into the woods. The scene became quiet and deserted, almost as if by magic.

A few hundred yards down the road, Goober and his bride approached the mill.

"We almos' there, Janie Rose," Goober said. "The mill's jest ahead on th' left. Hit's the first thing ye come to in Avery Cove."

He put his arm around her and pulled her close. "Are ye still cold?" he asked.

Janie Rose was wrapped in a blanket and had another blanket over her head, covering her bonnet and face with just her eyes exposed to the air.

"I'm better now," she said. "Kinda nervous though, seein' as how I'm gonna meet a bunch o' people for th' first time."

"Hit won't be nobody 'cept my aint and uncle," Goober replied. "We won't even stop at th' store."

About that time the mill came into view on the left.

"'At's th' mill up ahead," Goober said. "Won't be long now."

Then the sign caught Goober's eye. It reached from the ground up about six feet and was about eight feet wide. It was a sign that one could not easily miss.

"Whut on earth is *that?*" Goober said as he sat up tall on the seat. "I ain't never saw *that* b'fore!"

The surrey moved forward at a steady pace and the lettering began to become legible. Goober stared and stretched his neck forward. A look of wonder came over him. Finally, the surrey slowed and came to a stop in the middle of the road. He and his Janie Rose sat quietly, looking at the sign.

WELCOME
TO
AVERY COVE, NORTH CAROLINA
A COMMUNITY OF BROTHERLY LOVE
BIRTHPLACE OF
MAKEPEACE (GOOBER) GREEN
THE BEAR SLAYER

Goober settled back in his seat and looked at his bride.

"I hope to my never!" he uttered

And then from behind the sign, Will, Preacher Burden, Preacher Babb, and Roamer and Sweetie appeared. To Goober's amazement, people began appearing from every direction—from behind the mill, from behind every tree. The road was filling with people from all over the valley, and they were walking toward the surrey.

"Makie, who are all these people?" Janie Rose whispered through her blanket shroud.

"Why ... hit's Aint Sweetie, an' Uncle Roamer, an' Will, an' ever'body in th' valley!" Goober exclaimed.

He laid the reins on the footboard, took Janie Rose's hand, and they stepped down off the surrey.

Sweetie and Roamer made their way to the front of the crowd and had a private moment with Goober and his bride before the others surrounded them.

"*Come 'ere, Will, an' say hello t' Janie Rose,*" Goober hollered when he saw Will in the middle of the throng.

Will took Alice by the hand and started moving toward Goober, looking at Janie Rose as he went.

"There's something about her eyes," he whispered to Alice as they moved forward. "I know I've seen her before."

He studied her eyes as he slowly advanced, pulling Alice behind him. He flashed back to high school days and his time at the mill. He thought about the girls at his church and the daughters of the men who had worked for his father, and he just couldn't place her. It wasn't until he heard her voice that it clicked.

"Hey, Willie," she said when he finally stood before her.

Will was dumbfounded. He stood with his mouth agape.

"Have you forgot me?" she asked.

"*Prissy?*" He said. "*Prissy ... from the Cafe?*"

He turned to Alice with a look of confusion on his face before he turned back to Janie Rose.

"Goober's been calling you 'Janie Rose'," he said. "All I've ever known you by is 'Prissy'!"

"You and lots o' others," she said. "I met Makie when everybody was callin' him 'Makepeace'. That sounded kinda formal, so I just used *my* formal name back at him. He ain't never called me 'Prissy' cause my mama and daddy didn't never like it."

"But you were working at the company store!"

"Pearl got my job while I was in Raleigh with my grandma, so when I got back ..."

"You went to work at the company store!" Will declared. Then he realized Alice was tugging on his arm.

"Oh, Alice," he said, "I want you to meet Prissy ... Janie Rose, Goober's wife ... and Janie Rose, this is Alice Day. And uh ... uh *Makie,*" he said with a grin, "I want you to be the first to know...Alice and I are getting married!"

Goober's eyes lit up like candles on a Christmas tree, and he gave out a shout that caused Traveler to look around and whinny.

"*Y'all are gittin' married?*" he yelled. "*Fer sure?*"

Alice looked at Will lovingly and held on tightly to his arm.

"That's right, Goober," she said. "In the spring … when the flowers bloom."

Thirty-Six

SOMEBODY'S EXPECTIN'

Goober's sleep ended before dawn on Friday morning to the shuffle of Aunt Sweetie's feet going by his and Janie Rose's room. He had heard the sound hundreds of times before when he lived there as a bachelor, and he knew what would come next. At the instant he knew it would happen, there came the sound of a safety match scraping across the edge of a match box, and then from beneath his closed door, he saw the faint light of an oil lantern. He continued to listen, and sure enough he heard the door of the fire box on the kitchen stove open, the sound of wood being put in, the sound of another match, and the closing of the door. Aunt Sweetie was getting ready to cook breakfast.

Although the morning sounds were the same as always, and although the feather bed where he lay was an age-old friend, there was one big difference that morning. Lying beside him was his wife, sleeping soundly and breathing softly and rhythmically. He slid over next to her and put his arm around her. He was warm against the cold morning and she welcomed his closeness. She stirred slightly for a moment, and then her soft, rhythmic breathing returned.

Soon the shuffle of Uncle Roamer's feet passed their room, and in a moment he heard the banter of his aunt and uncle in the kitchen. He couldn't make out the words, but the exchange was cheerful.

He had almost drifted back to sleep when he heard the clatter of a frying pan on the stove followed by the sizzle of bacon. Over the course of a few minutes, the oven door opened and closed, and water was poured into the coffee pot. Then, as if on cue, there came the fragrance of bacon and coffee drifting in on the morning air.

Janie Rose stirred, stretched, and rolled over against Goober. She nuzzled into him and made a little humming sound, and then she sat up in bed.

"Oh, Makie!" she said. "What's that *smell*?"

Before Goober could answer, Janie Rose jumped up, put on her house coat and slippers and charged out of the bedroom with her hand over her mouth. She ran through the kitchen without a word and burst through the back door. Goober ran behind her as far as the kitchen, but he stopped and closed the door behind her rather than go outside.

"Whut's 'at all about?" Roamer asked from his chair at the table.

"Don't be s' nosy, Roamer," Sweetie said. "Mind ye own business."

"She looked a mite sickly t' me," Roamer remarked.

Goober peeked out the kitchen window into the darkness.

"She's been doin' 'at most ever' mornin' fer 'bout two weeks," he said. "I think I'll take 'er t' Doc an' see if he can give 'er a tonic."

"She needs t' see Doc," Sweetie said, "but they ain't no tonic 'at'll cure whut *she's* got."

"You know whut she's got?" Goober asked.

"I figger I do!" Sweetie said. "Your mama, she had it when she wuz expectin' you. Best as I can recollect, she got shed of it in 'bout nine months!"

———◆———

Esther sat at the kitchen table eating her oatmeal and staring off into space.

"Tomorrow's Saturday," she said, "… no school … we can sleep late. What would you say to a get-together tonight … you and me, Alice and Daniel, and Goober and Janie Rose?"

"Sounds like fun."

"Maybe a potluck supper," Esther mused.

"Tell you what," Will said, "I'll see them all today. You can bring Alice and Daniel with you on your way home from school."

"How about we make it a welcome home supper for Goober and Janie Rose, and Alice and I do all the cooking?" Esther asked.

"Sounds fair to me," Will said, "and I think Alice will agree. I'll see her first. What do you think about asking Demus? He makes a good apple pie."

"Gettin' better all the time," Esther replied. "Do we have any cream? If we do, I'll whip some up to put on the pie."

"I'm afraid not," Will said, "and we're gettin' low on milk."

He got up and poured a cup of coffee and sat back down at the table.

"You know, I've been thinking about things I need to do," he said, "and one of them is to buy a cow! What with Daniel being a growing boy and our family growing to four ... including you, of course ... a cow would be a good investment. I think I'll start lookin' around today."

"You just touched on something else we need to think about," Esther said. "This house isn't big enough for all of us, so I need to go see Preacher Burden about that house he offered me when he hired me."

"Now not so quick there!" Will said. "Remember that Alice will have an empty house when she moves in here. Maybe she would sell it to you!"

"It is a nice house," Esther said, "and it's close by ... but I'd have to sell my house in Wilmington."

She sat and thought while she finished her coffee.

"There's plenty of time left," she finally said. "I'm sure it'll work out for the best."

With her coffee gone and the clock running, Esther left the kitchen and went to her room. Will remained, sitting at the table with a stream of thought running through his head. Taking a wife would bring big responsibilities, he knew, but taking a wife with a son compounded the challenge.

In addition to a cow, he needed to think about a horse and rig for Alice, maybe a saddle horse for Daniel, and some pigs to provide meat for the table.

And if he was going to increase his livestock, he would need to provide additional food and shelter for them. He decided that what he needed was some sage advice from a long-time farmer—someone like Demus Whitedeer.

———

When Esther left for school, Will was not far behind. As Alice's house came in view, he saw Daniel charge out the door, cross the yard, and jump on Esther's buckboard on the fly. He chuckled to himself and marveled that in a few short months Daniel would be his stepson and his responsibility. As he thought about it, the chuckle turned into a mellow smile.

Alice was on the porch waving goodbye to Daniel as Will neared, and when she saw him, her wave shifted to his direction. By the time his wagon came to a stop at her house, she had moved to the yard, and when he got down she was there to embrace him.

"I'm going to have to ask you to marry me more often," he said.

She put her arms around his neck and pulled herself up on tiptoe to kiss him.

"And I'll say yes every time you do," she said.

When they were inside, Will lay out the plans for the evening, and Alice was most agreeable.

"You know, I've never really known Goober very well," she said, "much less Janie. He's such a character, and she seems so sweet that it'll be fun to get to know them, and of course," she added, "I'm so indebted to Demus that he'll always be welcome."

Then Will lay out his plans for additional livestock and a rig for her, and she listened with interest. She was particularly pleased that they would have their own cow.

Alice then excused herself and went to the back bedroom. In a moment she returned with a package that she handed to Will.

"Will, this is something I made a couple of months ago when I began to think there may be a future for us," she said. "If it's all right with you,

496

I'd like for us to give it to Goober and Janie as a wedding gift. If we do, I'll make us another one."

Will opened the package and unfolded a beautiful, handmade quilt sewn in the wedding ring pattern.

"It's beautiful," he said. "Are you sure you want to give it away?"

"Yesterday you reminded me that if it hadn't been for Goober, we never would have met," she said, "so yes, I'm sure."

"They'll cherish it," Will remarked as he examined Alice's delicate stitching.

With that part of his morning taken care of, Will reluctantly left and headed for Roamer's house to see Goober and Janie Rose. When he arrived, Roamer was in the stable, cleaning out an empty stall.

"Mornin', Roamer," he hollered as he approached.

"Well, look whut th' buzzards dropped outta th' sky!" Roamer said as he threw a pitchfork full of muck out the door.

"Where's Traveler?" Will asked.

"Goober took 'is li'l' missus in t' see Doc," Roamer said. "She wuz feelin' a mite poorly this mornin'."

"Hope it's nothing serious."

"Aw … she's prob'ly jest got a tetch o' th epizooties," Roamer said. "Travelin' does 'at t' some folks."

He propped on his pitchfork long enough to hear the plans for the evening, and he tapped his head with his fingertips, committing the plans to memory. Then Will was off to see Demus.

Demus met him at the door with a book in his hand.

"Another book," Will said as he walked in. "What are you reading this time?"

"It's a book about herbal remedies," Demus said. "I was brushing up on Panax quinquefolius … American ginseng. Come back to the kitchen and let me show you something."

Will walked back to the kitchen, and above and around the stove was a huge collection of gnarled roots, hanging on strings to dry.

"There's my gathering of ginseng for this year," Demus said. "I think it must be my best harvest ever!"

"Well, I don't know much about ginseng," Will said. "How much would you say you have there?"

"I count ginseng in taxes and books," Demus said. "There should be enough there to pay my taxes and buy a stack of books as high as your head, with some money left over."

"How long will it take you to read a stack of books as high as my head?"

"I probably won't read them at all," Demus remarked. "The way the kids are coming around to borrow books, I think I'll invest in books for them this year. I'm going to see if Esther will let me turn the selection process over to her."

"Well, you can ask her tonight when you come for supper," Will said. "We're having a welcome home party for Goober and Janie Rose, and the cost of admission for you is one apple pie!"

"I can afford that," Demus said.

———

Everything was ready, and all the guests were present—all except the guests of honor, Goober and Janie Rose.

"Will, do you think Roamer forgot to tell them about the party?" Alice asked.

"I doubt that," Will replied. "Roamer's mind is still pretty sharp. I'm afraid that Janie Rose may be sick. After all, she visited Doc this morning."

"Wouldn't Roamer have let us know they weren't coming?" Esther asked.

"You would think so."

"I bet Indians attackeded 'em on th' way here," Daniel said.

Demus rubbed his chin and thought.

"No ... I would have known about any impending Indian attacks," he said.

"I want some apple pie," Daniel declared.

Alice took a stance with her hands on her hips. "Get serious, Sonny!"

Daniel shrugged and went outside to play with Dawg.

Before long, Dawg let out a soft bark on the porch.

"That's Dawg's 'who's-that-coming bark,' " Will said. "They must be here."

Goober and Janie Rose ran up the steps and across the porch, anxious to get to the heat. Will opened the door, and they ran in without slowing down.

"We were about to send out a search party!" Esther declared.

"Give me your coats and hats," Will said. "Janie Rose, give me your blanket and I'll put it with the coats."

They took off their coats, and Janie Rose took off her stocking cap and scarf.

"Give me your hat, Goober," Will said, "and I'll put it on the bed."

Goober pulled his hat down on his head and gave it a little twist.

"I think I'll wear m' hat fer a spell, Will," he said. "M' head's cold as ice!"

Goober and Janie Rose backed up to the stove and warmed themselves while Will and Esther took care of the coats. Janie Rose looked around the room, taking in the place where Goober had grown up.

"Well, Janie Rose, how do you like Avery Cove so far," Esther asked as she reentered the room.

"Ever' body's been real nice," Janie Rose declared. "I think I'm gonna like it just fine!"

"Say, why don't we girls go in the kitchen and check on supper," Esther said, "and let the boys talk about boy things."

"Let's go," Alice answered. "I want to hear what Janie Rose thought when all those people popped out of the woods down at the mill."

The girls left for the kitchen, and Will motioned for Demus and Goober to sit down.

"Want me to take your hat now, Goob?" Will asked as Goober flopped into a chair.

"Naw, m' head's still cold," Goober replied.

"I've never known you to keep your hat on inside," Will said. "You're not getting sick are you?"

Goober raised up and peeked around the corner toward the kitchen.

"I ain't gettin' sick!" he declared in a whisper, and he pulled his hat off revealing a gauze bandage on the top on his head.

"Good Lord!" Will said, and he and Demus pulled back in surprise. "Is Janie Rose already poundin' on your head?"

Just then a commotion of squeals came from the kitchen, and Janie Rose peeked around the corner into the parlor.

"I told 'em, Makie," she said.

"Well, I might as well go on an' tell y'all too," Goober said. "We went t' see Doc 'is mornin' cause Janie Rose is gettin' sick ever' mornin'... an' he says Janie Rose is gonna, have a baby ... a little un."

Will jumped up, and Demus chuckled.

"*Goob! Congratulations!*" Will exclaimed. "*You're gonna be a daddy!*"

Demus chuckled again in his rumbling sort of way. "And when he told you, you passed out and cracked your head!" he said.

Goober squirmed in his chair, and his ears turned red.

"'At's 'bout th' size of it!" he admitted.

———

After they had eaten, "the boys" went in the parlor, and "the girls" stayed in the kitchen to talk about girl things.

"Demus, 'at wuz some good apple pie," Goober said as they were sitting down.

"I'll give your wife the recipe," Demus replied, "but the secret is in the apples. My pigs grow fat on those apples in the late summer, and I have enough left over to last 'til spring."

"Speaking of pigs," Will said, "I haven't put up any pork yet ... and I need to get a sow and start raising pigs here where I can corn-feed 'em."

"I have a pig trap." Demus said. "Why don't we go hunt a couple of pigs for you to put in the smoke house, and we'll trap a sow and a young boar and bring them back so you can raise some pigs here."

"How do you move a full-grown live pig?" Will asked.

"The trap is on skids," Demus said. "When we get the right pigs in it, we'll hook it to the horses and pull it back."

In the kitchen, the conversation was of a more feminine nature.

"Did Doc say when the baby is due?" Alice asked Janie Rose.

"He said early July. I was hopin' we could be in a house to ourselves when it come, but I guess we'll still be livin' with Makie's aunt and uncle."

"Sweetie will be good help," Esther said, "especially if your mother can't come."

"I sure wish my mama could have been here when Sonny was born," Alice said.

"Well ... are you and Will planning on a little niece or nephew for *me?*" Esther asked her.

Alice blushed and turned her head away. She tried to suppress a smile, but it came anyway.

"I want a baby for Will," she confessed. "Matthew and I tried to have a little brother or sister for Sonny, but we weren't successful. Will and I will plan and hope ... but planning doesn't always make it so."

Back in the parlor, plans were being made.

"Well, Demus, if you're in agreement then, we'll go hunting Tuesday morning and try to get a couple of pigs to cure for now. If we get an opportunity, we'll get three. I'm going to have to get used to including Alice and Sonny in my calculations."

"Can I go, Will?" Daniel asked. "Please!"

"You'll be in school," Will answered.

"Purdy please?"

"No, Sonny! But if is all right with Demus, we'll go trap the live pigs on Saturday, and you can go then."

"That's fine with me," Demus said. "Do you have plenty of salt for the ones we're going to cure?"

"I'll go get some tomorrow."

"How about hickory and apple wood to smoke them with?"

"I could use some apple."

"I'll bring you some. How about sage for the sausage ... and hot pepper?"

"Got plenty of that," Will answered.

"I still ain't much on huntin,' " Goober said, "an' since ye got he'p with 'at, I'll he'p out by a-fixin' up th' pigpen an' th' pig house fer ye ... an' I'll he'p out best as I can with th' curin' an' sech."

Will grinned. "You'll help eat some sausage too, won't you, Goober?"

"You can count on me!" Goober declared.

When school was out on Tuesday, Esther locked up and left for home with Daniel. She didn't know what to expect when she got there, but she knew that if the hunt had been successful, there would be plenty of work to do.

If there were pigs to be processed, it was a good day to do it. It was overcast and cold and there were no indications that the weather would warm again before spring. Soon there would be kettles boiling in yards and fragrant smoke rising from smoke houses all over the valley.

It had not been a good day for Daniel. His mind had been up on the mountain in the middle of the hunt, and school that day had been a waste of time for him. If it had not been for setting a bad precedent, Esther would have simply excused him early in the day and sent him off to find the hunters.

Esther pulled up to Daniel's house, but his mother was not at home. She pulled back onto the road and hadn't gone far when she and Daniel saw a column of smoke coming from the direction of Will's house.

"Gaw! Look at all 'at smoke!" Daniel exclaimed

"Look at all *that* smoke," Esther said.

"'At's what I said!" Daniel remarked.

"Daniel, you learned to talk beautifully, and now you're beginning to talk like the other boys," Esther told him. "It's not ''at smoke.' It's '*that* smoke.' "

"Whut's the difference?

"*What's* the difference!"

"'At's whut I said!"

About that time the house came into view, and they could see activity around the big black pot in the yard.

"We'll talk about it later," Esther said. "It looks like there's work to be done now."

And there was plenty to do. Will had enlisted the help of Demus, Alice, Roamer, Sweetie, Goober, and Janie Rose. R. Z. Ross had ridden up the road to investigate the gun shots he had heard, and had stopped to help as well.

A large hog and one a little smaller hung by their hamstrings from the tree in the yard. R. Z. was drenching them with hot water, and Demus and Will were scraping the last of the hair off the hides. They had been gutted, and Alice and Sweetie were processing the organs. Janie Rose was bravely doing her part by running back and forth to the house for knives and so forth, but mainly she was being schooled in the rigors of mountain life.

On some boards lying under the tree were the remains of another hog that had already been cut up. Roamer had put the hams, shoulders, and side meat in pans and was packing them in salt. He had put the ribs and back-bone aside to be cooked and canned. The excess fat he had trimmed from the meat along with the leaf fat from around the intestines would be saved until the next day when it would be rendered into lard.

Goober Green, the bear slayer with a weak stomach for such things, did his part and more. He kept the fire going under the pot, kept it topped off with water from the house, carried the heavy supplies for the ladies, and sharpened knives for everyone. When he was able to catch a short break, he fussed over his expectant wife who cooed over him in return.

When Esther and Daniel joined the crew, the speed of the process picked up. She and Alice moved to the kitchen where they began to cook the parts of the pigs that would be canned. They also began to cook some of the fresh meat for supper for all the crew.

By nightfall, all three pigs had been processed, and a supper of pork tenderloin, cornbread, and vegetables had been prepared. R. Z. chose to go home for his supper, and he took with him a section of tenderloin, some cleaned intestines for "chitins," and some snouts, ears, and feet for pickling. He also left with a promise from Sweetie that if he came back the next day, he could have some cracklings for cornbread after the lard had been rendered along with a pound of sausage.

———

Will and Demus waited for Daniel to come home from school on Friday, and then they were all off to the mountain with Demus's pig trap in tow. Don pulled the trap to the end of the river trail, and after some small trees and brush had been cut back, he pulled it on up the mountain to the spot where the pigs liked to congregate. The pigs had heard the noisy procession and were long gone when they arrived.

Demus chose a location under a low tree limb where the trap was placed. He set the heavy, wooden trap door and baited the spring mechanism with corn still on the cob. Then he tied a long rope to the trap door, looped it over the tree limb, and ran it up to the top of the ridge that overlooked the site.

"We'll come back early in the morning and see what we've caught," he told Will. "If we have one you want to keep, we'll drag it home, release it in the pen, and bring the trap back up and reset it. If we have a pig you don't want, I'll pull the door open with the rope and let the pig out."

Before they left they heard grunts and squeals close by.

"They're just over the ridge," Demus said. "We'll have some kind of pig in the morning."

The next morning they were back on the trail by first light. This time they brought both Don and Molly and a double-tree rig so that both horses could pull the trap with a pig inside. They also brought a piece of canvas to cover the trap and keep the pigs calm as they were being moved. The horses were left at the end of the trail, and Will, Demus, and Daniel moved as quietly as they could up the mountain side. Daniel was becoming an apt hunter, and Will and Demus were impressed with how he moved so cautiously through the trees.

Near the top of the ridge that overlooked the trap, they dropped down and crawled to the top. When they reached the ridge, they could see the trap with a large pig inside. Several other pigs were gathered around the trap try-ing to get in where the corn had been.

"That looks like the dominant boar in the trap," Demus whispered. "I assume you don't want him."

"You're right," Will whispered back. "Turn him loose."

Demus worked his way over to where the rope was tied off and slowly pulled it, raising the trap door. The boar sensed that he was being freed, and he backed out of the trap and looked around, grunting and sniffing the air. Immediately a sow ran into the trap and started rooting around for corn. A yearling pig followed her in and pushed up beside her.

"If that's a young boar," Will whispered to Daniel, "this is too good to be true."

He glanced over at Demus, who was looking at Will for some kind of signal. Will motioned downward with his hand, Demus dropped the door, and the pigs were trapped.

A symphony of squeals erupted as the two pigs realized they were penned in. They pushed against the sides and ends of the trap, but it held firm.

Will stood up and fired his revolver, and the other pigs, having been conditioned by seeing others killed by gunfire, scattered like ants.

"Daniel, go back and get the horses," Will said, and he and Demus went down the hill toward the trap.

"Congratulations! The young one's a boy!" Demus announced when they were close.

"They look healthy to me," Will said. "Do they look all right to you?"

"I'd say we did pretty well," Demus replied, "and it looks like the sow is already pregnant."

The sow turned her head and looked over the smaller pig toward Demus and Will.

"If pigs could frown, I'd say that sow was frowning at us," Demus said.

"Do you think she'll be hard to handle?" Will asked.

"As long as your pigpen is strong enough to keep her in, you'll be safe," Demus answered, "and if you keep dumping food in her trough, sooner or later she'll learn to like you."

While they were examining their catch, Daniel rode over the crest of the hill on Molly's back with Don trailing behind. The pigs squealed and charged the sides of the trap at the sight of the horses. The trap rocked back and forth, but it held together.

"Bring the canvas, Daniel," Demus said. "Let's cover them up and calm them down."

Demus and Will threw the canvas over the trap and secured it with a rope. They backed Don and Molly up to the trap and harnessed them to it. After a final check, they were on their way.

———

Janie Rose sat on a log watching as Goober made one last check on the pigpen and pig house. She watched as he shook each fence post and pulled on each strand of wire. She got up and walked over to the fence as he examined the pig house to make sure it would hold back the winter weather.

"That pig house looks fine enough t' live in," she said.

"Daddy wuz a good carpenter," Goober replied. "He took pride in 'is work wurther hit wuz a pig house er *his* house."

He ran his hand over a joint that had been pegged together, admiring how closely the pieces fit.

"I wish Daddy wuz here t' he'p me with all I got t' do," he said.

Janie Rose looked around at the house and outbuildings that Laddie Green had constructed.

"More and more I get th' feelin' that he is," she replied.

Goober's inspection came to a halt when he heard the trappers returning. When they crossed the river, the sound of the horses' hooves and the scraping of the trap runners on the wooden bridge caused the pigs to squeal at the top of their lungs. Esther, who had been working in the kitchen, heard the racket and ran to the porch to see the odd procession pull into the yard.

"Them pigs as big as their squeals?" Goober hollered to Will.

"Wait 'til you see!" Will answered.

Molly and Don pulled the trap up beside the pigpen and Will unharnessed them. He, Demus, Goober, and Daniel pushed the trap door up to the pigpen gate. Demus lifted the trap door, the pigs ran in, looked around, and went directly to the feed trough. A meal of oats and corn made them right at home!

———

A little while later after Janie Rose had gone in the house to visit with Esther, Will, Goober, and Demus were still sitting on the log admiring Will's pigs.

"Janie Rose wanted t' know why th' pig pen wuz s' far frum th' house," Goober said, "so I axed 'er if she had ever been 'round pigs b'fore, and she said she hadn't."

"Bring her back in a few days and let her catch a whiff of what a pigpen smells like," Will said.

"Sick as she gits in the mornin', 'at would really set 'er off," Goober replied. "Hit's bad 'nough havin' t' smell Uncle Roamer's pottin' soil in the parlor. I'm startin' t' think 'at's most o' her problem."

"Potting soil in the parlor?" Will asked.

"Uncle Roamer's gittin' ready t' plant 'is terbackie seeds. He's got 'bout two hunderd little pots in th' winders with the soil he mixes up in 'em. Keeps it s' hot in 'ere that steam rises off th' mixture."

"Smells bad, does it?" Demus asked.

"Well, course hit does! See … he gits sand frum th' river, an' dirt frum th' field, an' mixes it up with mule manure an' chicken droppin's. Makes th' terbackie might near jump up outta th' pots, but hit smells t' high heaven! He swears 'at's whut makes 'is terbackie chew s' good! Don't do nothin' fer Janie Rose's stomach, though."

Will and Demus chuckled and exchanged glances.

"I hope you don't mind me intruding, Goober," Demus said, "but I've been reading about herbal remedies, and it seems that the Indian women use catnip and peppermint in a tea for sickness during pregnancy."

"I hope to my never!" Goober exclaimed.

"And if you were to try that and it doesn't work, my book said that the Negro women in Africa use ginger root!"

"Why ... Aint Sweetie grows mint an' catnip in 'er garden," Goober said. "I'll git 'er t' brew up some fer Janie Rose."

Will turned to Demus.

"Remember when I stood up for you in church and you threatened to call me Preacher Parker?" he asked.

Demus laughed his deep, resonant laugh. "Uh ... yes," he answered.

"Well, I think I'll start calling you Dr. Whitedeer."

———————

S ince it had become a national holiday in 1863, "Thanksgiving" had never been celebrated in Avery Cove. That's not to say that the people of the valley were not thankful for each year's harvest, or that they didn't hold special celebrations in thankfulness for God's abundance. It is only to say that since it was President Abraham Lincoln who had proclaimed the fourth Thursday in November as "Thanksgiving Day," the people of the valley were not as attuned to the national celebration as they would have been had it been proclaimed by, say—Jefferson Davis.

There were still a few veterans of the Confederate Army living in Avery Cove, and there were more still whose fathers had fought under Robert E. Lee. They were not about to observe Lincoln's Thanksgiving holiday. They would celebrate their thankfulness in the old-timey way!

Of the many celebrations held in Avery Cove during the harvest season, the largest was held on the Saturday night after Will had trapped his pigs. It was sponsored by the Burdens and was held that particular year in a barn on one of the abandoned home sites belonging to the preacher.

The good preacher's annual gathering was especially popular because it was the only party of the year that had a band of professional musicians. This year, the group was the Linville Rangers, a rip-snorting bunch the preacher had booked two years in advance.

Will and Esther rolled into Alice's yard just before sundown on that special evening, and Alice and Daniel were waiting. They were bundled up against the cold, but it wasn't hard to see that Alice had gone all out to make herself pretty for Will. Daniel was spruced up too, and his hair was slicked back on his head with some of his father's tonic.

"Well ... look at you, Daniel!" Esther said as Daniel and his mother came down the porch steps. "Don't you look nice! Will you be my escort for the evening?"

All Daniel had to say as he climbed onto the rear of the buckboard was, "*Humph!*"

"And look at Daniel's mother," Will said. "If it's possible, she looks even nicer than Daniel ... and I'm sure Daniel would agree ... she's certainly prettier!"

Will jumped down and helped Alice up on the buckboard.

"Can I be your escort for the evening?" he asked tenderly as she took her seat.

"I'd be delighted, Mr. Parker."

"My hair feels like it has *bear* grease on it!" Daniel growled.

"Dan*iel!*" Alice said with a lilt on the second syllable of the boy's name.

Long before they arrived at the barn, the group could tell that the Linville Rangers were at least a loud group. The rhythmic thump of the bass fiddle and the raspy cry of the banjo reached out into the evening and pulled the buckboard toward the assembly.

With very few exceptions, every resident of the valley was there. Oil lanterns, hung from the rafters of the barn, provided ample light, and a large bonfire, burning in the barnyard, warmed the scene.

"Looks like a good crowd," Will said when he greeted the host.

"Far as we can tell, the only people not here are Granny Floyd and Demus Whitedeer," the preacher said. "Sad on both counts. Of course,

Preacher and Mrs. Babb aren't here ... but nobody expects them to come to a party where there'll be dancin'."

Granny Floyd, at ninety-six, was the oldest resident of the valley. She had not been out of her son's house in several years due to advanced arthritis, or as the valley people called it, "th' rheumatiz". Her son, Orville, would take her a piece of cake and tell her about the music and square dancin', and she would revel in memories of past celebrations.

As sad as the absence of Granny Floyd was, Demus Whitedeer's absence was even sadder to Will. Demus had been accepted by most when it came to church or council attendance, but there were still plenty of people who considered him out of place when it came to a social affair. Demus knew the social limitations of Indians and Negroes in that age, and he knew his plight was doubled by being both. He would stay in his limited place in order to be accepted in other, more important places.

The party from the very beginning was a total success. Cares of the tough mountain life were forgotten long enough for the people to wallow in joy. Old men clogged to the music on the wooden dance floor as toothless old women grinned and clapped time to the music. Young boys joined the old men in the dance and watched the elders' feet, trying to perfect their own style.

Everyone took a turn when it came time to square dance—everyone except Goober and Janie Rose. Goober refused to let Janie Rose exert herself in her delicate condition. Doc French tried to tell Goober that a little dancin' wouldn't hurt Janie Rose, but Goober would hear none of it.

"Waitin' till next year ain't a-gonna hurt neither one of us!" Goober exclaimed to Doc.

Esther found ample partners among her students. All the boys, even the most shy of them, managed to have at least one dance with the teacher.

Preacher Burden and Naomi even joined in. Naomi moved rather nimbly for a preacher's wife, but the preacher was a little less nimble as everyone would have expected the overweight preacher/storekeeper to be.

When it came time for the Linville Rangers to take a break, some of the old men flopped down on the straw in exhaustion. Others took a trip out to Roamer Robinson's wagon where refreshments were being served on the sly. Some of the toothless old women enjoyed their corncob pipe, but the majority of the crowd gathered around the table where cake and punch were being served. Preacher Burden and Naomi circulated throughout the group, shaking hands and hugging, reminding the Methodists that the celebration of thanks would continue the next day at the church.

Just before the music was to begin again, Preacher Burden called the group to order.

"*Ever'body listen up for a minute!*" he shouted. "*You men outside there and all you children runnin' around ... come in the barn and listen up. I've got somethin' important to say!*"

The men, women, and children all gathered in the barn, obedient to the preacher's call, and the preacher put on his serious face.

"*Sonny Day!*" he called out. "*Come here, boy!*"

Daniel froze where he was and pulled his head down between his shoulders. The preacher's call had scared him to death! Alice and Will looked at each other, wondering what was going on.

"Come here, boy," the preacher said more gently. "You aren't in trouble!"

Daniel inched over to the preacher with a frightened look on his face. The eyes of the whole of Avery Cove were upon him.

"Son," the preacher said as he put his arm around the boy, "the valley, for the most part, is here together ... and this is a good time for them to thank you for dispatching that mountain lion that plagued us for some time. Jasper Jeter has something he wants to give you ... and I want the people here to join in th' givin' with a solid round of applause!"

The crowd broke out into cheers and boisterous clapping as Jasper stepped forward and unfurled the skin of the cougar on the floor. It rolled out in front of Daniel with its head landing at his feet. It stared up at the boy through glass eyes, and he stared back with an open mouth and eyes as large as saucers.

The crowd moved in around Daniel and the skin of the beast. The other hero of the valley, Goober Green, worked his way over to Daniel's side and raised the boy's arm in triumph. Daniel was dumbfounded!

Despite Roamer's refreshments and the frenzy brought on by the presentation and the boisterous music, the behavior of the group was unusually good. When the party broke up near midnight, wagons rolled out toward home carrying joyful and thankful souls—the sons and daughters of the joyful and thankful people who had settled that place.

Thirty-Seven

A Christmas Surprise

"She'll make ye a good milk cow," Ollie Peeley promised as he and Will walked toward Ollie's barn. "Milk's got a lot o' fat in it too! 'Er butter's as rich as any I've ever saw!"

"Is she gentle?" Will asked. "You know, Alice Day and I are getting married, and she and Daniel will be milking her some."

"Hit's a good thing ye brought that up!" Ollie said. "Th' onliest quare thing 'bout this cow is ye have t' milk 'er frum th' lef' side! Ye milk 'er frum th' right, an' she's likely t' kick th'… she's likely t' kick ye!"

When they reached the barn, Ollie opened the door and propped it with a large rock. He opened the first stall on the right and propped it with the stick reserved for that purpose. The cow was standing in her stall munching hay from the feed rack.

"Tell me, Mr. Peeley, why do you want to sell this cow?" Will asked.

"Got another 'at'll be calvin' anytime. Don't need two milk cows!"

"How old is she?"

"I 'spect ye'd want t' know exac'ly how old she is."

"That would help."

Ollie rubbed his chin. "Hit's writ down in th' house," he said. "You stay rat here an' I'll go look it up!"

Ollie was off in a clip toward the house. The prospect of selling his cow had put a spring in his step.

Will put his hand on the cow's rump and felt the meat on her bones. He moved cautiously around on her "lef' side" and bent over to look at her udder. Then he squatted down and started pulling on her teats to see if all four were in good working order.

All at once the old girl turned her head around and looked directly at him.

"*Watch it thar, boy!*" she said indignantly.

Will jumped to his feet and looked the beast in the face. By golly! She looked and sounded exactly like Aunt Sweetie Robinson! She formed her lips into a perfect little circle and lolled her tongue around inside her toothless mouth.

"*Ye touch me lack 'at ag'in,*" she bellowed, "*an' I'll kick ye up side ye haid!*"

Will jumped back in horror and screamed! He jumped out of the stall, slammed the stall door, and ran from the barn, screaming as he went.

"*Will! Will! Wake up ... you're dreaming!*" Esther shouted as she ran into his room. She sat down quickly on the edge of his bed and put her hand on his shoulder. "That must have been a really bad one," she said. "You were screaming something about Sweetie and saying you didn't mean to do it."

Will sat up in bed and buried his face in his hands. When he had caught his breath, he began to chuckle.

"You ain't gonna believe this one!" he declared.

———◆———

While Esther was cooking breakfast, Will was getting ready for the day. He had been planning a trip to Burley for about a week, and he wanted to get an early start.

His search for a cow in Avery Cove had turned up no prospects. It seemed that the timing was just not right. His search, though, had led to a recommendation by at least two farmers that he see a dairy farmer in Burley by the name of Edwin Platt. Platt, he was told, was one of the first people in North Carolina to have a breed of milk cow called "Jerseys." He was told that the Jersey cows had been brought from England because they were the latest thing in milk production.

His trip to Burley had other purposes as well. With Christmas only two weeks away, he would do his Christmas shopping at the big general store. He had been thinking, too, that since he might not be able to go back to Burley again before spring, he would look for a wedding ring for Alice. Esther had let Alice try on one of her rings, and it was a good fit, so she was able to tell Will what size to get.

Demus had agreed to go to Burley with Will, partially for the companionship, but mostly to scout out the market price for ginseng. He was walking toward the road when Will approached his house.

"*Mornin', Demus,*" Will hollered.

Demus pulled himself up onto the wagon and lay his bundle on the seat before he spoke.

"Good morning, Will. These roads sure are better, aren't they?"

"If they're this good all the way to Burley, we'll make good time. What's in the bundle?"

"Food! Knowing you, you didn't bring any…and my bed roll."

"I brought a coffee pot and some dried beans. I was going to stop at Burden's and get some cheese and crackers and some canned fish."

"I have plenty … bread and jerky. Why aren't you taking Daniel?"

"I planned the trip on a school day on purpose, Demus. Gonna buy his Christmas present."

"He told me he wasn't going," Demus remarked, "so I asked him to take care of my animals … milk and feed the cow and feed the chickens and the mule."

"Good practice. Milking the cow is going to be one of his jobs when he comes to live with me."

The wagon rolled easily along the improved roadway. Even the horses seemed to enjoy the smooth surface. Time passed quickly, and by early afternoon, they were in Burley.

The first stop was the general store. Will got out his shopping list and made himself busy while Demus looked around.

Within 30 minutes, Will had bought a Winchester .22 lever action rifle for Daniel, a bottle of French perfume for Esther, and a dress for Alice. The rifle and perfume were easy, but the dress was a struggle. He finally found a mature sales lady who was very helpful in making the selection after he had discretely pointed out a female customer who was about Alice's size. The sales lady went to the rack and pulled out a light blue creation that Will loved.

"Can't wait to see her in that!" he told the lady as she was wrapping it.

He explained to the sales lady that he was getting married in the spring, and she was overjoyed to help him select a wedding ring from the jewelry case.

To top off his shopping, he bought several tins of mixed candy for folks like Roamer and Sweetie and the Neils, and a book about mushrooms for Demus.

On the way to the wagon, Will asked Demus if he had gotten the information he had wanted about the sale of his ginseng.

"Sure did," Demus replied. "I'll keep going to the Mast Store in Valle Crucis to sell my herbs. This store wants me to give them away!"

Edwin Platt's farm was about a mile outside of town. He greeted Will and Demus and told them about the Jersey breed as he was walking them toward his barn.

"Jerseys is jest a ideal breed o' dairy cow," he said. "They're sorta small and real gentle...purdy, too!"

He showed Will several animals that were already producing, and Will chose one named "Nancy," a small, honey-brown cow that had birthed her first calf about a week before. Will talked Mr. Platt into including a halter in the sale price, and a deal was struck.

"Want me t' milk 'er 'fore ye strike out?" Platt asked.

Will thought for a moment. "No, we'll milk her up the road."

It was almost dark when they reached the camping spot just beyond Burley. They gave the cow and horses some hay and gathered firewood. By the time it was dark, coffee and beans were boiling, and Nancy had been milked.

They sat down on a log by the fire and waited for the beans to cook.

"That's a good looking cow you bought," Demus said.

"She's gentle. I even milked her from the right side."

"You what?"

"Never mind," Will said. "Family joke."

"It's none of my business ... but why don't you and Alice go ahead and get married?" Demus asked.

Will told Demus how Daniel had wanted the marriage as his Christmas present, and how Alice was dead set against it. "I've learned that you don't try to reason with Alice about things like that," he said. "She wants to wait till spring ... 'when the flowers are blooming,' she says."

Demus took a deep breath and blew it out.

"And I've learned simply by reading that women can't be reasoned with when it comes to things of the heart. Seems like I have read too that spring marriages are traditional ... something about the rebirth of trees and flowers in the spring that causes women to get in a marrying way."

"Considering the fact that I've only known her for nine months, three or four more months aren't unreasonable, I guess," Will concluded.

"I'm sure you're right."

Beans, venison jerky, bread, and coffee with fresh milk made a good meal by the fireside, and a bed of hay in a covered wagon made for a good night's sleep under overcast skies.

———

The newly improved road had made a big difference, and Will decided to hurry the trip along because of the dark skies. His wagon, with the little Jersey cow walking behind, passed Burden's store shortly after noon.

The men who were congregated on the store's porch sat up and took notice as the pretty little Jersey passed by.

"Ain't never saw a cow lack 'at," one of them said. "Looks quare ... 'em big ol' horses an' 'at little bitty cow."

Will and Demus continued on, stopping only at Roamer's long enough to have dinner and split some firewood for Sweetie. Will finally got home and made Nancy comfortable in the barn, and then the snow began to fall.

———

The snow began slowly, spitting and sputtering those little hard flakes that the old timers said were a harbinger of a real winter storm. They were pinging on the tin roof when Will left the barn, and by the time he got to his house, the flakes were as big as biscuits.

The clock said 3:15. School had let out at 3:00, and he hoped that Esther hadn't remained after the children had left, unaware that it was snowing. He put his presents away in his room—all except Esther's perfume, which he hid in the loft above the back bedroom—and then he went to the window in the parlor and looked out. Instead of seeing Judy coming down the road bringing Esther home, he saw a genuine blizzard. The wind had picked up, and snow was blowing from the northwest on an almost horizontal plane.

He was concerned. Nobody should be out in a storm like this, he thought. He was just about to call Preacher Burden for advice when the front door swung open and Daniel and Dawg ran in.

Dawg shook himself and ran to the corner by the stove.

"*Did you get a cow?*" Daniel asked excitedly as he brushed snow off his coat.

"*What are you doing out in a storm like this?*" Will hollered.

Daniel looked puzzled. "I wanted to see the cow!"

"Does your mama know where you are?"

"I come straight from school!"

Will turned abruptly and went to the phone. He picked up the earpiece, turned the crank, and waited.

"Eunice?" he said. "Get me the Levees. ... Yes, it's really coming down. Yes, I'll wait."

He turned and glared at Daniel, who was still looking puzzled.

"Hello, Mrs. Levee?" he finally said. "This is Will Parker ... yes, it's quite a storm. Did you happen to see my sister, Esther, come by your house after school was out?"

Mrs. Levee indicated that she had been looking out the window since the storm began, watching for her husband to come home, and she hadn't seen anyone pass. Will thanked her and hung up.

There was urgency in his step as he turned and went for his coat and hat.

"Come on, Daniel," he said. "I'm going to take you home, and then I'll see if I can find your teacher."

At least the wind was at their back. They moved easily as they started down the road with Will clinging to Daniel and Dawg staying close. The problem was visibility. They had to concentrate to keep between the ditches.

It was Dawg who knew when they came to Alice's house. He eased away from Will and Daniel and started across the yard before Will and Daniel even knew they were there. Poor Esther, Will thought.

There was a dark object between them and the house that turned out to be Judy and the buckboard. Will relaxed a little when he saw that he would not have to continue further to find Esther, and his step quickened as he started up the porch steps.

Alice and Esther were standing, looking out the window, when Will and Daniel appeared out of the sea of white. They had an excited exchange, and then Alice rushed to the door. She opened it and grabbed Will and Daniel at the same time. She cried a little before she spoke.

"*Daniel, I'm tempted to give you a lickin'!*" she said. "*If I weren't so glad to see you, I'd do that very thing!*" She hugged him and brushed the snow off his clothing before she directed her attention to Will.

"Will," she said, "you always come through. Somehow I knew you'd take care of him. Are you all right?"

Will's teeth were chattering. "I'm alright, but some coffee would make me alrighter," he said.

He had his coffee, and he and Daniel filled the wood box. Despite Alice's pleas, he and Esther headed home with Judy and the buckboard. Esther sat on the seat, wrapped in a borrowed blanket while Will walked, leading Judy through the storm. He walked steadily all the way home without slowing down or taking a break. After all, he was a farmer, and farmers have to milk the cow on time—no matter what!

———

The snow continued through the night, and the temperature dropped like a rock. Goober's wild tales about animals freezing to death ran through Will's mind, making his sleep hard to come by. He lay awake with the sizzle of wind and snow beating on his window, thinking mostly about Alice and Daniel, though, wondering if they were cozy and warm.

When the clock chimed four, Will gave up on his fretful sleep and got out of bed. He pulled on his clothes and boots and went directly to the parlor stove to resurrect the fire. From the embers of the previous day he got a blaze to rise, and he piled on the wood and opened the damper. When the fire in the kitchen had been started, he put on his coat and hat, wrapped a scarf around his neck, and ventured out into the darkness with a lantern and a milk bucket.

It was hard going across the yard. The snow was almost to his knees. When he accidentally stepped into the ditch beside the road, he was in up to his waist.

The barn was surprisingly warm. The first thing he noticed was that the water buckets had not frozen. The heat from the bodies of three horses and a cow was enough to make the environment almost pleasant.

As appreciative as the animals were for their ration of food and water, Nancy was even more thankful to be milked. As Will pulled out the steaming white liquid, he thought about the convenience of having a cow, pigs, and a flock of chickens, and how he and his loved ones would never go hungry as long as the animals were there.

He thought, too, about Roamer and Sweetie and how they were fortunate to have Goober to take care of them. They were fast becoming old. What would they do, he wondered, when Goober had finished his work and was gone?

When the barn animals had been cared for, he turned his attention to the pigs and chickens. He boiled up a bucket of gruel for the pigs and filled the trough in the chicken house with mash. The chickens came down from their nests and perches to peck at their food, and when they did, Will noticed a curious thing—not one single bird had frozen to death on its roost!

———◆———

Two days of being snowbound were enough for Will. On the third day he got up, took care of his chores, and decided that he had to go out.

"I'm going over to see Alice," he told Esther. "Do you want to come?"

"Do I ever!" Esther replied. "We have to start planning for the Neils to come."

Will had tromped down a path to the barn by taking care of the animals, but he and Esther moved gingerly in that direction, each carrying two quarts of milk for Alice's growing boy. Nancy was being so generous that Alice would not have to buy milk from Preacher Babb anymore.

With the snow being almost knee deep, Will harnessed Don and Molly to the farm wagon. They, he correctly assumed, would have no trouble pulling through the frozen mess. They stepped high as they left the barn, and they were soon on the road, laying down hoof prints and wagon wheel tracks.

The snow lay firmly on the ground like a starched blanket. It covered the fields, leaving only the strongest of the wasted stalks standing above it. It still hung heavily on the trees and bent them into shapes that appeared painful and unnatural. Here and there the tracks of animals broke through the crusty surface. As for the smaller animals, they made their presence known by leaving holes in the snow's surface where they had burrowed upward to get their bearings, only to return downward and plough forward again.

Close to Alice's house the sun broke through the clouds and hinted at coming out to thaw the landscape. Will and Esther were looking upward at the hopeful rays when Alice stepped out on her porch and saw them coming.

By the time the wagon was in the yard, Daniel had joined his mother on the porch.

"I was beginning to think Sonny and I would be stuck here alone forever," Alice said.

"I was beginning to think the same thing," Will said as he climbed the steps to give her a hug.

Daniel went down the steps to give Esther a hand and help her with the jars of milk.

"You're becoming quite the gentleman," Esther told him.

Daniel lowered his voice to a quiet grumble. "Don't tell them girls at school," he said.

Alice and Daniel had been busy. On the front door was a wreath made of pine greenery and holly leaves and berries. In the parlor stood a Christmas tree decorated with memories of Christmas past and festooned with strings of popcorn that Daniel had grown, popped, and strung. In the kitchen, the table was cluttered with the makings of Daniel's Christmas gifts—cup sized mason jars filled with popcorn kernels.

Esther and Alice cleared a place at the table and began making a list of the things that would need to be done before the Neils came for Christmas. They planned a menu for various meals, compiled a shopping list, finalized sleeping arrangements, and talked about decorating. Then they settled on having a Christmas Eve gathering at Will's house. So that the Neils would be able to get to know their closest friends, they decided to invite the Burdens—including Peter Paul and Rachel—Roamer and Sweetie, Goober and Janie Rose, Demus, Doc French, and Preacher and Mrs. Babb.

Alice counted on her fingers. "When we include the Neils and the four of us that makes ... eighteen people! Where are we going to put them all?"

"We'll wedge them in," Esther said. "Some in the parlor, some in the kitchen. Will and Demus and Daniel can eat on a bed."

Amid all the planning and laughing there was a knock on the door. Will opened it, and there stood Demus with his hat in his hand.

"Demus! Come in," Alice called out from the kitchen.

"What brings you out?" Will asked.

Demus stomped the snow off his feet and came in. He went to warm by the stove.

"I was going to scout out a flock of wild turkeys," he said. "I wanted to see if I could talk Daniel into coming along."

"Can I, Mama?" Daniel pleaded.

"Don't see why not."

Alice told Demus about the Christmas Eve plans, and Demus got a thoughtful look on his face.

"I can just about guarantee a couple of turkey toms for the meal," he said. "One from Daniel and one from me. I'll even roast them!"

"We should invite you to eat with us more often!" Alice declared.

———

"We will arrive at your house on Thursday, Dec. 23. Merry Christmas," the telegram from Glenn Neil stated. The phone lines had been down between Burley and Avery Cove since the snow storm, and the telegraph service which had almost drifted into oblivion was coming in handy.

Will breathed a sigh of relief as he stuck the telegram in his pocket. He had been concerned since he hadn't heard from the boss.

"Naomi said to tell you that she's bringin' a coconut cake and a plum puddin'," Preacher Burden announced as he came from the back room. "I have your sugar, cinnamon, coffee, and baking powder right here. Gonna give you a discount since we'll be eatin' a good portion of it!"

"Hello, Mr. Parker."

Will turned to see Peter Paul Lamb walking up behind him.

"Call me 'Will,' " he said. "'Mr. Parker' was my father's name. It's good to see you, Peter Paul, and congratulations on your marriage!" Will stuck out his hand in greeting, and Peter Paul did the same.

The preacher beamed with pride from behind the counter. "Don't he look good?"

"Sure does, Preacher."

"And Rachel does too," the preacher said. "It sure is good to have 'em home."

"So how is Washington?" Will asked.

"Better all the time. We're moving to a house when we go back. Rachel's getting to be a real city girl."

His demeanor had changed. He had a look of confidence about him. The air of cockiness was gone, and in its place was a smile.

The preacher had changed, too. He wore a soft garment of acceptance over his body of authority. The struggle over Rachel had been won by both men.

———

Demus was in the barn milking his cow when Will stopped on the way home. He continued to pull as Will walked up.

"Hello, my friend," Will said. "Just thought I'd stop by and see if you're ready for Christmas. Only four days left, you know!"

Demus stopped milking and looked up. Will thought he detected a bit of extra moisture in his eyes.

"Will, I was just sitting here thinking. This will be my first real Christmas since Grandfather died. For years it's been just another day for me."

"I never even thought of that."

"Isn't it funny how things can change in an instant? For the past several years, the only way I knew it was Christmas was by hearing all the shooting on Christmas Eve. I had forgotten what Christmas was until Preacher

Burden read the Christmas story last Sunday ... and then those children sang! *My* ... how they sang! But this year ... I get to *celebrate* ... eat a meal with neighbors. Then when I come home on Christmas Eve night and the guns begin to roar around the valley ... I may just fire a few shots myself ... let ol' Santa know where I've been all this time."

Will nodded and looked away. His own eyes felt a bit damp.

"By the way," Demus said, "with that new cow of yours, are there any empty stalls left in your barn?"

"A couple. Why?"

"Just wondered. That's a fine barn, isn't it?"

He let his comment about the barn sink in, and then he went back to milking his cow.

G lenn Neil and his wife rolled to a stop in front of Turpin's mill on their way into Avery Cove. Under the shed, the saw was running, cutting a large beam out of a log. Caldwell, Goober, and two other men were intent on their work, keeping the log firmly attached to the carriage, and watching the sawdust fly. They didn't look up.

When the blade reached the end of the log, the carriage reversed and the timber lay bare of the slabs that had been cut away. Caldwell's two workers grabbed the end of the beam and muscled it onto a pile of others. Goober went immediately and ran his hands up and down the beam, inspecting it for defects. He pulled out a folding ruler and checked the dimensions up and down its length.

Glenn Neil nodded his approval and clicked his horse onward. The men were not even aware that he had been there.

"That Green's a hard worker ... good man," he told his wife.

When the length of the valley came into view, Neil stopped the phaeton again, and he and Mrs. Neil took in the view. He pointed to his right toward Fa'side, and she nodded and smiled. Then Neil's hand swept from right to left as he pointed out various homes and landmarks. From the look on her face, it was easy to see that Mrs. Neil was falling in love with the valley at first sight.

Neil took up the reins and clicked the horses onward again. They were closing in on their holiday with Will and Esther.

———

Alice removed her hands from the dishwater and dried them on a towel as she turned toward the front door. Before she could get there, the knock that had beckoned her came again.

When she opened the door, Roamer Robinson was standing with a basket in one hand and his hat in the other.

"Mr. Robinson! Merry Christmas!" she said. "Please come in!"

Roamer smiled sheepishly and stepped inside.

"Thank ye, Miz Day," he said. "I'll step inside so ye can shet th' door, but I ain't a-gonna stay. Is ye boy t' home?"

"No, he's gone turkey hunting with Demus Whitedeer," Alice said as she closed the door behind them. "Did you need him for something?"

"Oh, no ma'am. Sweetie sent me over t' bring 'im a little somethin' fer Christmas." He reached down in his basket and brought out a small package wrapped in butcher paper and tied up with red yarn. "Hit's sugar cookies," he said. "I know how younguns don't fancy fruitcake too much."

Alice smiled and took the package as Roamer sidled up close enough to her to whisper.

"They's *some* fruitcake 'at younguns don't have no business eatin' no how ... if ye know whut I mean."

Alice laughed. "I know exactly what you mean," she said. "He'll love these, especially since they're from you and Aunt Sweetie."

"Got a little somethin' fer you, too," he said, reaching into his basket. "I brung ye a jar o' Sweetie's mint jelly."

He handed Alice the little jar of the green jelly sealed with wax. A toothless smile spread across his face.

"I favor mine with biscuits," he said, "but some folks eats theirs with mutton er ham hocks."

"Thank you, Mr. Robinson. The cookies and the mint jelly will add a lot to our Christmas. Now," she said as she walked to the kitchen, "Sonny made a little something for you and Mrs. Robinson, and I'm sure he wouldn't mind me giving it to you."

She got one of the jars of popcorn kernels that was capped with a piece of red cloth and tied with a red ribbon and gave it to Roamer. His eyes lit up as he looked at it.

"I growed popcorn when I wuz a youngun," he said. "I like mine w' milk an' sugar fer breakfas'!"

He put his gift in his basket and turned toward the door. Then he straightened up and turned back around.

"Oh! I jest 'bout forgot," he said. "I brung ye somethin' else."

He reached in his basket and pulled out a bouquet of fresh wild flowers tied with a string. Alice's eyes widened, and she put her hand to her mouth.

"Mr. Robinson … where …"

"Oh, they come up in th' pots whur I planted my terbackie seeds. Hit seemed a shame t' jest waste 'em."

She took the bouquet and looked at it silently as Roamer shuffled out the door, across the porch, and down the steps.

"Mary Chris'mas," he said. "Me an' Sweetie'll see ye tomorry."

The "girls"—Esther, Alice, Sweetie, Janie Rose, Naomi, Rachel, Mrs. Babb, and Mrs. Neil—congregated in the kitchen and overflowed into the spring house. They fussed over and prettied up the dishes, platters, and bowls of food that covered every available flat surface.

The women were fast becoming a circle of friends, the greatest evidence of which was an edict by Mrs. Neil that she was to be called "Sal." To her acquaintances back home, her husband's business associates, and Mr. Neil himself, she had always been "Mrs. Neil," but that was going to change!

Amid the acceptance of Sal's name change, Mrs. Babb spoke up.

"Well if she's gonna be 'Sal,' then I'm gonna be 'Pru'! And the preacher can just get used to it!"

Over in the parlor, Preacher Burden spoke up.

"What in th' world is goin' on in there? It sounds like a bunch of hens cacklin'!"

Back in the kitchen, Esther opened the oven door and checked on the turkeys that were warming.

"Looks like they're warm enough," she said, and she removed the golden-brown birds from the oven and set them on the corner of the stove top.

"*Time to eat!*" Sal called out! Then she bent down to Sweetie's ear and whispered, "There's somethin' about this mountain air that makes a person hungry."

"*Demus, you and Sonny come slice the entree,*" Alice shouted.

Back in the parlor, Daniel turned to Demus with disappointment on his face.

"I thought we were havin' the turkeys we shot," he moaned.

The Christmas Eve supper was over. Every stomach was full, including Dawg's. Every available dish from three households was dirty. The house was a mess.

But more than the sharing of a meal, the importance of new friendships stood out. More important still was the celebration of the Savior's birth that had prompted the gathering. Without that event they would not have been drawn together.

All were quieter now, mellow in their fullness. The sofa and the two stuffed chairs had been given over to Roamer and Sweetie, and the honored guests, Glenn and Sal. The others sat on the floor or on kitchen chairs, or they stood and quietly talked.

Finally, Preacher Burden took a cue from Will and walked out before the group.

"Everybody, listen up for just a minute," he said as he put on his serious face. "Will has asked me as his pastor to once again share the Christmas story as it's written in the second chapter of Luke. Please listen as I read God's Word."

The preacher held his Bible out before him, but he recited from memory. "And it came to pass in those days, that there went out a decree from Caesar Augustus, that all the world should be taxed."

He went on to recite the verses about Mary and Joseph's trip to the town of Bethlehem, and how Jesus was born there and laid in a manger. He continued his recitation with the verses that told of the angels and the shepherds who went to worship the new-born King.

Then he turned to the book of Matthew and unfolded the story of the wise men who followed the star to Bethlehem, and his recitation concluded with the part about their gifts of gold, frankincense, and myrrh. Then he closed his Bible.

"My friends," he said, "we've already received the most precious gift of all this Christmas. Now, let's set about sharing our gift through service to others.

"And now," he continued, "my dear friend, Preacher Billy Babb has a few words for you."

"*Preach!*" Uncle Roamer cried out.

Preacher Babb stood and his big smile lit the room. His pearly white teeth shown like the stars above Bethlehem.

"No, Brother Roamer," he said, "I'm not gonna preach, but I am gonna wish a merry Christmas to all of you from myself and Mrs. Babb ..."

"That's '*Pru*', Billy!" his wife said.

"*You preach, Pru!*" Sweetie hollered, and her exhortation was followed by cheers from the other ladies.

A look of disbelief flashed across Preacher Babb's face, but the laughter of the group brought back his smile.

"Pru then!" he declared. "Now ... as you know, Sister Alice and Brother Will have announced their plans to be married in the spring. Think about this for a minute ... their marriage will not be the end of their love; it will be the *beginning* of a *lifetime* of love. In that spirit I want to remind you that Christmas shouldn't end at midnight tomorrow, it should last our whole life long. Just as the marriage of Brother Will and Sister Alice is a beginning, I want to urge all of you here to let this gathering be the beginning of a celebration that will last a lifetime! When next year comes, we'll have another celebration that'll take us to the next year ... and the next, and with each year's renewal, Christmas will live in our hearts forever!

"Now ... Sister Alice told me yesterday about something that happened to her that sort of reinforces my point. She said that out of the blue... in the middle of a snowy winter...Roamer brought her a bouquet of fresh spring flowers. She said it reminded her that the celebration of spring is taking place continually somewhere on earth. ... And just as we can celebrate spring in the bleak midwinter when there's snow on the ground, we can celebrate *Christmas* in July!

"And Folks, those flowers told Sister Alice something else as well. She had made up her mind that she wanted be married in the spring . . . but she took that bouquet of fresh flowers as a sign that she and brother Will should be married here...today...at this very place!"

A collective gasp went up in the room.

"I hope to my never!" Roamer uttered under his breath.

"And so," Preacher Babb said, "I want to invite you, on behalf of Brother Will and Sister Alice, to share this special time with them. I would like now to ask the members of the wedding party to come and take their places."

Will and Alice came and stood before Alice's preacher—Will on his left, and Alice on his right.

Also coming up to stand before the group were Daniel, who was to give the bride away, Esther, the bridesmaid, and Goober Green, the best man. Other than Preacher Babb, they were the only members of the gathering who knew that a wedding was to take place.

Except for Roamer who couldn't hold back his enthusiasm, the guests were stone silent, as much from shock as out of respect for the gravity of the occasion.

Alice handed Esther the bouquet of flowers that Roamer had given her. She and Will joined hands, and to the wonder of the guests, the ceremony began.

"Dearly beloved," Preacher Babb said, "we are gathered here today to join this man, Forrest William Parker Jr., and this woman, Alice Collier Day, in the holy bonds of matrimony. Who gives this woman to be wed?"

"*Me!*" Daniel stated emphatically, and he went to sit beside Demus on the floor.

"I hope to my never!" Roamer uttered again.

"Hesh up, Roamer!" Sweetie whispered, and she gave him a stern look.

Alice looked over at her son and nodded. Will gave him a wink.

Preacher Babb continued. "Is there anyone present who knows a reason why this couple should not be wed?"

Roamer looked around the room. "Nary a soul!" he declared under his breath, and Sweetie elbowed him in the side.

Preacher Babb's smile lit the room. He turned to the groom.

"Will, do you take Alice to be your lawfully wedded wife ...

Afterword

Will did take Alice to be his lawfully wedded wife, and Alice took Will to be her lawfully wedded husband. They promised each other that they would love, honor, keep, and be faithful until they were parted in death. Will placed the ring on Alice's finger, Preacher Babb pronounced them man and wife, and Will kissed his bride.

The men congratulated Will and slapped him on the back—all of them except Goober. The bond of brotherly love between them drew Goober forward to embrace his buddy, and the two of them—the unlikely bear slayer and the one whose life he saved—exchanged a quiet whisper.

The women all cried and hugged Alice, wishing her the best, but the biggest hug of all came from Esther, who had become more like a sister to Alice than a sister-in-law.

Alice and Will left in a shower of rice, and when the house was tidied and the dishes were washed, the celebration came to a close.

Doc French was the first to go. He went to check on Granny Floyd, who had been feeling poorly. He took her some special medicine—a piece of Naomi's coconut cake.

The Neils stayed with Esther, and they laughed and talked late into the night, planning for the day when they would be neighbors.

The Robinsons, the Greens, and the Babbs made their way home. They all wanted to see to it that Santa would find them sleeping when he came.

The Burdens and the Lambs had the longest ride, but their singing and laughter made it seem like the shortest. They didn't know it at the time, but Rachel was carrying the Burden's first grandchild. They could not have imagined how special their next Christmas would be!

Daniel went home to spend the night with Demus. When they got there they found that Santa had come and had left Daniel a Winchester lever action .22 rifle, a new winter coat, and a book titled *Survival in the Wild*.

For Demus, Santa had left a knitted sweater, a can of mixed candy, a book about mushrooms, and a jar of popcorn kernels. There was also an envelope from Glenn Neil containing a check in the amount of $25.00 with a note that said he should buy a book for himself and some books for the children of the valley. Demus tried not to show it, but he was filled with emotion.

The biggest surprise, though, came when Daniel went to the barn to milk Demus's cow. In the next stall over was a young pinto mare. On the stall door was a note that read, "To Daniel from Santa for being a good student."

Daniel opened the stall door and went inside with his lantern held high to see the glorious creature.

"Her name is 'Cherokee Rose,' " Demus said as he walked up behind him.

"Is she from Mama or Will?" Daniel asked.

"Neither," Demus replied. "She's from Santa, and Santa doesn't like for his customers to ask a lot of questions."

Daniel stroked the horse's neck and side and ran his fingers through her mane.

"She's the most beautiful horse I've ever seen," he said. "Will you please tell Santa 'thanks' from me, and that I love her?"

A smile came across Demus's face, and he laughed his big, thunderous laugh. "Consider it done," he said.

When the night had fully settled upon the land and the time for rest had come, gunfire began to ring around the valley. It started with a single shot from the south that was answered by several shots from the east. Before long the air was filled with salvos coming from all directions, blending and echoing into a clamor that Santa would be sure to hear.

And even though the jolly old elf had already made his visit to Demus's house, Demus and Daniel joined the cacophony by firing their own rifles as a show of their joy and thankfulness for their blessings.

As for Will and Alice, they had their Christmas day honeymoon at Alice's house, and then they went about the business of making Will's house a home for three and Alice's house a home for Esther. And they lived happily ever after in that house that Laddie Green built in Avery Cove, North Carolina—about four miles west of Burden's.

Made in the USA
Columbia, SC
26 February 2021